The characters and events portrayed in this book are fictitious. Any similarity to real people, living or dead, is coincidental and not intended by the author.

No part of this book may be reproduced, or stored in a retrieval system, or transmitted in any form or by any means, electronic, mechanical, photocopying, recording, or otherwise, without express written permission of the author, except for the use of brief quotations in a book review. No part of this book may be used to train AI or other generative text creation software. This author does not support the use of generative AI in print, art, or any other formats.

This book has only been authorized to be published through Amazon/Kindle Unlimited/KDP. If you come across this on any other website it has been pirated.

Edits by: Owl Eyes Proofs & Edits

Cover design: Get Covers.

Printed in the United States of America

©2024 Siri Pielski All rights reserved

Burn the bridges that no longer serve you.
I believe you can survive without them.

Content Notes

Dear Reader,

This book contains some heavy topics that are discussed or experienced on the page by more than one main character.

Those topics include:
Orphaned/Adopted child
Verbal and Physical abuse and assault.
Character Trafficking
PTSD Flashbacks/Nightmares
Panic Attacks
Self-doubt
Death Idealization
Toxic and Dangerous Sibling Rivalries
Cliffhanger Ending

Please note that this book also deals with the FMC learning how to be herself while trying to come to terms with all the new information and experiences she's being given. One of these includes the power of controlling her own sexuality. This book does feature MMFM Polyamory where two males are a mated couple, the female is an additional mate, and a third male is also courting the female.

Also know that the lack of the possessive s for Nikaius' and Priamos' name has been done intentionally and is not due to a lack of editing. I love my editor very much, but this is a stylistic preference you can pry out of my cold dead hands.

Characters/Places

Characters:
Morrigan Aegean (More-ih-gen Uh-jee-un)
Delaney Aegean (Dee-lay-nee)
Malin Aegean (May-lin)
Amara Ayrden (Uh-mar-uh) (nee Aegean)
Elijah Aegean (Ee-lie-juh)
Mae De'Lyon (May Day-Lee-on) (nee Aegean)
Nikaius Ayrden (Nik-eye-us Air-den)
Waric Cavanaugh (War-ick Kav-uh-naw)
Aslin Hawthorne (Az-lin H-awe-thorn)
Hawke Corviana (Hawk Core-vee-ana)
Aquila Corviana (Uh-quee-La Core-vee-ana):
Santiago "Santi" De'Lyon (Saun-tee-ah-go Day-Lee-on)
Imriel Gorlassar (Ihm-ree-al Gore-la-s-are)
Tarsenak Gorlassar (Tar-sen-ack)
Cadoc Kaan (Kay-dock Kahn)

Places:
Cav'Sara (Kayv-sar-uh): The continent on which Empathy takes place.
Be'Sal a(Beh-sah-lah)- The Northeastern province of Cav'Sara. It is bracketed by thes ea to the east and the Be'Sala mountains to the west and south.
Qu'tar - The town in which Morrigan lived closest to.

Kunmei (Koon-May) Southeastern province of Cav'Sara. It's the most central of the habitable areas nestled neatly between Be'Sala and The Pridelands.
(Family/Pack Breakdowns in back of book)

Contents

Prologue	1
1. Hawke	4
2. Morrigan	12
3. Morrigan	24
4. Hawke	30
5. Waric	37
6. Nikaius	44
7. Morrigan	51
8. Morrigan	62
9. Morrigan	71
10. Hawke	76
11. Waric	85
12. Morrigan	96
13. Morrigan	107

14. Nikaius	114
15. Morrigan	124
16. Morrigan	139
17. Morrigan	155
18. Morrigan	162
19. Morrigan	170
20. Morrigan	177
21. Morrigan	183
22. Morrigan	193
23. Morrigan	205
24. Morrigan	215
25. Morrigan	224
26. Morrigan	232
27. Morrigan	242
Stay Tuned	258
Acknowledgements	260
Clan Names/Vocab	261

Prologue

Priamos

The world was muted when Priamos woke. Nothing smelled familiar and though a chill ran through his fur, he felt hot inside. His side ached and when he tried to stand, his paws barely held him. Pain flared across his entire chest and no amount of licking seemed to ease the pain or help heal the wound. The world was silent in a weirdly muted way, but when he pulled himself from the sanctuary of the tree, he realized why.

More snow had fallen while he had been resting. It was a displeasing fact but one that he couldn't avoid. The setting sun above him meant that he might be able to make some distance towards the Lyon's den before morning rose and whoever had attacked him returned.

The mating bond with Earth still lingered in the back of his mind. He could still feel the brush of playful magic and almost smell the cinnamon and cedar scent of him, but it was dulled and muted in a way that made it so he couldn't pull on it to alert Earth to where he was. It was enough to let him know that his pack was alright, but not enough to get his mate's help.

He didn't know who the attackers were, nor why they were in his territory; all he knew was the puma's blood tasted wrong in his mouth and whatever magic they had used to prevent his healing was bitter on his tongue.

He was in desperate need of water, but he wasn't near any stream that he could hear and when he tried to lap at the clean snow around him, it burned his tongue, so he only paused to do it when the need outweighed anything else.

Walking wasn't easy. The slimy mud stuck between his toes and no matter how hard he tried to keep the regal footing of an alpha, he felt like a fumbling pup once again. His weight wasn't balanced and no matter how he tried to right it, his paws kept sliding away from each other, and he would flop to his chest, the pain searing up his entire body.

Nikaius wasn't awake yet, which meant Priamos had to figure out how to get somewhere safe to heal. The cold wasn't conductive to healing. Being without a pack was disorienting, and he didn't have any idea where he was. The area no longer tingled like his magic, nor smelled like his territory. It felt familiar, but he couldn't explain why. Though the night was quickly coming, the ranging colors in the sky were still visible to him. He didn't know what the colors were called, only that they were appealing in nature. He always enjoyed watching the sun set. By the time the sun had fully set, he finally managed to gain solid footing and found himself in rolling plains.

The view was familiar, the dense trees behind him giving way to grassy plains and high grass that he could easily hide in despite the snow. He and Nikaius had run similar paths when they were younger, but none of those times had been because he had fallen from a cliff after being attacked.

He grumbled as he kept walking, taking a deep inhale in an attempt to find out anything else about the area where he was. All warm-blooded scents had been washed away with the continual rain and snow that signified the winter season on the continent. Damp soil, snow, and the tang of his own blood were the primary scents that he could smell while his eyes adjusted to the dying light.

He was close to the Badlands and knew that he would have to tread carefully as they felt wrong and sucked the magic from one's veins. He would need to leave them quickly and safely.

His steps were uneven as he favored one shoulder, but he had found a steady pace and was able to cover more distance than he thought he would. When he finally needed rest, the sun was slowly peeking over mountains on the horizon, and his paws had finally met warm sand.

Chapter One

Hawke

Corinth Manor

The smell of snow was one of Hawke's favorite scents. It was as crisp and fresh as if one was breathing pure air without any lingering scents. It muted everything. Even when the world was already muddied by the dampness left behind by rainfall and ice, fresh snowfall made the world look bright and pristine again. Snow drew every dark thought from his mind and scattered it to the biting wind for another time. He stood at the front door overlooking the plaza below, watching the cloudy sky slowly darken as cotton ball fluffs of white fell from it. It was as close to flying as he could get in the winter. Though he loved the snow, the need for his animal was few and far in between in the winter months as the weather had the ability to turn treacherous within moments. He also didn't enjoy being cold. Though he would prefer to live in the constant warmth of The Pridelands, being Kielzer — an Avian changeling — meant he had the ability to be an emissary for Rekru'e leaders. And Nikaius was one of his very best friends which meant living in the south was a price Hawke was willing to pay to remain close to his sister and the pack, which now included *her* as well.

Thinking about Morrigan made Hawke's heart flutter, as if it was trying to replace his wild form to make him forget how bereft he felt without using it as often. He felt restless not being able to fly as much, but Morrigan was a good distraction from that. Since she had said yes to his request to court her, he had dropped the mental wall that dulled his senses to her.

In the beginning, Hawke had tried to block out anything to do with Morrigan, except what was needed to keep her safe. Part of it was for his own sanity to prevent himself from hyper-fixating on her when she didn't need another male panting after her. He also felt that hearing another's footsteps was enough to keep them safe. With everyone else it was simply a precaution, he was the captain of the guard and needed to remain alert, but unlike Nikaius and Waric, who had no problems keeping their senses open for everyone, Hawke didn't need to hear each inflection of Morrigan's heart, didn't need to obsess over what they might mean.

What Nikaius and Waric could pick up by scent, he could detect by sound. Though they were light on their feet when the time called for it, both men had heavy footfalls that were Atce' traits meant to draw attention to them. In their own home, they were unguarded, and the pace was usually slower but still heavy. Aquila's footsteps were lighter but still loud due to the footwear she chose. He knew his sister favored certain fashions most days, simply to make her status known when people began to question a woman being the leader of the ranks. It didn't hurt that she was his twin, and he could feel her no matter where she was. Aslin was sure-footed but lithe, her pace barely heard throughout the house.

Then there was Morrigan, who was none of the things the others were.

He could hear her soft, unsure pace as she walked by, and he assumed she didn't know he had returned. Before Hawke had arrived home, before Priamos took over, Nikaius had decided to try to sabotage what he and Waric had with Morrigan. Hawke knew that Nikaius struggled with keeping the negative voices at bay the closer Yasivr — the shifting moon — came to being full. It happened once a year and most Rekru'e let their wild forms free. Nikaius was the only Rekru'e that Hawke knew whose animal was an entirely different entity created by trauma. And when Yasivr got closer to fullness, Priamos got closer and closer to the edge until he snapped.

The last time it had happened, it had taken them a day and a half to find him. After Priamos' typical run, he had ended up at the home of Wren and Finn Falconer, the adoptive parents of Alya, Hawke's niece, who had imprinted on Nikaius as an infant. During times of great stress, he tended to gravitate to either Waric or Alya, depending on what thoughts were raging in his head.

Hawke hadn't been home when everything came to a head, having arrived shortly before Priamos and Waric left for their run. Waric had explained the situation to him while Morrigan had been in the bath. Neither had felt the need to bother her when she didn't seem upset or in need of comfort. With so many new things being constantly thrown at her and someone always being around, he knew that him hovering over her wouldn't be the best way to help her adjust to the chaos that was their lives.

She had only been with them a few weeks and had already been attacked twice within the confines of their home by a source of magic no one could explain. Typically, Hawke wouldn't need to be on alert in their own home because of the wards they had in place. They had elected for one of the few High Council approved uses of blood magic to create their wards. Only those who had been patched into the wards by drafters or existing members of the household could gain access to their home unaccompanied. Hawke wasn't exactly sure how it worked because he had never questioned it.

It had served its purpose until it hadn't.

The night before, Hawke had woken to the feeling of icy static crawling through his veins, and it had paralyzed him in his bed. It felt like he was standing in an ice storm, completely unclothed. Though it had only lasted a few moments, it allowed whoever controlled the magic to attack Morrigan. The magic felt similar to what he had felt when they were fighting the ice golems. It unnerved him to know that someone was targeting Morrigan. As the captain of the guard, he should have known how to prevent or combat the attack, but he had been just as helpless as Nikaius and Waric.

Letting out a soft sigh, he shook out the feathers of his wings and shut the door. Though he didn't have to have his wings out, they brought him comfort as an extension of himself. They had an extreme amount of nerve endings that could tell even the barest shift of pressure in the air. If he was paying attention.

With Aslin and Aquila gone, Hawke knew that he and Morrigan were on their own for dinner, but he didn't mind having to share a meal with only her. Perhaps he could convince her to let him take her to one of the diners in town, or on a picnic in the courtyard.

Making sure his pace was leisurely, and his steps were loud enough to be heard in the hallway, he turned from the door and sought her out.

He hadn't been completely paying attention to her steps when she had gone past, and he had assumed that Morrigan had retired to the study. He was concerned when he found it empty. Taking a breath, he closed his eyes and listened. Now that he allowed himself access to her, he could hear the faint flutter of her heart and the way she nervously tapped her toes on the floor. It wasn't a normal tap, but one where she would rest all her weight on one foot and kick the other back to tap her toes and the top of her foot on the floor. It was something he had never seen anyone else do, but it gave away her anxiety.

Knowing these things made it easier to find her in his room, staring out the large, picturesque windows that faced the town down the hill. The sun was setting and every few moments, a light would wink on, as if the stars were coming out to say hello despite the angry-looking clouds overhead.

It seemed that despite his efforts to make himself known, she hadn't heard him approach, and he took a moment to let his eyes wander over her figure. The knee-length, dark blue dress she wore clung to her curves, and her hair reached nearly to her waist in chaotic waves. The color reminded him of a few members of the De'Lyon pride who were descendants of the Kitzera tribes. The Kitzera tribes had died out shortly after the war, mostly due to the larger Rekru'e genes being hereditarily more dominant.

Being Santiago De'Lyon's advisor, Hawke had met Santi's wife Mae, who happened to be Morrigan's elder sister. Mae's hair was the same dark copper color, and Hawke knew that they had inherited the color from their father. Hawke, however, wasn't well versed in the family line of the Aegeans to know if Malin was a Kitzera descendant or not.

There were so many things Hawke wanted to say to try and ease the quick flutter of Morrigan's heart, but he didn't feel it was right to do so without her permission, especially when he knew that touch was her tether to other people's emotions. Though Morrigan had been believed to be magicless and marked as such with the *thaber* brand, Mae had confessed Morrigan's powers to him and Santi. She could sense people's emotions through touch.

"Your hair looks lovely. I don't think I've ever seen it down."

"The second night I was here, Nikaius helped me free the end from the braids." She didn't startle when he spoke, showing him that she had heard his approach and just hadn't acknowledged it, but turned her head to give him a sad look over her shoulder that gave away where her thoughts were.

"Braids?" He tried to remember how she had looked when she came to them, but his mind had been all over the place that night. So had his behavior, which he still felt like he might not have completely made up for, even though Morrigan had reassured him he had.

"Mmhm. I did something to anger my mother," turning back to face the windows, Morrigan wrapped her arms around herself, "she was always angry with me. I could breathe wrong, and she would find some punishment. That night, my hair had been in multiple different braids, and she used some magic to make them unremovable. I tried to remove them once, but I got lashes for it." Hawke sighed softly at the mental image that provoked. He was in awe of the strength that she had to not outwardly react to what he was sure was a painful memory. Or had she become so desensitized to it that it didn't really bother her anymore? Had she accepted what happened?

Guilt welled through him. Was it when he had been tasked by Mae to watch out for her? He remembered Mae's desperate plea for him to watch out for Morrigan to the best of his ability. He visited as often as he could. Often, it was more than once a week during the planning stages of his and Santi's ruse to get Morrigan into Santi's custody by tricking Elijah. However, he had only ever seen her in the kitchens in passing and had no idea of the cruelties she had suffered at her family's hands. How often had she been punished before or after his visits and he had no idea?

The thought turned his stomach, and he pressed a hand to his sternum, trying to will his pulse to slow as anger flooded him.

Morrigan seemed to know where his thoughts wandered before he spoke. "It was years ago." She assured him.

The need to comfort her almost outweighed his need to have her approval before he touched her, and he fisted his other hand at his side in hopes of hiding their shaking. "How many did you get?"

"How many what?" She turned her attention back to him, her posture relaxing a bit as she offered her hand to him. The simple gesture was all that was needed to break Hawke's resolve to not go to her. It only took him three strides across the room to be able to wrap his arms around her from behind, careful to keep his hands from her skin. She didn't need to know how tumultuous his thoughts were.

"How many lashes did you get when you tried to cut it?"

"Oh." She settled back against him and turned her attention back to the windows. "Nine. One for each braid."

Hawke wondered how many of those lashes scared her, but he didn't want to ask, didn't want to know how much pain she had suffered at the hands of people who were supposed to protect her.

"I didn't mean to upset you." Morrigan's voice was shy, and Hawke sighed when he realized he had fisted his hand in the fabric of her dress at her hip, and her hand was wrapped around the wrist of the arm banded across her chest.

"I'm not upset with you, Little Dove." Nudging his nose into her hair for a moment, he took a slow, deep breath, willing his warring emotions to settle before pressing a kiss to the top of her head. "No other harm will come to you under my watch."

"That's a hard promise to keep in this house it seems." She gave a soft laugh as she touched the bandage on her arm as a reminder. Hawke sighed gently, remembering the almost blackened state her skin had been in the night before.

They hadn't had much time to try to figure out what had happened. Hawke had been to their library and that of The Pridelands to try to find an explanation for the attack, but he hadn't found anything. And then he returned to Waric and Priamos leaving.

"You are a magnet for trouble." He teased, playfully tugging a lock of hair. She giggled and tried to swat him away, but she didn't get far with how he held her to him. Pinching her side earned him another squeal, and she laughed as she turned in his arms and gave him a gentle shove.

He grinned down at her as she gave him a playful pout. This was what he wanted. He wanted the bright, playful girl he had been told about and had seen creeping out between the clouds of her trauma.

"But now, you've given me even better access." Grinning, he nudged his nose against hers, earning him another laugh before she leaned up to kiss him gently. Curling his fingers into the hair at the nape of her neck, he pulled her closer, groaning at how warm and soft she felt against his suddenly aching flesh.

Typically, it would take him longer to feel physical attraction to someone, personalities were far more important than physical attributes, but with Morrigan things felt different. No matter who it was, it seemed she had ensnared everyone in their household who was inclined to pay attention to her. Forget Kitzera, perhaps she was one of the Velamo and called to them with an unheard siren's song. "You're so beautiful," he whispered as he broke the kiss.

"You—" She licked her lips as her jade eyes scanned his face, her smile soft. "You're not so bad yourself." Leaning up on her toes, she kissed him again, and he was helpless to deny her the entrance she requested as she nipped his bottom lip.

Pulling her closer earned him another squeak. When she pulled away, he paused, worried he had been too forward with her, but the grin that spread across her face eased the suddenly quick pace of his heart. Dropping down on her toes, she sized him up with a raised eyebrow. "Has anyone told you it's rude how tall you are?"

Hawke barked out a disbelieving laugh, blinking down at her as he tried to process what she had just said. "No, Little Dove, that's a first. What are you going to do about it?"

"I know what you're doing." Her voice was pensive, and he wondered what was going on in her mind as he watched her eyes scan him, then around the room, never settling on one thing for more than a breath.

Did she truly know what he was doing? Trying to ease her worry about others by selfishly drawing her attention to himself? He, Waric, and Nikaius held no secrets, and Hawke had let his curiosity get the better of him when it came to wondering if he could get her to make the sounds they said she made. Perhaps he could get something of his own instead. Mustering up more courage than he truly had, he returned her grin. "Is it working?"

"Perhaps." Her slow-spreading coy grin was the only warning he had before she shoved at him again. Though he was caught off guard by the action, he didn't budge, and her grin morphed back into her previous pout, her nose wrinkling. "You're supposed to move." She mewled.

"Oh, am I?" With a roll of his eyes, his own grin spread as he twisted a lock of her hair around his finger and tucked it behind her ear, leaning down to drop his voice to the same whispered level as hers. "Maybe you should try harder." He was purposefully putting himself in a position where her next move would be more effective without completely giving her what she wanted. She giggled, and her next push was harder than the last, and he accommodatingly stumbled back to sit on his bed.

"You little minx." Snaring her dress, he pulled, making her stumble forward and into his waiting arms. Sliding his hands down to anchor on her hips, he grinned up at her. "Still giving me better access."

"I..." her cheeks and nose turned pink as she blinked down at him, clearly having not thought her actions through to completion.

"You are always the one in control here." He reassured her, letting his grip soften so he could stroke his palms carefully up her sides.

Chapter Two

Morrigan

Corinth Manor

You are always the one in control here.

His words were like a warm balm, soothing the nerves she had become accustomed to when doing something new. Though things with Hawke had been ephemeral at first, once she understood the reason behind his behavior, she couldn't fault him for it. It was endearing that he had worried he had failed her without her ever knowing he was supposed to be caring for her in the first place. After he had confessed his part in her ending up in Kunmei, and his desire to be with her, she had learned she could easily anticipate his actions once he had stopped trying to distance himself from her. Though she had enjoyed the spontaneity of her encounters with Waric and Nikaius, Hawke was easy to predict. Her need for survival had given her the ability to determine the mood of her family but determining Hawke's moods wasn't a need for survival. He was someone she wanted.

Being in Kunmei had disrupted her life more exponentially than she had anticipated, and she was still struggling to find a way to settle into her new roles. So many new things, like kindness and free time and constant new opportunities, had come her way that she had found herself in a constant state of self-doubt. Knowing her place in her family and her daily routine hadn't changed drastically, so this uncertainty was something that she hadn't had to face at home despite her family's aggression.

She had gone into the Winter Moon Selection Night anticipating being sold to another form of servitude, but instead, she fell under the care of Lord Nikaius Ayrden.

Her expectations had been tossed out the window.

Having the freedom Nikaius and his pack afforded her was an adjustment she hadn't anticipated and was still learning how to appreciate to the truest extent.

Despite reassuring words and encouragement, every new step turned her stomach with anxiety, preparing to be reprimanded.

Finding comfort in being able to choose what she did was slowly becoming reality, but with that new reality came lessons she had never thought she would learn. Most important of those lessons was none of the rules and traditions imparted to her in Be'Sala had any effect on Kunmei.

The most jarring lesson had been the easy acceptance of her attraction to and being courted by more than one suitor. The thought had been alarming to her at first, and she had thought Waric and Nikaius were playing some type of cruel game with her, but after Hawke's confession and their easy acceptance of it, those worries had eased.

A little.

Aslin and Aquila had reassured Morrigan that it was alright to be with who she wanted to be with, but she still held some guilt about being attracted to Hawke while she was trying to figure out her relationships with Nikaius and Waric.

Reaching up, she cupped his jaw and pressed another kiss to his mouth. He wasn't as forward as Nikaius and Waric, instead deferring to her for almost every movement he made, and she appreciated it.

"Thank you," she whispered against his mouth. She owed him a million days' worth of gratitude for what he had done, despite her not knowing until after the fact. He was the reason she was free from her family and starting to build her own safety. It was still unsettling to think that she had only been in Kunmei for a few weeks, yet she felt more included and cared for than she had felt at home. Morrigan knew she needed to stop thinking of Be'Sala as home, but some days, she still thought she would wake up to find that the past few months hadn't happened.

Hawke's warm hands covered hers, and he pulled away to give her a smile. He was larger than Nikaius and Waric, yet he still managed to look boyish when he grinned. "You don't owe me any thanks. I'll be here in whatever capacity you need me to be, whether it be friend or guard or..." His eyes dropped away, and his shyness warmed her palms, replacing the heady arousal she had felt from him.

"Or?" His sheepishness made her bold, and she stepped closer. Leaning down, she brushed her nose along his before pressing another soft kiss to his mouth. As he hummed into the kiss, he dropped his hands back to her hips.

"Wha-t," he cleared his throat as his voice broke, "Whatever you want. You have me in whatever capacity you want me, Morrigan."

Pressing her forehead to his, she let out a soft sigh. She was eager for this next step with him, but she also knew it had started as him attempting to distract her from her melancholy thoughts. "I don't want you to think I'm using you."

"Use away," Hawke smirked, one of the loose braids falling into his face. Usually, he wore them twisted up into some type of knot on the back of his head to show off the shaved sides and back, but as it had gotten colder, he had transitioned to letting them hang loose when he wasn't actively guarding anything. Morrigan wasn't sure which way she preferred his hair to be. When it was pulled back, it showed off the strong cut of his jaw, but loose as it was right then, made him look younger and more boyish.

"Hawke." She gave him an exasperated look.

"I don't think that." He let out a soft sigh and tugged her closer by her hips so that her knees hit the edge of the bed. Hiking up her skirt a bit, she followed his direction and climbed onto the bed to straddle his hips before settling herself in his lap. "I know this is a weird situation for you." Hawke continued; his hands stroked through her hair before he cupped her chin so he could press a kiss to her forehead. "It's new and probably a little scary, but it's okay. No one is going to do anything you don't want them to."

"I know that."

"Do you? Because from this angle, it seems like you keep second-guessing yourself." He raised his eyebrow at her.

Sighing gently, Morrigan dropped her forehead to his shoulder and curled herself into him. "Because I'm afraid I'm going to make the wrong move or disappoint someone."

"We want you to be the most genuine and true version of yourself." Hawke didn't let her hide like she wanted to, nudging his nose into her hair, before shifting back to make her sit up again. His eyes searched hers as his thumb stroked along her chin under her bottom lip. Kindness and adoration were predominant through the connection she now had with him because of his touch. His arousal lingered in the background, sparking as she shifted, but nothing screamed dishonesty.

He continued with what he was saying before she could linger on the arousal. "Trying to be someone you aren't is the only way you're going to disappoint any of us. You want only one of us, just say the word, and we'll step back for them. If you want all of us, you can have all of us." The image of the four of them: her, Hawke, Waric, and Nikaius, tangled up in bed, sent a delicious throb through her, and Hawke laughed as if he knew where her mind wandered.

Morrigan relaxed into the next kiss he gave her, shifting forward when his hand pressed against her lower back. They were on more even ground sitting as they were, her chest pressed against his and able to see eye to eye. "I'm not a sharer in that aspect and have zero desire to see Nikaius and Waric naked any more than I must," he wrinkled his nose, which made Morrigan laugh, "but what you do with them is your own business. When you're with them, you don't have to spare me a single thought, and I promise you, they will tell you the same." He nudged his nose with hers again, and she let his words sink into her.

The more time she spent in Kunmei, with Nikaius' pack in general, she learned that she knew nothing about the world around her. She felt unprepared and inexperienced compared to everyone else she kept company with.

"I just don't want to be something you regret because I can't make up my mind." Being inadequate was a constant theme that was on her mind and though she was starting to take the members of the household at their word, reassuring herself was hard most days. A lot of her doubts came from a voice in her head that sounded a lot like her mother and sister. Somehow, whenever those thoughts came about, it seemed as if someone in the pack knew where her thoughts went and were able to pull her back from it.

Though cooking was something that had been her job at home, when she was in the kitchen of Corinth Manor, she sometimes fell into those thoughts, reliving the ire of her mother in the form of improperly flavored cakes—her mother often did this, stating that Morrigan had gotten it wrong even when the requests had been written—or something wasn't well done enough for her suddenly changing tastes. Aslin was a pro at suddenly coming up with a topic of conversation when this happened, even though it sometimes startled Morrigan.

Even the frankness of the conversation she and Hawke were currently having was a testament to her adjustment. She would have never had such frank conversations with past lovers, even though those had been few and far between and when she had been a teenager, before Amara had ruined that for her by telling their mother.

"I could never regret knowing you or anything that comes with that." His eyes searched hers and the honesty she saw there made her flush. For some reason, seeing his emotions so plainly on his face was a jarring reminder that not everything she had learned in her past was true. Her mother had consistently told her that changelings could hide their emotions and could manipulate the world around them to make others believe what they wanted, but with her connection to Hawke cemented by his touch, she could feel what he felt plainly on her skin.

"I have no magic." It was a lie that she kept telling herself, though they both knew the truth. She did have magic, was able to feel what others were feeling on her skin, but she was cut off or hadn't learned the other types of magic. She couldn't teleport or pull things from the ether like everyone else, and she couldn't feel any magic aside from a brief tingle when she touched someone.

"Magic isn't important."

Morrigan laughed. The notion was nonsense, and they both knew it. Magic was the most important thing because it created and powered everything. She knew he was trying to make her feel better, but it wasn't working. "It's literally the foundation of our world, Hawke."

"But it isn't what makes us the beings we are. You're still the kind person who hosts lessons for people to learn Common and helps care for children you have no tie to, despite the world thinking you have no magic. I'm positive your kindness doesn't end there." His hands smoothed up along her back, fingers somehow finding the exact spots where her physical scars lingered, as if he knew their location. It was still so new to welcome touch from anyone, but his hands were warm even through her dress, and it was comforting even if he didn't know they were there. "You're not less because of what you've been through, but more."

His words were nice, but they weren't going to erase years of inadequacy forced upon her by her mother and siblings. She wanted to believe him, but the thought of leaving herself open to him increased the uncertainty of her actions. "How can someone who is believed to have no magic and scarred be more?" If her family didn't think she was worth anything, why would anyone else?

Frustration burned away the feelings she had felt from Hawke a moment prior, and he killed the connection to his emotions by moving to settle his hands on her hips to push her back gently. "Get up." Alarm rang through her as she scrambled up from the bed and adjusted her dress. Had she said something wrong? Of course, she had. Self-doubt crept back in. Even though she was starting to feel safe with the pack, she knew there were limits and obviously she had crossed one. Crossing her arms over her chest, she watched him unfold himself from where he had been sitting to stand to his full height. When they had first met, he had been intimidating, all large and in charge with a grumpy demeanor, but now that she knew him, he didn't seem so scary. Except for the ever-changing expressions on his face as he thought.

Had he changed his mind? She wouldn't blame him if he had. It would be uncomfortable living in the same house as him if he had decided he didn't want her and that made her nervous. Could she remain unaffected by his loss if she had to see him every day?

Quickly stepping back, she allowed him room to stand, but before she could move any further, he reached for her, giving her a quick reassuring hug before leading her back over to the window. His presence was a warm one that had soothed her the night before when she had been caught in the throes of a nightmare that had been some sort of magical attack that no one could explain.

"Here's what's going to happen." He grinned, pressing a kiss to her forehead that felt like amusement and adoration, and turned her to face the windows again. "We're going to count your scars, and for each one, you're going to say something nice about yourself."

He was going to see her scars? Alarm rang through her, catching the breath in her chest for a moment as she stepped back. "I have too many." She protested.

"When was the last time you counted?" He raised an eyebrow, catching her elbow to tug her back to him. He didn't plan on letting her escape from whatever plan he had.

"I-I haven't." Why would someone want to count the scars left by another?

"Alright, then tonight, you'll know for sure." She jumped as he pulled her hair over one shoulder and pressed a kiss to the lingering mark Nikaius had left on her neck. Need throbbed through her, straight between her legs, as if Hawke himself had bitten her. His voice dropped to a low whisper that buzzed through her as he breathed them into her skin. "You can tell me to stop, and I will." His voice was low but held nothing but truth.

Did she want him to stop?

Anxiety still bubbled in her chest, turning her stomach at the thought of Hawke seeing her scars. He had seen them before, though, she rationalized. She had only been draped in a blanket when they ended up meeting in the bathroom after her night with Nikaius. He had been a bit rough with her, but she now understood why he had behaved the way he had. He was jealous that night when she and Nikaius had been together. The thought made something warm and soft settle over her. He had been jealous, but had only thought about the implications of Nikaius' mark on her, not the act they had been caught in.

Trying to swallow around the sudden lump in her throat, she nodded. While she was stressed about whatever was going on in his mind, she knew she trusted Hawke.

"I, personally, think you're lovely regardless of blemishes. I hold several myself."

"Guard things I assume?"

"Being friends with Rekru'e has its hazards." His voice was soft and warm against the skin of her neck before he pressed another kiss there.

She shivered as he tugged her zipper down, the cool air making her skin break out in goosebumps that were quickly soothed by the softness of Hawke's lips along the bared flesh, the feeling of his stubble a curious feeling. "D-does that count as one?" she asked curiously.

Hawke laughed. "No, darling, I need to get you out of this dress before it can really begin." Shock shot through her, and she grasped the bodice of the dress to her chest as she turned to face him.

"But won't people see?"

"The house is magic; it only allows what we want to be seen. Turn back around." He raised a challenging eyebrow before gripping her hips and physically turning her.

"I don't see how—"

"Morrigan." Hawke cut off her argument, and she let out a slow breath before turning to face the window again, the chill renewing as he finished unzipping her. "You can keep yourself covered and don't have to strip completely." His warmth left her, leaving her curious, but before she could turn to question him, it was back tenfold, his skin pressing to hers as his hand found hers. His fingers laced between hers before he pressed her palm to the window, his overshadowing hers. The shiver that shook her had nothing to do with the cold and was laced with comfort and arousal that left her gasping for breath.

"Don't move this hand. You can have the other one to hold your dress, but don't move this one." Hawke's command was soft, punctuated by lingering kisses on her neck and again on the brand that declared her magicless.

Even though she didn't feel quite settled yet, the sassy part of her had begun to feel more and more comfortable and had been rearing her head on occasion. She was still worried about getting in trouble, but... "What happens if I don't?" slipped from her lips before she could stop it.

Her breath caught as he chuckled, a low dark sound preceding his wide palms sliding along her bare skin, parting the dress further. "Do you really want to find out?"

"Maybe?" The way his lust thickened against her skin made her shiver, and her own rose to meet it, need rolling through her again.

Hawke ignored her, pressing a kiss to one of the scars. "One."

Oh, they were starting. Wracking her mind, she tried to think of something nice to say. "I... I think." She scanned the horizon outside the window. "I pick up on languages really quickly."

She felt his smile spread against her back. "You do."

He moved on to the next one. "Two."

"I... uh. I'm a fair baker."

"Very good baker, you're delicious." His teeth grazed the next one, and she pressed her palm more firmly against the window as he mumbled, "Three."

"I... Can I say I think I'm pretty?"

"You are pretty. Anything specific?"

"I..."

"That will count as two—" Hawke's voice was light and playful and made her giggle nervously as he continued to kiss her skin. She didn't know if he had found another scar or if he was just antagonizing her to comply with what he was asking.

"I like that I look like my father and Mae. It separates us from my mother and other siblings."

"That's a really good one." He shifted, moving further down her back. "Five?"

"Uh." His hands curled along her hips, stroking carefully along the bones there. "Madam Eda said I was a basic size for changelings. I know I'm not a changeling but hearing that I'm a basic size was nice. Especially after so many years of my mother forcing me into things that didn't fit."

"I think you have a lovely figure." He squeezed her before his hands wandered higher, up across her waist and up her ribcage.

"From you, that's a high compliment," she whispered. His hands tickled a bit, but she fought the need to move, deciding to focus on the adoration she felt in his touch.

"Why's that?" Curiosity tickled the skin of her ribs as he drummed his fingers.

"You're from Hawk's Keep in the Corviana Territory, aren't you?"

"I am."

"Your women are quite thin as well. The thought that you would be attracted to me isn't one I had considered."

"You'll find that not all of us hold up to societal ideals as the rest of the world does."

"So I'm learning." Even though she had started this—whatever it—with high anxiety, the longer Hawke's hands remained stable on her body, the more she sank into the acceptance that things were different here, and he saw her in a different light than what others once had.

Licking her lips, she sought out his reflection in the window, watching as he stood again. She hadn't realized he had knelt while addressing her scars, but that thought was fleeting as he stepped closer, his chest pressed flush against her back again. His hands separated then, one dipping lower as the other shifted up, his thumb brushing the underside of one breast that had her breath catching in her chest, and her lingering arousal flared back to life.

"You catch on to things pretty quickly."

"I like to think so."

"You only had five." The hand that wasn't at her breast trailed lower, his warm fingers tapping their way down her stomach and along the bone of her hip.

"Five?"

"Deep visible scars." His teeth found her earlobe, and her breath hitched as his palm spread across her breast, kneading it gently. "We'd be here all night if we were to count the small ones too."

"I...I'm not opposed to that." Her words were unsure despite her conviction to see whatever game he was playing through to the end. Hawke's fingers teased between her legs, and she leaned back to rest against him with a lustful sigh. Every emotion coming from him was nothing less than adoration and lust, two feelings Morrigan decided she wanted to sink into in that moment, or for him to sink into her.

"If you're sure." Removing his hands from her, he nipped the mark on her neck. His hands slid across her collarbones as he pulled the dress from her hands. Trembling, Morrigan let it pool around her feet, the slip going with it.

Turning her, Hawke grinned. "You're so beautiful. If I must spend every day on my knees reminding you, I will."

Shoring up some courage, Morrigan turned and smiled up at him. "I might take you at your word." His laugh was loud in the quiet room, so bright and open that it made her join him. His hands smoothed carefully down her sides and then back up before finding her chin again, pulling her in for a commanding, dominating kiss.

Like Nikaius, Hawke's size and warmth should be paralyzing, but his low murmured, "Come" made her melt. She wasn't even sure what he had meant by the word, just that heat seeped into every single nerve in her body and suddenly she felt like putty, ready to be molded and manipulated to whatever standard he needed.

Her shyness at being so bare was replaced by curiosity, a desire to chase the breathlessly wonderful feeling, but she also wanted to please him as well. As he stepped back, she followed easily, her breath catching the rough sound of her name on his lips. A soft plea slipped out as she reached for him again, intent on seeking out another wonderful, mind-numbing kiss from him.

A dark smirk curled his lips as his thumb brushed along hers again. "You know I've heard you before?" Her spine tingled as he drew her close, his words almost a kiss upon her lips. He turned them and before she could gain her footing, she tumbled backward onto the bed, Hawke following with all the ease of the predator she knew him to be.

Fates, she was going to be eaten alive by him, but she couldn't find one modicum of shame as she reached for him again. With her breath stolen by his kiss, his fingers pressed just barely over the edge to painful as he grasped her knee, tugging on it to spread her legs so he could settle between them.

Her heart raced, and she knew she was trapped, but she wasn't afraid. When he sat up, it felt as if she could feel his gaze; her body burned with each new inch of skin he gazed upon. They were quite the contrast; the rich skin of his hand wrapped around the starkness of her knee, but the trail his fingers traced drew her attention. Her gasp was loud as he settled closer, hooking her foot around his hip as he leaned over her again.

He was shirtless, but still wore the dark pants most guards wore, and it felt rough against her sensitive skin. "Hawke," before she could say more, he captured her lips in another kiss.

He kissed like a man starved, all tongue and teeth, with hands that grasped her skin tightly, sure to bruise. But she didn't complain, not when that desperate mouth sought to devour her neck right above Nikaius' mark. It was so strange that she could feel close to what she had felt when Nikaius had bitten her, but each pass of Hawke's tongue or teeth against it made sharp electricity shoot through her, as if scattering lightning through her veins from her throat to the tips of her toes and fingers back to her pulse between her legs, and her heart that hammered with it.

Hawke's nose nudged her ear, and he whispered, "I want you to beg for me."

Being pressed so thoroughly against him heated every part of her body, and everything throbbed as his hand crawled higher, squeezing at the fullness of her hip before snaking up higher. His lips and hands found different spots to tease her as one hand smoothed across his carefully shaved nape, her other sinking her nails into his shoulder, unsure whether to pull him closer or press him away. His kisses turned biting and her hand spasmed against him when he found the spot between her legs that made her toes curl.

"Oh Fates." She was absolutely gone and knew if he asked again, she would beg for the release he was teasing her towards.

Chapter Three

Morrigan

Corinth Manor

Despite countless amounts of reassurance from everyone at the house, part of her still felt like everything was a cosmic joke or some kind of test that she hoped she would pass.

But when his mouth found hers again, she readily arched up into him, pulling herself closer as she slid her hand up to grasp his shoulder and desperately rolled her hips, her own teeth sinking into his bottom lip.

Normally, all she did was think and feel, analyzing every emotion as it came to her, like Hawke's adoration and lust that tingled against her ribs where his fingers stroked teasingly under her breast. But when she was with someone like this, her own emotions seemed to drown out everything else and almost allowed her some peace from the outside world and let her just be.

She knew that they couldn't come back from it and while part of her was still terrified that there was some test between the three men that made her have to pick one or all, the other part was thrilled as she let herself just feel for a few brief moments before shifting to find his eyes again. Resting her forehead against his, she hummed softly, shivering as goosebumps chased his hand higher.

"You can't take this back later." He knew how she felt about Nikaius and Waric and she wanted— needed—his acknowledgment that he was very aware of her feelings for Waric and Nikaius but didn't care. She needed to know that he was willing to step over the line that would bring them from just courting to lovers.

"I'm not letting you leave here without being mine, Morrigan." He grinned down at her, his eyes bright as he spoke. Were his words a promise? His touch softened as he shifted to rest on his forearm, bringing himself closer to her to trace his fingers tenderly down her cheek, soft and patient, adoration and joy sinking into her skin at his touch.

"Right here in this space, in this room, we belong to each other and no one else." His words curled through her as she settled back to search his face. The way he said it, so breathless and raw, made his implication clear. He wanted her completely. Nothing about him screamed deception. "I just want you."

She was torn between laughing and crying over the way his voice sounded before he kissed her again. A torrent of emotions flooded through her as she shifted closer, moving to press her hips closer to him. She wanted him more than anything else at that moment, and she decided that like him, she would take what she wanted.

Awareness spread across her as a door slammed somewhere in the distance, and her wide eyes flew to his. She watched as he sat up on his knees and tilted his head, listening. After a moment, a slow grin spread across his face as he returned his attention to her, seeking out another kiss. "It's fine."

Though she had sex with Nikaius when everyone else was in the house, being aware that one of her possible mates could be the cause of the footsteps shuffling down the hall made her pause. In her distraction, Hawke's fingers trailed up along her arms, leaving a trail of goosebumps in their wake. Slipping his fingers in between hers, he pulled her hands up, pinning them above her head.

His lips found her throat again, teeth scraping along her windpipe in a move that made her entire body shudder and her voice break as she moaned soft and high. The potential that they might get caught should make her pause. While she was still getting comfortable sharing her affections with multiple men, she also didn't have any desire to be watched in such an intimate position. But it didn't deter her. With her hands pinned, and his lips on her throat, all she could do was give another sigh and shift under him.

She knew that the others were okay with her being with Hawke, but as he stroked his hand down her side, urging her hips to roll against his hardness once more, she still felt as if they were walking a dangerous line. Hawke's teeth found her earlobe and tugged, tempting her closer, and she gave into the thrill at the edge of the line they walked, her plea for more falling from her lips before she allowed it to do so.

Something about her request must have snapped the restraint within him because suddenly, his hand had a near bruising grasp on her jaw, and his teeth were sinking into the same mark Nikaius had left on the side of her neck. All teasing seemed to have left him as his other hand finally, *finally* dipped between her legs again, stroking her sensitive flesh in a way that made her feel as if his hand and mouth were attached by one line of devastating electricity.

All thoughts of remorse and anxiety fled as his thumb rolled over her clit and two of his fingers delved into her, his voice a dark growl. "Beg for what you want from me. I want to hear you say it. I want *them* to hear what I do to you." His words were possessive, but not in a way that disturbed her.

She was unable to settle, her nails digging into his skin as she rocked against his hand, a soft plea leaving her lips.

Hopefully. whoever had entered the house didn't hear them, or if they did, they didn't pay them any mind, despite Hawke wanting them to hear. His lips trailed lower to explore her exposed flesh, and a little gasp escaped when he nipped the bone of her hip, and she arched up into him as she tried to swat him away.

Hyperaware of the sounds of the room, her panted breaths mingled with the trembling air he exhaled against her sensitive skin, she hadn't registered his intentions but suddenly his mouth was between her legs, nipping at the tender skin of her inner thigh and everything else fell away.

It hadn't been long since her last encounter of this kind, except she had been fully clothed with Waric in the library and it had been a confusing surprise. She couldn't find any shame in the fact that she was enjoying this encounter just as much as she had with Waric. This time with Hawke felt different and new. Was it the fact that her hands met velvet tufts of feathers as she dug her fingers into the breadth of his shoulders as she tried to hang on to what sanity she had left? Or the thickness of his fingers and the way they curled into her just right, making her hips rock against him as he brought her way too close way too fast.

Feeling too small for her skin was a new sensation, and she couldn't quite find the proper way to lay as she rocked against him again, pulling him closer as his tongue, wet and hot, slicked over the sensitive nerves of her clit. When his fingers moved just right, she wanted to trap him there and beg him to never leave her again. Her fingers spasmed against his skin as she begged for just a little bit more.

His fingers curled again as he groaned into her neck, making her tremble before he pulled away. As she sat up, her protest died on her tongue as she watched him remove the rest of his clothing with quick, deft motions. A shudder rolled through her as his trousers fell to the floor. She took all of him in, licking her lips, mouth suddenly dry.

Taking in the nakedness of someone else was still a new experience but looking him over from head to toe kept the delicious throb inside of her thriving. As she reached out to touch him, he caught her hand and pressed a kiss to her palm before pressing it, and her, back onto the bed again. Collecting her hands in one of his, he pinned them above her head again, his grin spreading as he shifted her knees, tugging one up to hook around his hip as his cock nudged against her entrance.

His intrusion was slow, a barely there motion of his hips, as he made sure she was ok, but his patience didn't last long and with a snap of his hips, she was suddenly full. The sudden intrusion made her gasp and arch, the motion of her hips sinking him just a bit further into her and making him groan into her neck.

A giddy little laugh escaped her lips, chestier and breathier as she shifted again, rocking her hips in a way that shifted them again. But her motions alone were not enough. "Move..." She twisted her hands under his and dug her nails into his palm as she tried to move again. "For the love of everything, please move." The begging he had wanted finally fell from her lips. All the sensations he was giving her seemed to short-circuit everything else, lust and pleasure at the forefront, tickling her chest where his breaths heaved against hers and his lips teased at her ear, making her suddenly restless. She needed him to move more than she needed air.

"Shhh... I want you all to myself, remember?" His hand released hers and settled over her mouth, something she thought she wouldn't have liked, but the possessiveness she felt from him wasn't a burning brand like Elijah's had been but felt more like adoration, comforting and warm, and she found she didn't mind it. His other hand anchored to her hip so he could withdraw from her just to plunge back in. His hand muffled the noises she made, and his grin didn't leave his face as his eyes flicked to the door. Though she couldn't hear anything aside from her own blood rushing in her ears and his panting, it seemed like he was listening for something even though his hips kept moving in that slow, tantalizing pace.

Whoever had come home had figured out where they were but that didn't deter him as he found a pace that was slow and deep, the hand on her hip guiding her to work against him, encouraging her to meet him thrust for thrust. Once she had caught up with his pace, his hand moved, thumb finding the nerves where they met and pressed, making her hips jump in a way that had her throwing back her head as pleasure scorched through her entire body with the beat of her heart. Each hard thrust of his was met with a stroke of his thumb and the pace quickly threw her off the edge, her teeth sinking into the flesh of his palm as she tried to muffle the noise that escaped her.

He didn't give her any sort of reprieve before he pulled out and hauled her up to turn her to face away from him on her knees. Taking her hands, he pressed them against the headboard, his lips trailing down her spine as he stroked his fingers through her hair. "I want them to hear you scream for me." Heat flushed through her at the reminder that they weren't alone, even though he had shushed her only a few moments earlier.

Her first orgasm hadn't quite tapered off before he was sinking into her from behind, his pace hard and fast as he worked her higher and higher again. The angle was different and when he pressed between her shoulder blades, encouraging her to settle her chest on the bed, he hitched her hips up. The change in angle was everything the last position was not, hitting a different place than before that made her see stars with each deep plunge of his hips. Each motion drew her higher until her entire being trembled with the need to orgasm, but she didn't think she could. Not yet.

When his thrusts grew erratic, he fisted her hair and leaned over, pressing his lips against her ear to growl one devastating word as his fingers began quickly flicking and stroking her clit.

"Come."

That command was all she needed to break again, and she screamed her release into the room, unashamed of the sound as he groaned into her shoulder and came with her.

Chapter Four

Hawke

Corinth Manor

Hawke barely had time to clean them up and tuck Morrigan into his bed before he heard Waric's steps shuffle past the door again. It was the second time the male had passed by, and Hawke knew that he was waiting for a good moment to intrude. Waric's pace was unsteady and unsure, something that seemed out of character for his friend. The lack of accompanying footsteps warned him that Waric was alone.

While he wanted to stay and cuddle Morrigan, to give her the aftercare they had all accidentally set a precedent for her to not expect, he knew it was something that would have to wait a bit longer. Waric returning home alone was, unfortunately, more pressing. "I'm going to grab some water and a snack, okay? I'll be right back." He stroked his hand down her bare back, smiling when she gave a sleepy affirmative hum. He knew that she might be upset about the lack of care he had given when the marks he bit into her skin began to bloom, but he held only a small amount of remorse about it. The sounds she had made when receiving them were well worth her ire.

Tucking the sheet up around her, he pressed a kiss to her head before standing and shaking out his wings, bracing himself for whatever conversation was about to happen. Tugging his pants back on, he leaned over to press another kiss to Morrigan's shoulder before heading to the door.

Thankfully, Waric wasn't near the door when Hawke pulled it open. It gave him the chance to exit the room fully and shut the door before turning to find his friend. Waric was always pale, but the starkness of his skin was more defined, exhaustion evident in the darkness under his eyes. It had only been a few hours, but it seemed like ages had passed.

"I don't know where Priamos went." Waric speaking in Rekru'e was a red flag that sent alarm through Hawke as he watched his friend stare at the floor.

"He was with you earlier." Hawke stepped around him, leading them down the hall towards the kitchen. Even though they were speaking in Rekru'e, he didn't want Morrigan to overhear their conversation. She was smart and even though she might not quite comprehend what they were fully saying, he was worried she would catch their meaning well enough.

"I know, but you know how he gets. He wandered off but never came back." Waric followed, letting out a soft sigh.

"This isn't abnormal." The news wasn't new to Hawke. Priamos often wandered off to other territories for visits during his drops when he took over. Hawke had never really understood the way the moons and other moods affected the Rekru'e until he had lived with Nikaius for as long as he had.

Cav'Sara had three moons. Yasivr—the largest of the three moons—controlled shifting of Rekru'e kind into their wild forms. This was the moon that was quickly approaching and most affected the change. For Nikaius, however, his fluctuations were a little different and would often happen outside of the effects of that moon, depending on how much energy he had exerted over Priamos to prevent the change.

The other two moons controlled the ruts. Jahiy was four months after Yasivr and triggered a primals' need to breed, and Laz'mir followed four months after, influencing the change in other types of changelings, Hawke and Aquila included. Hawke was personally grateful that his animal wasn't affected at the same time as Nikaius; he didn't even want to begin to imagine the things that would happen if that were the case. Rekru'e tended to get very territorial around their mates, and Hawke knew that the way their situation currently stood, despite them being pack, Priamos might have an issue with Morrigan spending time with him. It was something they would have to approach as it came.

"I tracked him as far as The Pridelands' border. There was blood and the scent of others that I couldn't place."

"That's..." For Waric to not know the scents of others in this part of the territory was alarming. To get to the northern border, one would have to go directly through town to get there and because Kunmei itself was such a small town, someone, guard or civilian, would have noticed something amiss before then. At least Hawke hoped.

"I know," Waric let out a sigh, running a hand through his hair as he looked around the kitchen, licking his lips. "How's Morrigan?"

Hawke looked him over for a bit, trying to gather what he had meant by his question. Waric's heart was steady, there was no nervous or angry inflection of his voice and though his shoulders were slouched, and his arms crossed over his chest there didn't seem to be any tension within him. Nothing screamed that he was upset about the situation, but Waric was also one of the few people who could mask their emotions the best. He was able to control his physical form enough to change into other people, so if it hadn't been for his hearing and having known the man so long, Hawke wouldn't be able to anticipate his friend's moods. "The context of that question determines my answer, Waric."

The brunette laughed, shoving Hawke's shoulder, letting him know that there was no animosity between them. "Last time we talked, she was still a bit upset about Nikaius rejecting her proposal that he marry her to placate his father." Pulling some cheese and a hunk of meat from the fridge, Hawke set to carefully cutting them as he thought. He and Morrigan had talked about her plan to have Nikaius marry her to prevent Nikola Ayrden from forcing someone onto his youngest son. Hawke had agreed that it was a good plan. She wanted to be sure that their pack remained healthy and whole and having another newcomer entering their lives might not have settled as well as Morrigan had.

Nikaius had been further gone into the chaos of his own mind than any of them had anticipated, and his reaction had triggered the shift that allowed Priamos to take control.

"I'm not sure, honestly. I found her looking out the windows of my room earlier. She's upset, but I won't claim to know her thoughts on the matter. We can approach that topic later." He pulled a tray from the cupboard and set up the snack he had made before seeking out a water pitcher, glasses and some fruit he knew Morrigan would enjoy.

"How is her arm doing?" Waric asked, plucking a piece of melon from the bowl and crunching into it.

"Do you mean the brand or the burn?"

"Both."

"The burn is mostly gone; she's been putting a bit of salve on it. I haven't seen the mark on her upper arm though. I was careful to avoid it when I could." The night she had been attacked was one that replayed in Hawke's mind repeatedly, even though he had been reassured that there was nothing that he could have done. None of them had known what was happening. He had purposefully avoided touching it where he could because he was worried of how she might react.

Clearing his throat, he adjusted his hold on the tray and gave Waric a small smile. As a member of the pack, Hawke held affections towards his friends that he didn't with most others. It wasn't a sexual attraction by any means, though he could agree that Waric and Nikaius were very handsome men, but they didn't do for him what Morrigan did, which wasn't odd considering most people didn't do what Morrigan did. He had been party to some flings in the past, both male and female, but the attraction never lasted, and he had worried that Morrigan would be the same. But the connection he felt with her was different. It held a different sort of ease than what he had experienced in the past, like she had just walked into his life, declared she was going to stay and had kept her word, slowly melding herself into their lives.

Most of his relationships fizzled out because he was so busy bouncing between courts as an emissary and second-in-command, and most of his partners hadn't been satisfied with his abrupt departures, though they weren't entirely at fault for that. He had a serious lack of emotional presence as well, and if it didn't feel just perfect, he would easily let go when they decided he was no longer enough. It hurt a bit when things ended, but he hoped that with Nikaius and Waric also being in the picture, she might deign to entertain him for longer.

"I lost you there for a second." Waric waved his hand in front of Hawke's face, and he blinked.

"Yeah... Sorry." Blinking a few more times, he nodded. "I hate to be that person, but we might be able to coerce her into letting us look at it if we're both there. She hasn't let me see it since it happened. I don't know if it's some guilt she holds for making us worry or a fear she has that once we see it, something bad will happen. I know it unsettles her a bit, and it does me too. But maybe if we're both there, she'll realize the gravity of the situation. I think we've been doing her a disservice by not telling her that we're worried about it. I'll bring this to the room if you want to grab some of the salve and bandages."

Waric saluted him and turned to head in the opposite direction to gather the supplies.

Once he was sure he had everything he needed, snacks and water, Hawke returned to his bedroom, adjusting the tray into one hand to carefully push open the door to peek in before hip checking it to open more. Morrigan was still snuggled in his bed, sprawled out on her stomach with a pillow tucked under her torso and her arms wrapped around it. She looked peaceful, and he hated to break that peace to make her do something she didn't want to do. He was sure she had been tending to it, but he also knew that they needed to make sure it didn't get worse. Though the blackness of her skin hadn't seemed to spread past the bandage she had wrapped around it, they didn't know what magic had caused it, and the salve they had given her for it might not be what was needed.

His heart gave an unsteady little throb when Morrigan shifted to peer up at him through her hair with a shy little smile. She looked worn out but happy.

"I brought some food, Waric is bringing some salve so we can tend to your arm." His tone was soft, one he typically used on children, and he hoped she didn't feel as if he was patronizing her, even though he was, just a little bit.

"It's fine." She huffed, shifting away from him to tug the blanket up over her shoulders, attempting to hide herself from view before pressing her face into the pillow she was hugging.

"We still need to look at it Morrigan. I know you don't want to, but we can't risk there being any sort of residual magic to it." Hawke set the tray of food on the bedside table and sat on the side of the bed.

"Residual magic?" She shifted over onto her back, blinking up at him with an unamused expression. He knew that having people care about her was still new, but he couldn't help but smile at the disgruntled look she gave him as she brought the pillow with her, grimacing a bit as she tried to sit herself up with one hand. Sighing, Hawke reached for her right as Waric knocked at the door.

Hawke was worried about how Morrigan would feel with Waric seeing her in some stage of undress, but when she called out "it's open," that anxiety eased a bit.

He helped her sit up the rest of the way before reaching across the bed to pull his shirt from where it had been discarded and offering it to her. "Thank you." Morrigan gave him a slow, sweet kiss that stirred the fire in his blood once again, but Waric entering the room made her pull away. Shimmying out from under the blankets, she gave Waric a small smile as she passed him to step into the attached bathroom.

Both men watched her go before the door shut behind her. Waric turned a bright grin to Hawke, who laughed with him.

"She's fucking gorgeous, isn't she?" Waric mused aloud as he flopped himself down onto Hawke's bed. Hawke had worried for a moment that Waric would rescind his assurance that he and Nikaius were fine with him being in Morrigan's life and they would have a problem, but the leisurely way the brunette stretched out confidently eased some of Hawke's worry.

"She really is," he agreed.

"Hawke!?" Both men stood quickly at the alarmed tone in Morrigan's voice, but before either of them could move a step towards the door, it slammed open and Morrigan stepped out, her face flushed beet red.

"What's wrong, princess?" Waric asked, tilting his head at her embarrassed state.

"I..." Morrigan wouldn't lift her eyes to them, and Hawke stepped forward, reaching for her. She didn't really cringe away from him, but the motion was similar, and she frowned at him. "What on earth did you do to my back?"

For a moment, dread had made his insides turn cold before her words settled over him, and he realized what she meant. Hawke couldn't help the grin that spread across his face as she twisted herself around a bit to show off one of the bruises blooming on her shoulder. "Remember what you said to me when Nikaius marked you?"

Morrigan's eyes narrowed at him as she tugged the shirt on over her head. "No, why?"

"You said, and I quote 'It's a hickey. The healing salve you have will clear it right up.'" He reeled her in by the shirt, stroking one hand through her hair as Waric laughed beside them before he reached for her as well.

"I wasn't around for this conversation, what else did she say?" Waric's hand stroked through her hair as Hawke secured his hands on Morrigan's hips, pulling her flush against him.

"If not, I know other things that can heal or hide blemishes left on my skin by others. You forget this isn't the first time a man has left marks on my skin." He quoted. Morrigan's frown turned to an adorable pout, and Hawke leaned down to kiss her gently. "Didn't you also say something about it being the first time a man bruised you that you enjoyed? Judging by the sounds you made, I think you enjoyed earning those as well."

"Waric." Morrigan huffed, turning to the other male, but he laughed as well.

"Oh no. I'm not getting you out of this one, love. You started it with him, I'm just a deviously affectionate bystander."

"I hate you both," she groaned, pressing her face into Hawke's chest.

"You adore us." Waric pressed himself against her, bracketing her in between them as he pressed a kiss to the top of her head. "Now, let's look at that mark on your arm. I have a different salve that should block any residual magic if there was any."

Chapter Five

Waric

Cin Catriz, The Pridelands

Waric sighed, rolling out his aching shoulders as he trudged through the sand that led from the receiving platform into Cin Catriz, the capital city of The Pridelands and home to Santiago De'Lyon. It had been two days since Nikaius and Priamos disappeared and the night before last had been spent with Morrigan and Hawke, trying to ease his own worry about his mate.

The snow had fallen heavily in the two nights that had followed Priamos' disappearance and had blanketed the world in a way that Waric had no idea where to start. After he and Hawke had spent most of the day before canvasing the entirety of Kunmei's territory lines on foot, Waric decided he had to give in and ask for help.

Though Hawke was right and Priamos did tend to wander, Waric had always had the bond to defer to. In his mind, he typically could feel the crackling energy of Nikaius tied around his own thoughts. But it had been less like muted static that he couldn't quite catch a hold of enough to tug on.

Having the bond inaccessible for the third time in a month and a half was becoming a problem. Something was up and it had to be more than the constant storms that loomed over the Be'Sala mountains. Priamos was somewhere, without magic, possibly with serious injuries. If he had gone anywhere, it would have been to see Santi and Mae. With Mae's ability to heal by touch, and Santi's innate ability to be able to tell what was ailing someone by simply looking at them, the couple were the best healers in the entirety of the changeling courts.

While the platform he had arrived on seemed to be surrounded by miles and miles of endless sand, Waric knew that the entrance to Cin Catriz wasn't far. It had taken him a few times to find it when he had been first sent to train with the De'Lyon forces when he was a teen. The trick was not to look for it. You just picked a direction, closed your eyes and walked a thousand paces in whichever direction you'd chosen. Trusting the process and the one who gave you the invitation was hard at first, but the more Waric had practiced, the easier it became.

Taking a slow breath, Waric closed his eyes and turned, stepping off the platform in his chosen direction. One would worry they would easily get lost if they choose the wrong direction, but if the invitation was genuine, most people often didn't hit a thousand steps before they were greeted with the shade of massive buildings made into the sand.

Once he felt the temperature change, Waric opened his eyes to find himself in the central plaza of Cin Catriz. The homes in the square were similar to those in Kunmei, made of wood and brick, and the entire area was protected by large pillars and walls made entirely of stone. None of the buildings showed any sign of wear because they had been created with magic that prevented weathering and erosion.

Finally, looking at the paper he held in his hand, Waric found the address he needed to go to in order to find the library and took a slow, deep breath. He wasn't sure what he was going to do if Santi hadn't heard from Nikaius. He hadn't heard back from the Gorlassar nest to know if he had been there at all. He doubted it though. The De'Lyons were kin and closer to Kunmei than the Gorlassar home.

The library didn't look like a library from an outside perspective, simply a large house. It blended in with the homes around it, intricate wooden exterior included, but that had been intentional, a decision made when Santiago De'Lyon had taken over. Only a few people knew of its relocation and even fewer knew its whereabouts. The entrance changed daily, a portal hidden in a different shop or home within the city, and one had to request a meeting to be given access, which Waric had been granted when he had sent Hawke with the urgent request.

Warmth greeted him as he stepped into the library, the smell of ink and paper soothing away some of the anxiety Waric held in his shoulders and chest. It hadn't been long since he had been sitting at Nikaius' feet reading, as was customary for them to do, but the change of routine was starting to bother him a bit.

Rubbing his hand along his sternum, Waric hummed gently. He missed strong fingers threading through his hair. Morrigan's were fine, but there was something about the simple act being performed by a large hand that had killed people. Maybe Waric was a little twisted in that sense, but he enjoyed it nonetheless, after all, he had probably taken just as many lives. It wasn't something they took lightly, but it had always stirred a fire within them that when they came together, it would leave them mentally and physically in ruins for days afterwards. Morrigan coming along had deterred their own Selection Night traditions, so that sort of primal release hadn't happened in close to a year. Waric had hoped The Hunt—a Rekru'e Solstice tradition—would alleviate some of that beast, but he would need to find his mate in good condition before that happened.

Soren, the scholar who was also one of Santi's younger brothers, stood near a large desk, leaning on one hand as he grinned at the person he was talking to. It made Waric pause. The woman who was smiling up at Soren was almost identical to Morrigan. Her eyes and hair were only darker by a few shades, but the wrinkle of her nose as she laughed was the same. The cadence of her voice, soft but clear, was the same. Even her laugh was the same. Was this woman related to Morrigan somehow? She had to be. Waric had been ill the night it was revealed that Mae Aegean and Santi were true mates and had missed the confirmation ceremony the next day, so he hadn't been able to meet Santi's wife in person, but Waric assumed it was her.

Waric cleared his throat. As he approached, Soren rose, offering him a grin and a handshake. "Waric, well met."

Waric returned the greeting, but his attention was drawn by the woman who peered up at him with curiosity.

"You're the one who kidnapped my sister." Waric blinked at the sudden accusation and drew back as the red-haired woman stood, slamming her hands down on the table.

"Mae." Soren frowned, reaching out to touch Mae, but she slapped his hand away to stomp around the table and shove her finger into Waric's chest.

"No, I want to know what business you have taking my sister from her home?" Waric stood, dumbfounded, as he compared the similarities between Mae and Morrigan. They were both the same height, reaching almost to his shoulder but barely passing, but Mae was ferocious in her anger, and Waric wondered if there was a way to entice such a reaction from Morrigan. Their freckles were nearly identical, but some were hidden within her sister's tanned complexion. The sun had been kind to her.

"You're just as beautiful as your sister." Waric murmured absently.

Mae frowned at him for a moment, her finger still pressing against Waric's chest as her eyes flicked to his in confusion. "Is this some sick joke of yours? Does Morrigan know you were the ones who held her when she was branded?"

The memories that flooded to the surface then, of the small screaming thirteen-year-old he had tried to fight to return to. Nikaius had lost his mind when she was taken away and had bitten someone. Waric couldn't remember who. One minute they were being pulled away, the next, Bastian stabbed Nikaius. Priamos had lashed out and almost took out a lung. They both shifted and had fought furiously. It was only moments after that when Waric noticed their matching mark.

"We didn't kidnap her." Waric's brain finally caught up, and he cleared his throat. "Your brother, Elijah… He had brought Morrigan," Mae's breath hitched at the name, her eyes flicking between him and Soren for a moment, making Waric remember that 'Morrigan' hadn't been the name she was called for years. But it was her name, and he would use it.

They all had for months, and the name seemed to soothe some of the anger he could sense coming off Mae. "He brought her to Atce' Plaza to sell. Something happened, and she ended up in Bastian's hands."

"They tried to sell her? That doesn't make any sense." Mae's frown deepened as she crossed her arms over her chest, her disbelief evident in the stern set of her shoulders and the glare affixed on her face.

Waric watched her for a moment and tried to figure out why, exactly, she was so upset. Hawke had said the De'Lyon's were the masterminds. "I thought you would have known. Hawke said that it had all been planned by your husband." The downtrodden look on Mae's face disappeared at Waric's words.

"What do you mean?"

Waric frowned. Had she not known? Well fuck.

"Nothing. Slip of the tongue."

"Waric Cavanaugh," stepping closer, she glowered up at him. "What do you mean Santi had planned this?"

Oh shit.

"I think that's something you need to discuss with your husband. I only know secondhand details." Reaching out, Waric rested his hands on Mae's shoulders, hoping to will some of the fight to leave her. He wasn't as advanced as Nikaius in using his alpha powers, but he was still adept.

Letting out a shuddered breath, Mae shook her head. "Is she safe?"

That was a loaded question. "We've had two instances of someone targeting her with magic. First, it was an ice golem, and second, someone had gotten into her room and marked her. It left this dark black mark on her arm that we can't get to heal. It's almost like frostbite." He dropped his hands away from Mae's shoulders as she stepped back.

"That doesn't sound too safe to me." She turned on her heel with a huff. "I'm going to go have some words with my husband."

"Wait." Waric's voice broke as he reached out to catch her hand. He hadn't come for Morrigan, he had come for himself, to find his missing mate. "I came to see if Nikaius was here. He was attacked on the border, and we haven't seen him."

Mae's ire faded just a bit, but she didn't turn to face him, her voice dismissive. "He's not here."

Well, there went that thought. Where could Nikaius have gone? It wasn't like him to leave and not end up somewhere familiar. Where else could he have gone? Not only did he not want to go home without his mate, but he also didn't want to see the look on Morrigan's face when he returned with no word about him. Waric knew she was more astute than they all gave her credit for, but he wasn't quite ready to utter the words out loud.

Letting out a soft sigh, he dropped her hand, but she didn't move more than a few paces before she paused. Though he didn't want to admit it, he and Mae were in similar positions right then. He was looking for his lost mate, and she was looking for a connection to the sister she thought she had lost. "Is she happy?" she asked.

"For the most part. I know she misses you, and I'm worried about how much exposure to magic she's getting simply by being in Kunmei." Something in his words must have won her over because Mae turned to face him again. Her eyes focused on where he was twisting the fingers of one hand in the other, an anxious move Waric had developed as a child.

There was so much going on and though he was often the one who kept Nikaius and Priamos level, without the stability that they had developed, he was starting to feel like he was free falling. "We're doing our best to keep her safe. She's our mate, and we love her, why wouldn't we try our best to make sure of that? It's storming something awful in Kunmei and Be'Sala right now, but once the storms clear, I'll see about extending an invite to you so you can see her before Solstice."

"I would like that. Could I send her some things?"

Tension spread across Waric's shoulders and chest. Was this going to upset Morrigan even more than she already was? He would have to confer with Hawke and Nikaius to determine how they thought she would handle a gift from Mae. Clearing his throat, he nodded. "I can take something back with me if you'd like."

"She'll need something to wear for Solstice. I think I have the perfect thing for her." Her hand shook as she reached out to pull something from the ether. It was a black garment bag that looked a bit heavy. "It was my confirmation ceremony dress. It shouldn't need much alteration unless they've starved her in the year we've been apart."

"She's quite healthy, I assure you."

Mae gave a small smile. "Has she gotten used to changeling men?"

The question startled Waric, and he blinked at her in surprise. "What do you mean?" What did she know about their favor?

"The fact that you favor more to hold. I know my mother always gave her such a hard time about her size. My mother learned not to say anything to me or about her in my presence, but I don't know how awful they've been since."

"How did you assure that?"

"I might have stabbed her."

"You stabbed her? Your mother? Delaney Aegean?" Newfound respect welled within Waric as he laughed at the thought. Delaney Aegean was the most poised person he had ever encountered. The thought of how she would react if she was injured did not match the image Mae conveyed.

"Put my knife through her hand at the dinner table. Morrigan wasn't around to defend herself because it was shortly after she was injured. I refused to heal her until she apologized to me. Then threatened her that it would happen again if I heard her speak ill of my sister. She never said another word to me at all until I wed Santi."

"You have my utmost respect, Lady De'Lyon. I'll give this to the tailor so she can look it over and have Morrigan sized. If you hear from Nikaius, will you let us know? Something strange is going on, and I'm worried about his safety." He tried to remain composed as he asked, even though he realized his one lead had not been successful.

"If we find him, and he wants his presence known, we'll find some way to get word to you."

"Thank you."

Chapter Six

Nikaius

Unknown Area,
The Pridelands

Nikaius didn't know how much time had passed since he was last awake. He was vaguely aware of what was going on around him, but with Priamos largely in control, lucidity was something that Nikaius only held the barest grasp on. Trips from Kunmei to The Pridelands were typically quick with the portals from home, but walking it, particularly in his wolf form with an injured shoulder, made him slower, the world dragging as he continued to limp towards his destination: The home of Santiago De'Lyon.

Whatever the attackers had hit him with inhibited his ability to heal, which blocked him from being able to change back into his mortal form to teleport, but not enough to make him feel as if he were completely incapacitated. How someone hadn't found him yet was a mystery, especially with the wound on his shoulder steadily dripping. How he was still walking was entirely beyond him, but whenever he mentioned to Priamos that they needed to rest, he would shove Nikaius away to continue their trek. Nikaius was pretty sure they were surviving on nothing more than Priamos' determination and stubbornness.

At some point in his walk the day before, the woodland area of The Pridelands had tapered off and had become the rolling sands of the desert plain. Though it wasn't as hot as it would be in the northern part of the territory, the sun was still unforgiving, and Nikaius knew if he hadn't been in his wild form, the burn would have been so much worse. Being alone while trying to get to his destination, letting Priamos have primary control, gave him time to consider everything that had led up to the point where he was now.

His father wanted him to uphold the family tradition of marrying by the age of twenty-three.

It was a long-standing tradition that provided each lord with a living heir if something were to happen to them. Though they were mates, Nikaius' father refused to accept Waric as the person Nikaius wanted to marry. His father was focused on the what ifs of the world, instead of appreciating life as Nikaius and his pack had been doing. No, Nikola insisted that Nikaius had to find someone who could produce him an heir.

The fact that Morrigan knew about the tradition, as well as offered herself up to him, was a bit jarring, but the longer he thought about it, the more it made sense. Morrigan was that kind of person, the compassionate one who knew what it was like to be forced into doing things you didn't want to do to appease others.

He and the others had decided the night she entered their lives that they were going to let her find her own footing and decide what she wanted out of life with them. Sure, he could have reached out to Santi and Mae to have them retrieve her, but there hadn't been time.

There hadn't been time was the lie that he had kept telling himself, but realistically, there had been plenty of instances, including when Hawke had brought the letter to him to begin with. As a liaison between Kunmei and The Pridelands, Hawke had the ease of being able to go from court to court without needing to use any specific portal. It was old magic that had only been used by those who were chosen by the council. So realistically, on day one, he could have sent a letter to them, but he had allowed Priamos' curiosity and his own selfishness to continuously delay the inevitable conversation he would need to have with Santi.

Morrigan marrying him would solve more than one issue, but he didn't know how much of it was her genuine desire to help him or if it was something she felt an obligation to do. To him, it felt like the latter. Outside of him warring with Priamos, the doubts that crept in close to the full moons, and Morrigan being attacked, they hadn't really been able to spend a decent amount of time together. But most of that was his fault.

Despite his best effort to take things slow, Priamos had been too chaotic and close to the edge to control, so he hadn't really gotten to be in her presence for long without distraction, and it was a pity because the nights he did get a few moments to observe her just existing, he really liked the person she seemed to be.

A noise to his left drew him out of his thoughts and back into the awareness of the world around him. It sounded like a stone grinding against stone, and it sent chills down his spine the longer it went on. The sound made no sense in the wasteland that was the border between The Barrens and The Pridelands.

"Hey! Over here!" A voice in the distance made Nikaius pause, and he turned, searching for the one who had spoken. They didn't sound too far off from where he was.

"Oy, wolf boy!" The person was speaking Rekru'e, and Nikaius was glad to know that he was still in the Rekru'e territories. That meant that someone would know how to heal him. When Nikaius turned toward the direction he thought the voice had come from, he noticed a man he hadn't before. He was tall and dressed completely in white, only his eyes visible, but when he waved again, something familiar struck Nikaius. This had to be one of Santi's men. Something about him seemed more familiar than just his attachment to the De'Lyon tribe.

Stumbling his way across the sands, Priamos' paws finally met the cold marble platform the man had been standing on and a tremble rolled through him. It was weird that the marble was cold, but magic did wonderful things sometimes and now was not the time to contemplate how, or why, this man had randomly appeared with a hall of marble.

"You're quite the mess, man." The hand that reached out to stroke along the top of Priamos' head almost burned with how cold it was compared to his aching skin.

Nikaius wished he could shift and address his savior properly, but his injuries needed to be tended to first. When he had limped his way down the steps, the grinding noise began again, trembling the earth around him so much that he clumsily tripped over his paws and face planted onto the floor.

He wasn't mad about tripping over himself, the floor felt too nice, and he settled himself down, content for a nap. He was exhausted.

"Nope." A foot nudged him, and he gave a sleepy grumble. "We can't rest here. Someone is looking for you, and I don't know if you want to be found."

Someone was looking for him. The curiosity was enough to make him pull himself to his feet. He was so tired, but if this man knew how to heal him, then it would be worth whatever danger he might be getting into.

Despite being underground, the air was cool and fresh, as if he was still home instead of the desert of The Pridelands. Sighing softly, he followed the man further down the hall.

When they came to a room, the man began pulling off the white clothes he was wearing. When he was completely uncovered, relief welled through Nikaius. Silas De'Lyon grinned down at him.

Priamos gave a tired grumble, but he didn't have any energy to force himself forward to make sure that this person was actually who he appeared to be. Now that they had stopped moving, the throbbing in his shoulder was becoming deeper, matching the pace of his heart, and he wondered for a moment if there was an infection starting. Of course Priamos would push through, even with the threat of infection. Stupid wolf.

Silas seemed to know where Nikaius' mind had wandered, and he let out a soft sigh. "Come on, let's get you to the infirmary. I'll send someone to get Santi as well. I don't have the resources to treat you, but from the chatter I've heard, it's not safe to try to take a portal."

Nikaius wished he could shift back to his mortal form and ask what Silas meant, but someone else stepped into the room, carrying a large box of items. He couldn't see who they were, but they smelled familiar. Like an odd mix of his own pack, but he couldn't quite place the relation until she set down the box.

Mae De'Lyon was the spitting image of her sister, although she was taller and a bit slighter than Morrigan. The same freckles dotted her nose, and her hair was the same deep red color, but it only reached her shoulders. She smelled bright and summery, like fresh cut grass, and Priamos basked in the familiarity of it. It soothed some of the longing he held to be surrounded by his Earth and Sun again.

"Oh, what a sweet baby." Mae cooed setting down the stuff in her arms and crouching in front of where he sat. Priamos stirred to life, his tail giving a happy thump as she reached for him. While Nikaius tried to resist, tried to maintain some sort of dignity, Priamos had other plans and shoved him aside so he could go to Mae, plop down at her feet and bare his stomach to her.

How fucking embarrassing. The two warred for a few moments, but as usual, when they were in the wild form, Priamos won. They sat like that until another person entered.

Santiago De'Lyon's laugh matched his size, a loud deep sound that startled Mae, Nikaius, and Priamos, since none of them had heard him enter the room.

"I never thought I'd see the day when Priamos would submit to someone so easily." His voice was deep and held a thick accent as he addressed his wife in common.

"Priamos?" Mae jumped back as if she had been burned. "Like Nikaius Ayrden?" She frowned down at him, squinting her eyes to take him in.

Sure, they had been formally introduced, but they hadn't met while he was in his wild form because Santi and Mae had married shortly before Yasivr had been full. Rekru'e tended to be possessive of their mates when they were close to any of the full moons.

They had met in person about a month afterwards but that was prior to any knowledge that Nikaius had of Morrigan even existing, so he wasn't surprised that she was that thrown by the fact that he was there. Nikaius wasn't sure what day it was or where they fell within the cycle of the moon, so he had to tread lightly where Santi was concerned. Despite them being family, he knew that the older Rekru'e had status on him and could easily throw him from the court ,no questions asked.

"Aye, that's my youngest nephew that you're currently giving belly rubs to." Santi seemed to find the entire situation hilarious, which eased some of Nikaius' worry about him encroaching on territory at an inappropriate time. "What brought on the change this time, little wolf?" Santi's thick accent was for his wife's benefit, Nikaius knew this, but it was still annoying, and a little bit demeaning to be teased in another language.

Priamos took over again, rolling them so that he could give a low grumble at Santi's feet before settling them some distance away. Nikaius sighed.

You're going to pout now? Nikaius asked Priamos, who huffed again in the back of his head.

Home.

We can't go home yet, we're injured, and until we get mended, we'll be stuck here.

Mend then home.

Nikaius gave Priamos a mental shove, and the beast stirred with a grumble before returning to sit on his haunches at Santi's feet. Not being able to use words was frustrating, but Priamos nudging his head against Santi's thigh seemed to get the point across.

"Let's get you up to the infirmary so we can get you tended to; it doesn't look quite normal." Priamos gave a low grumble but followed as Santi turned to lead the way. Thankfully, there were no more stairs, but they still needed Santi's help when they reached the infirmary.

Once they were in the infirmary, Nikaius paused. There was no way they were going to be able to jump onto the table without getting a face full of floor. Again, he wished he had words because whining like a pup while pawing at his uncle's leg was a little humiliating, as was the deep chested laugh Santi gave as he easily scooped him up to set him on the table. Priamos had settled quietly in the back of his head, and Nikaius sighed as he shifted to lay more on his side.

When Santi prodded the area, it sent pain flaring through him, down to the toes of his front paw and back up across his chest. The area of pain had definitely spread, and he tried to grit his teeth against it. "You know I like picking on you, but rest assured, I get no pleasure from this sort of pain, nephew." The bitterness of the cleaning agent stung for a second, and Priamos flared to life, snarling and snapping at Santi. Pain in their nose made Priamos jerk back, and Nikaius laughed.

Santi had smacked Priamos on the snout.

"Don't make me treat you like a pup again. You go away and give me back Nikaius." The fact that Santi spoke to Priamos as a separate being reminded Nikaius that he was with an ally, regardless of what the world was trying to throw at him.

Mae entered the room then, carrying a bowl. Setting it down on the table next to them, she began pulling out tea bags. It didn't appear that the water was muddied enough for them to have steeped for a long time, so he wondered what she planned to do with them.

"Now I know it's an uncommon practice for us Rekru'e, but Mae has come up with this concoction that works at drawing out all manner of things. So, she's going to take the damp herbs and spread them across the main injury."

Nikaius looked from Santi to Mae and back. Santi was the doctor. Why was he letting his wife do most of the creating when Santi was just as efficient? Did Mae know about the plan that Santi had made to free Morrigan from her home? Had Elijah said something outrageous to Mae that would make her seek revenge on him? How did he know that the stuff in the herbs wasn't going to kill him?

His thoughts must have shown in Priamos' body because Santi laid a warm hand on his head, stroking through the fur behind one ear, a move that made them melt.

"Easy. She needs to clean it before she can heal it, Nikaius. She's the one with the magic healing powers, not me. I can make the things, but she can heal the wounds. That is why we're great together. Just let her do this, and you'll be right as rain."

Nikaius huffed, but he realized he couldn't do much of anything when he was literally being pinned by his uncle, whose animal was ten times the size of his. No man would want to fight Santi, and Nikaius was smart enough to join them.

Chapter Seven

Morrigan

Corinth Manor

After Waric and Hawke had left for the morning, the day seemed to drag by. She had made some bread and read a bit, but without the presence of another in the house, she wasn't quite sure what to do with herself, especially with a storm raging outside. After she had finished her book, she decided that maybe it was time to finally unpack the things she had brought with her that she hadn't had immediate use for.

Stepping into her room still raised the hair on her arms as if she expected the unexplainable magic to attack her once again. The last attack had been jarring enough that she hadn't entered the room since then. She knew she should shut the door, but the thought of possibly being locked in or attacked without a plan of escape unnerved her as she sat on the floor of her room and dumped everything out of the trunk. It wasn't any trunk that she had chosen, this one was infused with a unique form of magic that made it so that only she, Mae, and Santi had access to the hidden compartment at the bottom of it.

A small prick of her finger was all that was needed. There was no telling when someone would be home, so she knew she had to be quick. Standing, she made her way into the bathroom and retrieved the trimming shears that had been used on her hair only a few weeks ago. Morrigan was unsure why they hadn't been returned to Nikaius' room, but it was her luck that they were. Seizing them, she quickly made her way back to her room and settled back onto her knees on the floor, digging the blade into her middle finger with a soft hum.

It didn't hurt as much as she thought it would, and she hoped that wherever Nikaius and Priamos were, they hadn't felt it. A small part of her did, but she didn't want her privacy interrupted in that moment, afraid that the trunk would be something her men would seize if they knew about it. She had sworn to Santi that no one would know because it was illegal magic that could potentially send them before the counsel for punishment.

Letting the blood well for a moment, she pressed it to the centermost design. The bottom clicked and using the shears, she wedged the bottom open.

The books were still wrapped, aside from the one that sat beside her. She had been careless in leaving it out the week before, but by some magic, it had remained unscathed and was returned to her in pristine condition. Mae's pearls were still tucked carefully in the spot where she left them as well. Relief flooded her even though she knew only three people could get access to it. The bounds of others' magics were something Morrigan had learned not to underestimate, and she was sure there was some way for others to get in despite her sister's reassurances.

Pulling the books from their place, she carefully unwrapped them, stroking the cover of the fairy tales she had loved as a child. Each book was written by someone her father had known; a man named Glade Eversong who had gifted them to Morrigan on her fourth birthday. It was another secret she held with only Mae, as she had ensured that their father's love of reading carried on in herself and Morrigan.

Morrigan sighed. She missed her sister.

The book in particular that had caught her attention wasn't just one book, but several entombing the different variations of how their world had come to be, as well as tales meant to entertain small children, like tales of a princess who had been raised to hide her identity for she had inherited a power from each of the ruling families until she found true love who was able to set her free.

Morrigan stroked her fingers over the words, happy to note that the fading to them was minimal and she hoped, someday, to be able to share the secrets within the book with others. Maybe the children she and Aslin taught would be interested? The idea was appealing, but with the weather having taken a turn, Morrigan doubted there would be lessons for a little while.

Opening the book, she shifted to sit properly on the floor, tracing her fingers over the image the book portrayed.

"What's that you've got there?" Aslin's voice was warm and gruff, as if she had just woken up from a nap, and Morrigan found her blinking sleepily at her as Aquila walked by, stretching her arms over her head with a loud yawn. Hawke had informed her that he, Aquila, and Waric would be out for most of the morning due to training and debriefing, but Morrigan was unsure where Aslin had been or where she had come from.

"Books that were given to me when I was young."

"I didn't think you had anything valuable with you." Aquila's voice preceded her into the room and Aslin elbowed her as she passed. "What. No! I meant I'm surprised they let you bring anything with you at all." Morrigan bit the inside of her lip as she looked from them to the trunk and back. Closing it now would be suspicious, and she was sure Aquila had probably already figured it out. She was as astute as Hawke.

Setting the tray she had been carrying down, Aquila rested her hands on her hips and shook out her wings before looking around the room, ever in guard mode, even when she wasn't strictly on duty.

It was something Morrigan was slowly getting used to. There had been no guards in her mother's house, even though she and her brother held titles, their home was so far disconnected from the grid that one had to trek up the steep hill to get to their home, and no one had bothered trying to cause trouble in years. Being in Nikaius' home so close to everything made security a top priority for everyone in their household, except Aslin it seemed. The others were changelings though, and able to pick up more than she and Aslin could, whether it was Hawke's and Aquila's keen hearing or Nikaius' and Waric's sense of smell, or both species' ability to sense vibrations in the air around them. They were all things that were lost on Morrigan, but she was grateful to have people in her life who had those skills, even if they hadn't protected her the two times she had been attacked in their care.

Trying to remedy her suddenly dry mouth by swallowing, she turned her attention back to Aquila and Aslin. Right. She had been asked a question.

"I hid them when I packed. They didn't bother looking through my stuff because they didn't think I had anything I favored that was going into it." Reaching out, she pulled the box of pearls free to offer them to Aslin.

"Santi gave these to Mae when he first wrote to her. Their courting was quite like a fairytale. They met by accident because Mae and I were trying to make a run for it after she was told she was going to marry Bastian Ayrden. I got hurt, and we ended up meeting Santi. He and Mae are true mates that marked each other accidentally.

He wrote her a few letters and then she ended up visiting Mrs. Ayrden and getting stuck over there during a snowstorm. Some things happened with Solstice and then, the next thing I knew, they were getting married, and she was giving them to me for safekeeping. I don't think she's ever worn them because the time frame was so short between their meeting and their marriage."

"I'm sure she'd allow you to wear them if you wanted?" Aslin smiled as she opened the box to trace her finger along the pearls as Morrigan had done several times after Mae had left. Amara had almost caught her with them once and since then, they had been hidden away in the bottom of the trunk and only brought out when Morrigan had trouble sleeping.

"I would love that, but I don't want her to be upset if she knew I did." The necklace had never left its box, and Morrigan didn't intend to change that until she saw her sister again.

"You could write her a letter and ask? I think they would look lovely with most of the dresses we bought." Aslin closed the box and offered it back to Morrigan, who settled it onto her lap, slowly petting the velvet outside of the box.

"I've been trying to figure out what to say in a letter to her for weeks. I've written and rewritten one four or five times, and I just can't find the right words to say." Most of it centered around a fear that she would be upset, but also her confusion about where she stood with Nikaius. She didn't want to leave before she knew he was alright.

"You could tell her everything. I'm sure no one would hold it against you if you did." Aslin seemed to be in the same frame of mind as Morrigan, and she smiled as she settled more properly onto her knees, so they were closer to the same height.

"But I'm afraid that she would show up here." That really was the biggest concern, wasn't it? The thought of disappointing Mae and leaving before she knew what was happening with Nikaius warred within her.

"I fail to see why that is a bad thing." Aquila frowned, her eyebrows dipping in confusion.

"I..." Licking her lips, Morrigan clutched the book to her chest. "I'm scared of what will happen if she does."

"What do you mean?" Aslin moved to sit next to Morrigan on the floor and reached for her hand. Aslin's hand was cool and soft, but the only thing Morrigan could pick up from her was curiosity.

Morrigan looked down at their hands for a moment and let out a soft sigh. "I'm afraid she would be upset because I'm half in love with the brother of the man we were trying to escape," she admitted.

"If I know anything about sisters, and I have six," Aquila gave a soft laugh and leaned against the post of the bed, shoving her hands in her pockets as she smiled affectionately at the thought of her siblings, "it's that we really can't stay mad at each other for long."

Aslin nodded eagerly. "She's right. I ended up deciding that marrying a lord was not what I wanted, and my sisters were furious that I was passing up a chance like that. In the end, though, it opened more doors for them in the long run, and they forgave me."

Aslin and Aquila's sisters sounded amazing. "Mae was great; however, Amara always hated me."

"That's because Amara is a bitch." The look on Aslin's petite face made Morrigan snort loudly, a sound that sent the other two women into a fit of giggles as well.

"I don't think Mae will be upset with you. From what I know of her, I think she will be happy that you're happy." Aslin stroked her fingers through the end of Morrigan's hair before patting her shoulder gently. "Until then, we'll be your sisters."

It was a kind offer, but something felt off about it. Was it a thought made only of obligation and pity, or did they genuinely care about her? "Do you like me enough to do that, though?" The question was out before she could think not to voice it, and guilt churned her stomach at the hurt look that flashed across Aslin's face.

"What do you mean?" The tone in Aslin's voice had grown high and tight, and she pulled away from Morrigan, putting some distance between them.

Morrigan's heart flew to her chest as she looked from Aslin to Aquila, who looked confused. Fates, she shouldn't have said anything. She had gotten so used to speaking her mind with Hawke and Waric that it hadn't occurred to her that the rest of the pack wouldn't be as receptive. "Never mind." Gathering her things, she stood, but her paths to flee the conversation were blocked so she turned to face away from them, hands shaking as she tried to think of something else, anything else to deter the rushing sound of blood in her head and heat in her face.

"Morrigan."

"It's nothing. Never mind." Where did this sudden sense of panic come from?

"Hey, hey." Aquila appeared before her, and Morrigan jerked back but didn't get far. Aquila's hands settled on her shoulders before one slid up to cup the back of her neck. Her voice dropped as she tugged Morrigan closer, making a chill break out across Morrigan's skin. "It's okay, you're safe here. Whatever is going on in your head isn't what you think, Mor." Her hands were warmer than Morrigan had anticipated, larger too, but everyone in the household was different than what she expected, weren't they? The way her thumb stroked up and down the side of Morrigan's neck was reassuring, and Aquila only felt like concern. "It's just stuff you've been trained to think. You can speak your mind without this fear that something is going to happen. You're safe here."

Morrigan knew Aquila was right, no one had said anything about the things she said, but she still struggled with the fear that Aslin and Aquila would react the way Amara and Delaney had any time she spoke her mind. Getting used to speaking her mind to the men had been easy because all three of them were in constant agreement about how they treated her and how they expected her to treat them, but there hadn't been any serious conversations between herself and the two women in the room with her.

Taking a deep breath, Morrigan nodded, tears breaking free to roll down her cheeks and dampen the collar of her dress before letting her words come out in a rush.

"I didn't know if you just didn't like me or something because aside from when I'm helping you at the school, we don't see each other a lot." Her bottom lip trembled at the confession, but Aslin's laugh was not what she had expected.

"No... I... We like you; I promise. We just... Aquila and I..." When Aquila released Morrigan, she turned to Aslin, whose eyes flicked from Aquila to Morrigan and back as her face slowly turned red. "Aquila?" Her voice was an embarrassed squeak as she finally dropped her eyes to her feet and covered her face with her hands.

"With the men so distracted in entertaining you, we..." She took a step towards Aslin, who looked up at her with wide eyes before dropping them back to the floor. "Aslin and I found an opportunity to take some time to ourselves so we could foster our own relationship."

"Your own relationship?" Morrigan felt she was missing something as she looked at the two.

"It wasn't anything to do with you. I swear Morrigan. We just found ourselves with some spare time and took advantage of it."

"To foster relationships." Morrigan blinked at them. She felt like whatever they were talking about was glaring, but for whatever reason, she couldn't quite grasp it.

"With each other." Aquila grinned down at Aslin, who frowned at her a little.

"OH!" Realization hit, and Morrigan let out a little laugh, suddenly feeling silly. She had known there were feelings there, but for them to be able to foster that relationship was sweet. "That's lovely." It was. Being able to have time to get to know each other outside of prying eyes was something Morrigan had slowly been getting a taste of being with Waric and Hawke. She and Waric often spent time together in the evenings reading while Hawke was out doing night training that Waric didn't need to be part of, and she and Hawke often talked before bed.

Since the night she had been attacked, she hadn't slept alone. Which had made her time alone earlier in the morning feel a little slow, but she did have to admit being with the others soothed some lonesome part of her soul. Going from being constantly alone to never alone was exhausting, but she knew that everyone meant well in their desire to be near her. Whether it was concern for her safety, the desire to be near her because she was a novelty, or because they enjoyed her company, Morrigan didn't know. But most of the time, she liked the attention.

"We can definitely start sticking around more if you want."

"If you want. It feels weird to have my attention focused on so many people that I don't really know how to interact with people outside of my family. It's still something I'm getting used to."

"We could go Solstice shopping. I know you probably never celebrated because it's more of a mortal custom, but Nikaius' family often has a dinner, and the Council has a party."

"Will Nikaius be back in time for all that? My sister's birthday is coming up soon as well."

"He should be. He doesn't typically disappear for longer than three or four days; he's probably off wandering the territories or something. I think last time, he ended up somewhere near The Barrens because his fur was all singed on one side. He was fine, just looked really, really silly." Aquila laughed at the memory, shaking her head as Morrigan watched her turn to share a grin with Aslin.

Morrigan smiled. While it was reassuring that everyone in the pack had the same consensus about Nikaius' disappearance, Morrigan still worried, but she knew she would until he returned. There were so many things she was still learning in her new life and accepting things as they were was one she needed to settle into.

"I wouldn't mind seeing the market again," The idea of being around people was something she did enjoy, everyone in Kunmei had been so kind and welcoming to her, and as a member of Nikaius' household and possibly more in the future, she wanted to build good relationships with them as she did with Aquila and Aslin. Tucking the books and jewelry away into the top drawer of her dresser, she turned to face Aslin with a nod. "Is what I'm wearing acceptable?"

"Absolutely. You might want another layer though as it's quite chilly right now." Aquila pulled Morrigan's cloak from the ether and offered it to her as Aslin pulled her own on as well.

"We'll have to teleport if that's okay, the hill is steep, and the ice is a bit packed."

"As long as I have warning, I think I'll be fine." Nodding, Aslin reached for her hand, and they teleported to Kunmei's town square.

Once her feet touched down on the stone that decorated the ground around the fountain in the middle of the square, and her head had stopped swimming, Morrigan looked around eagerly. Every time she visited the square, she found something new.

The fun floral arrangements that had decorated the buildings lining the square from the wedding were gone, and in their place were sprigs of dark evergreen trees twisted along each doorframe. Morrigan had only seen Solstice decorations in books and reached out to touch the prickly needles of the closest bough.

Sure, she had experienced evergreens before in the woods around her home, but did they always look as bright and smell as fragrant as these? She wasn't sure and stepped closer to take a slow, deep breath in. It vaguely smelled the way Waric did, but different enough that she could tell it wasn't the type of tree he used. No, he smelled more like the cedar that was burned in the fireplace at home.

Home. It was weird to think that Corinth Manor felt like home now. Despite her earlier desires to leave and see Mae, she knew she would miss Kunmei and all the people she had come to know. They had eagerly welcomed her into their lives, and she was grateful for each person who smiled and waved at her as they passed. Being surrounded by people that cared for her, regardless of her status, was what Morrigan had always thought home felt like. It was how she felt when her father had been alive and whenever she had a chance to spend time with Mae.

"What do you get people for Solstice?" She had read about the custom recently in one of the books from Waric's portion of the library, but most of it was histories of how beliefs and traditions had come to be, not of what to give others. Gift giving was also a foreign concept to her as she hadn't received any since she was young. Her mother held the belief that birthdays were unnecessary after a certain age, and gifts were only to be given to flaunt one's worth.

"Whatever you think would fit them. I got Nikaius a new chess set and Waric a new book." Aquila's voice interrupted Morrigan's thoughts, and she turned to watch her friend pause to browse one of the windows of a shop. Aslin continued their walk, linking her arm with Morrigan's.

"I knit a new scarf for Waric each year. He likes the ones I make and has one of almost every color now. Last year, I bought Nikaius new riding gloves."

"Why do they ride horses if they can teleport?" Morrigan mused aloud, her attention drawn to a rainbow display of embroidery threads. She didn't know how to sew, and her knitting skills were subpar, but she did have an idea of something simple that she could make for each of them. They would only take a small amount of time, and she was sure if she asked, she would be granted the privacy to do so.

"Because there are places, like The Barrens, where magic cannot penetrate it. We can walk through there in mortal form, but Hawke and Aquila and Nikaius cannot go in their wild forms. The Barrens are so vast that going from one territory to another would take days, and horseback is usually the best mode of transportation when teleportation is not an option."

"Is that why Aquila mentioned Priamos' fur being singed?"

"Yes, he got too close, and it tried to dissolve the magic from him and force him back into his mortal form. That's why most neutral territories are within the limits of The Barrens or close to it. Magic is at its weakest, and it often prevents attacks and the like from happening there."

Shock tingled through Morrigan as she turned to stare at Aslin with wide eyes. "But it's neutral territory, would people really stage an attack there?"

"It wouldn't be the first time." When Aquila spoke, Morrigan spun around so quickly that her hair smacked her in the face, and she had to shove it aside to look at her friend. "But every time since their creation, attacks were made with weaponry, not magic. I've never actually seen someone attempt to use it outside of the receiving chambers."

"That's a relief, I suppose." Anxiety bubbled through Morrigan as she twisted her hair away from her face. She remembered Nikaius mentioning that as a lord, he was used to being targeted, but it still came as a shock to her that his words weren't in jest. In fact, she had been in the direct line of those attacks twice and no one could figure out why.

Throwing her hair over her shoulder, Morrigan decided to change the subject as a pang of hurt flared through her at the thought of Nikaius not being around. She knew she needed to accept that he would return when he was ready, and that she had more things to do than wait for a man. Turning to look at the display of threads again, Morrigan smiled. "Can we go in here? I have an idea of what I want to make for gifts."

Aslin made a high, gleeful noise and seized Morrigan's hand to drag her in before Aquila could comment one way or another.

Chapter Eight

Morrigan

Kunmei Plaza

Their trip into the shop was uneventful. Morrigan had gotten thread, and Aslin picked a few skeins of yarn to make Waric's newest scarf. The deep emerald yarn was apparently something she had been looking for, and she gleefully squealed over it for a few moments before they made their purchases. When they stepped out of the shop, Madame Eda was standing in the doorway of her shop, eagerly beckoning them to her. Dashing through the snow that was steadily following harder, Morrigan let out a loud, surprised giggle when she and Aslin found a patch of ice. Their arms went around each other, clutching each other tight until they could find their footing and slowly inched their way to Aquila whose laughter had drawn the attention of other shopkeepers who appeared at their own doors to see what the commotion was.

"You girls keep me young." Madam Eda laughed as she reached for Morrigan and bowed over her hand before doing the same to Aslin. It was a strange occurrence, but with Aslin unbothered by it, Morrigan let it go, allowing herself to be pulled deeper into the shop.

"I have a dress that you," she looked Morrigan over with a bright smile, "should be dying to see, but I feel as if you haven't been told about it yet." Taking her hand, Madam Eda brought Morrigan to the podium before turning away to pull a dress from where it was stored.

"Undress and close your eyes." The tone Madam Eda used was different than her normal stern commands, much softer than the last time she had been in the shop. Morrigan couldn't place why it made her nervous, but she obeyed, slowly removing her dress and handing it to Aslin before turning to face the mirror and closing her eyes.

The desire to peek was nearly overwhelming, especially with Aquila's soft gasp and Aslin's soft "Oh!" but Morrigan shifted on her toes a bit as she twisted the fingers of her left hand with the right.

"First you step in, and then the top is buttoned behind your shoulders. You can look, but don't peek in the mirror just yet." Morrigan's eyes flew open, but all she could make out was lots of white fabric. "Your undergarments will adjust once the dress is secure, so it will feel odd for a moment."

Morrigan wasn't sure what use she would have for a white dress. White and gold were her family's colors, more importantly, Delaney's colors. The actual Aegean colors had been green and gold, but ever since her father passed, Delaney claimed she couldn't stand any form of green because it reminded her too much of Malin.

Using the shoulder of the shop assistant, Aida, Morrigan carefully stepped into the bundle of white that Eda laid at her feet. The more times she visited the seamstress, the more comfortable she became with the routine of trying on dresses with someone's hands adjusting it to sit properly. In the end, few garments needed to be altered, and those that did needed to be taken in slightly, or the hem needed to be brought up. It was still a surreal experience to be easily sized after years of her mother telling her that the tailors would have to work too hard to custom make anything for her when Mae cost her enough.

The skirt of the dress was cool against her legs, a soft fabric that she didn't think she had worn before. Most of her attire was soft cotton blends. It felt like something she had touched before, but never worn. The overskirt was soft as well, but a different material. Both were similar to the fabric of dresses Aslin wore, which made Morrigan think that this was something special. Something expensive. When the skirt was settled on her waist, it was zipped up the back by Adia while Madam Eda helped Morrigan slip her arms into the bodice. The entire bodice was made of pearls, diamonds, and gold. Familiarity struck her as it was secured at the back of her neck.

Madame Eda had said that the dress was special, and as she ran her hands down the skirt, her stomach twisted nervously as her mind flashed back to Mae's nervous laughter when Morrigan had helped her into a similar dress on Mae's wedding night.

The back of the dress was open, and Morrigan felt Aida's fingers slide over her scars. There was sadness in Aida's touch, but it didn't sting like the deep sadness of someone who had been hurt. Instead, it tingled and mixed with curiosity for a moment before warping into the warm buzz of excitement that made a chill break out along Morrigan's skin. Madame Eda's smile matched what Morrigan now felt from Aida. "Go ahead and turn around, darling."

Morrigan hesitated. What if she was just imagining things? Would she be disappointed? Seeking out Aslin and Aquila, Morrigan found them near the door, Aslin's hands covering her mouth, looking like she was moments away from tears. Aquila's grin was broad as she gestured with her head for Morrigan to turn around, which Morrigan tentatively obeyed, taking slow, small steps to turn and face the mirror. Though she wanted to remain strong, her bottom lip trembled as she saw herself in what was undeniably her sister's wedding dress.

There was no mistaking the intricately decorated bodice that had been custom made for her sister. Delicate lattice work and filigree decorated the mesh that traced the sweetheart neckline underneath and spread up across her shoulders to be buttoned at the back of her neck and between her shoulder blades. She had been right in her assessment that the bodice was made of pearls and diamonds, traditional jewels of her mother's family.

Though she tried to hold it in, as she stroked her fingers along the jewel work, Morrigan couldn't help but take it as a sign from her sister and a happy little sob escaped her lips. There was no way they could have gotten that dress without Mae knowing. That meant that Mae had to have sent it with intention. "I wish she was here." Running her hands across her waist, she dipped her hands into the pockets she knew had been hidden in the skirt and was surprised to find something nestled in one of them. Pulling them out, she looked around the room, only to find curious looks from those around her. No one had known what this was.

Her hands trembled as she opened the small piece of paper to find a note written in her sister's hand. "Be happy and free." Her voice broke as she read the words out loud. That was all that was written on the paper, but she couldn't help but let the small bubble of concern shatter into happiness. Her knees gave out from under her, and she let out a happy little laugh that turned into a sob that she tried to cover with her hand.

No one said anything as she sat on the floor and sobbed. She had held onto so much worry and stress that her sister would be upset or wouldn't approve of the life she was trying to lead that she had never entertained the idea of Mae being happy for her. This had to be a sign that Mae approved of where she had ended up, right?

So many emotions burned through her, cold sadness at missing her sister twisted with joy that she had been gifted something that had been important in Mae's life. Her sister had cried over the dress, just as Morrigan was doing now.

She felt like the tears would never stop, but she knew that allowing herself to get out her emotions was something that she had never been allowed to do before. No one seemed inclined to stop her from feeling what she felt, and Aslin gently rubbed her back as she mumbled soft reassurances.

Morrigan didn't know how long she sat there, letting her tears ease months' worth of stress from her shoulders and chest, but when she finally managed to calm, she began to wonder why Mae hadn't just brought it herself.

She couldn't remember ever feeling as happy as she did at that moment. Her chest was on fire, her heart was in her throat, and all she wanted to do was laugh and cry at the same time, which came out in the form of a random noise that she couldn't describe as she clutched the note in her hands and pressed them to her heart as she observed herself in the mirror.

She looked everything like the bride her sister had been, except her face was splotched and red from the tears that fell as she tried to come up with any other words aside from, "How?"

"I don't understand."

"You don't know?" Madame Eda frowned and stepped closer, kneeling in front of Morrigan to take her face in hand. "Your mate was the one who brought it. Did he not tell you?"

Morrigan shook her head, smoothing her trembling hands over the dress again. No, no one had told her. How had he gotten it?

"I'm sure there's a reasonable explanation. Maybe it was meant to be a Solstice gift from your sister?" Maybe Aslin was right, and it was meant to be a surprise. She couldn't realistically confront Hawke or Waric while they were in a dress shop, especially not when they were still out doing rounds to check the boundaries for signs of Nikaius. And surely it hadn't been Nikaius who had arranged it, as he had still not returned.

Letting out a soft sigh, Morrigan rubbed the tears from her cheeks and nodded. Though she felt tired after putting so much energy into crying, she felt lighter than she had in days. "You're right. It's a sign that my sister knows I'm here, at least. I don't know how much she knows, especially if my being here was part of the plan that Hawke and Santi had set." She felt like their plan was something Mae wouldn't have approved of. She was always so vocal about how Morrigan was treated that Morrigan couldn't fathom why Mae would agree to it. But she did know where Morrigan was and that was something important. That meant that there was a possibility that she would see her sister again.

She felt silly being so emotional over a dress. It wasn't like it was her wedding she was trying on the dress for, and she knew that the tears were absolutely not needed, but they fell anyway. Having overwhelming emotions with nowhere for them to go had seemed to be the norm lately, but, according to Waric, having spent so much of her life constantly under stress would do that to someone.

Once she didn't feel as raw, she sniffled and wiped her cheeks with her hands.

"We can talk to Hawke and Waric when we get home." Aslin's voice was soft, and it stirred up the emotions that Morrigan was trying to fight.

"It's really very lovely. Is it acceptable to wear to a council event though?" She turned to ask Aslin, carefully running her hands over the bodice again. Her back and shoulders were bare, which was a little alarming, but Hawke had reassured her that no one would say anything about her scars. If they did, Morrigan was sure that one of her men would have words with that person and make their opinion as known to others as they had been in the bedroom with her.

"Others have worn far less to these events depending on the culture and who you ask." Aquila crossed her arms over her chest and looked at Morrigan over from head to toe. "But if you meant the color, it's perfectly acceptable to wear white. Solstice is the celebration of lights and that is why most brides who wed during Solstice choose white. I believe your sister Amara wore gold to represent the summer when she wed."

Morrigan hummed as she mulled over Aquila's words. Had it really been just under six months since Amara had wed Bastian? And less than a year since Mae and Santi's confirmation and union? Her life had changed so much in such a short time, and she could hardly believe it.

"You could always reach out to Mae and ask her for ideas regarding colors." Aquila suggested. "Surely this means that she knows you're here and is trying to open a line of communication with you."

"I'll do that when I get home." Eagerness and hope spread across her chest as she turned to smile at Madam Eda. "Let's adjust the hem for now. I'll write to Mae to see if she has any other color suggestions she'd like to make before we finalize, is that alright?" Madam Eda grinned at her and nodded.

"Of course, my child, whatever you want, we will make happen." Clapping her hands together, she turned away from Morrigan who watched as pins swirled around the room for a moment before the hem began to fold and pin on its own.

"I love magic," she giggled, turning her smile to Aslin, who grinned at her before resuming her perusal of the newest additions to the shop.

It was near nightfall when they returned home. Aslin and Aquila headed to the kitchen, announcing that they were going to cook and that Morrigan could relax for a bit before supper. Once she had returned her cloak and boots to her room and tucked away her gift making supplies on her bedside table, she headed for the library to seek out the letter she had been attempting to write.

She wasn't quiet when she entered the study, anticipating no one to be in there, but she found Hawke seated behind the large regal desk.

Morrigan frowned as she watched Hawke for a few moments. He seemed frustrated; his brows were furrowed, and his pen was pressed to his lips as his eyes flicked across the page, not settling on any one thing.

"Hawke?" With his keen hearing, Morrigan would have thought he had heard her come in, but he must have been so deep in thought, or had been ignoring her, Aslin and Aquila's return in favor of whatever he was concentrating on that he jumped, his frown turning to one of confusion as she cautiously approached. "Are you okay?"

"I..." he blinked up at her for a moment before letting out a slow breath. "Not really."

She shouldn't be surprised by his response. Out of all the members of the pack, he had been the one to not balk at being completely honest with her, but shock surged through her as he offered his hand to her.

It was a simple gesture that had developed between them in their time together. Hawke knew about her gifts and always made sure to defer to her whether his touch was wanted. She had come to realize that touch was a rare thing for him. After spending some time with him, she noticed he was friendly and open with the others in private, but he was rarely physical with them, except Aquila, who seemed to always initiate.

She took his hand and moved to stand beside him. He was so handsome, even when his face was set in a frown. Her eyes traced over him, taking in the brightness of his amber eyes against his dark skin and the freckles that spread across his nose and cheeks. They weren't nearly as noticeable as her own, but she had grown to love them just as she had learned to love her own through Mae. Ever since she had arrived in Kunmei, not a single person had commented about the blemishes on her skin, save for those that had been made in adoration when one worshipped her body.

The thought made her feel hot, the images from the nights that had passed flooding her mind. Perhaps she could distract him from whatever caused him misery in the same way he had distracted her? Before she could voice the thought, he spoke. "I'm struggling to understand this." He tapped his fingers on the letter he had received earlier. It had been labeled as urgent by Silas when he had delivered it, but Hawke was the only person who was in power enough to receive it.

The tug on her skirt drew her into his lap, and she reached for the missive as she settled.

"How can I help? Is it common? You know I'm teaching the classes; I don't mind tutoring you in private." She scanned it for a moment and frowned at him. "I'm not well versed on my Rekru'e, Hawke. I don't think I can translate it accurately."

"No. I can read it. It just doesn't… I don't know how to explain it." He shifted, wrapping his arms around her waist and tugging her closer so he could press his face into her back.

"That's alright, you don't have to explain. I can just read it." Settling her hand on top of his, she gazed over the letter again, letting her thumb stroke along the back of his hand as she tried to ignore the surge of embarrassment that heated its way up her arm.

Affection mingled with his embarrassment, and he shifted so his cheek was against her back. "It sounds silly, but the words just don't connect right in my brain when I read it."

"But if I read it, then it's fine? Even if I don't translate it?"

Hawke nodded. "Rekru'e is my first language. I'll understand, and we can test your pronunciation at the same time." He gave her waist a pinch, and she squeaked before elbowing him gently and shifting to settle in his lap again.

Reading Rekru'e aloud wasn't as hard as it once had been; the lessons she had been attending with the children were paying off. However, her understanding and ability to translate words on the fly was still severely lacking.

After she had finished, Hawke hummed, nudging his nose in her hair, which made her giggle. "What was it about?"

"It's a request from a couple of the towns for check-ins on the dams and such that hold off water from the lakes in the mountains." Hawke's voice was soft and low, as if he didn't particularly want to answer her, but he did anyways.

"Can we answer that request?"

"We don't have the jurisdiction to, it's Be'Sala territories." Morrigan sighed as she rested back against him, allowing herself to be shifted so she sat more comfortably in his lap, but where she could see his face.

"Hawke?"

"Hmm?" His gaze was focused on some point across the room, even though his fingers trailed slowly up and down her arm.

"What are your duties as an emissary?" She was curious to know how he performed his duties without being able to comprehend what he read.

"I don't have to read anything if that's what you're asking." He smiled at her and nudged her temple with his nose. "It's okay to be curious. Typically, if things arrive, it's for Nikaius or Santi, and Commander Aquila handles all orders for our guard."

"That's convenient, isn't it?"

"We've staged it that way on purpose. Unlike Nikaius and Santi, we know that people would question my capabilities just as you are."

"I..." She felt awful questioning him. She knew how it felt to have people assume you lacked worth because you couldn't do what they did. "I'm sorry. You're right."

Hawke gave her a small smile and reached over to press a kiss to her temple. "It's alright to be curious. I don't think you think less of me for it."

"Quite the opposite really. I don't think it's necessary to try to force yourself to do something that our society deems a requirement. You've found ways to live around that, and I find it admirable."

"Your ability to live while feeling the emotions of others is admirable as well, please don't forget that." He pressed another kiss to her forehead and shifted back so he could rock them slowly in the desk chair, making Morrigan giggle.

Chapter Nine

Morrigan

CORINTH MANOR

Hawke was gone when Morrigan woke the next morning. His side of the bed was cold and judging by the height of the sun in the sky, she had slept for a considerable amount of time. It was still weird not to be required to get up at a certain time to prepare the meals and house for the day, but it hadn't been that hard of a habit to break.

Her first few days in Kunmei were met with a constant onslaught of nightmares, an attack on her life, and an entire upheaval of her life and routine. The first week or two had completely thrown off her sleep cycle and the more she got to know the pack, the less comfortable she became sleeping alone. She had somehow gone from feeling unsafe every day of her life to seeking out the safety the others provided for her. Thinking back on it felt weird because she had lived her teen years in fear of everyone that she met but had eagerly sunk into everything the pack had to offer.

Perhaps there had been some trick of alpha powers that had seeped into Nikaius' words the night they met. *You're safe and allowed to be who you are here.* He had told her, and it hadn't taken her long to believe him. Even though she had been attacked twice, she still felt safe within the walls of Kunmei, as long as she wasn't alone. A pang of longing spread through her, and she let out a soft sigh as she rolled over and sat up on the edge of the bed.

After confirming her attraction to her men, she had rarely slept a night alone, especially after the last attack that had happened when she was sleeping. The mark on her arm still stung, and whatever had burned her skin lingered, the salve they had on hand only took the pain away but did nothing for the blackness of her skin.

It hadn't healed in the four days since it had happened. Neither had they heard word from Nikaius.

Standing, she stretched and tried once again to pull something from the ether. Every morning since she had come to Kunmei, she had been trying to see if she could actually perform the things the others did. She could finally get the mundane things like the lights and water and stove to work, but that was about as far as her powers went. She was utterly useless to the pack, and she knew they knew it, but she had hoped that maybe being exposed to magic would help her figure out how to do the things others were taught in their teens.

Mae had tried to teach her, but it had been to no avail. No matter how many times she held out her hand and tried to fuse her powers with the world around her to pull from another place, it never worked. Aside from when they had been attacked, magic only felt like a slight buzz on her skin. She had no idea what she was supposed to be feeling or how she would know her magic was connected. Staring at the dress she had hung over the chair for the morning, she reached out her hand and tried again, but still nothing. No tingle of magic, no touch of fabric, nothing.

Letting out a frustrated sigh, she padded across the room and snatched the garment from the chair to get dressed.

The house was quiet when she left Hawke's room, and her steps echoed on the stone floor as she made her way up the hall. She knew that Hawke, Waric, and Aquila were probably off somewhere holding court or training, but that didn't explain where Aslin had gone to. A quick search of the house came up empty, so she decided to check the courtyard.

She hadn't been in it since the day she had tried her hand at making it change and was curious what it would look like when she peeked inside. The snow had turned to muddy slush with the endless rains outside, and she hoped that maybe the courtyard would still be the soft pristine fluff of white it had been then.

Taking a slow breath, she settled herself, hoping to see something new. She was curious if the courtyard would change like they said it did, but she doubted it would work for her. If it didn't, then no one would know.

Turning the handle, she pushed the door open, closed her eyes, and stepped outside.

The rush of water met her ears before a warm breeze touched her face. Opening her eyes, she took in a surprised breath as she looked around.

Under her feet, springy grass gave way to coarse sand that made her toes itch and the rolling waves of the sea. The air smelled briny and damp, and she felt like she was four years old and holding her father's hand again. She had never learned how to swim, but the one time she remembered visiting the sea, her father had let her and Mae kick and splash in the surf as he followed close behind.

Missing her father and Mae wasn't a new feeling, but it burned a little less when complete warmth surrounded her from the balmy breeze and bright sun. Hiking up her skirt, she rushed forward to sink her feet into the damp sand and let the surf crash against her shins. It was cool, and the bubbles tickled as they fizzed and receded back from where they came.

"Hello?" Aslin had to be nearby, but the only sound Morrigan could hear was the rushing of the waves.

She hadn't heard animals in the snowy courtyard, and she wondered if there would be any in the water. Aslin had said that the courtyard provided fruits and vegetables to the town when they were in need, did that extend to fish in the sea spread out ahead of her? It had no end, and all she could see was miles and miles of blue. She knew she should be grateful to have the pack, but still she wished her father and Mae could be there to experience this with her.

The bright sun lifted her spirits some, and she let out a slow breath before backing away from the sand so that she could sit in the shade the trees provided. She hadn't had much experience with warm summer days, but this met every one of her expectations, and she slowly sank down onto her back to enjoy the warmth.

The warmth was soothing and settled her in a way the fires in the hearths had not and made her drowsy.

"Morrigan?" She didn't remember falling asleep, but she sleepily blinked up at Waric as he leaned over her with a lopsided grin.

"I've been looking for you for an hour. I thought you would have been with Aslin." Instead of making her get up, Waric moved to sit next to her.

"I thought she was in here. I woke up, and the house was quiet, so I figured she was in here somewhere."

"No, no one was here but you when I came in."

"I wonder who chose this then."

She was still groggy and shifted so she could move closer to him. Laughing gently, he moved so she could rest her head in his lap, and he could stroke his fingers gently through her hair. "You had to have. Aslin was in the kitchen."

"She wasn't there when I looked earlier. And we both know it doesn't work for me like the Mundane magic of the rest of the house."

"Maybe your powers are getting stronger, and you did it without realizing."

"Don't be silly. My magic isn't that strong."

"I'm not trying to placate you, Morrigan. I genuinely think the longer you are exposed to magic, the stronger it will get. You've only been with us a few months."

"I was exposed to magic all the time at home though."

"Not as extensively as you are here. Plus, if I remember right, a direct connection to an alpha can nullify whatever the mark does to you."

Morrigan sat up quickly. "What do you mean 'whatever the mark does to you' I thought it was just a brand."

Waric stared down at her for a moment before his eyebrows dipped into a frown, and he looked away from her, out towards the rush of the waves. "Do you want to learn how to swim?"

"Waric, what do you mean? What does the mark do to people?"

"It's nothing Morrigan, forget I said anything."

"No. I will not accept that response, Waric. You just said the mark does things that a connection to an alpha can nullify." Standing, she brushed the sand from her dress but before she could get a step or two, Waric seized her wrist and pulled her back to him.

"It's really nothing, Morrigan, forget it." His tone dropped, and she could feel the tingle of warning in his voice on her skin. It was the same feeling she got from Nikaius and Aquila when they were trying to soothe her.

Betrayal flooded her, followed by anger that he would try to use alpha commands against her.

"Don't you fucking dare." The realization at what Waric was trying to do made her blood run cold and then hot as every kind thing she thought about Waric shattered. How long had he been using his powers on her without her knowing? Wrenching her arm away, she shoved him with all the strength she had. When he stumbled, she turned and fled, angry tears burning her throat and eyes. She was not gentle or quiet as she slammed her way into the house.

Slamming the door behind her, she turned. "Aslin? Hawke?!" Her voice broke as she fought back a sob, not knowing if she had the power to call for someone as Waric and Nikaius did.

Chapter Ten

Hawke

Corinth Manor

The house's magic alerted Hawke that something was wrong before he had heard the call. It was a buzz of magic that started between his wings and twisted its way up around his shoulders and down through his fingers. It was something the other members of the house would feel as well. It was what he had felt the night Morrigan had been attacked in her room. Rolling his shoulders, he shook out his wings and gave a small apologetic smile to the jeweler he had been conversing with. "If you'll excuse me, my lord calls." Dipping a quick bow in parting, he took a deep breath, pictured the hall of Corinth Manor and pulled on his magic.

Flying was the only thing Hawke enjoyed more than teleporting, but they were two entirely different feelings. Flying made him feel like he was one with the wind, able to soar on whatever wind current he could find. Teleporting was stepping through the ether. His entire body felt alive, like static was touching every single one of his pores from his scalp to his toes.

Despite teasing Morrigan when they had first met, Hawke had been terrified the first time he had done it on purpose. The first teleportation was often an accident, and he was surprised that Morrigan never experienced it, even an accident, before she was branded.

As his feet settled, and he came back to himself, he heard the slam of another door before he saw Morrigan run around the corner. She barreled straight into him, letting out a loud scream as her heart beat quickly in her chest. She looked windblown, and her cheeks were red, as if she was on the verge of tears. Alarm burned through him, and he turned, suddenly on alert as he tried to figure out what she was running from. Were they under attack again? Where were the others? Guilt welled in him. He shouldn't have left her alone. Court could have waited, or he could have woken her, but he knew that the nightmares that plagued her cost her the sleep that she needed.

The door to the courtyard slammed open and Hawke tensed, ready to retrieve his sword from the ether as he turned Morrigan so she was behind him. He had faster reflexes than most things that could be thrown at him. He had worked hard for that honor.

Nothing, however, had prepared Hawke for Waric to be the one to barrel through the door. Skidding to a stop, Waric frowned. Hawke looked over his shoulder at Morrigan, who had curled herself against his back. Why was Waric chasing her? If this had been some game that they were playing, the house wouldn't have alerted him. She had to have called him to raise an alarm that he could feel.

"Morrigan? What happened?" He needed to get a clear idea of what was going on before anyone did anything rash.

"What does the brand do, Hawke?" Her voice was timid, as if she wasn't sure she wanted to know the answer, her foot tapping anxiously on the floor.

"What?" His brow furrowed as he tried to make sense of what Morrigan had asked.

"It doesn't do anything, Morrigan, it was a slip of the tongue." What had Waric said about the mark that had upset Morrigan? Looking at Waric, he studied his friend, trying to see what answers he could gather about what had happened. Waric looked frantic, concerned and apologetic, the starkness of his face and the rhythm of his heart giving away his nervousness more than his rigid posture.

"What does the brand do, Hawke?" Morrigan's eyes were bright and glassy when he looked back at her, as if she would start crying at any moment, and Hawke's confusion deepened.

"It—" He paused, trying to consider how to answer. Honesty had always been his policy, and he was inclined to answer her truthfully. He thought Nikaius and Waric had already told her the nature of the brand on her skin, of what it did to her. As he went to answer, Waric cut him off.

"Hawke." The warning in Waric's voice would silence a lesser man, but Hawke wasn't intimidated. He hated lying to her, knowing that those lies would only cause future problems. He also knew that he needed to be diplomatic about how he approached it. They were already keeping Nikaius' status from her. He refused to keep this from her, even if it appeared Waric wanted to. The truth about her magic was something that directly affected her because it was the reason she was treated the way she was her whole life.

She needed to know the truth, even if that truth damaged her relationship with Waric and Nikaius.

He just wished he didn't have to be the one to tell her.

He had seen what knowledge did to others, intimately knew the aftermath of those realizations.

Hawke had to assume that Mae didn't know either.

If he didn't tell Morrigan, she would pull away from him, but if he did, he'd be betraying Waric's confidence. No matter what he said or did, he would be upsetting one of them.

Letting out a slow breath, he turned to run his hands carefully down Morrigan's shoulders, slip his fingers through hers, and pressed their foreheads together. He felt like there was no right answer that would appease them both. He only knew which one was more important. He knew he could withstand whatever Waric could throw at him, it wouldn't be the first time they had come to blows over something, but Morrigan only deserved kindness.

Settling himself in his decision, he shook out his feathers before slowly stating, "It nullifies residual magics."

"Hawke." Waric growled, his tone dangerously low. Hawke saw him step forward from his peripheral vision. This wasn't the kind man that Hawke had grown up with and something was terribly wrong, but Hawke didn't let him get too close to them, shifting to push Morrigan behind him again. Hawke had made his choice.

"She deserves to know, Waric. I understand you hold guilt for the part your family has played, but she deserves to know. This affects her more deeply than it does you. Her life is more important than your shame." Feeling Morrigan tense at his back and watching Waric straighten, his jaw setting in an angry frown, Hawke knew they both were listening.

"I would have thought that you would have already told her. Are your feelings more important than her understanding?" Hawke sighed heavily and watched as Waric's jaw ticked as he ground his teeth before he turned and disappeared into the void.

Fucking coward.

He was leaving Hawke alone to confess the news. Of course he was. "Let's get something to eat and then talk, okay? I'll tell you whatever you want to know."

Morrigan's soft sniffle made him turn, and he let out a soft sigh as he pulled her close, wrapping his arms around her shoulders and stroking his fingers through her hair. "What happened?" He tried his best to keep his frustration out of his tone. He didn't want her to misinterpret his warring emotions as being directed towards her, and he was careful to only stroke his hands through her hair and run them along her shoulders, trying to give her comfort but not wanting to touch her skin to skin until they both had control of their emotions.

His need to protect her warred with the knowledge that stepping between the two with only emotions and no logic could potentially make the situation worse. Without someone to reasonably sort out the motives of each of them, their house would remain divided.

"He..." Morrigan's voice broke as she tried to explain. "He tried to use those stupid alpha powers on me. I felt them on my skin." She hiccupped out a soft sob that squeezed Hawke's heart in a vise grip. Why would Waric do that? Was he really that worried about her knowing the truth? She already felt like her family had betrayed her. Knowing they had willingly made the choice wouldn't affect her as much as Waric worried, or so Hawke hoped.

In all the time that Hawke and Waric had known each other, he had never known Waric to use his gifts on anyone but Nikaius. Was his mate's disappearance affecting him so strongly that it was clouding his judgement? Hawke knew that he had spent the morning before trying to figure out what exactly had happened to Nikaius and had come home with nothing to report. It had been four days since any of them had seen him, so it made sense that Waric was worried.

But trying to use his powers to avoid a serious conversation was not something Waric would have ever done in the past.

Taking a grounding breath, Hawke shifted back to look her over. Her face was red, and her eyes glistened with unshed tears. Though he was frustrated with Waric for dropping a huge bomb on Morrigan just before disappearing, Hawke understood, a bit, why Waric was behaving the way he was.

Taking her hand, Hawke tugged her towards the kitchen. "I can't excuse his behavior, and it's not my story to tell, but I can answer questions you have regarding the mark and it effects." It had been so long since Nikaius and Waric had been separated for more than a day. Waric was typically the one who held Nikaius together, but Hawke knew that it was a routine that Waric held dearly because his own experience with dysregulation was one he wasn't proud of.

"The basic use is to mark those who don't have any powers, or they don't have acceptable powers." Though he didn't have any plans for what he wanted to make, he pulled some vegetables from their place and knives from their block. He had noticed that when Morrigan was upset about something, she tended to end up in the kitchen.

Morrigan sniffled and nodded, pressing her palms into her eyes as she struggled to understand what he had said. "Didn't have acceptable powers?" Morrigan questioned as she accepted the knife he offered her, and she started chopping the carrots, taking a shuddered breath.

Hawke's hands shook as he turned to look around the kitchen. He wasn't quite sure what he was looking for but being able to look away from her for a moment to gather his thoughts helped. Most of his instincts screamed at him to gather her in his arms and steal her away to his room, to prevent Waric from seeing her until she was ready, but he knew that he was projecting his own anxiety. He was worried this fight with Waric would set her back emotionally and cause her to pull away from them. As much as he hated the idea, he still didn't feel it was a good reason to lie to her. "Mmm. We recently found out that some families chose to mark children whose powers they don't accept."

"Does it take away their powers?"

"Typically."

"I wonder why it didn't work for me." He knew it was a big thing for her to openly acknowledge the powers that she had, after spending most of her life being told they didn't exist or pretending as such.

"I think it might have, sort of. You still can't pull things from the ether, and I know you haven't teleported yet." She flushed, her hands stilling for a moment as she looked up at him. "However, you and I and your sister know that you still have your fate given powers. I believe the Fates intervened in more way than one at your Culling. I think they prevented the mark from blocking your powers and gave you your fated mates at the same time."

Her breath caught in her chest as her eyes flew to his. Tears glistened on her lashes, and he wanted to reach up and brush them away. He did so tentatively, unsure if she would want the comfort or pull away from him.

Morrigan sniffled as she turned her face into his hand, nuzzling his palm. "I still don't really know how I feel about people believing my powers exist outside of Mae."

"I can understand the trepidation about that. You've held them so close for so long that it's almost second nature to keep them hidden. Waric is the same way. He's done some things he's not proud of and puts so much energy into balancing Nikaius out that he sometimes forgets that just the act of being Nikaius' stability gives him purpose." Morrigan sniffled again before pulling away, turning her attention back to her task.

"That doesn't sound like a good reason to be in a relationship." Morrigan mused, her eyes focused on the potatoes she now carefully sliced.

"Oh, no. it's not like that. They've loved each other since they were children and before Priamos came into the picture, but being sent to train on different sides of the continent broke them both a little." Hawke gathered a pot full of water and set it on the stove to cook. He knew how to make soup pretty well, and with the vegetables that Morrigan was cutting, he was thinking maybe they could make his favorite. "It's not my story to tell, but Waric gets just as much balance from Nikaius as Nikaius does Waric. It's what makes the dynamic for two alphas to work."

"I feel like I will never stop learning new things about the Rekru'e." Morrigan set aside what she was cutting to reach for a bag of potatoes to cut.

"I still find myself learning things about them as well, and I've lived among them since I was small." He hadn't learned until a few weeks ago that Nikaius had accidentally gotten too close to a flame as Priamos and singed his fur off. The bald spot wasn't obvious on Priamos because his fur was so thick, but on Nikaius, it was evident any time he tried to grow a beard.

"How old are you?" Hawke blinked at her, having not expected the question.

"Aquila and I just turned twenty-five." Their birthday was October second, nearly right in between Morrigan's June and Nikaius' December birthdays.

"So you've been here a while." She raised her eyebrow at him a moment before resuming her cutting.

"I have." Hawke gave her a smile, nodding. "Ten years."

"And you said this is out of character for him?" Morrigan's question wasn't surprising, but he knew she was trying to assess why he was behaving the way he was. Morrigan was kind and was probably thinking of ways to help Waric instead of being angry with him. She had a right to do both, but she also had a right to know the whole truth.

"It is." Hawke set aside his knife and reached for Morrigan, carefully nudging his hand against hers. When she accepted it, he tugged her closer. She could feel his nervousness, but he knew she needed the truth. She deserved it. "We don't know where Nikaius is, and Waric is struggling with it." Morrigan's brows knit in concern as she blinked up at him, the mask of concern tempted Hawke to kiss her. He knew then wasn't the time and place to follow through with those thoughts, so he continued with his explanation. "I know it doesn't excuse his behavior, but he's worried. The last thing we heard was that Priamos had been injured near the edge of our territory. We followed his scent as far as we could, but when we hit near The Barrens, everything just smelled like rot. Waric went to a couple of friendly courts to see if Priamos had turned up, but no one has seen him. Waric still has a bit of access to their bond, so we know he's alive, that's about it."

"And no one knows anything?" Her eyebrows rose with her question, and her gaze searched his face. He knew that she could sense what he was feeling through touch, but he also knew that unless the situation called for it, he didn't really hide his emotions from his face either.

"No."

"Why hasn't anyone said anything about this? Do Aslin and Aquila know?"

"They don't. We were trying to keep it quiet until we knew for sure what was going on, but we haven't found any leads and with Waric's behavior..." he wasn't apologizing for Waric, but he had hoped she understood where the man was coming from.

"I have a bit of an idea what he's going through." Morrigan looked pensive. Hawke knew she would understand, had been counting on it. Morrigan needed to know, and Waric needed someone to tell him that how he was feeling was okay, even if his actions weren't. "I struggled a bit when Mae left with Santi. It's hard to not have near constant communication with someone who is your whole world."

"It is." Hawke caught her eye and gave her a shy smile. "Luckily, my world lives with me more days than not." Joy warmed his chest as Morrigan's cheeks and nose turned pink.

"Aquila is lucky to have you so near." She returned her attention to what she was doing, but Hawke let out a low laugh and caught her chin. He had expected her to flinch, but as he tipped her face up, he only got the endearing blush and wide eyes. Pressing a gentle kiss on her lips, he smiled. He knew she was trying to deflect his attention from herself, but he refused to let her demean herself. "I'm lucky to have you here." He muffled Morrigan's nervous giggle with another kiss. "Waric is lucky to have you too." Resting his forehead against hers for a moment, he settled himself.

If someone had asked him to predict his reaction to his partner being with others, he would have probably scoffed at the idea, posturing that he would never agree to something like that. But here he stood, knowing that Waric needed Morrigan more than he did at that moment, and it didn't bother him. "You should go talk to him. He should be groveling for your forgiveness, but he'll probably make himself sick with stress first."

Morrigan didn't pull away, only leaned back a bit to search his eyes with her own. "Has he done that before?"

"He may seem all big and bad, but he doesn't handle high levels of stress well."

"Clearly." She stepped away from Hawke with a low, sad hum. "We need to be at our strongest if whoever attacked Nikaius comes back. I know we have our guard, but someone will need to run the court if Nikaius doesn't come back soon."

Nodding, Hawke remained silent as he watched Morrigan gather a tray and loaded it with a few of the biscuits she had made the day before, as well as a jar of sweet jam. He wasn't positive, but he had an inkling that the conversation Waric and Morrigan were about to have wasn't going to be an easy one for either of them. But Hawke knew that Morrigan would handle it with a kindness and grace that he wasn't entirely sure she realized she had.

"I'm in constant awe of you," he whispered as he carefully caught her elbow and pressed a kiss to her head. "You've gone through so much, but you continue to be your most genuine self, no matter the circumstances."

Her expression softened, and she gave him a tentative smile. "At some point, choosing kindness becomes easier than choosing violence. The longer I'm here, the more I'm learning that the only reactions we can control are our own." Pulling away from him, she gave a smile and collected a few more things for her tray.

"You say that like it's a bad thing, Little Dove."

He thought she was going to walk away and leave the conversation at that, but when she reached the door, she turned to smile over her shoulder. Her next words were simple but sucked the air out of the entire room.

"It's not when you love someone."

Before he could comment, she was gone.

Chapter Eleven

Waric

Corinth Manor

It only took Waric a matter of minutes to realize how extremely he had fucked up.

His head was a mess, and he hadn't meant to snap at Morrigan. He was typically good at keeping himself together, but Nikaius' disappearance was getting to him more than he cared to admit.

It had been four days of constant worry. He constantly felt like he needed to vomit, and no matter what he did, he couldn't expel the nervous energy that coursed through him. While running was usually a stress reliever, he found that it only made him feel worse because while he usually didn't have a goal in mind, this time he hoped he would find Nikaius along his path.

The nights had been sleepless, with constant recurring nightmares of their separation leading him to wake multiple times in the night to check the bond. Nikaius and Priamos' magic was faint but still there; however, the longer they were apart, the more agitated Waric found himself becoming.

Looking around the bathroom, he shook his head, trying to rid himself of the anger that welled within him. Whatever had attacked Nikaius was going to pay.

The magic he had sensed at the site where Nikaius had been injured smelled bitter, burning his nose whenever he inhaled. It had been years since they were separated without communication. Part of him finally admitted that he feared that Nikaius wouldn't come back. The last time he had felt such cold, all-encompassing fear was the last time they had been forcibly separated by Nikola Ayrden and Waric's father, Cedric.

Same gender mates weren't rare by any means, but some families still abhorred it to the extreme, including Nikaius' and Waric's fathers.

He stared at himself in the mirror for a moment. He hadn't realized how bad he looked. Dark bags under his eyes, and his face more pale than usual, he wondered why Morrigan hadn't commented on it. Had she even noticed? Things had escalated so quickly that he hadn't really had time to think about his actions or anything else. It seemed all he could do was put his foot in his mouth.

Gripping the side of the sink, Waric fought the nausea that twisted his stomach. He could have seriously injured Morrigan by trying to use his powers on her when he wasn't in control. There had been times in the past where he had done some bad things because he wasn't in control. He actively fought against remembering those times and had regretted the outcome immensely every time he did. Having Nikaius around soothed the angry beast in his own head.

The fact that he didn't have an animal was one of the turning points in his relationship with his father. When he was a child, they were as thick as thieves, being Cedric's only son, but when Waric had first shifted, it hadn't been the same as it was for his sisters. Instead of cervids like the rest of his family, Waric was able to change shape into other beings. His first shift had been startling, having woken up with a wild combination of his family's features at age seven. It had taken him more than twelve hours to find himself again, but no matter how much he tried, he could never channel an animal for himself.

While every other family member was able to find an animal within them; elegant deer, solid and stable moose, and even elk, were among his family member's wild forms, Waric hadn't been bothered by the fact that he was different. Once he had figured out how to manage them properly, Waric felt like he had earned some power for himself. His powers were entirely unique and the pride Waric felt knowing that all the people who looked down on him and doubted him were grossly underestimating his abilities.

Waric had never felt less than his siblings, at least not until the day of his own Culling. He knew some of what Morrigan felt, having been forced to stand in front of everyone to have his abilities tested.

Because Waric believed he had passed the tests because he had performed the way he was told to, exhibiting his powers in what he thought was a spectacular fashion, the last thing he expected was for his father's loud declaration that Waric's powers were not of use to their family. Cedric then volunteered Waric to be branded.

Waric hadn't understood how the brands worked until then. He, like the majority of people he knew, thought the brand was only used as an indication of someone having no magic.

To know that his father felt so little care for him that he tried to make that decision was what fractured Waric' belief in his father.

At the time, his uncle had been his saving grace, his mother having begged her older brother to declare Waric his future heir as he had no children of his own. Waric and his uncle had never actually met before that moment, but that declaration had saved him from experiencing what Morrigan fully had. His uncle's choice set his life in motion to be in near constant company with Nikola Ayrden and his family. Cedric had intended for Waric to befriend Bastian Ayrden; he had never outwardly shown any disapproval of Nikaius.

Until they had received their mating marks.

Waric had kept the true nature of the brand to himself until he was nearly twenty, ashamed of the fact that his family were the main creators of such a vile practice that included dark blood magic that cut one off from the ether that granted their powers.

He knew Hawke had mentioned Morrigan having powers, had seen his friend defer every touch he gave to her control. But he had never believed it until he had felt the silky feeling of her magic against his.

His hands spasmed as he remembered the feel of it, like a cat wrapping itself around his palms and up his arms. It had been warm and a little wild, and his first instinct had been to extinguish it. Was it to control her or to protect himself from it? He didn't know.

His stomach gave a painful turn, and he retched into the sink, bracing his head in his hands as every vile thing his father had said to him welled up and wrapped themselves around his throat, strangling his sob from him.

Where was Nikaius? He needed Nikaius.

Would Morrigan forgive him?

He had extremely fucked up, and he had no idea how to fix it.

His stomach turned again, bringing up what little lunch he had had, combined with stomach acid that burned his throat and nose as he gagged on it.

"Waric?" His name on Morrigan's lips made his resolve crumble as his knees gave out from under him.

"Holy Fates, Waric?!" Something crashed to the ground before she entered his line of sight, worry etched on her pretty freckled face. He loved those freckles.

Warm hands on his face startled him from his thoughts, and he jerked back, carefully wrapping his hands around her wrists before he dropped them, remembering she could feel his emotions through his touch.

"Don't touch me." He jerked away from her, using his feet to gain some distance between them. "Please don't touch me." His hands wavered as he held them up, unsure whether he wanted to touch himself or her or nothing at all. Looking up at her, he saw the hurt look on her face, and he realized he needed to clarify. "I don't want to hurt you."

"You're not going to hurt me, Waric." Morrigan's voice was confident even though her bottom lip trembled. But Waric knew the truth.

He already had hurt her.

"You don't know that." A sob broke from his chest as he shook his head. "You don't know what I'm capable of. I killed my father. I was out of control then, and I'm not in control now." He felt like his chest was being cleaved in half by his own hands. He couldn't breathe, but he couldn't not tell her, couldn't keep the words inside. "Nikaius is the only person who never thought me to be mundane or ordinary. He always told me I was remarkable. I started to believe him until we got separated."

His gasping sobs filled the air, and he wanted Morrigan to hug him, to hold him, but he held himself back, held himself away from her. He didn't deserve her comfort, didn't deserve her touch.

"They stole me from my bed the night they separated us. I still have nightmares about it. I still have sleepless nights where I wake up in The Pridelands instead of in my bed." Another sob broke free as the fear of that night flooded through him again, pulling a full body shudder from him as he tried to get up. He needed to get away from her before his emotions took over in full force, and he hurt her more.

"I'm not proud of the person I became during that time." His stomach fought against him, and he stumbled as he tried to find his feet, leaning over the sink again. "I will never be able to make amends with the lives I took. I might keep Priamos in control, but that control keeps me balanced."

"Waric." The sound of Morrigan's voice was soft and soothing in a way Waric didn't understand. She was supposed to be afraid of him, of what he had done, and what he could potentially do. She should turn and run in the other direction.

"I returned home to visit my mother." Waric started. Maybe telling her would make him feel better somehow. Running the water in the sink to clear it only threw him further back into the memory.

The room was cold. It hadn't been occupied long enough for the fires to adjust, but Cedric Cavanaugh, and Waric's uncle, Greymane Hawthorne, stood expectantly when Waric entered the room. The water from the fountains on the terrace just outside the doors rushed softly, a sound that calmed Waric even with the high tension in the room. He did not want to be at this 'meeting' but knew it needed to be done before he could spend the night getting reacquainted with his mate.

His mate.

Ever since he had noticed the mark, he had been ecstatic. When he and Nikaius had discovered they could talk telepathically, even over the great distance they were apart, it had only solidified their bond. Though Nikaius had never said it, Waric knew he felt the same. It was in the warmth of Nikaius' magic brushing along Waric's mind when they were talking, and the way Nikaius' voice sounded. To have a fated mate was more than any dream Waric could have ever asked for, especially once he became aware of his father's disdain for not only his magic, but himself as well.

Greymane's grin was almost completely hidden by the bushy beard on his face, and Waric hesitated as he threw open his arms with a loud "Welcome, Nephew!" The energy in the room was charged with the crackling of power the three of them gave off, but Waric felt no fear.

"I'm glad to be back, Uncle." Dipping his head courteously, Waric shoved his hands into his pockets. "I had hoped to speak with mother for a moment before I returned to Kunmei."

"Return to Kunmei? What nonsense do you speak?" Greymane's brows dipped together as he looked Waric over curiously. "Your place is here now, boy."

"There will be no returning to Kunmei. You are to take over as your uncle's heir. That has always been the plan, son." Though Cedric Cavanaugh was nearly a head taller than Waric when he had been sent away, Waric was now nearly his height, the span of his shoulders just a bit broader.

"What plan? I was forcibly taken from my bed, drugged, and forced to spend four years in The Pridelands. I was never informed of, nor agreed to any sort of plan. I am no one's heir, and I have no intention of leading anything." He trembled with barely restrained rage, disbelieving the fact that they had the audacity to think things would have changed for him. He wasn't as intimidated by the man who stood before him. After having partied with the De'Lyons, he would not be afraid of another man, unless Santiago De'Lyon himself issued a challenge. He held more respect for Santi in his pinky finger than he did for either of the men who stood before him.

"Is this about that stupid mark?" Greymane crossed his arms over his chest, his skin unmarred by any scar or mark of any sort. Neither he nor Cedric knew what it was like to have a mate bond as neither had ever had the privilege.

"The bond, and Nikaius, are a blessing from the Fates. I refuse to put either of us in jeopardy by ignoring their will." Where was his mother during all this? Though it was their family home, he had yet to catch a glimpse of her, but he was sure if she was home, she would have heard the three men, as they were not quiet. If she had heard them, she would have come to see him, never resisting an opportunity to see her son. He looked around, wondering if maybe he had missed a sound indicating where she was.

"The Fates do not exist, boy. Your mother has been feeding you nonsense since you were young, and it will stop now."

Waric's blood boiled. Had they done something to her? He hadn't heard another sound in the house aside from the two men. Where was his mother and sisters? "Do not talk about my mother as if you know her. You appeared out of nowhere to prevent me from being branded. You prevented me from losing my magic, and I appreciate that, but I never agreed to any of this."

"You did agree to this when he kept you from being marked as a common piece of trash." Cedric rose to his full height, stepping closer to Waric so that they were toe to toe. Waric could smell the brisk pine scent of him, as well as the acidic scent of whatever liquor he had ingested. When he was younger, the combination would have made him cower.

Now, it made him angry.

"I did not agree to anything! You agreed to it on my behalf when I was a CHILD because you had no use for me." Jabbing his finger into Cedric's chest, he raised his voice. "YOU made this choice. Not I. And I have zero intention of going along with anything you say when you would rather have me not exist. I know you intended for me to die at the hands of a De'Lyon so you had grounds to challenge their young high lord and take over their lands for your own plot. We haven't told anyone because I wished for years for it to not be true. But I've seen the letters to Regan De'Lyon myself, Father, and I am no longer a child or a willing pawn in whatever schemes you have planned." He gestured wildly around the room, happy when he saw his father step back, saw the flicker of fear in his father's gaze.

"You no longer have any power here because I. AM. NOT. AFRAID. OF. YOU." A wild current of air twisted around him. The static in the room heightened as Cedric's jaw clenched, but Waric refused to take a step back or drop his eyes to disengage. He knew he was the one with power. His heart raced with it, and his skin prickled with the energy that encompassed him.

His words enraged Cedric, whose eyes widened before he drew back a hand back. Pain exploded across Waric's mouth and jaw, and he jerked back in surprise as a different sort of energy twisted from the point of impact as his father punched him.

"If you do not do this, your mother will pay gravely. You do still care for your mother, don't you?" Cedric threatened, eyes dark with malevolent promise.

Waric's mind blanked, pure blinding rage encompassing him. He would willingly take all the abuse in the world if it prevented Cedric from turning it towards his mother. His whole life as a child had been spent getting his father's attention in any way he could so that it wasn't on his sweet, caring mother.

Waric had learned from a young age that Cedric hit his wife, had witnessed him do it more than once. Sometimes the belt was turned on him when he tried to fight for her. Waric had made it his mission to make Cedric's life a living hell. It gave Nikaius so much anxiety when Waric openly challenged Cedric and that was something he would have to make amends about in the future.

Tonight, however, was the end of Waric's desire to be what his father wanted. He would steal away his mother to Kunmei if it meant protecting her.

He was DONE. The first time his primal shift happened, he had thought he was going crazy, thought he was going to die with the sheer amount of pain that encompassed him as he shattered into a million pieces before fusing back together in a new form.

Something his father and uncle didn't know was that he had learned how to pull animal forms. Not just one, but all of them. At first, the wild forms had been volatile, but he had figured out how to control every one of them, had been determined to control them.

This time he didn't feel that control. He felt like snarling, felt anger, frustration, and hurt. While he had known not to hope for it, part of him had believed his father would be proud of the man he had become. Instead, all the pain and negative emotions he had felt his entire life exploded from him.

The world blacked out, reality completely falling away as his entire body erupted into blistering, searing flames that left every part of him devastatingly scorched.

"I'm not afraid of you." His voice was loud and harsh, and Cedric looked terrified. He took a step back, his eyes wide as he stared at Waric.

Waric lunged at him, his grip unrelenting as they tumbled to the ground. Waric growled, low and dark as he bellowed again, the statement loud and deep and pulled from somewhere low in his stomach, summoning all the powers his own alpha form allowed him. He wasn't sure what form he was in or how much damage he could do. He could feel nothing but heat.

His mind only focused on making sure that Cedric could never hurt them again. "You will no longer hurt me. Or her. Or anyone else." *Cedric stilled below him as his power met Waric's.*

Waric blazed through it, absorbing it instead of bowing to it. The power coursed through him, and his fingers sank through Cedric's pale throat.

"Never again." *Waric swore. Cedric shuddered, his breath gurgling before it cut off abruptly as Waric clenched the hand inside of his throat and pulled.*

The sound in the room died away as some dark, feral part of Waric purred in the back of his head. Dropping the esophagus, he looked down at his father, then the blood that ran down his mating mark to drip off his elbow.

He thought he would feel something, some kind of emotion at finding his father dead by his own hand.

But he only felt relief.

He knew he would regret his actions later, but he had other business to finish. Locking his eyes with his uncle's, he brought his own hand up to lick the blood from his fingers. Warmth engulfed Waric's back, and he stiffened, his words dying on his tongue. He had forgotten himself as he told his story, forgotten that he had been trying to apologize to Morrigan.

"Greymane looked me in the eye. Declared I was unfit to lead any territories and left to tell the rest of the court heads what I had done." Waric didn't want to turn around, didn't want to face her, afraid of seeing her expression. What would hurt more? Her pity or disgust at his actions? The knowledge that he had already hurt her twisted his stomach painfully, but the worry that she would never look at him made him tremble. Though she needed to know Waric was terrified of moving in case he did something wrong, in case his actions terrified her. "They couldn't reasonably charge me with anything, as it was deemed a family matter, but the damage was done. The damage I had caused, was done."

Her hands were warm as they wrapped around him before they tracked up his chest, stopping to rest over his heart. "You're here, and you're safe now." Morrigan's voice vibrated against his back and all feeling returned to him, a surprised sob tearing itself from his chest. She didn't smell like fear, and he was more relieved than he could possibly say.

He didn't deserve her kindness or understanding, didn't deserve anyone's peace and kindness after what he had done.

But he wanted it. He wanted her.

The power she had over him was the same power Nikaius had, but she didn't have the same history. Could he let her claim and hold that power? Could he trust her?

Without thought, he extracted himself from her grip, then turned and dropped to his knees in front of her. If she wanted power over him, he would allow her to take it. Throwing his arms around her hips to hide his face in her dress, he finally, *finally*, let the sobs completely take over. Allowing himself to break was hard. He was always Nikaius' strength and stability because it helped him keep his own chaos in check, but Nikaius wasn't home, and he didn't know when he would be back. He needed to find stability in himself instead of depending on another to give it to him. He needed comfort, needed softness. He needed Morrigan.

He hadn't allowed himself to cry over what had happened that night, but allowing himself to do so now was freeing. Freeing and painful. He felt like he was being skinned alive.

Coming back to himself after crying wasn't as hard as he had expected and provided some form of clarity. He needed to be stronger for her. What Waric had with Morrigan needed to be different than what he had with Nikaius. He had erred in his expectation that both situations would be the same, that Morrigan would need the same things from him that Nikaius did.

Morrigan didn't need him to be her stability. She had depended on herself for far too long to need someone else to be that. They had been developing a good relationship before his behavior, and he liked to think that he eased some of her own anxiety, had earned himself several smiles when she seemed to be far away.

Though she had depended on all of them for some emotional comfort, her entire being didn't depend on being something for someone else. Ever since she had joined them, he had watched her find herself in ways that he wished he could.

Maybe accepting that Nikaius was currently unavailable was something he needed to do so he could be better not for her, but for himself. The possibility of hurting her was just as devastating as if he had raised a hand to Nikaius. But Nikaius could hold himself against

Waric's moods, as Waric could defend himself against Priamos' volatility. Morrigan did not have the experience for the darker sides of magic, which meant he needed to be in better control of himself. He needed to do better for her.

He would do better for her.

Waric knew he didn't deserve her forgiveness or the warmth her hands provided as they stroked through his hair, nor whatever words she said that he didn't hear over the sound of the rush of blood in his head. "I'm sorry," he whispered against her stomach before pulling away to look up at her.

Tears shone in her eyes, her nose and cheeks were red. Her bottom lip trembled. "I'm so unbelievably sorry, Morrigan." Waric whispered, his hands curling into the skirt of her dress. "I'm not myself right now. It's no excuse, I know. I will spend every waking moment trying to make it up to you."

Morrigan's touch didn't waver as she looked down at him, reaching her hands out to cup his face in her hands, brushing her thumbs against his cheeks. "I think you need to forgive yourself first, Waric. You have so much pain and hurt lingering just under the surface."

When he tried to pull away, she held him still, shaking her head. He had never seen anyone with eyes that were as bright a green as hers, and he felt like he could stare into them forever. "You can't heal when you're still hurting." She whispered

Climbing to his feet, Waric rubbed his hands over his face before offering his hands to her. "Maybe we can heal together then?" He wouldn't blame her if she refused his touch, but he was elated when she stepped forward and took his hands.

"Take a deep breath. We'll get through this together. Okay?" Closing her eyes, Morrigan did just that, and Waric eagerly obeyed, taking a slow, deep breath.

Fates, he loved her.

Chapter Twelve

Morrigan

Corinth Manor
- Starsgard

It had been six days since anyone had seen Nikaius. The stress of it had started breaking down their household. Waric had lost himself in his grief and tried to use his alpha powers on her, and she had learned the truths of what her brand from the Culling did. It felt like their entire life had been put on pause once she knew the truth of Nikaius' disappearance. It had been on hold for so long, but with a key member of their pack missing, it seemed even more so.

It hadn't been long since she had heard Waric's story, and her fingers still burned from the searing pain she had felt from him as he relived what had happened to him. She couldn't imagine being in that mindset as long as he had been and couldn't fathom how deeply wounds like that hurt.

Knowing that there was a high possibility that her mother had chosen for Morrigan to be marked during her Culling was a new fragment of reality that Morrigan hadn't mulled over for very long. For the life of her, she couldn't figure out her mother's thought processes on the matter. She had been told it was because Morrigan was magicless and was some shameful secret.

Delaney would have had to request for Morrigan to be marked or had set up the conditions in which her failure would be documented. Something didn't add up.

She had settled into the bath, gaze flicking over the hills and forests outside the full wall windows as she tried to let the hot water soothe away some of the hurt that still lingered inside. While she liked to believe she was strong, she still felt like she was off-kilter. She had believed her men to be infallible and perfect, but the more layers she peeled away, the more she learned about them, and herself. They were all just as damaged and a little broken, just like her. Betrayal by family seemed to be a running theme between them, but that only meant that she could understand them as they understood her. They all had that commonality, which made their relationships even more poignant. They were working on themselves while also helping each other become the best versions of themselves.

Soren had come to provide some updates for them. It had been a week of rain, non-stop shifting between freezing temperatures at night and endless rain during the day. A lot of the rivers and streams were near their breaking points. To not have their lord on call put her and everyone else on edge, so she understood.

Hawke had sought them out, to give them the news, and Waric had left to join him. Before he left, he had pressed a gentle kiss to Morrigan's forehead. He felt nervous, and she knew it would be a while before he truly trusted himself with her again.

The water of the tub rose slightly and Morrigan stiffened, getting pulled out of her thoughts by it's churning. Looking up, she spotted Waric sitting on the edge of the tub, his pants rolled up to the knee with his feet in the water. "Nikaius will be home soon," Waric promised. His gaze turned to the large windows as well, and he let out a soft sigh.

Giving him a small smile, Morrigan dipped herself under the water for a moment to rinse her hair before moving to sit in the tub in front of him, resting her arms on his knees. He reached out carefully, his fingers brushing tentative adoration across the freckles on her cheeks.

Courting typically dictated that a female should accept the courtship of one male, but when both males were a mated pair, the norm had been driven away once the topic had been explained. She hadn't had much time to grasp what it really meant to be courted by two men who were also together. Add in a third and the world just seemed to tilt more on its axis.

She couldn't regret the decisions she had made. It felt right to spend time with Hawke as she had Waric and Nikaius, and she knew the three held no hard feelings between the three of them. Hawke and Waric both had been very vocal about the fact.

"I'm so tired, Waric." It had settled deep within her bones, started from the pinpoint area of Nikaius' mark, and spread across her entire body. She was getting rest, Waric and Hawke making sure of it, but she still felt unsettled and lost. It was weird not having Nikaius around after so long.

"I know, love. He'll be back soon. We've gotten word—"

Before Waric could finish, a door down the hall slammed open. "Waric?! Morrigan?!" Aslin sounded frantic, and Waric easily cleared the lip of the tub as he stumbled out, summoning a robe from the ether for Morrigan before flinging open the bathroom door.

"Aslin??" Morrigan climbed out carefully and pulled on the robe. She had barely made it into the hall when their friend slammed into Waric with a sob.

"The dam... the boundary dam. I just got word from Sable in Barnam that the dam isn't anticipated to hold through the night."

"Barnam? That's in Be'Sala?" Morrigan knew of the territory at the base of the mountain but hadn't known it was populated. "I know they said they were close, but is it that bad?" Had Waric and Hawke been keeping other things from her?

"They're not doing anything! They've petitioned Bastian, but he's refusing aid. Every head has refused them aid." Aslin's energy was frantic, and Morrigan reached for her.

"Even the De'Lyons?" Morrigan's voice broke at the question. She had known there were petitions being made. Hawke had explained to her that they couldn't offer aid, as it was another lord's territory, but Morrigan felt like that logic was flawed. Saving people's lives was everyone's job.

Aslin shook her head. "They're too far away. The aid won't arrive in time. There are children there, Waric. Families."

"I..." Waric looked between the two with a frown.

"We have to help them." Morrigan turned to Waric too. "Please tell me there's a way to help them?"

"I... I can't make that call. You both know that." Because Waric had killed his father and Greymane had made sure his nephew would never be in power. "I'm not a court head."

There had to be something to do, some way to help. Nikaius was the head of this court, and he was currently unavailable. Who all knew he was missing? "Isn't there some rule or law about someone taking over a court if their lord is indisposed?" Surely there had to be something she could do since Waric couldn't make the call.

Petting Aslin's hair, she tried to mull over all the things that she had overheard since her father's death. Anything that could help them.

What did she know about court politics? Nothing really.

The only information she knew was Santi had claimed The Pridelands when his great uncle had died. His uncle had no children and left behind no next of kin, so Santi was the closest and most eligible person to take the position, and no one objected. Bastian was Nikaius' next of kin, and Morrigan knew better than to reach out to him. That wasn't an option.

"There has to be something. I don't know a lot about court politics. I would think you, Waric, as his mate, would be able to stake claim when he is gone." Would his uncle's declaration make him unfit by proxy as well?

"It doesn't work like that though." Aslin sniffled, running her hands over her face with a deep shuddered breath.

"Why not? It's the same as being next of kin, isn't it?" Morrigan searched Waric's face as she thought. Aslin had mentioned that the neutral territories a few days earlier, and it had Morrigan thinking. "What about the Neutral Territories like Atce' Plaza or Starsgard??"

"What about it?" Aslin asked. She had calmed down a bit, but her face was still splotchy and red, and despair still curled through her as Morrigan reached to brush her tears away. Where were Aquila and

Hawke? Hopefully, they were safe from the onslaught of the storm that had been upon them for the last few days.

"It's neutral territory, right? Can't we just bring everyone there? No one person has a say over who can do what with the area, right? I mean, I'm sure there are some rules to it, but this is an emergency, and if there really is no one else, I will make that call." She couldn't just let those that lived in a forgotten area suffer because their lord refused to help.

"There will be objections."

Something heavy and unseen settled over Morrigan's shoulders. This was a large thing to even consider. She didn't know anything about leading people. She did know, by proxy, what was needed to orchestrate a large party and a wedding. It would be similar, wouldn't it?

But was this a burden she was willing to claim as her own?

Yes.

"I don't care about the objections. I'm in the position to make that call when no one else is. Legally, despite what my brother and mother claim, I've still got a title to my name, right?" Waric's grin spread across his face, and he surged up to press a hard kiss to her mouth.

Pride welled through the kiss, and Morrigan gave a little laugh. The time for being scared to make choices of her own was in the past. Even though her hands shook, and anxiety turned her stomach, in this moment, this is who she wanted to be. When she had first entered Kunmei, Nikaius had told her she was safe and allowed to be who she wanted to be.

But who was she?

She no longer wanted to be the terrified, obedient girl she had been forced to be under her mother's care. She wanted to give everything within her power to save people who could not save themselves. Taking a deep breath, she tried to quell the flight of angry bees in her stomach. She needed to be bigger than her own emotions. She was terrified of messing this up, the entire world feeling cold for a moment as she followed Waric back into her bedroom. Underneath that terror was a determination she hadn't known she was capable of.

This was a big moment. This would bring her out of the shadows and throw her in the radar of others who might not approve. Her mother might hear about it. Would Delaney come on her own? Would she try to force Morrigan into submission again?

No.

If she wanted to be seen as bold and capable, she needed to stop being scared of others. She was Morrigan Aegean. From what she remembered of her father, he was bold and caring and kind, and she wanted the world to know she was her father's daughter. She wanted to be Mae De'Lyon's sister. Bold. Fierce. Free.

Freedom often came at a cost, and now that she had been given a taste, she wanted to cement it and shout it to the world. "We can do this." Though she was reassuring herself more than either party in the room, she said it again, chanting it as a mantra in her head. She couldn't do it alone though. "I'm going to need as much help as I can get."

"We've got you." Aslin voice was soft but strong, and she turned to Morrigan's armoire to gather clothing to dress Morrigan in.

Morrigan's hands trembled as she looked at herself in the mirror and picking up a brush to run it through her hair. It looked darker when it was wet, and it made her feel a bit separated from her sister and father. Surely, they would support her decision. Nikaius' had told her once that he believed she would be a good leader.

Was he right?

Where was he? He needed to be here to defend people. She needed his help.

Taking a deep breath, she willed her hands to steady as she carefully twisted her hair out of her face. This was a choice she was making not only for herself but for the people of Barnam as well.

This choice would change everything. She wouldn't have the anonymity of being a nobody in Nikaius' court. Others would learn of her existence, and it would raise questions. Was she ready to face those questions? Give the explanations that would throw her mother and brother into another full-blown scandal?

With the mark on her shoulder, no one would believe her capable of leading anything. She would prove them wrong.

"What are your orders, my lady?" Morrigan jumped, having not realized that Waric had left until he reappeared at her side. She had anticipated something less battlement, but dressed as he was, she remembered that Waric was just as much a part of the guard as Nikaius was. They held a lot of power between the two of them.

"Oh, Fates, are we actually going to do this?" She took a solidifying breath and nodded, this time saying, "We're doing this," with conviction. They were doing it, and no one could stop her. Waric smiled.

"We'll stand by your side in whatever you decide." Waric reached up to gently touch her cheek. He did so unerringly, this time not afraid to show her what was lingering under the surface. His resolve and confidence were warming.

"We have the option to help people where others are refusing. I couldn't live with myself if I didn't at least try." Morrigan dropped her robe and accepted the undergarments Aslin provided. She stepped into the gown that Aslin lowered for her before turning so she could be laced in. It was one of her more formal dresses.

"Aslin..."

"It's not ideal, but they need to see your kindness as leadership." Aslin explained. She was right. It didn't scream monarchy but was a bold royal emerald that would definitely draw attention. When one looked at her, there would be no doubt that she was the one in charge. She hadn't worn fine things when she was growing up, but as she lifted her chin and squared her shoulders, she was able to see her sister in herself again.

Mae had been beautifully bold in every way. Morrigan hoped that her pride in herself would make Mae proud as well.

"I don't really think I can lead anyone. This will be temporary at best. When Nikaius comes back..."

"You'll do great." Waric's hand grasped Morrigan's hand, and he nodded. The steady confidence that welled up her arm through their joined hands was encouraging. "Call for the guard. They will appear." Warmth seared through Morrigan. Waric's faith in her was unwavering, and she appreciated it so much.

Morrigan nodded, took a slow breath, and called, "Hawke? Aquila?" Her voice broke at Aquila's name. Aquila was her friend, and Hawke her lover, she didn't want to command them, but she also knew they'd understand. They appeared moments later, both looking dazed and confused before realizing something was amiss. Both were already dressed in their mantles; she must have pulled them from the evening muster.

Aquila and Hawke looked stunned, but Waric grinned, pressing a kiss to her temple. "You've got this. In this moment, with just us here, you can do no wrong."

Morrigan nodded and when Aslin finished the back of her dress, she stepped forward, hand still tight in Waric's even as she lifted her head to declare, "I've taken leadership of the court in Nikaius' absence." Her gaze met Hawke's, and her mouth went dry. His concern was evident on his face, his eyebrows raised in surprise as he took her in. She could almost feel his assessing gaze before his eyes returned to hers. It felt as if he was trying to see her soul, and she fought the urge to nervously pick at her nails. Could he see what she felt? He didn't look upset, which was a relief, but as his eyes locked with hers again, he seemed guarded, like he wasn't sure what to make of her at that moment. His lack of approval would hurt, but Morrigan's mind was made up. "You said we couldn't do anything about this, but I refuse to accept that. Starsgard is neutral territory. Gather as many people that can create portals as you can that can teleport to Barnams. We have lives to save."

Hawke searched her gaze for a moment before it flicked to Waric and Aslin, then back to her. "Can we speak alone for a moment?" His words made her heart fly to her throat, and she gave a shaky nod. Hawke was always the voice of reason, always wanting to know all the details before deciding about what to do. It was something Morrigan was grateful for as she knew she was prone to making emotional decisions.

Waric pressed a kiss to the top of her head before following Aslin and Aquila out the door.

"Are you sure this is what you want to do?" Hawke stepped closer and reached for her, always deferring the first move to her. Stepping into him, she nodded. Hawke let out a slow breath before taking her face in his hands so he could press their foreheads together. All he felt like was worry, and she hated that she was the cause. "You can't come back from this, Morrigan. This isn't some one-time thing. Your name will get out. You will be under a mass amount of scrutiny because of your existence. They will try to pick you apart from every angle, including your relationships with other people." She knew he was right; she had seen it happen time and time again from the sidelines during her mother's parties.

Sighing softly, Morrigan curled her fingers around his wrists and tipped her chin up to kiss him gently before stepping closer and hugging herself closer to him. "There are people that need saving, Hawke. Whether I do or don't want to do something is beside the point right now. These people need us, and if I'm the only person that can make that call, then I want to do it. I have Waric on my side, and hopefully you as well."

"You'll always have me, Morrigan. Always." He gave her a gentle squeeze and stroked his hand over her hair. Once the racing of her heart slowed, and her resolve firmed, Hawke finally stepped back. Taking one of her hands in his, he stepped into a bow, pressing a kiss to her knuckles. "We have an elite force that can be ready in thirty minutes."

"Thank you, Hawke." Morrigan spoke breathlessly, her bottom lip trembling as tears welled in her eyes. He gave a swift nod before vanishing into the shadows again.

Once she had composed herself a little, she stepped out into the hallway seeking out the rest of the pack. "Where do we plan on bringing everyone?" Aquila asked.

"I know we can't bring them here. After we received a missive about this the other day, Hawke explained to me that even if we were to provide asylum, Kunmei doesn't have the resources. I did some reading because I was trying to figure out the other court's motives. There are so many people in power, I didn't understand why they can't help." Shaking out her hands, she tried to remember everything that she had read. Having open access to Corinth Manor's library as well as the archives in town had been a blessing, and she surprised herself with how much she had learned since she had joined them. Politics and history weren't something she had quite delved into yet, but she had done some reading about the neutral territories.

"Do you think Starsgard will suffice? It will hold more people and it's neutral territory, so it will take some time for others to find us and form an argument." Morrigan looked at Waric and Aslin, who nodded. "Perfect. I know it's late, but we need to rouse anyone who can help. We'll open Starsgard to everyone. I know we do not have many here, but if there are others that need help, they shall be welcome as well. Aquila, send your quickest scouts to as many low-lying territories as you can. I don't know much about Be'Sala's geography, but if that dam fails, we can only assume that Barnam won't be the only one in the way."

Aquila bowed and disappeared. Aslin's fingers made quick work of braiding Morrigan's hair into something simple but out of the way. Morrigan had no intention of just observing, she was going to help just as well as anyone who volunteered their time. "I'll go set up a portal close by," Aslin whispered, and Morrigan nodded before turning to where Waric waited.

"Your compassion will save us all." Waric whispered when they were alone again. He seized her around the waist and hauled her to him, pressing a searing kiss to her mouth. Something clicked into place then and warmth bloomed through her. Was this what love truly felt like? Being able to trust someone so deeply and have their trust in turn?

"I'll sound the alarm and make sure everyone knows where to go. Aslin will be with you, so the house will expand to allow rooms as needed. Be safe." His words warmed her. So many things were going to need to be talked about and decided, but the fact that Waric still stood beside her even when his own mate was absent meant more than she could voice. The entire pack's acceptance of what she wanted to do wasn't something to take lightly.

"I'll be here. You be safe." She replied, and Waric gave her a mischievous grin. She couldn't leave without telling him, though they still had some things they needed to work through, she needed to acknowledge how she felt. Just in case things went poorly, and it was some time before they saw each other again. Before he could turn to leave, Morrigan leaned up to throw her arms around Waric's neck and pressed herself to him, kissing him with the hope that conveyed everything she felt for him.

When they separated, his grin returned, his forehead pressing to hers gently as she slid her hands into his. "To be your mate is an honor," she whispered, her bottom lip quivering. It was scary to accept such a thing, jumping feet first into the unknown, but that seemed to be the theme for her tonight. Warmth spread up her arm and when she looked down, stars were scattered across her skin encased in stippled flames that curled up her forearm, the same stars that spread across Nikaius' wrist as well. Waric's mark. With another kiss, Waric disappeared into the void.

"Aslin," turning, Morrigan found her friend grinning, holding her cloak, "we've got things to do." She accepted the cloak before taking Aslin's hand.

Chapter Thirteen

Morrigan

Starsgard

Morrigan had expected her first venture to Starsgard to include sweeping views of the castle, but she and Aslin ended up exiting their portal into a room that was nothing but dark stone. Some of the walls had varying shapes and figures drawn into them, but she didn't know what they were for. She was a little disappointed that it wasn't as grand of an entrance as she had imagined, but there were more important things to do than to satiate her curiosity. She would have time to explore when things settled down some.

Ten past midnight, the first people from Kunmei began arriving. She wasn't sure what she had expected, but she was surprised to encounter mothers with barely awake, bleary-eyed children, and sleepy teenagers. Some of the mothers looked just as tired and exasperated, their frowns making Morrigan feel guilty for rousing them from their beds, but she knew that they were safer in Starsgard than down in the lowlands of town.

The rest seemed to be alert, though their children fussed, and a few teenagers looked ready to fall back to sleep while standing.

Though she had expected some form of frantic energy of anger and high stress, Morrigan was surprised to realize that she knew each by name as they greeted her. When had she learned so many people? "Ladies, I'm so sorry to have roused you from sleep." Though she was nervous about speaking, her voice was stable. "The water levels of the rivers have risen to catastrophic levels."

"My husband said that the guard had been called?" One woman asked.

"I do not wish to lie to you, and I don't know how much I'm supposed to say, but I'm going to need your help. We're planning to evacuate all the low-lying areas to save as many as we can, not only from our court but others as well. I do not expect anyone to help if they do not wish to, but I cannot do this alone. If you wish to find a room and stay with your children, please do. I just want everyone to be safe."

"My lady, it's a privilege to be called upon to spread the kindness we have received here. Please don't fret." Abbigale's mother, Molly, patted Morrigan's hand, calm and patience soothing her frazzled nerves through the contact. Morrigan nodded. "Let me pop Abbigale back to bed, and I'll be right down."

"We're with you, my lady." A young male with a wild mane of red hair and pale cat ears perched on top of his head grinned at her. "How can we help?"

Clearing her throat of the happy tears, she smiled at him. She didn't know when she had come to love these people as her own, but each face she saw that she knew made her want to cry from joy. However, now was not the time for tears. She had a job to do just as everyone else did. What use could she put young adults to? "Thank you Gryffin. Can you cook? We need the kitchens staffed. The weather is terrible, and I don't know if the people of Barnam have lost connection with the magic grid. We don't know what condition they will be in when they get here. Not to speak ill of others, but their lord has refused them aid. I want to be prepared for the worst. We need soup and warm beverages. Is that something you are comfortable with?" His eager nod eased Morrigan's worry before he and a few others headed in the direction Aslin had sent them.

Looking around, she realized there were curiously few men around but before she could ask about it another, more important thought came to her. Turning to those who lingered in the hall, she asked, "Where are the healers? Do we have healers here?"

A few raised their hands. "Good, let's set up an infirmary. Simple magic should be enough. I don't anticipate anyone being seriously injured, but it's best to have some idea of what we're looking for. Triage the most susceptible first and then branch out from there. I trust you to divvy up who does what based on talents." The group nodded, and Morrigan smiled as her nerves settled a bit more.

She could do this. It was like preparing for a party that her mother had hosted. Chin up Morrigan, we can do this. "Aslin, do we have an inventory of what we have on hand?" That was the most important thing for any event. Knowing what you have and what you need.

"I'm not sure what is where. We can always pull things from other places if we need to."

"Let's take stock of what we can find first. Most importantly, we're going to need blankets and warm clothing." Morrigan turned to face the receiving hall as a whole. The room was large and made of dark stone similar to the marble of their bathroom back home. One wall had large windows that overlooked the courtyard and a door for physical entry into the building. The two side walls were undecorated, and the back housed drawings of different wards and symbols. Morrigan knew they aided in the ability to teleport and use portals into the room, but she didn't know explicitly what any of them meant.

Molly returned, and with her were several others who were either mothers to the young adults or had found somewhere to put their children back to bed. "There are some supply closets on the upper floors, we can gather whatever we find."

"Yes, thank you. I think our primary needs will be blankets and clothing. We don't know what they will be able to bring with them." A handful of women disappeared as others branched out in the hallway that joined the reception chamber to the rest of the castle. Curiosity was eating at her, making her skin tingle and itch with the need to explore and learn all she could about it, but she knew there would be time for that later. She needed to do something to ease the feeling, but she also knew now was not the time to dip into the old habits of allowing her emotions to take over. She needed her wits about her and rationality on her side. Tomorrow could be for exploring. "Aslin, how many rooms does Starsgard have?"

"This main floor has the servant's dormitory to our left, this receiving room, a dining hall to our right with the council room off to the right. The kitchen and two additional chambers make up the rest of this floor. Upstairs are the king's and queen's suites and ten large guest rooms separated by a guard dormitory. There are other structures on the property, guest houses and the like for when big gatherings happen, but I don't know what condition they are in."

"And how many people can fit into one dormitory?" Morrigan didn't know how many people they were expecting, and while she hoped Starsgard would be big enough, she knew that some things didn't go as planned.

"About a hundred each, but we can shift walls and stuff if we need to." Aslin pulled a tablet of paper from the ether and showed it to Morrigan. It had the layout of the floors and the rooms on each. Morrigan scanned the image trying to get a better idea of what needed to be where.

"We have our own families from Kunmei here, plus whoever will be coming from Barnam and other towns. Let's open as much of the second floor as we can."

Aslin dragged her finger over the page and Morrigan watched as the layout changed. Was Aslin just making a plan, or were the rooms changing as she plotted them out? Before Morrigan could break away to satiate her curiosity, Aslin frowned up at her. "The king's and queen's suites can't be moved."

Looking over the floor plan, Morrigan hummed. "That's alright. We can find the maximum use of that space." Turning at the sound of footsteps entering the room, Morrigan smiled at the women who appeared near them, each carrying baskets of blankets. "It won't be perfect, but it's hopefully only temporary." She smiled at Aslin over her shoulder before gesturing to the group. "Set those over there, please."

"Not to interrupt, but you mentioned finding use of space?" Cressida, one of the women who was in Morrigan's class, spoke up, and Morrigan nodded in encouragement. "Perhaps a nursery should be a priority, my lady." She smiled as she patted the back of the babe who cooed from the sling on her chest. "We would probably have more hands if we had childcare."

Morrigan smiled, gratefulness spreading through her at the suggestion. While she tended to try to be a one woman show in the kitchen for her mother's events, she knew that with large events came large responsibilities and help was always needed. "That's a great idea, thank you. Let's allocate the queen's suite for that. I don't know much about what would be needed in a nursery, so I will leave that set up to you if you'd like?"

"I would be honored. A couple of us will go and do that now and let the others know. We'll have more hands than you'll know what to do with." Morrigan laughed, accepting the offered hug. She carefully touched the light blond hair of the baby with adoration for both him and his mother. While she loved children, she had only tended to them on rare occasions and didn't really know the ins and outs of daily life with one.

Another group appeared with more bedding. "We have a nursery being sorted, an infirmary set up in the dining hall, and sustenance being prepared in the kitchens. If you all wouldn't mind helping me sort this, I think we might be able to be ready for whatever this night throws at us."

Though they didn't know what the night would bring, Morrigan was happy to finally to realize that she was as much a member of Kunmei as those that were helping her.

"Morrigan?" Aslin's voice was tentative, and Morrigan turned to her with a smile.

"Everything will be fine, Aslin."

"I know I just..." Reaching out, Aslin caught the nape of Morrigan's neck and pressed their foreheads together. "You're doing amazing," she whispered.

Joy soared through Morrigan from the point of contact at their foreheads down to her toes as she let out an unrestrained laugh.

This was where she belonged. This was what home felt like. She had felt it with Mae, but now she some how had found it on her own with out any blood connections near.

The Kunmei Guard arrived half past midnight, just as Hawke had promised. All carrying children. "We were directed to the children's home first, my lady." Was the only explanation she received from a blonde guard as a hastily wrapped baby was passed to her before he disappeared again. Other guards arrived with older youth who also carried the youngest amongst them. "I'm going to need help." There were so many children. "We're going to need help." Careful of the child she carried, she dashed to the door.

"We have children, I need more hands!" Women in the hall who had been trying to sort through provisions in the storerooms stopped what they were doing, much to Morrigan's relief. The kindness people exhibited was beyond anything she had ever experienced.

In the next round, with the baby still cuddled against her chest, she caught one of the teenagers who came through carrying a toddler with a babe wrapped to her chest. "Please, what is your name?"

"Angelica, miss."

Morrigan looked around, and her bottom lip trembled. "Angelica, How–How many of you are there?"

"Twenty-five ma'am."

"Twenty-five..." It broke her heart to know so many children were without parents. There was no way. How was that possible for a village she hadn't known even existed?

Could she protect them all when the inevitable backlash hit?

She knew their—her—guard would do its best, but she knew she would need more. Another figurehead to back her claim to provide asylum to those in her care.

She watched a plain clothed male she knew, Cassian, step through the ether to hand two children off to his wife, Jyn, with a kiss. How Jyn had known where to be and when was curious, but Morrigan couldn't help the pride that spread across her chest as more plain clothed men and women began coming through.

Capable civilians had gone to help the guard. That was why her people seemed to be so few. Letting out a watery little laugh, she turned to survey the controlled chaos around her.

The room was too crowded, becoming too full too quickly, so she willed the receiving chamber to open up to the dining hall next to it. Surprise lit through her as the wall vanished and people began to spread out. Some looked up from what they were doing, but no one seemed too fazed by the vanishing of the wall.

"I need someone who knows The Pridelands." Aslin had said that Santi was willing to provide aid but wouldn't arrive in time. Hopefully, she would have enough time to divert them.

"I do, miss," Angelica passed off the children she held. "I'm willing to help, and I know your story is similar, miss. My parents defected from Be'Sala to The Pridelands when I was young. High Lord Santiago De'Lyon has me patched into his wards. I can be there in minutes."

"If you're sure?" Angelica nodded.

Each moment in the presence of the gathered people surprised Morrigan more and more. "Grab yourself some warm clothes and a coat, then please go as swiftly as you can to The Pridelands. Call Santi and Mae De'Lyon personally. Tell them Morrigan sent you and that we need their help." Angelica nodded and then she was gone.

Chapter Fourteen

Nikaius

Unknown Area, The Pridelands

Kunmei was the same as it had been since Nikaius was a boy. He wasn't sure what he expected when he stepped through the portal that would bring him home. Maybe for the scenery to have changed or the lake to have dried up?

He was now the Lord of the Kunmei and with that came responsibilities Nikaius had learned to handle by watching Bastian.

Bastian, whose temper always led his actions. Bastian who always put his own needs above those of his people's. Though he and his brother didn't agree on much, Nikaius had always paid attention to what he was doing and how he conducted himself.

Mostly to learn what not to do, which his father was not pleased about.

Nikola Ayrden always seemed to be displeased by Nikaius, which led to Nikaius being sent off to train in a territory that was not his. It was the reason why Nikaius was finally setting foot in his territory four years after having earned his right to it. His father was waiting for him, but Nikaius had someone more important to see. Someone that was lifetimes more important than listening to whatever rubbish his father wanted to spout: Waric.

Lifting his arm to the sky, he watched as the silver stars of his mate mark shimmered in the moonlight. It had been years since they last saw each other, but they hadn't been separated. Not really. Especially not when you share a mate mark with your best friend.

Hearing Waric's voice in his head had been as jarring the first time as it had been hearing Priamos. He had been in the middle of sparring with another male when Waric had started narrating different hand to hand combination names. Nikaius had been so distracted, he had earned himself a nice scar from where he had been cut with his challenger's sword. But once Nikaius was used to the whispers and inside jokes, it helped him feel closer to his mate, helped him feel not as alone.

Nikaius wanted nothing more than to see his mate. He had played the scenario of seeing each other again over and over in his head, allowing his excitement to build.

Although Waric had been very fluid with his sexuality, even at fifteen years old, Nikaius hadn't been sure where he settled. He had been with both men and women before as was common for Rekru'e who went through ruts and heats, but nothing had felt life changing or appealing. It was mostly a means to an end. Would it be the same with Waric?

Dropping his arm, he turned to look around the clearing. This was where Waric had suggested they meet. It was where they had first met and went anytime they wanted to be away from all the happenings in life. They needed to figure out how they were going to navigate the new life they would lead with Nikaius being the head of a court. They had talked about their ideas a few times, from abolishing the trade of thabers to forbidding the Culling. They had thrown so many ideas around that Nikaius wasn't sure which was most important anymore. They all were important, and they would talk about it, but that was after Waric met with his father. He had no idea what the meeting was about, but he knew that there was bad blood there as well.

While they had been away, Waric's sister married another, and his cousin absconded responsibility, leaving Waric as the only eligible heir to their family name. But Nikaius knew that Waric had no desire to lead. Nikaius had protested that they could better achieve their goals together if they were both heads of state. Waric had disagreed. He didn't want the power that came with such a task because he had seen how power changed his father and Bastian.

A crackle of energy encompassed the area announcing Waric's appearance in the clearing via teleportation before his voice broke the silence. "Nikaius?" *Nikaius turned, finding Waric only a few feet away. His heart gave a hard lurch, and he felt like the wind had been knocked out of him. Throwing himself into Waric's arms, he laughed, pressing a hard kiss to his mouth.*

His joy was short-lived as Waric hugged him back, burying his face into Nikaius' neck and taking a deep, shuddering breath. Pulling back, Nikaius frowned as he took in Waric's appearance. The first thing he noticed was that Waric's hair was longer, the ends curling along his shoulders and falling into his eyes. The second was that he was covered in blood.

Alarm rang through him as he stepped back to hold Waric at arm's length, his eyes flickering over his mate's body trying to find some injury that was responsible for the blood splashed across his clothes and face. "What happened?"

"I killed him."

"Killed who?"

"My father. He swung at me, and I killed him. My mother will never forgive me." *Though Waric didn't cry, he did tremble hard, his entire being shaking under Nikaius' hands, not meeting his eye. Nikaius could sense the stress he was under, could smell his scent turn acidic as his hands trembled.*

Taking Waric's face in his hands, Nikaius pressed their foreheads together, trying to will some calm through their bond. This was not how he wanted to spend their first night back together. He had expected hugs, kisses, conversations, lying next to each other on a bed for hours. He had imagined hard conversations and talks of their futures.

Waric broke their touch and wrapped his arms around Nikaius' waist. Though he seemed unwavering, Nikaius allowed Waric to cling to him, pressing his lips to the side of Waric's head as he swayed them back and forth. Nikaius willed Waric to just be for a moment, to allow himself the time he needed to process what had happened and what the future looked like for them. Waric didn't need a solution, he needed to be grounded, and Nikaius was content to do that, to be the stability Waric needed while he pieced himself back together. They would address what their next course of action would be when Waric was calmer. Where was Cedric's body? Were there witnesses? Would people be coming for Waric? He could hear the tumultuous thoughts and phrases and words that made barely any sense through their bond that gave evidence to Waric's panic.

Nikaius wasn't sure what needed to be done, but he would happily do it once Waric was in a better place to make decisions.

Nikaius wasn't sure how long they stood there, waiting for Waric to gather himself as the water in the lake crashed against the shore and frogs croaked nearby. Finally Waric pulled away, rubbing the drying blood along his own jaw. "Some reunion." Waric sighed, his frown pulling deeper as he looked around.

"We have our entire lives to make our reunion perfect, Waric. All I need is you here." Nikaius pressed another kiss to the side of Waric's head before lacing their fingers together with a grin. "You don't have to worry about going back, Waric. We have our own home; we can call Hawke and Aquila and make Corinth Manor our own."

Nikaius' knew his attempt at humor would probably fail, but it hit its mark enough to get Waric finally smiling as he leaned up to press a kiss to Nikaius' mouth. It had been so long since he had kissed someone that he forgot how quickly it could ignite a fire within him, Suddenly ravenous, he leaned into the kiss, dropping Waric's hand so he could fist both of his own hands in the too long hair at the nape of Waric's neck. Priamos rumbled in the back of Nikaius' mind. They needed to get the scent of another's blood off him. Waric needed to smell like him, and only him. Priamos was sure that would make everything better.

Waric growled low in his chest, and Priamos responded with his own grumble.

Mate. *Priamos purred.*

Mate. *Waric agreed, his voice a low hum in Nikaius' head as he nipped Nikaius' bottom lip.* Nikaius gave his own rumble as he returned the bite and tugged with his teeth. Waric stumbled into him and suddenly they were chest to chest. Waric pulled him closer, deepening the kiss as his hand dug into Nikaius' hair and their hips met firmly, making them both groan.

Kissing wasn't something that naturally turned him on, but with Waric, the opposite seemed to be true. Kissing Waric felt like his every nerve ending was on fire, and he would never be satisfied with just one kiss. Perhaps it was the mate bond. There were so many things he didn't know about mate bonds, only that he and Waric had been in each other's thoughts, that they weren't ever truly apart.

Mate.

Saying the word, even in his head, seemed to be enough to cement their bond further. He had read how mate bonds were like imprints, once fully accepted, the hearts synched and the bond grew more solid, giving them each the ability to be with their mate in an instant. Whether that meant that Nikaius could pull Waric through the bond or if Nikaius would go to him, Nikaius was unsure. He waited a breath, and then two before he finally felt it. His heart slowed, making his entire body tingle with energy before it skipped a beat and resumed its pace.

Waric laughed as he pulled away for a breath.

"I love you." He whispered. Nikaius had known how Waric felt about him, he had said it before, when they were children and through the bond when they were apart, but Nikaius had never said it back. He had never been sure of his feelings for Waric because the only love he had grown up with was that of his mother. What he felt for Waric was different, more, somehow.

When he thought of Waric, his heart got light, and he felt like he would shed his skin in the pure sensation of joy every time he thought about the life they were going to live, but confessing one's love was something Nikaius felt like he needed to do in person. Though his nerves almost prevented him from saying anything Priamos gave him a mental shove that made Nikaius laugh before he kissed Waric again.

"And I love you." The giddy laugh Waric gave made Nikaius' heart soar. He wanted nothing more than to continue to make Waric laugh and smile and promise eternal happiness to the one the Fates had blessed him with, but he knew more pressing things needed to happen.

Pulling away, Nikaius frowned, licking his lips as he looked over Waric again. Blood was splattered across his chest, neck, and the side of his face.

He thought he would be disgusted by the sight, but he was surprised to learn he wasn't. In fact, pride swelled through him as he looked at Waric again.

His bold, fierce mate had finally retaliated against his abuser. He had taken back the power that Cedric Cavanaugh and Greymane Hawthorne had taken from him countless times in his youth. Power that Nikaius wished he could take back from his own father for having restricted him from his mate for so long, but his own retribution wasn't important right then.

His mate was a rumpled mess but powerful in his own right, and Nikaius wanted nothing more than to bow to him, to show him exactly how he saw the man standing before him. But first, they needed to eat and bathe.

"Let's go home." Nikaius whispered, giving Waric another kiss before tugging him through the ether into the manor that would become their home.

Nikaius startled awake, reaching for Waric, forgetting where he was. He tried to settle back into the memory he was dreaming of, tried to dream himself back into Waric's hug. He missed Waric even though it couldn't have been too long since he had been gone. The room was dark, and he could hear muffled voices and footsteps outside of the room, but all he could smell were the bitter and soothing herbs and himself. He wondered if he was still confined to the back of his own mind and if Priamos was still in control.

It didn't feel like they were trying to battle for the same space anymore, and Nikaius sighed as he shifted onto his back. His pain had settled into a shallow ache centering in his shoulder, which gave him hope that he was finally healing. Some of the smaller injuries had infection setting into them that Mae had been able to cleanse with a tincture and salve that Santi and Mae created, but the large wound that took up most of the front of his shoulder hadn't been touched by her healing magic.

After a thorough exam by Santi, they determined that whatever he had been hit with was some sort of dark magic they didn't have an explanation for. When Priamos had been in control of their body, being able to tell Santi and Mae what he was experiencing was impossible. They had given him some form of sedative in an attempt to help him sleep off whatever other side effects the wound was giving him. The sleep and healing must have had placated Priamos enough to let Nikaius shift back to his human form.

Blinking into the darkness, he stretched, realizing that he finally had his body back. Lifting his right hand up into the air above him, he flexed his fingers with a sigh. The silver stars on his wrist caught the faint light of the embers in the hearth, and he let out a slow sigh as he contemplated the shimmering stars and the dream he had just woken from.

Being raised Rekru'e, it hadn't been a surprise to either of them that they had been mated, but neither had thought it would be to the other. They never had time to explore what the mark would mean to them because when Nikola caught sight of it, he sent them to train on opposite sides of the continent. Waric had been sent to The Pridelands, home of Nikaius' uncle Santiago De'Lyon. Nikaius assumed he hadn't been sent there because Nikola was worried about favoritism. Instead, Nikaius was sent to train with the Velamo in Kemerseli, with the Gorlassar nest.

Shortly after Nikaius' fifteenth birthday, Nikola insisted he and Waric participate in a Culling just as Bastian and Santi had a few years before. The Culling was an archaic practice where, at thirteen and a half, faekind were tested to determine their magical worth. It had been a tradition since the fall of the Veil after the war, but it never felt right to Nikaius. Though his thoughts probably came from a place of privilege—he hadn't shifted until he was forced to at fourteen but had remained unmarked—he felt that just because it hadn't happened to him didn't mean he needed to approve of the practice. He had watched friends get marked and sent off when he was younger.

The Culling was something he and Waric wanted to abolish.

Waric.

Nikaius sighed with longing. This had to be the longest they have been separated from each other since they were sent to different training camps as teenagers, the longest they hadn't been able to rely on each other in years.

Though they fought like animals the first few weeks they trained, Nikaius quickly earned the respect of Tarsenack Gorlassar, who was the heir to the Gorlassar Nest. Tarsenack had quickly become an ally for Nikaius' plight to have the Culling abolished as his own father had been victim to it. That was how Nikaius had learned that mating bites and marks often nullified the effects of the brand.

Until then, neither he nor Waric had known that the brands also canceled out any magic that the bearer had, and some families chose to mark their weakest family members even if they did have powers. He and Waric were also pretty sure they had some tie to the young girl they had held when she was branded.

Something in Priamos had snapped when they marked her, and he woke up a few days later to find that he and Waric had marked each other while they held her.

Remembering that turned Nikaius' thoughts towards Morrigan. Since he had bitten her at the beginning of his rut, did that have some effect on her powers? Hawke mentioned that Mae had told him about Morrigan's powers, and that somehow the brand hadn't stopped her from being able to use them. It seemed she was only cut off from the mundane powers that all fae had, like teleportation and pulling things from the ether.

He hadn't gotten a chance to see the mark on Morrigan's arm, having been out running when she was attacked, and she had worn long sleeves the morning after. He was curious to know how it was healing and if it was the same as his. Hawke had mentioned that it looked like someone had burned their palm into her arm and that was how his own injury felt, like someone had taken hot pieces of magic and etched them into his skin.

Nikaius wasn't sure how long he had been away from Waric, Morrigan, and his family, but he knew it had been a few days at least. Desperate to talk to them, desperate to check on them, he searched in his mind for his bond to Waric. He could feel Waric in his mind, springy and bright, and gave it a little tug. The resulting flood of emotions made his breath catch painfully in his chest.

The first emotion that flooded through was fear. It wasn't fear for himself though. It was a worried and concerned fear. Nikaius tried to get a glimpse of what was going on in his mate's head, but it was a jumbled chaos of words that Nikaius didn't have the right headspace to translate accurately to figure out what exactly was wrong, but he knew his absence didn't help.

He needed to get home.

Groaning softly, Nikaius sat up, trying to roll out the ache in his shoulders, then he stood carefully, unsure if his legs would support him after having been in his wild form for so long. Tentatively putting his weight on one foot and then the other, he stretched himself to his full height, glad that he seemed able to support himself.

Having been to The Pridelands numerous times since he was a pup, he was familiar with most of the spaces inside of it. He had known that the De'Lyon pride had different magical abilities, and that the entrance to the library changed daily. He also knew they were incredibly protective of their space and people, but he'd never known them to have secret areas under the sands.

When he reached the door, he took a moment to listen, trying to see if there was any indication of where he truly was. Someone was pacing in front of the door and when Nikaius pulled it open, Mae paused in her steps, blinking up at Nikaius in surprise.

"Mae?"

"Nikaius." He watched with curiosity as Mae flushed, running her hand through her hair. "How are you feeling?" Her attention was on her feet, and Nikaius took a deep breath, trying to catch some scent that would give away the cause of her nervousness. Looking over her shoulder, Mae surprised him by dipping under his arm and entering the room, snapping the door shut behind her.

"I'm feeling better, thank you." Nikaius stepped back and the fire in the fireplace roared to life with the lights overhead, brightening the room. "Are you alright?" She smelled worried, the same feeling that tickled the back of his mind when he turned into Waric's bond again. Why was everyone around him worried?

"I am well. But..." Licking her lips, Mae smoothed her hands over her stomach and wiped them on her legs. "We don't know what it means yet, but Aeron is looking for you."

"The Valkyrie?"

"Yes. He appeared at the house shortly after Waric visited the library."

"Is Waric okay? And Morrigan?"

"They're worried, but fine." Mae's expression didn't change. "Aeshira came to us looking for some of her kin the day we found you. She said that Aeron and his troops went to investigate the disappearances because they're becoming more noticeable but hadn't heard from him in days."

That Aeshira was missing people was concerning because the Valkyrie and the Velamo tended to have a shared hive mentality. Pack mentality like what he held with Hawke and Aquila was more primal based and mostly feelings. The Velamo and the Valkyrie grew up in each other's minds and it made them the strongest force Nikaius had ever met.

Mae continued speaking, drawing Nikaius from his thoughts. He watched her twist her fingers in her hand as she spoke, a habit he had noticed Morrigan had as well. "After she left, Aeron appeared, saying that he had visited your home to speak with you about something urgent, but you weren't there. I didn't say anything to him about Aeshira coming to us because it was suspicious. Silas thought so, too, and he went to tell Santi but ended up finding you instead."

Realization dawned Nikaius then. "That's what Silas meant by him thinking I didn't want to be found. I wonder why there's a disconnect with the Valkyrie. I know Aeron was on Bastian's side about the court division, but to have his troops completely cut off from Aeshira is treasonous."

"We don't understand either. Santi doesn't want to let you travel unless we know that the magic that marked you won't track you back to your pack, and I'm worried about how it would affect Morrigan."

Did Mae not know about Morrigan's injury? "Did Waric not mention?"

"Not mention what?"

Rubbing his hand over his mouth, Nikaius wished he hadn't said anything, but he knew she deserved the truth. "I don't know how many days I've been here, but the night before I was injured someone attacked Morrigan in her sleep. I think it was with the same type of magic as this," he gestured towards his ruined shoulder. "We have no idea who or what it is that keeps targeting her, or why."

"We don't know what kind of magic this is either, but I'm beginning to wonder if Aeron has something to do with it. He returned just a bit ago claiming that there was no one at your home. Santi said to leave it, but something isn't adding up, and if Morrigan's not home, then where is she?"

Before Nikaius could respond, the burning tingle of awareness spread across him and he turned, blocking Mae from view with a low growl as a windblown, drenched young woman appeared in the room.

"Lady De'Lyon, Morrigan needs your help."

Chapter Fifteen

Morrigan

Starsgard

The clock struck three before things settled down. Morrigan took volunteers to take shifts keeping an eye on the receiving room, just in case others from surrounding towns got the news that she was offering haven to those who needed it at Starsgard.

"Two hundred and seventy-six people, Morrigan." Aslin's voice was soft as she checked the numbers once more. "We've saved two hundred and seventy-six people. Mostly females and children."

"Where are their men?" Morrigan swayed side to side, the baby still fast asleep against her shoulder as she looked around at the people who mingled. The number of females and children outweighed the males even with her own in the mix.

However, now that they were dry, she couldn't tell hers from the ones who had come.

That was the way it should be.

"Morrigan..."

"There's a reason why Bastian and others refused to provide aid, Morrigan." Hawke had finally returned, and relief flooded through Morrigan as she turned to greet him, accepting his kiss as he approached. He felt like pride and hope, even though his words were low and sad. He looked down at the small being she held and rested his hand over hers. "They're on the outskirts of what we believe to be an encampment."

"An encampment?"

"Mmm... We believe one of Be'Sala's training camps is somewhere higher up on the mountain." Hawke looked around, dropping his voice a bit. "It's all just speculation, because we can't get in to know for sure, but it's the only reasonable explanation to where people are disappearing to. Men as far as The Pridelands have been going missing for years. We have people trying to get in to find out for sure, but there's no telling what will happen. Even though we have people looking, no one seems to be able to actually find anything."

"Who all knows about this? Why isn't this wider spread knowledge?" She searched his eyes as she tried to find a motive behind something being kept quiet. If people were missing across multiple courts, that was a treasonous offense that needed to be dealt with.

"We're keeping it quiet to not give false hope." Hawke pressed another kiss to her head before turning to survey those that had gathered with them. Morrigan hated that she understood their motives, even as unfair as it was to the families who had lost someone.

She dared to think that perhaps her father would be amongst one of the people missing. But he had been gone for sixteen years. There was no way.

Instead of questioning him further, Morrigan nodded, trying to force her yawn down, but not prevailing.

"You look like you could use some rest." Aquila had returned. Thank the Fates.

"I will when everyone is back safe." She was waiting for Waric to return with Silas and the rest of their guard.

"Waric is right behind me." Aquila promised, and Morrigan nodded, looking around again.

"Here you are. I was wondering where he had wandered off to." Sable, one of the women whom Morrigan had met earlier in the night that helped tend the children's home, appeared at Morrigan's elbow, offering her hands. "I'll take him so you both can rest."

Morrigan nodded again, carefully shifting so the babe didn't wake when he was transferred. "What's his name?" she asked softly, brushing dark hair from his sleeping eyes.

"We call him Bec."

"Good night Bec. Good night, Sable."

Morrigan watched them leave before yawning again and rolling her shoulders. It had been a long evening and while most of the house was quiet and nearly everyone was asleep, Morrigan wanted to wait for Waric. She wanted to make sure he came home, and that he was okay before she let sleep take her.

"You're exhausted." Hawke's arms wrapped around her from behind, and he pulled her to him, bracketing her in his warmth as she yawned again.

"I need Waric to come home before I go to bed. We don't know where Nikaius is, so I need him to be here where I know he's safe."

Hawke lifted her right hand, sliding his fingers through hers before kissing the back of it trailing his lips over the stippled flames and stars along her wrist. "You'd know if something happened to him. You'd feel it, or the mark would disappear."

Embarrassment flooded through her as she blinked at him. "I don't know anything about this sort of thing, Hawke." He didn't feel like he was upset, but she had to ask, regardless. "Does it bother you?"

"That you're wearing his mark? Not at all. Like I've said before, having multiple men in your life isn't uncommon here. Having multiple marks is rare, but either way, there's nothing wrong with any of it. No one will fault you or those you choose, me included." His nose brushed along her ear before he pressed a kiss behind it. "He'll be here in the morning."

"I want to wait."

"You're practically falling asleep on your feet."

Morrigan gave a sleepy hum, then rested her head back against his shoulder as she closed her eyes. "I can sleep here until he returns." She gasped as Hawke turned her to face him.

"That's an unacceptable answer."

"It's really—Hawke!" She screeched as he scooped her up over his shoulder, his arm banding around her legs.

"Off to bed with you. Say good night."

"Put me down!" Kicking her feet was useless and only earned her another laugh from Hawke as he turned away from the receiving room and headed down the hall.

"What are you doing!?"

"I'm putting your sassy ass to bed. You need to be well rested, and we both know Waric will be upset if you stay up and wait for him when you have a nice warm bed he can crawl into later."

Morrigan huffed, knowing that he was right and when Waric came home, he would seek her out before anyone else. They hadn't had time to talk about the mark and what it meant.

She didn't know how Hawke managed the stairs with her squirming and giggling, but she squeaked again as Hawke tossed her down onto the bed. The moment she stretched out on the bed, however, all the tension eased from her as exhaustion crept in.

"There, see. Can barely keep your eyes open." Hawke carefully tugged her shoes from her feet before seeking out something from the dresser. "Here, sit up, and I'll get you out of that dress."

Morrigan laughed sleepily. "I don't think I have the energy for that tonight, Hawke."

"So, you admit you are tired." He pulled her up by her shoulders to wedge himself behind her, his fingers working quickly to undo the laces and zip of her dress.

"I admit nothing," she sighed. Flopping back against him, she gave him a sleepy smile.

"Come on Princess, you can go to sleep once you're out of your dress."

"You just like taking me out of my clothes," she teased.

Hawke laughed and moved from behind her to grasp her knees and pull her to the edge of the bed. She drooped backwards playfully, stretching out across the bed in an attempt to resist his pull. "But I'm sooooooo tired." She let herself be limp as he grabbed her arms to make her sit up, and she giggled as she fell back when he let go.

Letting out a loud sigh, Hawke stepped back, stretching his arms above his head and letting his wings flare before relaxing again.

"Fine," he groaned, drawing the word out as he shook himself. "I suppose I'll go find my own quarters to sleep in if you're not going to cooperate."

"Noooo." Morrigan didn't feel any embarrassment as she wiggled herself up from the bed to reach for him. "I'll behave. I promise." Not anticipating the edge of the bed to be so close when she moved to stand, she slid from it and found herself suddenly on the floor. Hawke's seriousness broke, and he guffawed as he reached for her.

His laughter teased her own as he helped her from the floor and let her finish removing the dress. Tugging the borrowed shirt over her head, she situated herself before wrapping her arms around his waist. "Thank you for that."

"Any time you need laughter, my love, I'll always be here to provide." Wrapping his arms around her, he pressed a kiss to the top of her head.

Being called 'my love' did a funny thing to her heart, but before she could think about it too deeply, Hawke returned them to the bed and sleep found her quickly.

Waric returned sometime during the night.

Morrigan remembered waking briefly as she was jarred in the bed and Hawke's soft "careful" that rumbled under her cheek. Waric's warmth and soothing scent enveloped her. Before she could feel embarrassed about the position she was in, their soft voices and someone's hand in her hair brought safety and calm that lulled her back to sleep.

Waric's soft breathing greeted Morrigan when she woke, and she hummed gently, turning to curl herself against his chest, happy that his return hadn't been a dream. She didn't remember what Waric and Hawke had talked about, and she wasn't sure she wanted to find out just yet. The cool air meeting her back was a clue that Hawke had probably already gone for his morning muster.

Waric's breathing hitched for a moment before his arm slid across her shoulders to pull her closer. "Morning." His voice was scratchy from sleep, and it sent a chill down her spine.

"Morning." Morrigan's voice was soft, not wanting to disrupt the peace that had settled around them in the night.

"You did great last night," he whispered like he was telling her a secret, his nose nudging into her hair.

"Everyone was so helpful."

"That's what good leadership does."

"You and Nikaius are doing great."

"You are part of it now, and you did spectacularly,." His fingers trailed down along her arm before snagging her hand and lifting it so they could both look at it. Across his wrist, silver stars glistened, matching the ones on her own wrist. She stared at their marks in wonder as he laced their fingers together and brought them to his mouth, pressing kisses along each knuckle.

The motion made her heart flutter, and she sighed softly, guilt welling through her. "It feels weird without Nikaius here. Won't he be upset? Hawke already knows."

"Nikaius has got to sort out his own shit before we approach that, and Hawke was aware of the situation long before either of us were. Everything will be fine." Waric seized her knee, tugging her closer so that her leg was across his hips. His hand slid up to settle along the curve where her thigh met her backside, fingers teasing along the undergarment she wore. When her breath hitched in surprise Waric gave a mischievous smirk. "I promise. Nik will be home sooner than you think."

Though she was unsure of his words, she allowed them to soothe her worries for a moment, happily sinking into his kiss and enjoying the leisurely way his fingers stroked along her skin.

The sound of giggling children running past the door made Morrigan stiffen, but Waric didn't seem to mind, pulling away, the grin still in place. "There are children here."

"Twenty-five orphans from Barnam." A little sting settled in her chest again at the thought, remembering what Hawke had told her the night before. People were missing and he and others were trying to find them. Hopefully, they would find them soon. Until then she knew her focus would need to be on finding some way to help those children and the others that had been uprooted because of the flood.

"Mm. Hawke passed on the numbers." Waric rumbled. "We have just over three hundred people here, and the rain doesn't seem to want to let up anytime soon." Waric's grin seemed a little out of place, but as he seized another adoration filled kiss, she remembered that before Nikaius had gone missing he had been the easy going one of her men, always with a smile. Was he slowly returning to her? Morrigan watched him climb out of bed, admiring his lean back and the way his muscles rippled as he stretched. The silver stars of his and Nikaius' mating mark shimmered as he rolled his shoulders. He wasn't as broad as Nikaius but almost as tall but she knew they were quite evenly matched in many ways, and she briefly wondered if his prowess in bed would be just as exquisite.

The look Waric gave her when he turned to look over his shoulder sent a shiver down her spine, but before she could truly react, he seized her legs and pulled, earning a loud squawk of surprise. Her startled response did nothing to ward him away from taking her foot in his hand and pressing a gentle kiss to her ankle. "I've instructed the guard to get to whatever low-lying towns they can find." His kisses drew higher, and she could feel him grin against her skin. Fates, he had a wicked mouth. "I told them to try to evacuate." His nose brushed the side of her knee. "The dam won't hold through the day." He smoothed his hands slowly up her thighs, shifting her nightgown up over her hips.

"There's no way to fix it?" Talking was the last thing Morrigan wanted to do, but she continued to play the game, gasping as his teeth teased her inner thigh.

"Mmm. No... We don't have drafters." His voice sounded like his mind was a million miles away, but his next words, "Gods, you smell so divine," made her body flush hot.

"Drafters..." Morrigan's word ended on a sigh as she arched when she felt his mouth on her through the cloth of her undergarments. "Waric..."

"Shh. I have yet to show you just how in awe of you I am." She knew there were more important things that needed to happen, but those thoughts fled as he shoved the cloth aside, and his tongue stroked across her clit. She forgot how to breathe for a moment as he delved his fingers into her, lapping at her clit with quick strokes that spread electricity through her from the point of contact.

When he sucked and hummed against her clit, her head fell back with a soft groan. "Oh Fates." Her hands found his hair as she ground her hips against his mouth, gasping every time his fingers curled within her.

Though it hadn't been long since she had been with Hawke, every experience she seemed to have with her men was entirely different, and she was surprised at how quickly Waric was able to wind her up. His motions drew her so close to the edge so quickly that all she could do was rock against him and tremble as she sought her end. As she came,

Waric growled against her, wringing more gasps and a shiver from her as he took all she gave him.

When Waric returned to her side, she gave a soft, sated smile, but before she could reach for him to return the favor in some way, a knock sounded at the door.

"That must be Hawke with the report." Waric groaned pressing a kiss to her temple before adjusting himself.

Just in case it wasn't Hawke, Morrigan straightened her shirt and pulled the blankets up into her lap as she sat up, watching Waric answer the door.

Stepping in, Hawke gave Morrigan a once-over that made her blush before he offered an envelope to Waric. Morrigan wasn't sure when she had started noticing it, but as Hawke sat next to her, and Waric started reading the missive, the air changed.

Hawke reached out, tucking some of her messy hair behind her ear as she watched Waric start to pace. She wasn't sure she wanted to know, but she knew she needed to. "What is it?" She asked in a whisper.

"We were right. The dam failed about an hour ago. Most of the other low-lying towns seem to have been abandoned long before now, thankfully." Relief mixed with devastation flooded through her at Waric's words. The people of Barnam had come so close to losing their lives. Hands trembling, she reached to take Hawke's, settling it in her lap. She wasn't sure how he was able to compartmentalize his feelings like he did, but she appreciated the stoic calmness that sank into her skin. They had done the right thing. She wasn't sure how long they would be safe in Starsgard, but at least they were all alive and together for now.

After sitting in silence for a few moments Morrigan decided it was time to start her day. Pressing a kiss to the back of Hawke's hand she stood from the bed and stretched. "Have we heard any word about Nikaius?"

"I haven't." Hawke admitted with a frown. "I'll ask around to see if anyone has heard anything as I back to my rounds." Snagging Morrigan by the hips he stood to wrap her up in his arms for a moment. "I'll be around if you need me." Morrigan gave a small nod and accepted a kiss before watching him leave. It was still so strange for her to feel so many wonderful things for more than one person.

Pulling open the closet, she sighed happily to see clothing that was better suited to her than the shirts Hawke had found before. The room they had claimed was the king's suite, so she hadn't been surprised to only find men's clothing the night before, but having tapped into the castle's magic must have encouraged it to adapt to what she needed during the night.

"I felt him for a brief moment last night, which means he's still alive. I'm hopeful that we will see him again soon." Waric ran his hand through his hair before setting the letter aside to look her over for a moment. "I think today should be about contacting drafters to see if there is anything that can be done to restore or divert the river. Unfortunately, the only ones are in other courts, so finding someone might prove difficult. Hopefully, we will have enough time to figure out housing for everyone once the storm settles." Waric pulled clothing out of the drawer in the dresser: simple pants and a shirt.

"I sent someone to reach out to the De'Lyons. Hopefully, they'll come." She held out a simple dress, tilting her head as she looked at it.

"We'll see." Waric frowned before stepping into the closet and pulling out something different. The dress was a bit more formal but still simple. "This will be better suited for today. You're the ruling lady here, you should look the part, even just a little. If other heads of court should come to see what was going on, especially those who refused aid, it would be harder to negate your power."

Morrigan nodded, licking her bottom lip. "What if I do something wrong? Or someone more powerful than me arrives?"

"As of today, in the eyes of our people, you are equal to all others who dare trespass on our territory. You have me, Aslin, Hawke, and Aquila here to back you up. Our people know you. They trust you and will stand with you as well. I think the loyalty of our people and those of Barnam will surprise you."

Morrigan nodded and pulled the dress on. It was well fitted to her, clinging to her chest, and cinched at the waist with starry gems before falling free to her ankles. The emerald color was lovely, and the sleeves hid her mating mark. The cuffs were adorned with silver stars as well.

It was short enough that she wouldn't have to do anything special for shoes, so she slipped on a pair of gold flats and smiled when Waric gave her a once-over and nodded. He seized her by the waist, pulling her close before placing a kiss on her forehead. "Beautiful. I'm sure Aslin has an idea of what to do with your hair, so I'll fetch her so I can meet up with Hawke and Aquila for a report. I'll also inquire about the request you sent to The Pridelands." Morrigan nodded and sought a kiss before they parted, Morrigan heading down the hall to find Aslin and Waric to the guard dorms.

"Morrigan!" Right as Morrigan had reached the second room of the queen's suite, her friend's voice came from the room she had just passed. Backtracking, Morrigan frowned as she stepped into the room. Aslin appeared, breathless "I... I found the vault." In Aslin's hands was a half circlet adorned with the same stars that decorated Morrigan's dress.

"What vault?" Had Aslin turned into a thief overnight?

"There's a vault in the queen's suite that only the lady's maid of the ruling household can access."

"But you're not a lady's maid?" Aslin's logic seemed flawed, but Aslin just grinned at her, offering up the headpiece.

"I'm close enough, apparently." Aslin giggled.

"You're my friend Aslin, not a maid."

"It doesn't have to be a literal maid, Morrigan."

"Then why say it?"

"Do I not help you pick what to wear and do your hair?"

"Yes, but that's because I don't know the dress styles like you do."

"I guess that qualifies me. Do you want to wear this or not?" The hair piece glimmered as if it was adorned with a dozen stars directly from the sky. Morrigan had never worn something so fine. Was she allowed to? Would it hinder her plans for the day?

"Can... Is there a way to wear that while also not having to worry about being prim and proper? If I'm going to be Lady Aegean, I want to be the part, but I also want to be relatable to my people. I do not wish to be my mother or any other lord or lady who frowns upon their people and never interacts. I plan to help make food and entertain the children, just as anyone else would. I will not be a distant ruler. This is temporary, and I want to maintain the respect we have for each other."

Aslin nodded, surprise lighting her eyes before she made quick work of settling the adornment in Morrigan's hair, twisting the front of her hair away from her face to intermingle with the stars as it fell down her spine. It was a half braid, with the rest of her hair hanging loose, and Morrigan loved it.

"Perfect." Aslin nodded. "Absolutely perfect. Today will be a day like no other."

Morrigan's hands shook as they made their way down the hall. There would be no turning back from this if she went through with it. If their people accepted this, she would officially be the head of Kunmei until someone took that title from her. She would willingly give it back to Nikaius when he returned or pass it to Santi when he arrived.

She hoped she would have the right people backing her, but she was still terrified. She wasn't trained as a lady.

The two guards who stood at the door to the Great Hall wore white tabards over their leathers. The tabards were new, but before she could comment, they were bowing and pulling open the doors for her.

"Good morning, my lady!" Several people called from where they sat, eating breakfast. Older children and young adults played cards at one table, and the younger children were coloring and drawing at the table next to them. No one seemed to be too shaken by the night's events, and she was thankful that it seemed everyone had settled.

Before she could enter the hall, one of the women who was helping in the nursery walked by, trying to soothe the infant Morrigan had been handed the night before.

Her heart ached.

"Is he unwell?" she asked, and the woman frowned up at Morrigan.

"No, we just haven't been able to get him to settle since he woke this morning. He's been fed and changed. Poor baby." Cooing softly, Morrigan reached for him.

"Here, I'll take him for a while. Maybe a change of scenery would do him some good."

"Oh no, you don't have to do that, my lady. I would hate for your dress to get ruined if he were to get sick."

Morrigan laughed, taking the cloth from the other woman's shoulder, and tossing it over her own before taking the crying babe. "There we go darling." Carefully settling him against her shoulder, she rubbed her hand along his back in slow circles as she returned to what she had been about to do. "I'll return him if he gets too much. You have other children you need to attend to. He'll be fine with me, I promise." Without allowing room for argument, Morrigan stepped into the waiting hall.

People rose to greet her, some carefully touching her hand or patting her arm as she went. Not one of those touches held malice or anger, only gratitude and happiness. Morrigan wasn't sure how long she could go without being completely overwhelmed by touch, but she needed to trust herself and her ability to manage it. She knew she was stronger than what she gave herself credit for. Remembering that was the hard part.

She knelt on the floor to receive forehead presses from many of the children. Physical touch was something she was still getting used to but had eagerly accepted where the children were involved. She hadn't quite had the reasoning explained to her, but she knew it was a connective form of affection and often received them from Waric and Hawke when they desired closeness. Nikaius had done it a few times as well.

Morrigan wasn't sure when Aslin had reappeared, but her hand was a constant presence at Morrigan's elbow or shoulder, and she knew if Aslin deemed something as a threat, they would be teleported out in a second.

By the time she made it up to the head of the room, she was near tears. The amount of support and kindness she felt through the touches of the people was overwhelmingly positive.

These were her people.

She could do this.

"Everyone..." Her voice shook as she tried to address the room. "Everyone." The room fell silent, and she adjusted her hold on the now-sleeping baby on her shoulder, patting him and swaying as a way to alleviate her own nervousness.

"Everyone, thank you so much for the overwhelming amount of support you have shown, not only to those who needed our help, but to me as well." No one said a word as she slowly paced from side to side, meeting the eyes of the gathered one by one. "Many of you know that where I come from, I was not treated as a lady, and I don't know anything about the finer things in court, but the fact that you immediately fell in to help me was more than I could ever ask for. I'm so proud to be a member of your court and to know that you have faith in each other that I didn't have in myself. " Many people nodded, familiar and unfamiliar faces alike.

"I... I'd like to have the pleasure of being your lady until my time to lead ends. I will be the leader that you can come to if you need anything. I want to hear what you have to say and how we can make this court, right here and right now, a better place." The banners overhead rustled as if there was a breeze flowing through the hall. "I know I probably won't have any bearing over this court once we return to the rest of the world, but until the time comes when the title is stripped from me, let me fight for you now." The room was silent, all eyes on her and the babe in her arms. "I'll graciously take any objections, any comments, concerns, or critiques that you may have." Her stomach turned, but she knew that what she wanted was not to beg for their faith like those who came before her. She didn't want to force their hand, she just wanted to be one of them.

"I will not turn a blind eye to injustices or to harm that is being brought to you. I would hope I proved that last night, so you know my words are true." Passing the child off to Aslin, she kicked off her flats and stepped down from the platform to the floor below.

This was what she really was meant to do. Care for others the way she had only been cared for by her sister before coming to Kunmei. She was still terrified everything would be for naught, but really, there was nowhere else she wanted to be.

Gasps rang out as she dropped to her knees, tears welling in her eyes. "I've never felt like I've truly belonged anywhere before, but maybe that was because I was meant to be here. Here and now, whether you declare me or not, I deliver myself to you. I will fight for us until my dying breath because you are what it means to be kind and generous and loving, and I refuse to be anything but those things. I refuse to be anywhere but here, with you, my people, in any capacity you wish to have me." She dropped her head, bowing to those she wished to call her people.

"You'll be my lady until my dying day," Aslin knelt beside her, baby and all. The room shimmered for a moment, and Morrigan's tears fell.

The faith her friend showed was insurmountable and, above all else, that was what she needed the most.

Or so she thought.

Motion made her straighten, anticipating an objection. Instead, she found Waric kneeling in the center of the room. The white-clad guard knelt behind him.

The.
Entire.
Guard.

While the hall was large, it was unable to hold the vastness of the guard when already filled with those that had arrived in the night, but even out in the hall, men and women adorned in white knelt before her.

"You will be my lady until my dying day."

Morrigan sucked in a surprised breath, her bottom lip trembling as she mouthed the words "Thank you." Her voice no longer worked.

A ripple happened then, and others rose from their seats to join the guard. Her hands trembled more as she let out a happy sob.

The air gusted again, and Morrigan watched in shock as the white tapestries that hung along the walls and overhead shimmered, then changed to emerald, with silver stars decorating their faces. The tabards the guard adorned changed before her eyes as well. They accepted her, and the house, it seemed, had as well.

Waric and Aslin stood together, both reaching to pull Morrigan by her elbows to her feet. Morrigan accepted Bec back from Aslin, holding him close as her lips trembled.

"You were perfect, darling." Waric crooned, pressing a kiss to her temple.

The door to the receiving room swung open, and Angelica quickly entered. "My lady! Lord De'Lyon has agreed to come. They wish to be met at the gate." Morrigan nodded, a bit embarrassed but unbothered by the tears that broke free and rolled down her cheeks.

Santi had arrived.

"I'm on it," Waric nodded before Morrigan could say a word, then pressed another kiss to her hair before he and the guard exited the room. Hawke and Aquila returned to the receiving chambers to receive updates from those who guarded them.

Once the room settled again, Aslin held out her hand to Morrigan, who took it and proclaimed, "I present to you Morrigan Aegean, Lady of Starsgard and protector of the Enclave."

"Koea of Barnam!" Several people called out and others echoed before a cheer went through the crowd. She didn't know what the word meant, but it seemed positive. The hall erupted into applause and Morrigan cried, pressing her face into the dark hair on Bec's head as she curled into Aslin's side and let out a hiccupping sob of happiness.

The air changed suddenly then, and a voice from too close declared, "I object."

Chapter Sixteen

Morrigan

Starsgard

Bastian Ayrden stood uncomfortably close, his grin sending a thrill of surprise through Morrigan. When had he entered the hall? How had he even gotten in? There were guards in the receiving chamber, and Waric was headed to the gates to let in Santi and his guard.

"How did you get in here?" Morrigan asked. She had only met Bastian Ayrden once, during selection night, which felt so long ago.

"You forget, little girl, I'm patched into the wards because I own this property. This house and these people do not belong to you, nor will they ever." Murmurs spread through the crowd, but no one bowed. Not a single person bent their knee to this man who held more power than she did.

She had just promised to defend these people from those who sought to do no good, but now, facing the man who had threatened her life and carelessly tried to throw away the lives of those in the room, she wavered. Challenging a lord could prove to be treasonous.

Taking a step back, she took a quick glance around the room, hoping that Waric had returned, or Hawke and Aquila were nearby. Uncertainty flooded through her as her stomach churned with anxiety. Only Aslin was with her, and though she stepped up to stand next to Morrigan, she did not challenge him herself. She couldn't. Aggression towards court heads was frowned upon. Morrigan had heard stories about events that had warranted the death of the person in lesser power. Morrigan's hands trembled, and she tried to soothe some of that nervous energy by gently patting the back of the child, who made a soft noise against her shoulder.

"It's alright," she whispered to him, trying to reassure herself that she was doing the right thing. That this would provide a better world for the people they had saved. Perhaps if she stalled long enough, Santi would appear.

Though Morrigan wanted nothing more than to defer her power to someone else, hadn't she just asked these people to trust in her to protect them? Taking a slow, deep breath, she nodded once again and settled herself.

She needed to approach this with logic, not emotion, but she also needed to stand her ground. The lives of the people she had already saved were more important than her own discomfort. Putting her conviction where her mouth was and proving to these people that she was going to fight for them needed to be her focus because there was no one she refused to surrender to more than Bastian Ayrden, except maybe her own family.

Raising her chin, she took another step back, more for Bec's safety than her own. "I'm not some simpering woman, Bastian Ayrden." A few people gasped because Morrigan did not use his title, and despite the unease, she forced herself to not care. He didn't deserve respect for the way he had willingly sentenced people under his care to death.

"You cannot come in, claiming to be the primary power here when you were willing to let people, children, die." She gestured towards the crowd. No one stood out separate from the others, and she knew, from the looks on her people's faces, that this was the right move. They would defend those who could not defend themselves.

"I see none of my people here." Bastian scoffed.

"That is because the people here are not your people. They are MINE as I am theirs. This is neutral territory. I'm upholding that neutrality." Voices of agreement rose from the crowd, but Bastian scoffed.

An eerie giggle echoed through the room, and Morrigan's attention was drawn from Bastian to Amara, who she hadn't realized had come. Everything within Morrigan froze. All she could feel was the heavy sensation of foreboding that came with seeing her sister's face.

Having spent a while in Kunmei, Morrigan forgot that she could have a visceral reaction to someone, but as Amara began to speak, Morrigan's heart flew to her throat. "Hello, Lizzy. I knew you would be so jealous of me that you would try to sleep your way to the top, but I didn't imagine it to happen so quickly."

This was typical Amara talk, something that shouldn't shake Morrigan as much as it did. She had seen and been on the receiving end of more than one of Amara's tantrums. The complete chaos her powers could create was not something she wished on these people. Morrigan handed Bec to Aslin, stepping in front of them both when Amara's gaze followed her as she continued speaking, "Elijah said he had sold you as a broodmare to Nikaius, but I hardly believed anyone would buy you. Must have been pity." The energy in the room chilled, as if someone had left a window open, and Morrigan realized she needed to do something. Amara was dangerous, and these were all jabs at her. Things that Waric, Hawke, and Nikaius had assured her weren't true. "What's it like begging for scraps?"

Morrigan wished her mind would work faster, try to figure out something that could diffuse the situation without anyone else's help. Hadn't she just told Hawke that she was learning the only reactions she could control were her own?

She could choose how to react to Amara's behavior. She needed to react opposite of what Amara expected. Morrigan was no longer a victim to be played with, and they needed to know that.

"You tell me." Aslin cut in. Her voice was hard as she adjusted her hold on the baby in her arms. Morrigan frowned at her friend over her shoulder, but Aslin's eyes were locked onto something above them. "These people have chosen Morrigan. This castle has chosen Morrigan. Look at the proof before your eyes. Look up."

Morrigan's eyes followed, and hope flared through her. The house was still decorated in emerald and silver, not the Ayrden sunset. Ether shimmied for a second before Hawke and Aquila finally appeared.

Lifting her chin, Morrigan took a deep breath. While she knew she would need more than just some colors and her guards at her back, she felt supported and capable once more. "At this moment, this is my house. This house and these people have chosen me, not you. If you have come to take it, you will have to take it by force. If that happens, you will never have full control because those collected here will not respect you."

Pain flared as Bastian backhanded her before grasping her chin harshly in his hand and pulling her close by her face. His anger burned her skin like acid, and her breath caught as it burned down her throat. "I do not need respect when I have power," he spat.

Fighting past the vile feeling of Bastian's ire spreading across her jaw, Morrigan laughed. She hadn't been afraid to die by his hand at Selection Night and now she felt even more fearless knowing that this wouldn't go the way Bastian wanted.

"Power cannot buy respect, and you can't force trust. Your power is useless." She seethed, grasping Bastian's wrist and digging her nails in. If he intended to hurt her, she refused to let him come out unscathed.

The room erupted into chaos, but before Aquila and Hawke could reach them, the doors to the hall slammed open with enough force to knock one of them free of its hinges.

The ripple of power that flowed through the room made everyone scatter, pressing as far to the walls as they could.

"Unhand. My. Mate." Waric's voice was joined with the rough voice Morrigan knew just as well.

Nikaius had returned.

Relief flooded through her so harshly that she collapsed to her knees, sucking in a deep breath as she became free from Bastian's hold. Nikaius was bruised and battered; claw marks littered most of his chest, and his shoulder looked as if it had been torn apart. The blackened state of his skin was nearly identical to what her arm looked like. He looked like he was just slowly returning to normal.

Waric and Nikaius weren't alone. Her guard, wrapped in green, was joined by golden guards of The Pridelands, and at Nikaius' side was none other than Santiago De'Lyon himself.

Bastian said something, but Morrigan didn't hear as she shot to her feet, a devastating amount of relief suddenly suppressed the fear and acidic sting of Bastian's touch she had felt only moments ago. Shoes forgotten; she made her way across the room.

She wanted to be angry, to yell at Nikaius about how he had left them and how they had needed him, but now that she saw him, all that escaped was a loud sob as she crashed into him. All the stress and worry seeped from her when he wrapped his arms around her and hugged her close.

Part of her felt like she needed to be stronger, to not fall apart the moment one of her men appeared, but Nikaius had been gone for so long. He smelled like rain-soaked earth and bitter healing herbs, but his heartbeat against her cheek distracted from that.

"I've got you. We're here, and we're whole. I've got you." His hands trembled as he pulled away to card them through her hair, his anguish and sadness spreading across her skin, mingling with love and adoration that made her heart flutter.

"We still have no idea what's happening. I don't know who attacked you, but they used the same kind of magic. Santi and I were talking theories, but then we got the call about you and that falls to the wayside. Santi almost didn't let me come back."

"Aye. He's not fit for travel, but that cannot be helped." Santi spoke for the first time, and Morrigan turned her attention to her brother-in-law.

"Do you have any ideas—"

"Nay, but I believe there are more important things to focus on at the moment."

Nikaius reeled her back to him, scooping her face up in his hands and pressing an adoring kiss to her forehead. "Did you really take over the court while I was gone?"

Morrigan gave a shaky nod. His voice reminded Morrigan that Bastian was still seething at the head of the hall, but she didn't want to pull her attention away from Nikaius just yet, afraid he'll disappear again while she's not looking.

"That took a lot of courage. I'm proud of you." The feelings she got from Nikaius mirrored his words. "Once we get this all settled, then maybe we can revisit the idea of your proposal?"

Morrigan hummed in affirmation as she wrapped her fingers around Nikaius' wrists to center herself on him. "I'd like that. If I had known what you were going through, I might have waited a bit longer."

"There is no one to blame but myself. Once we figure everything else out, we can get married wherever and whenever you want, even if it's tonight on that dais." Waric laughed behind her, and she smiled. There were still conversations that needed to be held, and she would need to check in with Waric and Hawke before making any rash decisions.

"I object." A new voice sent ice skittering down Morrigan's spine as she turned to find Waric. Instead of Waric, her eyes locked on Elijah, who stared back at her from Bastian's other side. "As the eldest family member of her estate, I object to this union."

Air caught in her lungs as she stared at her siblings, tall, fair, and regal, as they stood on either side of Bastian. Something about the way they stood made her think back to an image she had once seen of someone's depiction of gods. But they were not gods. They were people who had made her life a living hell since she was thirteen. They had made her sick with anxiety and the vicious dark emotions that twisted in their minds. They sucked the very air from the room and all she could focus on was them.

Had they come to take everything from her? Had they come to take her home? Surely someone would say something if they tried, right? Though Elijah was right and unmarried, she was still technically a ward of their estate, but she no longer felt that was the role she was meant to play.

Elijah raised an eyebrow, and Morrigan took a reactionary step back that landed her against Nikaius' chest, a low threatening grumble erupting from his throat.

No. She wasn't their ward anymore. She had taken control of her own life, and she wanted nothing more than to prove that to anyone who thought they could take it away from her. She was happy and comfortable and wanted to stay. How could she fight for the people of Kunmei and Barnam if she couldn't fight for herself?

Years of repressed anger and betrayal replaced her fear, shattering like ripping out painful shards of glass as she pushed away from Nikaius. "I'm no simpering woman," was what she had declared to Bastian mere minutes ago, and yet the sound of her brother's voice had made her just that.

No. Lifting her chin, she prepared to face off with Elijah. She could be embarrassed about the way she shrieked, "You can't object to shit!" later. The moment the words left her mouth, everything crackled around her. Reality shattered. Those painful pieces of terror and self-doubt, insecurity and inadequacy, every harsh word and abuse lodged themselves into her skin and heart like fragments of ice lodged deep within her. Her entire being was torn and bloody and broken.

As suddenly as she had fallen apart, she found herself again, toe to toe with Elijah.

All the pain was suddenly gone, and she stumbled, surprised at the change, and turned to look around herself. "What?" Shocked, she backed up a step, running her hands over herself. There was no blood, no shards of glass or emotion or ice to make sure what had just happened was real, and she wasn't hallucinating. Nope. She was still solid.

Had she actually just teleported?

Before she could seek out one of her men, Elijah's hand shot out to grab her throat. The anger in his grasp threw her back to the night in the alcove. He had sent her to her death that night, not knowing what the outcome would have been but wanting to be rid of her just as fiercely as her mother had. She was treated as nothing more than a burden to them ever since Mae had married. Her body flashed cold, as if she was back Atce' Plaza only seconds before he had sent her to her death.

A buzz of static curled its way up the mark on her wrist, and she gasped back to awareness. If she could teleport there, maybe she could teleport away. The thought was fleeting, but resolution settled within her stomach. No. She refused to let herself fall back into that pit of despair that she still ached with. Though relief had been swift, it still lingered in the background, ready to take over once again.

"Morrigan?" Hawke's voice reminded Morrigan that she wasn't helpless anymore.

As she had done on Selection Night, Morrigan swung out with her foot and caught Elijah in the knee hard enough for it to buckle. Freeing herself, she kept her hand on his wrist and stepped away, using his own forward momentum to wedge her knee into his back in a move she had seen the guards use in practice. She hadn't realized that they tapped out prior to any permanent damage. With her entire weight on his back, his shoulder made a sickening crack, and he dropped to the floor.

The sound made her stomach lurch, the feeling of him going limp like nothing she had ever experienced before wracking through her body.

Oh Fates.

She had seriously injured him.

Oh Fates. Scrambling off him, she looked around the silent room before turning to flee. She suddenly found herself in the chambers she and Waric had shared the night before and bolted into the bathroom.

She wasn't sure how long she sat on her knees emptying her stomach and dry heaving before someone pulled her hair away from her neck and placed a wet cloth across her clammy skin. "Ya did some real damage there, Firefly." Santi's low, warm voice made Morrigan start sobbing all over again.

"I don't know where you learned either of those skills, but I'm gonna tell you I'm proud of you. Someone will no doubt say something, but you have an entire court who is saying you were attacked first." His large hand smoothed up and down her back. His presence was so soothing. It was different than that of her men, more paternal. Letting out a soft cough, sure that her stomach would remain where it was, she turned into Santi, wrapping her arms around his middle to bury herself against his chest.

"I've missed you."

"And I you little lady. But right now, we have bigger things to do besides a family reunion." He pulled away and ran his hands over her hair to cup her face. Santi's broad grin soothed her a bit more. "Yer pack is out there worried about you. I told them to let me check on you while they handled," he made a vague gesture towards the dining hall, "*that*. He attacked first. The important people know this, and you are safe. We just need you calm for what happens next." Taking the cloth from her neck, he used it to carefully wipe her face. "There, lovely. I don't think you have anything left to lose, do you?"

Morrigan wasn't sure if he meant with her stomach or in general with a court waiting on her. Taking a slow breath, she nodded and accepted Santi's help to stand. She was a little unsteady but was confident she wouldn't need to throw up again.

Heads turned her way as she entered the room from the chamber off one side, and she shied away for a moment, but Santi's presence at her back was reassuring. He was the largest man she had ever met, clearing Hawke's height by several inches, and to know he was with her brought comfort.

At the table set up on the dais, at the end of the hall where Morrigan had stood previously, sat Bastian with Amara to his right. She wore the same calculating grin she always wore, brown hair perfectly straight down her back and blue eyes not once leaving her husband's face as he spoke quietly to her. Amara looked happy, but Morrigan couldn't fathom why. Did their personalities and desire for chaos coincide that well?

Aquila and Hawke stood at the foot of the dais, but Morrigan was unsure whether their positioning was to keep Bastian and Amara from her people, or her people from Bastian and Amara. Either way, she was grateful they were there. Hawke looked as if he trembled with fury, but when he caught sight of Morrigan, the tension eased from him, and he gave her a relieved smile. She reached him first, curling her fingers between his, accepting his worry and relief as it flooded through the connection their skin made. She needed some of his stoic strength and knew he needed to know she was alright. "I'm fine," Morrigan whispered, resting her forehead against his shoulder for a moment with a soft, slow breath. "We're fine."

"Everything will be fine." Hawke's hand left hers and tipped her chin up so he could press a gentle kiss to her mouth. She was shocked by the public display of affection, but she couldn't fight the way she melted into him as his teeth nipped her bottom lip. He was so warm, and she felt his agitation ease with each small kiss he placed upon her lips. "You're beautiful, and you are mine." Someone scoffed in the background, but they ignored it.

She knew what he was doing, and affection welled within her. "Of course, I am." Giving his hand a squeeze, she gave him another quick kiss before turning to Aquila, who stood next to Hawke. Aquila gave Morrigan a grin and an affectionate eyeroll before dismissing her with a wave of the hand. Wrinkling her nose at Aquila, Morrigan turned to seek out the rest of her pack.

Aslin sat in one corner with the school-aged children, helping them with their lessons. It seemed like the disruption did not affect the peace she had tentatively created as much as she thought it would.

Waric entered from the kitchen, carrying a large tray of bread with three children happily giggling around him, each carrying their own item. He grinned when he saw her and detoured to her to press a kiss to her temple. "Everything is fine, I promise." Shifting the tray to one hand, he gave Morrigan's a squeeze before returning to his duty. He felt calm and confident. That was reassuring. She would feel a bit better if she could read emotions across distances and know what kind of mood Bastian and Amara were in.

A squeal from her left made Morrigan turn, and her heart fluttered at the image of Bec happily sleeping against Nikaius' chest in a wrap while Nikaius held one of the toddlers balanced in his large palm above his head. The child was just high enough that they could reach Nikaius' face and giggle when he would playfully bite at their tiny fingers. Little Alya clung to his leg as well, engaged in a conversation with a friend while Nikaius stroked his fingers through her hair.

"Now that we're all here, we can discuss the stupidity that is you thinking you can run a court and attack a lord. What do you have to say for yourself?" Morrigan turned as Bastian stood and prowled forward, but Aquila and Hawke stood in his way.

"I've said all I need to. You will not agree with anything I say." Morrigan turned back to watch Nikaius approach. Carefully, he dislodged Bec and offered the babe to Morrigan, who cooed when Bec scrunched up and gave a tiny whine.

"Oh, little love I know." Something about having him close brought her joy, but she couldn't put a finger on why that was. She had never really considered the thought of having children, but really, she did enjoy being around them. Especially ones as small as Bec. After giving Bec kisses on his cheek, Morrigan curled him close to her chest and allowed herself to be pulled to Nikaius so he could give her a snuggle of his own. His nose nuzzled into her hair as he pressed a kiss to her temple. "I'm sorry." Nikaius whispered before adding another kiss. They both stilled as heavy footsteps approached.

"You can say all you want, Bastian, but this is neutral territory. She is the one enforcing the neutrality." Bec startled, letting out a cry when

Santi spoke, and Nikaius offered a low grumble, his hand resting over Morrigan's that seemed to soothe the babe.

Santi stepped in front of Morrigan and Nikaius, settling his hands on his hips. The pose drew his height up and his shoulders out, making him impossibly larger.

He was the alpha of the alphas, and she knew, just from the way the energy crackled through the room, that if they had decided to let nature run its course instead of following traditions and rules, there was no doubt that Santi would devastate any opponent he would face.

Except maybe a dragon, but Morrigan had never met one old enough to shift.

"This isn't even your territory, Lyon. The only way any of you can have any say is if there is a vote conducted by heads of state." Bastian snapped, turning his attention to Santi as if the larger male was the one he had an issue with.

"It's neutral territory." Aquila pinched the bridge of her nose, her exasperation evident on her face as if she had already attempted to explain it to him once.

"I'll put it to a vote." Nikaius grinned as if he knew something they didn't.

Bastian scoffed. "Fine, but it will be a draw, which means we will take this to council because I doubt they would want some nobody running a court."

"Aye. At least our votes will be cast, won't they? Smooth along the proceedings at council." The grin Santi threw over his shoulder matched the one Nikaius wore.

Something was happening, but Morrigan couldn't figure out what.

"If we don't win, we have other places to move people, right?" She whispered to Nikaius, who gave her a small wink and offered her the sling he had worn Bec in as he turned his attention to those gathered, sliding his hand through the ends of her hair before stepping away. She tried to cling to him, to find somewhere to catch and hold so he couldn't get far. Though he seemed fine, Morrigan still worried that he would disappear if she let him go too far.

As if he sensed her sudden distress, Nikaius caught her hand and pressed a kiss to her knuckles. "I'm not going anywhere." When he dropped her hand, he moved his to rest against her lower back. It wasn't full body contact like she desired, wishing she could keep his warmth near, but it was still a tether to him, a reminder that he was there.

"Council vote is now in session." As Santi spoke, Waric shushed the children in his care and sent them over to the other side of the room where the rest had gathered with their caretakers.

"We're here to decide the fate of Starsgard. It's a dedicated neutral territory that typically does not have a head of court. But Morrigan Aegean has shown an exemplary determination to uphold the mission of Starsgard to keep this territory truly neutral."

"Aside from her assaulting a lord."

"One could argue it was warranted." While Morrigan's attention stayed on Santi, who paced to the middle of the room, Waric had returned to her side, his fingers curling gently into the hair at the back of her neck. His thumb picked up the same soothing motion that Nikaius' was doing along her lower back, and it settled her a bit, the mark on her wrist tingling at the connection she shared with both of them.

They would need to talk about the marks in more depth later on, but for now, she tried to pay attention, even though their heat encased her so well.

"Be that as it may, she has no proper training or bearings to lead a court." Bastian tried to argue.

"Be that as it may," Santi stated mockingly, "you were the one who suggested the vote in the first place. Aslin, can you take a note for us?" Santi rolled out his shoulders and turned to face those gathered, raising an eyebrow at Aslin in question.

"Yes, my lord." Aslin seemed so happy to pull a pad and paper into existence, and her grin stayed in place as she began writing carefully. Once she was finished, she grinned and shifted her stance, raising her head a bit as she spoke again. "Most of those gathered know how these things work, but I shall explain anyway for the record. The pen requires blood to note your vote." Shocked, Morrigan frowned as she looked at Nikaius and then Waric. She had thought that all blood magic was forbidden! Santi and Mae had sworn Morrigan to secrecy over the chest she had. Was it only okay when dictated by the council? That seemed to be the case with the marks, and now for this? Waric and Nikaius were looking at each other. Nikaius had his eyebrow raised at Waric, who grinned even though Aslin continued speaking. "You prick your finger and write your vote. It is binding until it is unbound by another vote to contest it."

"How do you prevent blood illnesses?" Morrigan whispered to Bec, who watched everything with sleepy brown eyes. She hadn't intended to get an actual answer, but Waric leaned down and whispered, "Magic" into her ear, which sent her into a little fit of giggles. He shushed her by pressing a gentle kiss to her mouth before their attention was drawn back to Aslin, who had finished her explanation.

"Lord De'Lyon as the furthest down on in the alphabet you shall cast first." Aslin offered the pen to Santi, who happily took it.

"I vote in favor of Morrigan Aegean becoming the preceding lady over Starsgard and Atce' Plaza." He wrote on the pad and then stepped away to offer the pen to Nikaius.

Nikaius' eyes danced between storm and ice as he turned to address her, pen held in his hand. "I told you that you would be a fantastic leader someday. I think today is that day. I vote aye in favor of Morrigan Aegean, Lady of Kunmei and Barnam."

Bastian scoffed and stomped his way down the stairs of the dais, shoving Hawke and Aquila aside before snatching the pen from his brother. "To get this ridiculous thing over with, I vote nay. Amara, come cast the Aegean vote on behalf of your brother so we can leave." Amara tentatively stepped forward, confusion marring her pretty face as she reached for the pen herself.

It was obvious she hadn't realized she would be involved, but when her eyes moved from Bastian to Morrigan, the confusion disappeared, and her gaze hardened again. Pricking her finger, Amara scoffed, and declared, "Nay" before scribbling on the page.

But the blood didn't take. The confusion returned, and she looked from the page to Bastian and back with alarm. "What is the meaning of this?" Bastian snatched the book from Aslin and turned it over. "What sorcery is this? Have you jinxed it?"

Hawke and Aquila appeared behind Aslin, Aquila snatching the book back from Bastian with a look that could kill.

Nikaius stepped up next to Santi, his arms crossed over his chest as Santi laughed. "She is not of Aegean blood."

"What nonsense do you speak?" Amara's voice was high, her hand flying to grasp at the family crest she wore around her neck. Morrigan rounded on them as well, eyes wide, her squeaked, "What?" being drowned out by Amara's protest.

"No one ever questioned why Elijah and Amara don't hold any resemblance to their father or other sisters. Except my wife and I when we tried to get custody of Morrigan once we wed." The matter-of-fact way Santi spoke jarred Morrigan a bit. She knew that he and Mae had tried to fight for her. They had visited as often as their mother would allow, but that did nothing to save her from things that had happened at her mother's hands. "Turns out that Malin Aegean only fathered two children. Neither of them is Elijah or Amara. Mae and Morrigan Aegean are the only blood heirs to the Aegean name, and only they can speak for their family."

"What?" Amara's, Bastian's and Morrigan's voices merged on the word. None of them could believe what he had just said.

"Which means legally, Morrigan is the only person in this room who can cast the fourth family vote needed to make this vote official." Aslin took the book back from Aquila and offered it to Morrigan.

Morrigan froze. They weren't meaning what she thought they did. There was no way that SHE could speak for their house. Nervous butterflies took flight in her stomach as her gaze bounced from face to face.

Aslin nodded encouragingly, and Waric kissed the top of her head. Nikaius stood with Santi watching as Bastian and Amara whisper shouted to each other, gesturing wildly as they did. They had been hedging their bets on Amara having that vote. Finally, her eyes settled on Hawke. While Nikaius and Waric were her adventure and her joy, Hawke was her stability. With approval from the three of them, she believed she could do anything as long as they were with her.

"Do you really think I can do this?" Morrigan's hands shook. Though she hated that he was always delegated to the voice of reason, Morrigan realized this was the reason why he was the emissary for Nikaius and Santi. Her emotions were all over the place, and she knew that the Rekru'e were holding themselves back, yet he and Aquila seemed like they were the most unaffected. They both maintained their positions at Aslin's back despite the angry lord to her left.

"I think that you know your own mind better than any of us, Morrigan. We all believe you capable, but it's not we who hold the pen.

We can't make this choice for you. You are the only one who can speak for yourself and what you desire. We're just here to support you with whatever choice you make. Yay or nay."

Morrigan's bottom lip trembled, and she let out a slow breath through her nose. Hawke's ability to say exactly what she needed to hear must have been gifted to him by the Fates.

Having confidence in herself was all she needed, and she didn't know what that confidence would change, but she was willing to try, not only for the people of Kunmei and Barnam, but her pack and most importantly, herself.

"It only hurts for a moment, I promise." Aslin whispered, giving her a shy smile as Waric took Bec to free up both her hands.

"Aye," she whispered softly before pricking her finger with the pen and writing her answer on the line after Bastian's.

It stayed.

At first, nothing happened.

Nobody moved.

Morrigan expected something, although she didn't know what really. The book to disappear in a cloud of smoke? It sounded ridiculous even to herself, so she didn't voice that thought. She reached out, curious to know if the ink was actually her blood, but the book snapped shut and she jerked back, startled.

"It's been decided, three ayes to one nay in favor." Tucking the book under her arm, Aslin grinned and offered her free hand to Morrigan once more.

This time, Morrigan felt more confident. She finally had something that was hers, that she had gotten on her own merit, not because it was handed down to her by her sisters or mother. Selection Night had truly been the new beginning she had briefly dared to hope it would be.

Looking over her shoulder, Morrigan sought out her pack. Hawke and Aquila had joined the Rekru'e men. Santi grinned at her while Bec snuggled against Waric's shoulder. Waric's other arm was draped over Nikaius' shoulder. Nikaius winked at her. She hadn't had time for them to talk about anything. Everything was happening so fast. She hadn't intended for it to get this far.

Really, she had truly intended to give up control to Santi or Nikaius, whomever came first, but now they seemed content to let her have this. So many things were about to change. Santi gave her one of his broad goofy grins and a thumbs up. Morrigan giggled before turning her attention back to Aslin.

Alright. Time to do this for real.

"Once again, I present to you Morrigan Aegean, Lady of Starsgard, Mediator of Atce' Plaza, and Controller of the Western Keep."

"Protector of the Enclave!" Waric's voice rose with several others.

"Savior of Barnam," rang out once again.

Behind her, Bastian scoffed, and a loud crackle signaled he had left. For a moment, Morrigan wondered why it had made a noise that time and not the prior, but she didn't feel like asking. That would come later.

The air in the room changed again, but not in the oppressive manner it had before. It lifted into something light and freeing, and Morrigan felt as if she could finally breathe.

Being declared the head of something meant she was truly free from the family that had treated her so harshly. She was finally no longer the girl who had been trodden on and beaten into place. Waric, Hawke, and Nikaius had been trying to show her that, even when she was afraid the other shoe would drop. She had learned so much in the span of less than an hour, and there were so many questions that she needed to ask, but for a short moment, she let it all pass and turned to greet her people once again.

Chapter Seventeen

Morrigan

Starsgard

What felt like hours had only been moments. The rain still poured outside, Nikaius' hair curled at the ends in its dampness, and Morrigan's hands still shook as she accepted congratulations and support from those around her. Bec had been passed off to one of the caretakers overseeing the nursery to be put down for a nap, and Morrigan missed his soothing weight. It had been grounding in her nervousness, but now that she had been left to her own devices, she wasn't sure what to do with herself.

The entire day felt like some sort of wild fever dream. Suddenly, she felt too overwhelmed by everything going on in her head. Everything had happened so fast and even though she had been the one in control, it still felt like the world was moving and she was not. The world warped. She was happy, why was this happening now? Sucking a deep breath in through her nose, she let it out, then turned on her toes and sought out her shoes.

Turning, she jumped when she found Waric behind her, grinning from ear to ear. She shared his smile, but the constant influx of touch mixed with events of the morning had caught up with her, and she suddenly felt tired. "Can I have a few minutes?" she asked, shaking out her hands as they tingled with nervous energy.

She probably had more important things to do than panic, and she wanted to try to get her sudden weariness under control before she took on any more from the day.

"Of course, the kitchens are that way, or I can escort you back to the room." Waric looked worried as he gestured towards the kitchen but gave her a gentle smile.

"The kitchen is fine. I just need..." She couldn't adequately explain what she needed, only that her skin ached from where touch had reoccurred, and her throat and face still burned from Bastian's and Elijah's putrid touches.

A few people called soft greetings when she entered the kitchen, but no one commented when Morrigan picked up one of the chef's knives and began carefully cutting potatoes. Despite it being a task that had been forced upon her at a young age, cooking was something that cleared her mind. You could only focus on what you were chopping, or you would get cut.

Without asking, someone set a bowl of some sort of marinade in it next to the board where she cut, and she gave a small smile before sliding what she had chopped into the bowl.

Breathe in.

Half the potato.

Slow breaths lead to a calm heart. Mae's voice echoed in her head. Mae had been the one to teach Morrigan how to regulate her body.

Breathe out.

Quarter the halves.

A calm heart leads to a steady body. She dropped her shoulders away from her ears and took another breath.

Breathe in.

Cube the potato.

A steady body leads to a steady mind. She stopped trembling.

Breathe out.

Potato in the bowl.

A steady mind can handle anything.

The world quieted as she repeated the words in her head and actions with her hands.

She was down to the last potato when fingers carefully touched her hand. She looked up, surprised to have not heard anyone approach.

Nikaius.

The contact was warm and sent contentedness mixed with calm tingling up her arm. It didn't add to the rawness of what she had been previously feeling, which meant either her attempts at focusing had worked or his touch did not affect her in the same way.

Both would reasonably make sense.

"Morrigan?" His voice was soft, like he was uttering a secret, and his eyebrows were knit in concern. The way he said her name was her undoing, and she let out a loud sob before setting down the knife and throwing her arms around his waist. The wall within her shattered again when he wrapped his arms around her and held her close as she let the tears fall. All the stress and fear seeped from her, mingling with the sheer overstimulation of the past few days. She was a tangled mass of emotions and desires but felt each one acutely. It felt so different to experience them herself rather than secondhand.

Cold fear twisted in her stomach, making her curl her fingers tighter into Nikaius' shirt. She was so afraid of being too close to him but also of losing him. It was born of confusion about where they stood. There were so many new things being thrown at her from every angle. She was so happy he was home but also worried about how he would feel knowing that she had taken over his court and that she was mated to Waric. Would he be bothered by her growing relationship with Hawke as well? He felt different in a way she couldn't truly explain. There was less of an edge to his touch where his fingers stroked across her nape, warmer and lighter than before.

As if she had summoned him with only her thoughts, Waric's warm fingers slid across her shoulders, and his body bracketed her between him and Nikaius. The warmth was soothing despite the sob that she tried to muffle. He stood close, his forehead pressed against where her neck and shoulders met, so that they were connected skin to skin as his hands stroked slowly up and down her arms. She knew that Waric had been even more upset than her when Nikaius disappeared, and she felt a bit guilty taking all of Nikaius' attention. Neither of their emotions warred with each other though. Waric was calm and accepting, spreading warm concern and adoration across where their skin met as he whispered soothing little things into her hair while they swayed a bit. Nikaius' emotions fluctuated a bit between some form of cold sadness she couldn't place the reasoning for, and extreme joy as he adjusted his hold on Morrigan so that they were both settled closer into Waric's embrace as well.

"Gotta get those big emotions out." It hadn't been the first time they had been in this position. The last time had been after she and Nikaius had slept together. It seemed choosing things for herself was the catalyst to disrupt the stability of her emotions, not that there had been too solid of a foundation prior.

"We've got you. Let it all out." Nikaius rested his cheek on top of her head as his voice rumbled soothingly.

Waric and Hawke had been her foundation while Nikaius had been away, and she was unsure how they all would fit together now that things had changed.

The fear of retaliation from her brother bled to the horror that caught in her chest. She had seriously injured him, and she cringed at the memory, pushing away from Nikaius to shake out her hands. She had punched Elijah before and received lashes for it, but she couldn't imagine the punishment that would come from having injured him so extremely. Shaking her hands out did nothing to alleviate the memory of the feeling of his shoulder giving way.

Disgust drowned out that horror. She wasn't sorry for her actions. It had been a snap reaction to all the things he had ever said and done to her. Anger flared so powerful and hot that she couldn't quite tell it apart from the pain of betrayal. She pressed her forehead against Nikaius' chest, hiccupping as it burned her throat. Waric had stepped back when she did and now stroked his hand slowly up and down her back. His presence was soothing, even if she wasn't wrapped in him.

She had been lied to. Her entire existence was even more of a lie than the one she had spent fifteen years living. They weren't even her siblings.

Was Mae—No. That thought was not allowed to go any further. Santi had said that she and Mae were the only children of Malin's. It sobered her. How much did she not know about herself? How much did Mae know but hadn't been able to communicate? "I want my sister. Please?" Her voice broke at the end of the sentence and Nikaius' look of concern melted away. He looked as if he was going to cry himself. His eyes searched her face for a moment before he cupped her jaw gently in his hands and pressed his forehead to hers.

"I'd bring you the Fates if you asked." Her heart gave a leap at his words, and the affection she felt surged through him tingled along her skin. She pressed her cheek into his hand, giving a little sniffle that earned her a smile from him. Nikaius looked at Waric over her shoulder, and Waric's hands curled themselves around her waist, pulling her against Waric's chest.

Waric cuddled her close, resting his cheek on top of her head as he swayed them from side to side. "I've got her." She felt Waric nod and gave another of her own. Taking a slow breath and letting it out through his nose, Nikaius leaned forward, pressing a gentle kiss to Morrigan's mouth before reaching for Waric. The motion was reminiscent of Waric's when Priamos had come to her during her panic attack in Madam Eda's shop. They both grumbled as Nikaius snagged the back of Waric's neck with his right hand and Waric reached for him. They shared a kiss, and it eased some of the worry Morrigan had about there being some form of rift between the three of them. Using her right hand, she slid it up Nikaius' chest to mirror their connection, curling her fingers along the nape of Nikaius' neck, her fingers overlapping through Waric's. Affection, adoration, and love warmed her hand, and Waric's free hand curled carefully around her throat, connecting the three of them through touch. Everything they felt was the polar opposite of her own emotions, each twisting through her, combatting the sting of the burning hate and distress and anger that had singed her insides after her brief time with her siblings.

She wondered for a moment if the touch she received from others affected her mentally. Living in Kunmei had been primarily positive, and she has started feeling healthy and whole inside and out, but the moment Bastian's skin touched hers, everything came crashing down around her.

"I'll go speak with Santi," Nikaius whispered, nudging his nose against Morrigan's temple before stepping away from them. As he left the kitchen, Morrigan took a slow, deep breath.

Affection surged to the surface for her sister's husband. He had come when she had needed him to, regardless of whether that was simply because of his love for her or if Nikaius had some part in it. Clearly, they were friends, and Nikaius and Waric having a friend like Santi made her feel a little more settled.

Her adoration for Waric and Nikaius wasn't muted now that one had left and the other remained, nor had her affection for Hawke. They had all come forward to show support for her in different ways, just as her need for them differed. Hawke was her stability and strength, deferring to her to know her own mind. Waric was her joy, despite the issues they had a few days before, most of the time he was the one to lift her spirits. And Nikaius was her heart. He had been the catalyst to every single event that led her to building the strength she felt she had. He had started on the path to believing she was capable of being her own person, and she couldn't wait to see who she would become with their guidance.

This was exactly where she wanted to be, despite whatever bumps in the road led her there. Turning, she curled herself into Waric's chest, letting the tears fall but no longer feeling the urge to sob.

Waric rocked them slowly from side to side, gently soothing her, giving her time and silence to think.

"I teleported," she whispered as Waric's hand stroked slowly up and down her back.

"You did." Waric pulled away a bit to stroke his hand through her hair and gently cupped her jaw.

"I don't know how I did that." She gave a small smile.

"I don't think any of us do." He pressed a kiss to her forehead before pulling her back to him.

"I... I'm the head of a court." She let herself settle back into him, tucking her hands up under her chin.

"You are." Waric swayed them from side to side.

"I... My siblings aren't my siblings." When Waric remained silent on the matter, she began to wonder how much he knew. How much did any of them know about her? "Mae was right, and my father was watching out for me." Her voice broke, and the tears renewed. She hiccupped a little laugh despite the sob that threatened to bubble up again. "I don't know how to lead people, Waric." The reality of the situation made her pull back, to shake out her hands again, the feeling of being impossibly large in her own skin returning, an unending feeling of nervous energy and the need to move renewing. She pulled away from him to turn and face the kitchen. Surely there was something else that needed to be done. Something to keep her hands occupied so she could steady herself again.

Somehow, Waric knew what she needed and offered up a bushel of carrots from one of the counters. She wasn't sure what they wanted done with them, but it seemed that a stew was being prepared. She could skin them and figure out how they needed to be cut later.

Taking the smaller knife from Waric, she took another deep breath before carefully stroking it down the large carrots to remove the outside layer.

"I wish he was here." Irrational longing spread through her. No matter how much she wanted her father, he wasn't coming back. He had long been buried, and with his burial, her sense of safety and love had gone with it. Mae had filled the void as best she could but that deep need to have someone else looking out for her had never settled. Not until she had come to Kunmei.

"I know, sweetheart." Waric moved so he was in her line of sight again, rubbing his hand slowly up and down her back. "I know, but you must know that you irrevocably have me and Nikaius and Hawke on your side. I'm pretty sure Hawke would burn the world for you. Aquila as well. Aslin probably wouldn't kill for you, but she might poison someone."

The image of Aslin trying to poison someone made Morrigan giggle. Her friend could easily get away with something like that.

"There, see. You've been thrown a whole lot of chaos in a short amount of time. You're allowed to feel overwhelmed. I'd be concerned if you weren't." Morrigan gave him a watery little smile, and he nuzzled his nose into her temple, giving the top of her ear a little nip.

They stood like that for a few minutes. She no longer felt the need to sob, but the tears still flowed as she thought about how much her life had changed. Waric stayed close by her side as she slowly regained some semblance of balance and felt less raw.

Chapter Eighteen

Morrigan

Starsgard

Morrigan didn't know how long they stood in the kitchen, Waric watching over her while she tried to expell all the negative energy that burned through her. "Do you want to go see the baby?" Waric's voice drew her from her thoughts. "It's been about an hour, I'm sure he's awake by now. The nurse said he's been exceptionally restless for a newborn."

"I thought all newborns were restless for a bit?" Morrigan sniffled as she set down the knife and offered the carrots to one of the people who was helping in the kitchen. She felt guilty having not asked about Bec as

Waric had been the last person to have him, but he was glad to know he was safe still. Waric smiled and wiped the tears from her cheeks.

"Changeling newborns typically imprint within the first two or three days after birth." Waric took the bowl of potatoes and set them aside before grabbing a damp cloth to carefully wipe off Morrigan's hands. "According to Sable, he's not been with anyone long because he's failed to imprint on anyone." Once Waric deemed her hands clean enough, she dried them and allowed him to tug her from the kitchen.

Morrigan smiled as she watched their marks glitter in the light of the rooms they passed before they headed for the stairs.

"Did they say what happened to his mother?" she asked. It must be a hard decision for a mother to leave a child so small, and Morrigan assumed it wasn't by choice.

"She caught an illness before he was born." Sable whispered as she stepped out into the hall just as Morrigan and Waric made their approach to the room that had been set up as the nursery. She must have overheard their conversation. Bec fussed in her arms, little pitiful sounds that made Morrigan's heartache. "They had to take him early, and it's been making it hard for him to imprint on anyone else. He's been through four homes already." Sable sighed, rocking from side to side. Bec keened softly. Despite being snuggled close, he seemed restless.

"And he's how old?"

"Just shy of a month."

"Waric said that it wasn't typical for changeling children to go so long without imprinting. What happens if they don't? Is it just pack semantics? Because I'm sure—" Sable cut Morrigan off.

"They fail to thrive. Imprinting is a basic survival instinct. The imprint secures them to this world. It's deeply ingrained in their entire being. It's how they learn to regulate their body temperature and temperament. It's much like a mating bond. The hearts synch."

Morrigan frowned at Waric. Her heart felt no different than it always had. He just grinned, reaching out to run his fingers gently along the back of Bec's head.

"Isn't there something someone can do?"

"Not unless he imprints on someone. He's barely eaten more than necessary to survive. The only time he's been calm was when everything was happening with the storms."

"The storms? Do you mean the flood? How long was he calm then?" Waric's eyes finally caught Morrigan's, and he gave her another one of his slow grins. Something was going on in his mind, but Morrigan was battling the need to reach out and take the babe from Sable.

"Aye. He's been more calm being here." Bec's soft keen turned into a distressed wail, his fist lodging itself in his mouth as he cried over it.

"This is calm?" Morrigan ran her fingers along Bec's little cheek, and he turned towards her to suckle one of her fingers for a moment before wailing again. "He was perfectly content with us earlier. Right as rain. Does that mean he's imprinted on someone here? We'll have to see if we can figure out who!" Excitement and joy welled through her. This would be one child she could help of the twenty-five that needed homes. "I'll take him and see if we can find out who."

Taking Bec from Sable, she kissed one of his chubby little cheeks before curling him close. "Leave it to me. I'm sure we can figure out where you need to be, yeah?" She spoke softly to Bec, who cooed as he snuggled into her shirt.

"Morrigan."

"No, really. I'm okay, he's okay. I'm sure it has to be someone in the vicinity." Despite her setbacks caused by Bastian and Elijah, Morrigan felt like finally she could do some good again and help the small child in her arms find his home.

Before she could turn to step away, Waric caught her elbow. "Morrigan."

Tears welled in her eyes, and she blinked at him in confusion. "Don't you dare tell me it's too late for him. I refuse to accept that, Waric. There's got to be a way. If I can get through all the nonsense that's been thrown at me the last fifteen years, I have every hope that he can to. I'll find them." Though part of her felt cold at the thought of giving up the snoozing child in her arms she knew that it would be for the best to get him with a family that would guarantee his survival. From everything she had just been told she knew that time was of the essence when getting him to imprint, and that scared her. What if they found the person and it was still to late? Holding Bec a bit closer she forced those thoughts away with a shake of her head. No. She refused to accept that as even a possibility.

"Sweetheart." Waric's forehead met hers, one of his hands sliding around the back of her neck as the other rested atop hers on Bec's back.

"I'll find them." Curling Bec closer, she sniffled again; her emotions still too raw from the chaos they had been moments ago. "I refuse to let anyone under my care not survive this if I can help it, Waric."

"Oh, you silly girl." Sable laughed, offering the blanket and a bottle one of the younger women held. "Stop and listen to your mate. You're the imprint."

"Me?" Morrigan pulled away in shock, looking between Sable and Waric in confusion. Bec still fussed, but the sound was different, and she frowned. "I can't be... I'm not a Changeling."

She gripped Waric's wrist, the world twisting for a moment as she tried to catch her breath. There was no way that Sable was correct. Her wide gaze flicked from Sable to Waric and back, trying to find some semblance of teasing in their gazes, but found none.

"You're still a mortal being with two Rekru'e mates. I'm sure they can help you figure out the logistics of raising a Changeling. What did you expect to happen when you have children?" Sable said.

"I can't have children. That's irrelevant."

"What do you mean?" Waric asked as he frowned at her, accepting the bottle from Sable and offering it to Morrigan. Frustrated, Morrigan snatched it away from him before adjusting so she could cradle Bec and offer it to him. He eagerly took to it, and Morrigan smiled softly at him before remembering that she was having a very important conversation with her mate.

She looked over her shoulder to make sure they were alone as Sable returned to the nursery.

"Before coming to Kunmei, I'd never been offered any form of contraceptive before. I was a pawn in my mother's games for years, when Mae was otherwise occupied and couldn't defend me. I would certainly have had a child by now if I could have them."

"Morrigan..." Waric's voice was low as he looked around.

"No, Waric. I'm not an idiot. I know nothing about how Rekru'e stuff works, sure, but there have been enough times where something would have happened, and it hasn't."

"It's more likely that your mother was lacing something with contraceptives to prevent that from happening." Nikaius' voice interrupted them from behind and Morrigan jumped, turning to face him.

Her breath hitched as she caught the stoic expression that Nikaius held. Why did that thought hurt? Was it because it was another thing that Delaney had done to her without her consent? It was one more thing she now was unsure about when it came to her own self and body. She was learning so many things that were changing her, making her more of a stranger to herself, and she wasn't sure how much more change she could take before she would lose herself completely. She wasn't sure where her anger came from, but she huffed and passed off Bec to Nikaius with a bit more force than she should have and stomped away from them towards the king's suite.

"Morrigan?" Hawke frowned as he approached, but Morrigan ignored him in favor of slamming the door to their bedroom shut behind her.

Now that she was questioning herself more, the whole conversation about children felt ridiculous. She was unprepared for anything that she was being given, and she wasn't sure how much she could truly handle. She wouldn't know what to do with a child. She only had brief memories of her father, and she refused to be like her mother. There was no way she could become someone as cold and calculating as Delaney. Morrigan not being Delaney's child made her behavior make a bit more sense, but it was still something Morrigan had just learned about herself.

There was no way she could take on a baby. She now had courts to rule while they waited for Bastian's threat to come through regarding the council being summoned. There was too much to do and not enough of her to go around as it was.

She would have to fight to be taken seriously, throw in a baby and they never would, would they?

"Morrigan?" Hawke's voice was muffled by the door.

"Leave me alone." Running her hands through her hair, she turned to pace away from the door with a sigh. Why was this the thing she wanted to fight them about? They had been nothing but kind and caring and supportive, but if they learned that she felt like she was slowly losing herself because everything she thought she knew was lies, would they still care for her?

"That's not how we do things, princess, and you know it." Waric pushed open the door, letting Nikaius and Bec in first. Nikaius seemed absolutely besotted with the tiny boy in his arms, talking softly to him in Rekru'e as Bec blinked up at him with sleepy brown eyes.

Hawke followed them, letting the door shut behind him as he offered his hand to her. "Talk to us. I know a lot has happened in a short amount of time."

Silence settled in the room like a heavy blanket on her shoulders. She wasn't sure how to express what was going on in her head, afraid of whatever she would say, taking another piece of herself with it. Was she becoming a stranger or her true self? She had yet to figure that out, but she still feared the outcome.

Right now wasn't completely about her though, was it? It was more about Bec's fate.

"Adding a child on top of trying to claim two courts is too much. Aslin mentioned the Western Keep earlier in the territories I'm now over, and I want to investigate that. I'm afraid that we won't have long in Starsgard with Bastian's threat of bringing the Council to us looming overhead. If the Keep is livable, I'm hoping we can petition to have it be the new home of the residents of Barnam. If my geography is correct, it should be close to where Hawke said the supposed encampment was. Adding a baby into the mix isn't really responsible." She dropped down onto the bed, letting out a soft sniffle as she pressed her palms to her eyes.

"We'll be here to help. We can figure everything out." Nikaius' words were soft as he reached for her hands. She hadn't seen him pass Bec off to Waric.

"The only people who take me seriously right now are in this room, plus Aslin and Aquila. I'm afraid if I take on too much, something will fall by the wayside." Morrigan protested as Nikaius' words fell on deaf ears. Everything was too much too soon, and she couldn't help suddenly feeling like she was drowning again. She wasn't equipped to deal with any of it. "I don't want to bring more chaos into our lives."

"Are you more worried about yourself, or about us?" Hawke asked softly as his eyes flicked from where Waric stood by the door swaying with Bec to Morrigan.

"I'm worried about all of it. Our lives are already in chaos. There are so many things to do, and my attention cannot be in multiple places at once. Everyone seems to keep forgetting that I have no idea what I'm doing on a daily basis, why would now be any different?"

"Morrigan." She was sure Nikaius' voice was meant to be soothing, but it didn't feel that way. Whatever calm he was trying to give her made her feel itchy and raw again. "I'm pretty sure we unanimously voted towards you doing whatever you want to. You tell us what's needed where, and we'll go there. It's entirely your choice. No one is going to tell you what to do. No one is saying you can't do this."

"No one's saying I can!" Morrigan snatched her hands away and stood, crossing her arms over her chest as she moved to walk away from him.

"I am! Morrigan, are you not hearing the words I just said?" Nikaius stood quickly, grasping her elbow to turn her to face him again, his voice rising. Bec startled, letting out a loud cry, and Waric glowered at them both before he started murmuring in soft Rekru'e to Bec once again.

Nikaius' hands settled heavily on Morrigan's shoulders and didn't relent as she tried to pull away. He wasn't listening to her. None of them were listening. Did none of them realize she was screaming inside? All these things were adding one on top of the other to further obscure her from herself.

Who was this person who had willingly taken on so many tasks? Had they given her too much power in choosing for herself? Why would they do that when she was whittling down into nothing of her former self? How could they not know?

"You don't have to do any of this on your own! No one said you can't be involved!" The hair on Morrigan's arms raised with the tone of Nikaius' voice, and she took an alarmed step back when his power sank into her skin through her clothes.

His emotions ranged from frustrated to concerned to adoration that didn't fit with the others. She had never been able to feel someone's emotions through her clothes before. It was a jarring sensation that brought her focus from her own mind to their point of contact. What was happening?

It pulled all the negative energy from her, leaving her breathless.

"Nikaius, calm." Hawke stepped forward, resting his hand on Nikaius' shoulder. "Emotions are already high. We don't need to be yelling at each other." Something about Hawke's words deflated the anger that was rising in her as she looked around the room. It sounded like her heart was in her head, as if she would pass out at any moment, but finally taking in her surroundings gave her more clarity.

Nikaius had just come back and was still healing and yet here they were shouting at each other. Was he really angry with her? Why was she angry?

Hawke was right. She wasn't completely in control of her own emotions and hadn't been for the last few hours. The moment she thought she would be okay, something else happened, and she hadn't had time to sit and process what those things meant. She was trying to do all the processing and actions at once when it came to her instead of compartmentalizing it for later.

As Nikaius reached for her, she stepped back again. "Don't touch me." Her words weren't as vicious as her last ones, but more of a quiet plea. His touch would just confuse her more. It wasn't his fault. None of them held any fault in this.

Nikaius' voice was softer as he offered his hand. "When have I ever told you no?"

"Less than a week ago when I proposed to you." Morrigan bit out, her heart racing as she tried to calm herself. None of this was planned, and every time she tried to make a new plan, another factor came into play.

"Name one other time." Nikaius crossed his arms across his chest, head tilted as he raised an eyebrow at her. "Do it. I'll wait."

Chapter Nineteen

Morrigan

Starsgard

Morrigan paused. When was the last time he had told her no since before the rejected proposal? When had any of them told her no? Her lips parted as she tried to think back.

"I know you're not used to getting what you want, and maybe that's what this little temper tantrum is about." Nikaius snatched the dress at her waist and pulled her to him, sliding his hand into her hair and pressing his forehead to hers.

"It's not—" Morrigan tried to look away, but his other had caught her chin to force her gaze to remain on him.

"You threw a baby at me." Nikaius raised his eyebrow, Priamos' light eyes mingling with Nikaius' blue.

"Slammed the door too" Hawke chimed in with a grin. Morrigan wanted to argue with him, but Nikaius' hold on her hair tightened, and she stilled.

"And stomped your foot just now. That was cute, by the way." Nikaius' voice was lower, his words brushing against her lips. Morrigan huffed, but the hold Nikaius had on her didn't relent. More of Priamos came through, and Morrigan could feel his power throb through her across his bite mark, down to the fingers connected to Waric's mark, and down through her core.

"That was." Hawke's laugh was soft. She knew if she was in danger, Hawke would have stepped in again, like he had when their emotions were doing the talking, but she also knew that Nikaius' hands had never hurt her before, and she didn't anticipate his power to do so either.

"Listen. Are you listening?" Morrigan gave a small nod. They weren't mad at her. No one was mad at her about the things she had chosen. They still saw her the same.

"Imprinting isn't something that was planned, but we've all been a part of it before, and just because a child imprints on someone doesn't necessarily mean that they have to parent them, Morrigan. We're just trying to give you the choice to decide what you want to do."

"What do you mean?"

"Alya is my imprint." Nikaius confessed.

"She is?"

"Mmhm. She's actually Hawke and Aquila's niece. It wasn't expected, considering she has a large family. The Corviana nest had ten children." Hawke and Aquila had eight siblings? That was a lot. Morrigan blinked up at Hawke in surprise and realized that outside of Aquila, she didn't really know much about Hawke. She would need to remedy that, but Nikaius continued. "The likelihood of her imprinting on me instead of her family was extremely low. Like a ten percent chance of happening. I was also only nineteen. I was still new to ruling Kunmei and with her being Avian, it was just the better option to find a Kielzar family. I can't teach her things like how to fly and other things that Avian children needed to know. I see her regularly though because the bonds between imprints tend to cause some irritability and instability if ignored for too long."

Reaching out, Nikaius carefully took Morrigan's hands. "What I'm saying is there are other options. Alya is content and happy living her life with her parents, even though she is aware of the bond we share. It's a normal occurrence here in Kunmei, and if you're not prepared for it, we can figure something out. I imagine he'll be a Kaan with where he comes from but that will come with his naming. You'd just need to see him every now and then just to soothe the chaos of the bond."

"I don't want to be a distant mother or ruler or any of it. I didn't exactly have the best role model of what a good mother is. I'm afraid this would separate me from others too much. I want to be involved." Why did the thought of giving Bec to someone else to raise make her feel heartache? She didn't think herself capable, but she also wasn't sure she wanted anyone else to do it.

But with everything else, she was terrified that one position would overshadow the other and something would be neglected in her attempts to figure everything else out.

"No one says you can't be involved. I literally just told you there are options that have worked in the past." Nikaius' frustration bled through whatever calm he was trying to offer her and burned its way up her arms.

"Let's just take this one step at a time. There's been a lot happening, and I think we're acting with more emotions than logic right now." How Hawke's voice was still calm during all this Morrigan didn't know, but she was happy at least one of them was still holding onto some semblance of peace.

"Let's start at the beginning." Waric suggested, moving to sit on the bed not far from where Morrigan and Nikaius stood facing off with one another, even though Morrigan no longer felt the need to fight. They weren't mad at her. They weren't trying to force her hand or change anything about her.

They were just trying to get her to make the choices for herself.

"Do you want to remain head of these courts? Yes or no?" Nikaius asked.

"Yes, but—"

"Yes or no." Nikaius cut her off, taking a step closer. "Do you want to have control over what happens at the Western Keep?"

"Yes." She didn't know what her part would be, but she did want to be a part of it. There were people who could potentially use that space.

"Do you want to protect everyone in your domain?" Waric's voice joined, but Morrigan couldn't turn to look at him.

"Yes." Her heart pounded in her chest. Admitting these things was scary.

"Good girl." Nikaius' words caused a curl of pleasure and made her bottom lip finally quit trembling.

"Do you want that baby?" Hawke asked from over Nikaius' shoulder. He still stood close by, Morrigan assumed as more of a moderator than anything else. She wasn't sure why she had doubted them.

"Yes, but—"

"Oops. I take back the praise." Nikaius murmured.

"No..." She was sure the revocation was a tease, but she didn't want him to not praise her. It had been so limited in her life.

"No, you don't want the baby?"

"Nikaius." He was ridiculous.

"Morrigan." He was messing with her now, a slow grin spreading across his face.

"Do you trust us to have your back no matter what chaos you bring?" Hawke asked.

"You shouldn't—"

"Do you?" Waric interrupted.

"Yes." Though she felt like she might be sick from the admission, her entire body trembled as she came down off the endorphin high of her panic. She knew she trusted them implicitly, even when she forgot her own head.

"You understand we would support you in anything you wanted to do?" Nikaius' voice softened as he reached out, gently touching her elbow.

"Yes."

"Good girl. Do you want that baby?" Nikaius pressed his forehead against hers and closed his eyes. The tether she hadn't realized was between them snapped so suddenly she gasped, and all her senses snapped back to her.

Hawke's hand found hers and felt like calm. Morrigan couldn't begin to fathom why Hawke was being so calm about the entire thing. She had already disrupted their lives enough, throwing a child into it would cause more upheaval, wouldn't it?

But they hadn't seemed to have missed a beat in their lives, had they? Shame flared through her at the realization that she had been so in her head that she hadn't realized that their world hadn't stopped when she came into their lives. Hadn't Nikaius stated that being attacked was all in the day's work of a lord? Hawke and Waric had both mentioned that having multiple partners wasn't uncommon, and even Nikaius seemed mostly unbothered by the fact that she had taken over his court in his absence.

While her entire world had been turned on its side, she had expected all the upheaval to have the same effect on them. But the changes she saw in herself weren't ones that were happening to them as drastically. Every single, small change altered her path, but the only thing that had changed for them was her.

They were offering her the options that they were readily okay with offering, and none of them came with consequences.

Having been so misguided in life was disorienting. Every single breath she took was seen as an offense to her family and that had greatly skewed her interactions with others. She was constantly afraid that one errant move could crumble the foundation she had built with the pack.

But now they were showing her that though things were changing, they weren't as life altering as Morrigan had made them up to be. She wasn't alone. It wasn't her versus them. It was them against everyone else.

Four people could easily take care of a baby, six if one included Aslin and Aquila in the mix. She had control of the courts, but she could defer that power back to Nikaius or Santi as she had previously thought she wanted to do. Oh Fates, how had she been so selfish?

"Do you want him?" Hawke asked again, his lips brushing against the knuckles of the hand he held standing beside Nikaius.

"Yes." Her bottom lip trembled, and she pulled her gaze away to seek out Waric, who stood close by, swaying as he talked to Bec.

"We'll be here every step of the way, princess. Whatever you choose, we're here to support you." Hawke reached out to catch Morrigan's chin and drew her into a soft kiss. "Waric?"

Waric offered Bec to her, smiling as she carefully took him and pressed a kiss to his head. "If you want to do none of the things, then you don't have to. If you want to do them all, you can, we'll navigate that too." Waric promised.

"You have an awful lot of confidence in me." Morrigan settled onto the edge of the bed, adjusting Bec so he could finish eating, her little finger slowly stroking his cheek as she held his bottle.

"We have every reason to have a lot of confidence in you. You have several courts in your hands. You could conquer the world if you wanted." Hawke said.

Morrigan snickered, shaking her head. "You're ridiculous."

"And you're beautiful, baby and all." Nikaius sat next to her, reaching out to stroke the dark hair out of Bec's eyes. "I'm sorry I grabbed you. I let my frustration get in the way of my point."

"I'm sorry I yelled at you. There are so many new things cropping up that I felt like I'm drowning. So many lies are coming undone, and I don't know who I'm going to be when they're all gone. It's terrifying."

"That is terrifying. So is admitting them and asking for help." Waric looked from Morrigan to Nikaius and back, signifying that his words were meant for both of them.

Before she could respond, a knock at the door made Morrigan jump, startling Bec in the process. "I've got it." Waric went to the door and spoke with whoever was there before returning to the bedroom and offering Nikaius the envelope in his hand.

"Hey, let's go put the baby to bed." Waric distracted Morrigan by cupping her chin in his hand and stroking her bottom lip gently. "It's nothing bad, I promise."

Standing, Morrigan nodded, adjusting the drowsy Bec to her shoulder.

"It's fine, I promise." Nikaius pressed a gentle kiss to her mouth before turning to pull Hawke across the room so they could discuss the missive.

Letting out a soft sigh, Morrigan nodded and stood. "Do we have to take him back to the nursery?" She knew that whatever Nikaius had received would be important and was probably the summons they had been waiting for since Bastian's departure. There was no way he had gathered the council so quickly, but Morrigan had seen wilder things happen in shorter time frames.

"We can set up his own nursery here and back home and wherever else we go. That's a perk of magic, Morrigan." Hawke reached out to snag her elbow, pulling her to him before he pressed a gentle kiss to her forehead, her nose, and finally her lips. "Don't think too much about it," he whispered. "Let yourself be happy and let us be the reason why."

Giving him a small nod and another kiss, she turned to follow Waric from the room.

Chapter Twenty

Morrigan

Starsgard

Bec cooed softly as Morrigan rocked him in the chair Waric had manifested for her.

They were in a small room between the king's suite and the guard dormitory that she had been told was a safe room for the past king. If there was ever any danger, he would retreat into that room and wait for his guards to protect him.

Though the room had multiple entrances, and they had come in from a different door, Waric had made it so that the only door in and out of the room was the one attaching it to their bedroom. Which eased Morrigan's mind, so she didn't have to stress about someone accidentally waking him by walking into the wrong room, or by children seeking out places to hide.

The dresser, bassinet, and day bed were all made of dark wood that was similar to what decorated Nikaius' room in Kunmei. Though Waric had made there be only one entrance, the magic of the house had added a window that she had cracked just a bit. It created some airflow, but not enough to chill the entire room to an extreme temperature. She wondered if it held the same magic as the ones in Kunmei.

Morrigan's favorite part were the soft, light green tones of the room. Green was her favorite color and to have that be incorporated made it feel even more perfect. She was happy that she and Bec had a place of their own.

"We're going to make the world better little one, just you wait." Morrigan whispered to him as she watched his sleepy little eyes blink slower and slower before they finally closed. She stayed like that, smiling down at him while his breathing evened out.

Once he was fully asleep, Morrigan winced. Now came the hard part. The last time she had moved him, he had startled awake, and she had to start over again. This time, learning from her past mistakes, she carefully stood without adjusting him to her shoulder as she had previously. Her steps were cautious as she made her way to the bassinet, but as soon as his back touched it, he began fussing.

Frustration burned through her, stinging her throat and eyes with unshed tears. She was out of her depth and as she scooped him back up, she swayed, patting him on the back as she tried to get him to calm down again. This was another reason she didn't think she would be good at being a mother. The only example she had was her own mother, who always seemed frustrated or upset with her without recourse. Morrigan didn't want to be like Delaney, but there she stood, frustrated, unable to figure out how to keep an infant asleep long enough to put him down. Sniffling, she fought back the tears she could feel building.

"You've been in here for a while, everything alright?" Nikaius' voice was warm and full of affection; Morrigan could hear the smile in his voice. Her shoulders relaxed as he approached, goose bumps spreading across her skin as he neared. Being close to him was soothing. Though they had been apart for a few days, it had felt like lifetimes to Morrigan because so much had happened in the span of those few days. She was sure Waric had felt the same. Had Waric and Nikaius already talked about Morrigan's and Waric's mark? What about how Waric's automatic reaction to telling her about the mark was to try use his alpha powers against her? She wished she could hear into the minds of others instead of just having connections to them through touch.

"He won't let me lay him down." The admission felt a bit like defeat, and she was waiting for him to condemn her. She was making Nikaius aware of her inadequacy in the realm of parenthood, and a small piece of her expected him to snatch Bec away any second.

Typically, she was able to pick up skills after a bit of repetition. She had picked up on writing Rekru'e pretty quickly and most recipes only required a bit of tweaking to come out perfect if they didn't the first time.

Caring for a child wasn't something Morrigan had been given a lot of experience in; it wasn't something she couldn't just pick up with repetition.

"Show me what you were doing?" Nikaius asked her gently, kissing her cheek.

Bec had finally settled down, and Morrigan felt a little silly with Nikaius watching her every move. She had to remind herself that he was only watching to figure out how to help. He wasn't there to judge her or criticize her.

"Wait." Nikaius whispered as he caught Morrigan's elbow, preventing her from moving away. "How does the mattress feel under your hand?"

Morrigan hummed as she thought for a moment. "Kind of cool."

"Alright. Now imagine what that would feel like to someone who was still figuring out how to regulate his temperature, which is currently based on yours, and his own body and skin in the process. What do you think that would feel like?"

Oh! Poor little guy. Morrigan felt bad for not realizing sooner. The nature of the effects of imprints was another thing she was still trying to learn well. "Probably very cold. How can we fix that?" She turned to look at him, waiting for his suggestion, and watched the way the soft smile spread across his face. She had missed his smile.

"Pull your hand out slowly, bit by bit until it's out. That will give it time to warm a bit before you set him down." As Nikaius carefully guided her hand out from under Bec's back, the babe stayed quiet, only squirming a bit before his breathing evened out. Gleefully, she threw her arms around Nikaius' waist and hugged close to him.

"Thank you," she whispered, careful not to raise her voice. "I know it wasn't his fault, but I was getting frustrated. You had perfect timing." She could hear the tinge of regret in her own voice, hoped Nikaius didn't catch it and question her about it.

"We were waiting for you. After the third time he started fussing, I decided to come see if I could help."

"So, you are all aware I'm a failure." Her lip trembled as she pulled away from him to cross her arms over her chest. Knowing that the men she loved knew about her struggle hurt her pride a bit. It wasn't uncommon for her to react emotionally.

Nikaius pressed a kiss to her forehead. "You're not a failure. You're still learning. I can guarantee you that no one knows what to do right off the bat, except maybe my mother, but she's an anomaly. You're doing fine."

Thinking about meeting Nikaius' mother, or any of her men's families, suddenly seemed daunting and terrifying. "Oh gods. What is your mother going to think of me when I meet her?"

"She's going to adore you, I promise. I know she's mentioned trying to get close to Amara." Morrigan's breath caught for a second. What sort of nastiness had Amara been spreading about her? Did Nikaius' mother know who she was? Before she could voice these concerns, Nikaius continued, his words putting her at ease. "She doesn't feel like there's a true connection there, simply polite acquaintanceship. Which is exceptionally odd considering they visit quite often according to her."

"How often—"

Aslin appeared in the doorway, her cheeks flushed as she panted a bit, out of breath. "Excuse the interruption, but someone is asking to speak to you."

"I'm sure it can wait a few minutes." Nikaius grumbled, stroking his hand through Morrigan's hair.

"I'm afraid it can't. They claim to have come from near the Western Keep."

"The Western Keep?" Though it was one of the neutral territories, Morrigan wasn't aware that there was a connection between the keep and Starsgard.

"That's what they're saying." Aslin responded with a nod. Though they could teleport, Aslin looked as if she had run the entire way to her.

"The male is very wild, and his female companion is demanding to speak only to you."

"To Nikaius?" Morrigan looked up at him as he frowned down at her, nervousness twisting in her stomach at his expression. It didn't seem like something that would upset Nikaius. Who were these visitors? Were they refugees from one of the towns that were in the way of the flood? Hawke had assured her that everything in the path had been cleared out, so perhaps they had left to seek refuge prior to the dams falling and just now made it to them.

"No, to you Morrigan. She asked for you by name." To her? How did anyone outside these walls know her name? Taking a deep breath, she tried to let her exhale take her anxiety with it.

The intimate moment between her and Nikaius was over, and duty called. Would she ever get used to it? Leaning over to stroke hair from Bec's eyes, Morrigan gave him another smile before following Aslin from the room, Nikaius close on her heels.

Aslin must have spoken to Hawke and Waric first as neither waited for them in the empty hallway. When they descended the stairs, Morrigan paused for a moment. The entire area felt strange and off. Her skin buzzed a bit, almost like it was falling asleep, and she noticed the floor was eerily quiet. The upstairs living areas had been full of children playing and families chatting, but once she hit the bottom stair, she noticed that the halls were empty. She could hear the murmurings of conversation, but nothing like the livelihood of the morning.

Something was wrong.

"Oh, thank the Fates!" Morrigan jumped at the loud exclamation, knocking backwards into Nikaius as they stepped into the infirmary. A woman with short cropped dark hair stood quickly, her soaked clothes dripping on the floor as she rushed over to Morrigan.

Hawke appeared at Morrigan's side as the woman's companion, a large male in one of the beds who tried to rise, snarled and growled at Nikaius and then Waric when he stepped forward.

The woman interrupted them, pulling Morrigan's attention back to her. That odd magic that tingled her skin remained, becoming almost uncomfortable until the woman took her hands. "We need your help, my lady. We came to warn you..." The woman's words faded as Morrigan focused on the cold hands in hers, shock singing through her veins when she realized she couldn't feel anything from the stranger.

Most people who came to them felt like fear and then relief for being given somewhere warm to be, but this woman felt of nothing. It felt wrong, almost suffocating, like being locked in a closed room with a blindfold. Morrigan wanted to pull away, but she felt bound to this woman in a way she had only felt once before. At her Culling.

It felt like her skin was stuck, like if she pulled away, she would fall or dissolve into nothingness. The world muted, the only sound was the roaring of blood in her head and her heartbeat in her chest as she tried to pick up something, anything. Her hold tightened on the hands that held hers, and she felt like she was trembling as she was met with a dark abyss of nothing. It wasn't cold or hot, it just was. Morrigan had never figured out what exactly her powers did or how they worked, but she had always known that she felt them in her hands and up her arms to her heart. Now everything was hollow and empty. Like she was plunging her arms into a deep cavern with nothing to touch on any side.

The world warped before everything went black and she gasped, panic choking her as her knees hit the floor beneath her. Suddenly, she was in a room all alone. She couldn't see anything and couldn't feel anything either. She couldn't breathe as she ran her hands over her arms, through her hair, trying to feel *something* but none of it felt real. It was like she was locked in her own mind and there was nothing within but effervescent smoke. She tried to scream, but no sound passed her lips.

Chapter Twenty-One

Morrigan

Starsgard

Suddenly, sounds came back in a deafening roar of chaos. Shattering of glass and growls. Someone screamed. A flurry of motion happened around her, but she couldn't concentrate on it, only on trying to find herself again. Morrigan.

She was Morrigan, but was she really? Fear made her feel cold, her entire body trembling with it. Who would she be without her powers? Most of her interactions growing up had been guided by touch. If she couldn't interpret how people were feeling, would she be safe?

What would she lose if she never got it back?

Every sound echoed in her head, and she had to press her hands to her ears to get some relief as panic finally found itself in her chest when warm hands found her cheeks. Concern shattered the darkness and when she opened her eyes, Waric knelt before her.

Relief thawed some of the fear as she looked at him. Waric and Hawke and Nikaius would keep her safe. Aquila and Aslin too. She was safe with them, and they cared for her, no matter her condition.

"Morrigan?!" His voice brought everything snapping back, and she was finally able to catch her breath.

"Waric!" She threw herself into his arms, tears of relief rolling down her cheeks as she tried to bury herself in his warmth.

"What happened?" Nikaius was crouched next to them, his face pale and eyebrows knit with worry. When she looked up, Morrigan saw Hawke standing in front of them with his wings flared. They would keep her safe, no matter what.

She forgot how threatening Hawke could look and realizing the contrast between her stoic guard and her sweet lover made Morrigan chuckle.

That chuckle broke through the pressure that surrounded her, and she took another deep breath. "I don't know." Brushing away the tears as they fell, she scanned the room. Nikaius offered his hand to her, to help her stand, but she shook her head. Electing to sit for a few more moments would allow her to be confident in her ability to stand later. "I couldn't feel anything from her." Her voice was a broken whisper, her throat hurting as if she had been screaming. Maybe she had been. The lack of feeling still lingered in her palms and fingers, and she shook out her hands as she tried to rid herself of it.

"That's only happened one other time, and that was at my Culling."

Waric and Nikaius looked surprised by this, and Hawke lowered his wings slightly to look over his shoulder at her. "I don't like this."

She didn't either, but despite what had just happened, Morrigan wanted to hear them out. Once she felt stable enough, Morrigan stood, rubbing her hands on her dress. She could feel the coarse material under her palms, but she still couldn't feel anything from Hawke when she stepped around his wings and rested her hand on his arm. Had the woman taken her magic somehow?

The young woman was standing near the edge of the bed of a male who was nearly as large as Santi. Her face was pale and streaked with tears as she looked on, her face horror struck. No, Morrigan didn't think what she did was on purpose. If it was, they would have fled.

The male shared nearly the same coloring as Hawke with dark skin and black hair that was stringy with wetness. Though Hawke's skin was mostly unblemished, the man's skin was covered in varying designs that sparked Morrigan's curiosity. She couldn't remember the last time she had seen tattoos of any type since it wasn't all that common.

His chest was bare, and Morrigan recognized the burn there as it was similar to the ones she and Nikaius had. It looked as if someone had tried to pull his heart from his chest and failed; the blackness spreading like five fingered claws tearing up his chest, neck and across the right side of his face. As if thinking about it made it react, her arm started to burn, and Morrigan hissed in surprise, pressing her hand over it.

How the man had not completely lost his eye was beyond her, but she did not know his experiences. She didn't want to assume he couldn't see from that eye, especially since it was just as black as the mark, but the sight made her unease worse. When their eyes met, it felt like she was being pulled into the abyss, a strange disconnection from the world making her panic renew, and she stumbled back, breaking their gaze before she noticed he and his companion were signing between themselves.

They signed quickly, and while Morrigan understood sign, theirs was quick and not a lot of what they said made sense. They were talking about something, but she couldn't quite catch the meaning, and while she was afraid to get too close, she was curious to know what they were talking about.

Morrigan took a step closer, but Waric's hand caught her elbow. "Careful." He warned. Usually, she would blaze full speed ahead, but he was right. After that one encounter, Morrigan wasn't sure she wanted to touch either of them.

Waving her hand, she got their attention before signing: "Who are you?"

"You know sign?" Nikaius asked with a surprised laugh as he crossed his arms over his chest and stepped into her line of sight. "But you didn't know Rekru'e when you joined us."

"It's a separate language than Rekru'e, but of course I know it. Mae does too. We learned for Imriel."

"Gorlassar?" Hawke frowned at her in confusion. Morrigan was under the impression that Hawke had interacted with Imriel, the younger male having been brought up in different topics of conversation before.

"Yeah. They say he was touched by the Fates. He can't speak. We learned to better communicate with him, but what this man—"

"Ben," Ela interrupted, "We've been calling him Ben. He picked up sign from us. It's just that a lot is going on right now, and we need to sort our thoughts."

"Us? Who is us?" Morrigan asked as she took a step back and looked around. She didn't want to be ambushed by someone else. Crossing her arms over her chest, she tucked her hands under her arms. Unease crept through her, the thought of someone appearing in the room suddenly and touching her without her permission making her cautious.

"My name is Ela. My sisters are still in the encampment." Ela responded, her brows knit in confusion at Morrigan and her men. "I'm really sorry about what happened. I don't know what I did." She looked at her hands as if she had never seen them before, her eyes wide as she held them out and turned them over.

"A lot has happened that we're not sure about right now. Let's try to address things one step at a time." Though Morrigan was nervous to have any of her men leave her, she knew the wounds Ben had would need to be tended to. "Nikaius, can you get Santi so he can look at Ben's wounds?"

Nikaius' face showed what Morrigan felt. He looked like that was the last thing he wanted to do, but Waric tugged at his hand, lacing their fingers as he tried to lead Nikaius away.

"She's got Hawke. It will be fine." Waric tried to assure Nikaius though his gaze flicked back and forth between them.

"I don't like how he smells." Nikaius admitted in a low voice. "They both smell wrong."

"I've got them." Hawke told them while Morrigan frowned at their retreating backs.

Once they had left, Morrigan turned her attention back to Ben and Ela. She kept her hands tucked away, feeling like she was trembling but not wanting to see the evidence for herself.

Typically, she would go to them and embrace them to try to find a way to help them, but she was also scared of what their touch could do, or what hers would do to them because of Ela. Looking up at Hawke, he seemed at a loss as well, his eyebrows low, and his jaw ticking as he ground his teeth.

"I'm sorry. We've had so many newcomers into Starsgard that things haven't quite settled." Morrigan rocked nervously on her toes, not daring to stray far from Hawke's side, but unable to release the nervous energy that was buzzing inside of her. Nikaius was right, everything sort of felt wrong, but not in a way she could readily express with words. It was almost as if it made her skin itch. "Where did you say you were from?"

"A town called Hillcrest. Well... it was Hillcrest." Ela's voice turned sad as her gaze dropped to her hands. Had they lost their home too? Morrigan felt sorrow for them. "It's in The Barrens." Ela continued. "Right outside of what I think is called the Western Keep?" Morrigan turned to look at Hawke over her shoulder. She knew the quick upward flick of his eyebrow signaled that he was listening, even though he said nothing. He was allowing Morrigan the right to lead the conversation but still stood tall with his hand on his sword, ready to defend her if needed.

Investigating the Keep had already been on the list of things Morrigan wanted to achieve. Learning that there were people living in The Barrens just outside of it was an alarming thought that needed more investigation.

"How did you end up here?" Morrigan asked, taking another step forward to pull a chair near the foot of Ben's bed. It was a daring move, and she sat tensely. Everyone was on edge, but she didn't want anyone to feel unwelcome despite her need to be cautious. Hawke followed close behind and stood at her back as she sat.

"I found Ben, well... Ben found me at my home in the forested area of The Barrens, with that large dark wound across his chest. I thought no magic could exist in The Barrens, so surely a wound like that would heal on its own because the magic that caused it would be removed, but it hasn't." If Ela didn't know what had caused the wounds and if The Barrens, a place that Morrigan had been told sucked the magic out of someone, hadn't removed it, there was something larger than simple magic at play.

Morrigan looked at Hawke with wide eyes, afraid they would never find an answer.

"The storm took out my home," Ela added.

"I'm sorry to hear that. Perhaps there will be a way to restore it once the rains settle." Morrigan was unsure whether she wanted to be too familiar with the newcomers, but she had planned on reaching out to see what could be done to provide homes to those who resided in Starsgard once the storms had settled down.

Perhaps they could find something for Ben and Ela as well? Maybe further away from everyone until they knew what had caused the issue with Ela's touch.

"It was some time ago, I assure you. I'm not quite sure how long ago, actually. Time has been a bit weird to us. While fleeing, we stumbled across some kind of camp between Hillcrest and the Western Keep. There were some men there. One looked like your dark-haired male, that's why Ben reacted the way he did." Morrigan stiffened. She only knew of one man who looked like Nikaius. Did she mean Bastian? "There was a man with light gray wings with him as well. They allowed us a few nights' rest in their camp. On the third night, Ben had gotten up for something and walked in on them talking to Kumnei."

"The God of Mischief?" Shock flooded through Morrigan as she looked back at Hawke in alarm. "I don't know much about him; I've only heard the name spoken by Nikaius when I incorrectly spelled Kunmei in Rekru'e."

"The gods are long dead." Hawke stated, his uninterested mask falling from his face as he looked between them.

"That is what he saw. The fact that he knows Kumnei's name, but not his own, is what led me to seeking out someone else." Suspicion began to rise. The man didn't know his own name but knew the name of a god that was believed to be dead?

She wanted to give them the benefit of the doubt, and Ela being in contact with a god would make her negating touch make more sense.

Ela glanced between them, wrapping her arms around herself as she shifted closer to Ben. The way he smiled at her reminded Morrigan of her men and the different grins they gave her when they found her particularly amusing or for no reason at all.

Even if there was something suspicious, there was no way Morrigan could deny the love they shared.

After another deep breath, Ela spoke again. "We fled in the night, in between shifts with the guard, and were gone before morning. We made it to the border at daybreak and came across a portal in Cav'Sara that brought us here."

"Why here?"

"We had overheard asylum was being granted here, and we hoped to acquire it as well. Gods cannot interfere with the affairs of man."

"Does Ben believe himself a god?" Hawke asked, his tone was almost dismissive. It seemed like he didn't believe the story they were telling.

Was she believing them too easily?

"We don't know if he is or not. We call him Ben because we don't know his actual name. He can't speak, and when I tried to teach him how to write common, it doesn't come out correctly, just illegible symbols."

Even though she didn't fully believe them, curiosity replaced Morrigan's nervousness. She wanted to see what they meant. "Hawke, can you get us some paper and a pen, please?"

"Can you not just pull it yourself, my lady?" Ela asked. Morrigan flushed.

"I cannot. I don't have access to that type of magic," she admitted, fighting back the shame she suddenly felt. Having people point out her lack of magic and her giving a rebuttal was easy because it was a response to something. Openly admitting her fault to a stranger who possibly wouldn't understand made her nervous.

"I thought you had to have magic to be the leader of a court?" Ela looked Morrigan over, but her gaze wasn't a nasty assessment like one Amara often gave, but of curiosity. "I don't have magic either. Being raised in The Barrens takes all the magic out of you." Ela admitted as she looked over at Ben, who watched them cautiously.

"Here you are." Hawke offered Morrigan a pad of paper and a pen that she accepted with a smile.

"My name is Morrigan." She wrote her name in Common and in Rekru'e on the paper before gesturing to Hawke. "This is the captain of our guard, Hawke." She wrote his name as well before offering it to Ben, setting it tentatively on the bed and quickly drawing her hands away to settle them in her lap. If he really was a god, she didn't want to know what his touch would do to her.

"You can go ahead and show her." Ela encouraged, resting her hand on Ben's for a moment before pulling away. "I don't think she'll understand either, but it's better than the others." Morrigan assumed Ela meant those they had met at the encampment near the Western Keep, and it made her sigh softly. They had been through a lot and deserved the benefit of the doubt. It couldn't be easy being through what they had. Though they might be delusional, they still deserved compassion.

She watched as Ben's eyes scanned the paper, tracing the lines with his fingers before taking the pen. Morrigan assumed he was trying to copy them, but what he wrote looked nothing like either of the languages she had written. Though her lines weren't perfect, his hand made the correct movements, but the result was not the same.

It hadn't changed magically before her eyes, but something had happened that she couldn't explain.

He frowned, setting aside the pen. "I see the letters, but they do not come out. Only this." He signed. His brows furrowed as he tossed the paper and pen back down the bed towards her, grimacing as he sat back.

"I've seen something like this before, I think. But I don't know what it says." Hawke murmured, carefully tucking his cheek along Morrigan's as he leaned over her shoulder to look at the marks on the page. His skin felt warm and pleasant, and she was happy to note she could feel his curiosity tingle and mix with her own.

Morrigan was unsure if Hawke meant he didn't understand because of the language itself or of his own stressors with reading but before she could ask, he continued, "I think it might be the language of the gods."

"The language of the gods?" Morrigan gave a little laugh at the absurdity of the name itself and how perfectly it aligned with Ben and Ela's belief that he might be a god.

The thought only lasted for a moment. She had watched him directly copy what she had written, watched the stroke of his pen, but it hadn't come out like hers had. Why else would Ben only be able to write in the language of the gods?

"Mmm." Hawke hummed as he picked up the papers and looked them over. "A long time ago, it was believed that people who were deaf had encountered the gods because mortal beings cannot hear their voices without being deafened." Morrigan's mind went to Imriel. He had been born without his hearing. "Those that cannot speak are believed to be the reincarnations of gods. It's all based on ancient thoughts that no longer really apply though." Hawke rested his hand on the back of Morrigan's chair. "Only a few believe that anymore though. People can lose their hearing or voices by illnesses or exposure to too much magic for too long."

Morrigan watched Ben and Ela as Hawke spoke. It didn't seem like Hawke's words upset them even though they gave each other uneasy glances from time to time.

Santi entered the room, drying his hands on a towel with a grin. "What's this I hear about gods being amongst us?" He smiled at Morrigan before turning his attention to Ben. The dark-haired male growled at Santi, wrapping his hand around Ela's arm to keep her close, but Santi seemed unbothered by his reaction.

Nikaius gave his own grumble from the door, and Morrigan frowned over her shoulder at him. She knew he was being protective of her and the others, but she really didn't want a fight, not when Ben and Ela could possibly provide insight into the Western Keep and its surroundings.

"You look like quite a mess, my friend." When Santi spoke, Morrigan wasn't sure if he actually knew Ben, or if he was trying to get on their good side. It was probably the latter, but she couldn't help but smile at her brother-in-law's exuberance.

"We were trying to figure out if Ben was writing the language of the gods and how to interpret it." Morrigan admitted. Santi was the head of The Pridelands and was a wealth of knowledge. Hopeful that Santi might have a lead, Morrigan took the paper from Hawke to give to him.

Looking at it for a moment, Santi hummed. "I have an idea of who we can reach out to to see if they understand what is being written, but I'm not sure if the Valkyrie will be any help. Aeshira is usually quick to respond to summons. You could send someone to her to request an audience." Morrigan had never spoken to a Valkyrie before, and despite the seriousness of their situation, Morrigan felt a bit excited at the possibility of meeting one.

The Valkyrie were larger than life women who were believed to be the soldiers of the gods. No one knew how long they lived for, but Morrigan had read that their leader Aeshira was older than her grandparents but didn't look it.

Knowing she needed to temper her excitement didn't deter Morrigan's smile as she stood. If Aeshira did come, perhaps she would have insight into the nature of Ela's touch taking away Morrigan's powers. Was it because of her life spent in The Barrens? Or was it some form of magic from the gods that she had inherited?

Clearing her throat, Morrigan stood and collected the paper from Santi. "Santi is good at what he does. Let him tend to that and then you can join us for dinner." Morrigan gave Ben and Ela a soft smile before turning to exit the room.

Turning to Hawke once they were a few doors down from the infirmary, she shook her hands out again. Being out of the room made the tension leave her shoulders, the tingle of magic slowly receding from her skin the further away they got. Feeling was slowly starting to return to her arms, but she still felt the gaping hollowness that lingered. "Do with that what you think is best," she gestured with papers in her hand towards Hawke. "If what they say is true, we need to treat this on a need-to-know basis." Stepping closer, she curled into his side, careful to keep her hands to herself but needing his warmth. "I would like for us all to meet after dinner." Nikaius gave a nod as Waric crosssed his arms over his chest. It would be a huge thing to call her first meeting, her stomach turning with anxiety over the thought, but she knew it needed to be done, especially since she didn't know how long they would be safe in Starsgard before Bastian made good on his threat.

Chapter Twenty-Two

Morrigan

Starsgard

Morrigan's breath caught as she sat up in bed. She had only sat down for a moment, just to ease the ache in her feet. But the room around her was dark, and she felt like she had slept a while. She was too warm and a bit disoriented as she looked around.

A wave of anger flooded through her that wasn't her own. It felt different from any anger she had ever experienced, not a bitter burning sensation, but rage that made her feel hot inside. She didn't understand the anger because only Bec was in the room with her. She must have fallen asleep while she had been waiting for Bec to do the same. Now, he was sound asleep in the bassinet, sprawled out on his back and snoring softly when the rage hit again. She stood, checking on Bec one more time before intending to find some explanation for the sudden feeling, or to find help.

This emotion almost felt like her own, the feelings deep within her and twisting to burn her throat. This wasn't her anger, but she couldn't figure out whose it was, couldn't figure out why she was feeling it when she wasn't touching anyone. She had been outwardly angry only a few times, and it wasn't a feeling she ever wanted to feel again, especially with what happened the last time her anger got the better of her. For a moment, she wondered what Elijah's state was, but that anger suddenly turned to arousal, halting her steps as it stung like electricity through her before she had even reached the door. Brief images entered her mind, as if she was viewing the situation through another's eyes. A hand wrapped in dark hair, while the other banded around their throat. She stumbled as another image came through. It looked like Nikaius, his dark hair was wrapped around a pale hand, and he groaned as his face was forced more into the material under his cheek. Was she having a vision of some sort?

She needed to find Nikaius, needed to know that he was ok, needed to know that the emotions currently coursing through her were not real. As she exited Bec's room and entered the sitting room of the king's suite, she noticed the bedroom door was ajar, and there were grunts and growls coming from inside as if there was a struggle happening in the main bedroom. It reminded her of when they had encountered the ice golem, making panic sear her throat. Were they being attacked again? She stepped forward, determined to figure out what was going on. As she went to call out for Hawke, her breath caught in her throat and knees trembled with the wave of anger mixed with arousal as Waric's voice met her ears.

"You made her cry, you worried the rest of us, and you let your brother get the better of you when you knew to come to me. We all know ways to help get those thoughts out of your head. You don't have to do these things alone." Heavy breathing was the only response.

Another wave of arousal made her pause before she reached the bedroom door and the impact of flesh on flesh sounded again. Were they fighting? Pushing the door open a bit, she watched Waric raise his hand and smack Nikaius again. Right on his bare ass. Both men were very naked, and Morrigan realized what was happening. Embarrassment canceled out the other feelings for a moment, and she took a step back. They were having sex while Waric reprimanded Nikaius.

Tilting her head a bit, she carefully stepped forward to edge the door open, just a bit more, hoping to get a clearer view so she could fully see what was happening.

When she had thought about them together, Nikaius was always the one in charge, the one commanding Waric to please him. It was Waric on his knees, hanging onto Nikaius' every command, pleasing him however he could, and in turn pleasing himself.

When they were together, Waric was normally sitting at Nikaius's feet, or deferring to him for instructions.

Instead, it was Waric behind Nikaius, pushing him down into the bed, turning his backside red with loud slaps that had her wincing. Wincing and longing to see more. For a split second, she wondered if this was new, something that they were trying, but Waric's practiced motions and whispered narration, however, proved that he had skill in what he was doing.

Nikaius gave a low groan that reminded Morrigan of the night they had been together like that, bodies twined together. Seeing them together was sending arousal trembling through her that she tried to block from her mind.

All her relations with her men had been individual encounters, but as she watched Waric and Nikaius moving together, her body flushed hot at the thought of what they would do to her if she was with them, if she was in between them. She'd never engaged in multiple partners before, emotionally or sexually, and the thought made her curious, made her want. But she wasn't brave enough to ask Waric and Nikaius to be together with her at the same time.

Hawke had mentioned previously that he wasn't interested in being with Nikaius and Waric, but she wondered if something would ever happen between the four of them. Whose hands would go where? She had enjoyed every time someone's lips touched her skin, what would having three mouths on her feel like? Her breath trembled at the thought, the harsh arousal she was feeling morphing into something hot but soft. She could almost feel someone's tongue between her thighs. Was there a way that that would work? Did she want it to work?

Another smack of flesh on flesh brought Morrigan back, making her jerk away from the door as the tantalizing thoughts still twisted in her head. Would there be time to explore those thoughts now that she had taken on Bec and the courts? She was still worried about what influence those things would have on her life that she hadn't stopped to think about the fact that the relationships she held were still new as well.

Though she contemplated interrupting them so she could figure out why her emotions had suddenly gone haywire, the longer she watched, the more she wondered if it was more than just sex between them. Waric's reprimanding words weren't stuttered with anger and the strike he gave Nikaius didn't seem to actually be injuring him. Though Nikaius' skin was red, he didn't seem to be fighting or arguing with what Waric said. They were both deriving pleasure from this. Even if she wasn't sure of their motives, Morrigan knew that Nikaius had taken the same potion she had, which lasted for thirty days and would cause damage if consent was revoked by either party.

This realization made her nervous to interrupt. Perhaps Hawke would be a better option? He might know what was happening and possibly provide some relief to the ache building between her legs.

As she turned, intending to return to Bec, she ran straight into Hawke's chest.

"Hawke!" she gasped in surprise, trying to keep her voice low so as not to alert Nikaius and Waric that she was there, watching.

"I was coming to see if they had made up yet and instead, I find you." His amber eyes flicked from her to the open bedroom door and back as his grin spread. "Are you snooping, Little Dove?"

"I..." She flushed as one of the men in the other room groaned again, making her skin flush hot. "No?" Her denial wasn't convincing to her own ears.

Hawke drew her close by the hip, his grin turning darker as he also caught the sounds. Leaning down, his nose brushed her ear as his voice dropped so he could whisper darkly against her skin. "I didn't take you as the voyeuristic type, Morrigan."

Waric had stopped speaking, and the only sounds were their groans and flesh meeting flesh. "I felt anger and then..." Her voice died away as she tried to find words, her mind torn between listening to the sounds in the bedroom, trying to explain herself to Hawke, and the need burning through her. "And I..." She had somehow thought it into existence again and another wave of heat flushed through her so strongly she had to brace herself with one hand on Hawke's arm, trying to maintain some semblance of composure. She had never been able to orgasm without touch, but with the way the arousal kept twisting in her veins, the less sure she was that she couldn't. "I don't know what's happening," she whispered, licking her lips and daring to look up at Hawke again, eyes big and pleading, silently asking him for help.

Reaching down, Hawke laced his fingers through hers and lifted her hand to kiss the stippled silver flames that decorated her wrist. A shudder curled through her, and Waric groaned in the other room. "When a mate bond is solidified, strong thoughts and emotions can slip through. Waric is probably projecting and didn't realize you had access to it yet." His eyes danced as he looked her over, gaze lingering on her curves, on her lips.

"What do I do?" Her attention waned as Waric said something else in the low, growly voice he had used with her before. Her body was burning up, she needed relief. Maybe Hawke would guide her away, would help ease this need inside of her.

"Well, we could do one of two things." Hawke's grin grew, and he pulled her closer using his hand on her hip so that she was flush against him, a move that made her realize that something had aroused him as well, but she didn't know if it was her arousal or the scene unfolding in the bedroom.

"Uh-huh?" Though she knew she should resist, the temptation of his fingers on her hip made her press her forehead against his chest. She knew she shouldn't, that she would be embarrassed if they were caught, but she wanted Hawke to continue.

"We could leave and let them have their privacy…" That should be the only option, shouldn't it? Morrigan frowned up at him in confusion, but his grin remained as he let go of her fingers to tuck a lock of hair behind her ear. He leaned forward, his teeth nipping the lobe in a way that made her gasp. "The other option," his voice was low and slow, leaving her hanging on his every word as she tried to concentrate on him while also trying not to shiver with the pleasure that curled through her at the sound. "We can assuage that arousal while we watch." He turned her, making sure she had a full view of the activities happening in the bedroom beyond the door.

"Watch? I thought you said you didn't want to see them naked." She didn't know why she remembered that part of their conversation, but the thought died away as her attention snagged on Waric again.

Something about watching the muscles in Waric's back and thighs flex as he pressed into Nikaius was tantalizing and watching made her mouth dry. Each press of his hips caused a flash of arousal to flare through her, and she realized that Hawke must be right and the bond between her and Waric had somehow come to life. She hadn't been prepared to feel his arousal through it or anything at all. She was woefully unprepared for the bond and wondered why none of them had warned her about it. It was also only a few hours after it had happened, and Morrigan knew so much had happened in a short span of time, so she could understand the lack of preparation even though it was jarring.

"I might have lied a little." Hawke's laugh rumbled against her ear. What part had he lied about? Shock snuck through her as his palms stroked down her shoulders and over her hands before securing over her hips, pulling her snug against him as well. "They're more physical than what I like to be." His fingers drummed against her hips before wandering lower to slowly gather her skirt as he took a step back. As wrapped up in him as she was, Morrigan stumbled but followed until she felt him kneel behind her.

The ache between her legs flared hotter as his hand found skin and stroked gently up, across her thigh. "I'm not fond of being touched," he admitted, "but touching..." His hand squeezed her thigh, rolling the muscle in a way that made her shudder, his fingers so close to where she wanted him to be. The ache was unlike anything she had experienced before, like she had been kept on edge for hours even though only minutes had passed. She was ready to beg for relief.

"The quickness of your heart shows your interest. I wonder how much we could get away with before they realize we're here?" Morrigan's mouth was dry, and she couldn't find the words to respond, her mind distracted by the renewed sounds in the bedroom. It was still dark where she and Hawke were and the only light was what was in the bedroom, bathing Nikaius and Waric in the glow of the fire.

She contemplated resisting; it felt like an intrusion to be spying on an intimate moment, but the twisting sensation of arousal made it hard to care. Hawke knew Nikaius and Waric better than anyone else, and if he truly believed Nikaius and Waric wouldn't have a problem with it, then maybe she should give in. She was so desperate for relief.

His hand finally found its home in the space between her legs. She knew she was already wet, her own arousal twisting with his and with Waric's, making her tremble.

"You're so wet," Hawke murmured against her low back before pressing a kiss there. "Keep your eyes on them, watch how nicely Nikaius takes him." Hawke's fingers sank into her as Waric thrusted into Nikaius again, and she gasped, wrapping her hand around Hawke's wrist. She wasn't sure whether she wanted to encourage him deeper or to pull him away. Waric's pace was slow but hard, and Morrigan's eyes were glued to them even as Hawke pressed his fingers into her again, immediately picking up the same deep but slow pace.

"Imagine riding one of their cocks like that. You'd be helpless to do anything other than take what they give you." The way Hawke's fingers curled made her tremble. Did he... Did he want her to do that to him?

Maybe that would soothe the fire in her blood. While his fingers felt great, they weren't enough. Daringly, she licked her lips and whispered, "Show me." She refused to look back at him, afraid that if she saw his face she would balk at the thought, but his responding groan preceded him pushing her away so he could stand.

"You do know that if they see you, they might decide to join?" His lips followed the whisper of the dress's zipper down her spine.

The thought made her tremble. How would that work? Who would be where? Did she want that? Taking a shaky breath, she nodded and let the dress fall from her shoulders. Agreeing to this was akin to deciding to take over the courts. It wasn't a step backwards to give herself to Hawke, or to any of them, but another step forward into who she wanted to be. She wanted to be kind and gracious and compassionate, but she also wanted to be spontaneous and brave. She wanted to feel beautiful and desirable. She wanted to love and be loved.

Hawke's mouth chased the chill across her shoulders and down her back again. "You're so beautiful." His hands left her body, but before she could turn to inquire about what he was doing, she heard his belt hit the floor with a thud. The rustle of fabric was the only warning Morrigan had before Hawke was guiding her back. "Here, sit carefully."

His knees widened her stance before pulling her to him. "Here." Shifting back some more, Hawke tapped the back of her knee. "Step back to kneel." His voice was a low grumble, and she frowned, turning to look back at him. Someone groaned in the bedroom and the arousal flared again, pulling a soft gasp from her. Hawke patted the cushion next to his hip. "You'll have more control if you're kneeling instead of trying to use the floor."

She wasn't quite sure what she was controlling, but as she got a full glimpse of Hawke in his nakedness, the thought fled her mind for a moment. How she had gotten so lucky to have three very handsome men interested in her was something she wondered often, but there was nothing like seeing the power they held just under their skin. Like Nikaius and Waric, Hawke was all lean muscle, and she couldn't help turning and reaching out to smooth her hand up his chest. He felt hot under her palms, and she watched as goose bumps broke out across his skin, his head tipping back as he groaned softly.

"If you don't get up here, you're going to miss all the fun," he teased, even though he made no move to prevent her from touching him.

Another wave of stimulation hit her, and she gasped as it hit deep between her legs, as if someone had stroked their fingers from her clit all the way up to her throat and back. "Fates." She panted, daringly letting her hand stroke down lower, taking his cock in hand.

He was hard, and his hips twitched when she stroked him, a hissed breath escaping through his teeth.

Morrigan turned at the sound of strained gasp from someone in the bedroom and watched as Waric's hand wrapped around the dark locks of Nikaius' hair and pulled, a throb rolling through her that matched the tug nearly perfectly. Was she able to feel what Nikaius felt through Waric's bond as well?

Hawke's hands on her hips brought her back to herself, and she gave a shaky nod. She felt ready to combust or dissolve into a puddle of goo.

Cautiously, she let Hawke turn her before she shifted back so that she could kneel on the settee, straddling Hawke as his hands slid up her sides and back.

"Easy." Hawke guided her down, and she gasped as she felt the head of his erection press into her slowly. The position was similar to the last time they had been together, and she groaned softly as she braced herself with her hands on his knees.

The fullness she felt as he adjusted her hips provided some relief but also renewed the heat that curled its way across her body.

One of the men in the bedroom groaned, drawing Morrigan's attention back to them as Hawke shifted so that she could settle more directly on her knees. Hawke's hand on her shoulder pulled her back so she would sit up properly, and she shuddered as it changed the angle. "You can control the angle and the depth here." Hawke whispered against her shoulder before giving her a gentle nip.

Adjusting again sent a zing of electricity through her, and she gave a breathless laugh as she did it again. For the next few moments, she experimented with the different positions and depths, trying to figure out one that satisfied some of the ache enough to make her groan softly. But just his cock wasn't enough.

"Touch me," she pleaded as she rocked her hips against his. Hawke's hands came up to weigh her breasts in his hands, his lips peppering kisses along her neck as his own hips shuddered with her, meeting her next motion with a thrust of his own that made her throw her head back with another high groan.

Hawke's own heavy breathing muffled the sounds from the bedroom and Morrigan startled, tensing as a warm wet tongue swiped its way across her clit.

"Ohhhh." The word rolled out of her in a giddy laugh as she rocked her hips, seeking out the sensation again. She didn't know who was between her legs, eagerly lapping at her clit, but that made it even more tantalizing because the light from the bedroom had died away, taking any visibility with it. The thought of being unseen made her bold, and she slid her fingers into sweat dampened hair and pulled.

"We're going switch positions," Waric's words ghosted across her lips, but before she could seek out a kiss, Hawke was shifting her up, off his cock, another's hands pulling her off her knees. Before she could begin to feel indignant about being manhandled and moved, she was pulled back to sit fully again. Hawke pressed his cock back into her, sinking deeper now that she wasn't as spread open as she previously was.

A hand stroked its way up her calf before tugging, causing Morrigan to shift her weight to one foot, leading her to depend more on Hawke's strength to keep her from falling.

All thoughts of her balance and potential embarrassment fled her mind as her knee was hitched up over someone's shoulder and the warm tongue returned. "You're such a good boy." Waric murmured. Morrigan wasn't quite sure where he was in relation to them, but his words told her that Nikaius was the one between her legs. Nikaius' low grumble was all the warning she got before he went all in, lips and tongue and teeth teasing every part of skin he could find between her legs as if he was ravenous.

Though Hawke had said that he wasn't one for touching, he gave his own low groan before hitching his hips a bit, giving an actual thrust that tore a high keen from Morrigan's throat.

The tension that Nikaius was creating with his mouth, a twisting sensation of shocking nips with his teeth being soothed by his broad warm tongue, paired with the rough slide of Hawke's cock, made her see stars, and she could feel tension building in every part of her.

Waric's soft cedar scent was all the warning she had before he captured her mouth in a kiss, his hands stroking their way up along her chest to brush over breasts with a teasing flick to her nipple. When she jerked, Hawke groaned, his hand finding her hip and digging into the skin there. Though the pain was acute, it added to the other sensations, but anytime she tried to move, tried to actually participate, she felt uncoordinated and would lose the delicious friction and chaotic spiraling burn that crackled under her skin.

"Shh," Waric soothed her whine with another kiss before his lips trailed down her neck, opposite of where Hawke's breath panted against her skin.

She knew she wouldn't last long. Their coordination was impeccable, and when Hawke shifted her again, pressing himself impossibly deep, Nikaius' lips wrapped around her clit and sucked hard, shattering all that tension in the span of a single breath.

Her fingers dug into Nikaius' hair and twisted as the nails of her other hand dug into Hawke's leg. She felt like she needed to stop moving but couldn't control the roll of her hips or the way her head fell back against Hawke's shoulder when Waric's teeth found the mark Nikaius had left on her shoulder and bit.

She felt like her orgasm took forever, wringing every last drop of energy from her body before everything faded to nothing more than a throbbing ache. This new feeling had nothing to do with arousal and everything to do with the weird position she was in.

Letting herself relax against Hawke, she trembled as Nikaius' tongue swiped along her clit again. "Mmmh." Shifting, she used the hand in Nikaius' hair to push him away. "Enough," she whispered, trying to shift away from him, but unsure how to really untangle herself from the position she was in.

The room was still as they paused to catch their breath, and as loathe as she was to break the content silence, she needed to speak up. "My hips hurt," she whispered softly. Hawke's loud laugh startled her, and his hands wrapped around her stomach to adjust them both.

"You just effectively had a foursome, and that's the first thing you say?" The humor was not lost on her but while Hawke teased her, someone took her elbows and carefully helped her stand, both her and Hawke taking in sharp inhales when he pulled from her.

She had yet to figure out why her mind was quiet after engaging with them, but something about the closeness of each of them made her feel safe.

Right then, though, she felt sticky and sore. Hawke groaned as he stood as well, pressing himself against her back before directing her to look back at him to seek out a kiss. "You're amazing. I'll be right back." His footsteps echoed as he entered the attached bathroom.

"Are you okay?" Nikaius' voice was gravelly as he stood, trailing his hands up her legs before taking Hawke's place at her back, wrapping his arms around her to hold her from behind.

"Mmm." Morrigan gave an affirming hum as she let herself be swayed back and forth by him.

"I'm sorry for upsetting you." He breathed against her skin. "I know I said it earlier, but I feel like I need to say it again and again."

"I understand what happened. It's alright now. We're all together and whole and that is all I need," Morrigan answered. Because that was the truth. If someone were to completely unravel their reality, all she would hope to keep would be her pack and Bec. The rest of the world could be in upheaval, but as long as she had them, she knew she would survive whatever was thrown at her.

As if he knew she was thinking about him, Bec cried from the next room, though it didn't disrupt the peace. "I've got him." The water in the bathroom shut off and Hawke returned to the room. He sought out another from Morrigan kiss before she heard the door to Bec's room open.

"Wait!" Morrigan gasped as she took a step forward. "Put some clothes on."

Nikaius and Waric laughed. "That's what you're worried about? He's a baby, he doesn't care if Hawke is wearing clothes." Waric quipped, reaching out to tuck a lock of hair behind her ear.

"I..." They were right and now that she thought about it, Morrigan laughed as well, the sound soft and filled with happiness. True happiness.

The lights flared to life enough for her to see but not enough to be blinding, and Waric stepped in to hug her as well. Letting herself be pulled to him, she gave a soft hum, the sentiment of her being happy with her men renewing.

Hawke returned a few moments later, still completely naked but carrying Bec cradled in one arm and a washcloth in the other. "Let's get you cleaned up." He offered Bec to Nikaius, who grinned and scooped up the child to snuggle his nose into one of Bec's chubby cheeks.

As Waric and Hawke helped Morrigan clean up and dress in something more suitable to sleep in, she watched Nikaius and Bec with a swell of affection.

Right here was exactly where she wanted to be.

Chapter Twenty-Three

Morrigan

Starsgard

The morning found them still snuggled in bed, Morrigan's cheek resting on Waric's shoulder as he stroked his fingers through Nikaius' dark hair. She knew she would need to get up soon because Hawke had gotten up with Bec when the morning light was barely beginning. She had protested, trying to insist she do it since Nikaius was the one who put him back to bed the night before, but Hawke gave her a gentle kiss and bid her to rest some more. Though she felt guilty, it hadn't taken her long to drift back to sleep, with Hawke's voice a low rumble in the next room over as he tended to Bec.

She was so happy that they had so readily taken to helping her care for Bec. She knew the situation was new and that it would take time to develop a routine, but to see it happening so quickly set her mind at ease.

Yawning softly, she snuggled closer to Waric. The quiet was soft and peaceful, and Morrigan wanted nothing more than to spend the day just like that. But it didn't last as a soft knock at the door shattered that peace, and Morrigan looked to Waric, who sighed and pulled himself away from them to go answer it.

Nikaius stirred, blinking sleepily as they listened to Waric's quiet voice at the door.

"We'll be there shortly." The door clicked shut, and Waric turned, leaning against it as he let out a heavy sigh. "Santi has returned."

"Where did he go?" Morrigan asked, shifting onto her side to watch him pull clothing from the dresser.

"He went to inquire with Soren about the location and layout of the Western Keep." Waric rolled his shoulders as he tugged on a pair of underwear followed by black pants. "If what Ela said is true, and she and Ben came from that direction, we might be looking at a huge lead for where the others are disappearing to."

Nikaius scoffed. "I don't think we should be indulging him in the thought that he is a god. The idea itself is ludicrous."

"I'm not saying that." Waric settled his hands on his hips as he looked from Nikaius to Morrigan and back.

Morrigan frowned as she watched the two of them stare each other down. "We were supposed to have a meeting about this last night but..." Her cheeks flushed as her mind flashed back to the night before, renewing the shallow ache in her hips.

Nuzzling into her shoulder, Nikaius laughed gently. "We can set something up after breakfast."

Nikaius sat up slowly, leaning over to press a gentle kiss to Morrigan's mouth before disengaging himself to get ready for the day ahead.

With a soft sigh, Morrigan nodded and pulled herself from the bed to stretch. Waric stepped over, pressing a kiss to her forehead and offering her fresh undergarments to put on before following Nikaius into the bathroom.

Fates, she loved them. There was no limit to the things she was willing to do for them and their people. Slowly dressing, she smiled as she thought about the night before. She had never thought she would be in the position she was in, mated to one male and in a relationship with two others. Her life was chaotic, but it was hers, and she was proud of that despite all the questions that still lingered.

"Morrigan?" She didn't realize she had been staring at the door of the bathroom for several moments until Aslin's hand waved in front of her face.

Blinking in surprise, Morrigan turned to her friend with a shy smile. She had been so lost in her thoughts that she hadn't heard Aslin enter the room. "Sorry, my mind wandered. If I have any say about it, I think we might be set to travel today, and we don't know what the state of the Western Keep will be."

"You plan on going with? I thought you would choose to remain here with the others. This isn't something we're typically a part of."

"I want to be there. It's part of my territory, and I want to make sure nothing is overlooked when it comes to the lives of our people. Do you really think they will be interested in finding livable rooms?" Gesturing to the door, she shook her head. She loved her men, but they had one-track minds, and she knew this. "No. They'll be assessing threats and getting as far into the territory as they can. I want to see what it looks like to be sure it's even habitable. I'm sure Waric would agree with me." Aslin smiled but didn't say anything, watching as Morrigan pulled clothes from the closet and started to dress.

"We still have some things to figure out, like who is going to stay and protect this realm while we're off discovering another." Waric entered the room and snagged Morrigan's hair to give it a playful tug.

Morrigan gave him an affectionate smile and a gentle kiss. "I don't know if I'm allowed to, but if things go according to plan, I intend to let the people of Barnam have the Western Keep. But I need to know what sort of state it's in and be able to make plans for when we manage to get drafters involved. I want to be sure it's entirely livable."

"That's a good plan. We'll talk about it after breakfast." Nikaius adjusted his shirt sleeves as he stepped out of the bathroom. He pressed a kiss to the top of her head before following Waric out the door. Morrigan giggled as Waric exited the room, crowing a low good morning to those in the hall.

Once she was dressed in something that was comfortable but would be warm enough if they decided the day warranted travel, Morrigan twisted her hair away from her face and pinned it back with another clip from the queen's suite vault.

When she stepped into the additional room to find Bec gone, she frowned at Aslin, who smiled. "I think Hawke brought him to Sable when he woke up this morning." Morrigan gave a noncommittal hum as she straightened the blankets on the bed. "I thought he just put him back to sleep after tending to him."

Patting her arm gently, Aslin headed back into the main sitting room. "I saw them meandering down the hallway earlier. He may not look it, but Hawke adores children. We all do."

Before Morrigan could fret too much about it, Aslin cut in, "You've had a long couple of days, Morrigan, the baby will be fine without you for a few hours. But if you do want to see him, I'm sure Hawke tucked him into the nursery when he left for his rounds." She knew Hawke would take care of Bec, knew he would ensure the baby was safe, but she still needed to see him with her own eyes.

Her steps quickly took her to the nursery and as they entered, Sable was walking around singing a soft song to Bec as they wandered the room. When Sable caught sight of them, her smile widened. "Look who's here! I told you she wouldn't be too long, didn't I?"

As she accepted Bec, Morrigan smiled down at him, pressing a gentle kiss to his forehead and nose before curling him close. Her heart felt fuller than she could ever remember. She still felt unsure about what her capabilities were and how long her happiness would last, but she knew the truths that were laid in front of her. She had an amazing pack by her side and several things she could call her own, including the small baby who eagerly snuggled closer. Bec seemed to be doing better than before, not nearly as fussy as he had been. When Sable offered a wrap for Morrigan to use to tuck him in close to her, Aslin helped her hold Bec as they figured it out together. Nikaius had made it look so easy the day before, but it took some getting used to. It was simple enough to learn, and she liked the fact that she could have her hands free while also holding him close.

Having Bec so close to her and Waric's mark on her wrist made her feel like she had somehow cheated the Fates.

It made her thoughts go dark, wondering if all the happiness, the sense of safety, would need to be paid back.

"He's just been fed so he should be alright for a little while," Sable informed them.

Morrigan gave an appreciative smile. "I'm so happy everyone is doing well."

"Me, too, my lady. Me too."

Greetings were called as they entered the dining hall. Morrigan wanted to tell them her plan to resettle them in the Western Keep, but she didn't want to get their hopes up.

She and Aslin ate breakfast quietly, Morrigan wondering where her men had disappeared to. It was hard to remember they all had their own jobs to do until they were gone doing those things.

As they were finishing up, Aquila sat next to Aslin with a smile. So much had happened in such a short amount of time that Morrigan felt bad for not having had time to spend with her friends.

"Is everyone settling in alright?" Morrigan asked Aquila, who gave Morrigan a bright grin.

"For the most part, yes."

"Uh-oh. That doesn't sound good." Aslin murmured around a bite of her eggs.

"Nothing we can't handle."

"Is it the people from Barnam? Is someone causing issues?" Morrigan set aside her fork, having eaten her fill of the eggs, and turned to face Aquila.

"No, a few of the guard, actually."

"That's..." Morrigan couldn't find the right word. She did understand their trepidation about being under her leadership when their lord was present, but she didn't know how to remedy that.

"Like I said, we've got it covered. I believe you said you wanted to hold a meeting. When you're done, I'll escort you. The others are already there." Nerves flooded to the forefront as Morrigan looked at her two friends. There were important decisions to be made, and realistically, she was the only one who could make them.

Taking a deep breath, she stood, careful not to jar Bec as she did. He fussed a little bit, but after a few gentle pats, he settled back to sleep. She was amazed at how much he actually slept since they had gotten him settled, and she couldn't be happier that it was with her. They still had to find homes for the other children, but that would come once they figured out the status of the Western Keep.

Aquila and Aslin stood as well, and Aquila led the way out of the dining hall. The meeting room that had been set up was two doors down from the dining hall, across from the receiving room. "Why aren't we using the council chambers?" Morrigan asked softly. The night they had arrived in Starsgard Aslin had told Morrigan about the room off the dining hall.

"There are more people who want to be heard involved than typical council meetings." Aquila gave Morrigan a grin. "That's a good thing, I promise."

As they approached the room Morrigan's nerves flared again. There was conversation happening inside, they didn't seem serious, just casual conversations as they waited. Would the ease of conversation change once she entered? She hoped not.

She paused just outside the door, trying to solidify her mind, trying to keep her heart calm as Aslin entered on her own. Stepping into the unknown was terrifying. But before she could actually step into the room, the word *thaber* caught her attention. She could barely see the guards that stood next to the door, ones in her own green and gold.

Oh Fates. She had known it was coming, but to have it spoken in a conversation she couldn't really understand was jarring. Stepping closer but still out of sight, she was able to catch more of the conversation.

I know she's thaber, but she saved so many people, Ty. The Rekru'e was spoken in a harsh whisper. He was defending her.

That doesn't mean anything. She shouldn't be here at all. She doesn't have powers, so why should she be in power? Bastian said—

Morrigan's blood ran cold as she took a step back, disengaging from the conversation. Her hands trembled against Bec's back as she tried to determine the best course of action. Bastian had clearly gotten into the ear of some of their men. She could let Nikaius or Waric handle it, or even Aquila and Hawke. She looked over to see Aquila only a few steps away, her posture rigid as she ground her teeth together. She had overheard as well.

"Aquila?" Morrigan asked softly. This was putting her friend in a poor position. Her caramel eyes found Morrigan's.

"You know not all of them believe that, right?" Aquila asked, catching Morrigan's elbow and pulling her a bit further away from the door.

"I know. But now I'm worried about how many people Bastian has gotten to."

"We can say something to Nikaius and Waric about it," Aquila suggested. "I've been trying to get rid of him for ages, but he hasn't done anything warranting dismissal."

"I..." Morrigan looked back towards the door. "No one will take me seriously if we do that." It was a truth that Morrigan had thought about. She had claimed the courts and asked the people to trust her. If she had one of her men do her bidding, how would that look? They hadn't heard what was said, and that was another problem all on its own. But she needed to know she could trust the people serving her as well. Clearly, this male was no longer trustworthy. She needed to put her foot down and make it known that she was serious about her role, no matter how scary it was. "Can I trust you to back me up?" Locking eyes with Aquila, Morrigan made up her mind about what needed to happen. Taking a steadying breath, she gave a small smile. "I'm about to do something crazy."

A grin spread across Aquila's face. "I have an idea about what's about to happen. I love crazy." Dipping into a bow, Aquila gestured for Morrigan to stay where she was before stepping into the room.

The way Aquila barked "Attention" startled Morrigan, who stared up at her with wide eyes. She was going to have the whole room's attention on her. Oh Fates. She couldn't back out now. "My lady, Morrigan Aegean has the floor."

Morrigan stood frozen to the floor for a moment before she caught sight of Nikaius, who gave her a bright grin and a subtle jerk of his head, encouraging her to step into the room.

Okay. She was doing this. Taking another deep breath, she stepped into the room. Santi was the first to give her a formal bow, his left hand over his heart and bowing at the hips. Nikaius, Waric, and Hawke followed suit. The others gathered paused for a moment before dipping into formal bows of their own. Surprised, Morrigan looked at Aslin, who appeared at her elbow after she floundered for a moment. "Dip your own curtsy or just acknowledge them." Aslin whispered.

Morrigan had never been the one being bowed to, so it didn't really occur to her that only the role had been reversed for her. Dipping her own curtsy, Morrigan gave Santi a thankful smile. "Thank you."

As she accepted Aquila's offered hand, Aquila smiled, whispering, "I've got you."

Giving a shaky nod, she turned to the two males who stood closest to the door. "*You there,*" her voice shook for a moment as she tried out the words in Rekru'e. She knew speaking their language would make the sting even worse. When her gaze flicked to Nikaius and Waric, they both looked concerned but stayed where they were. Turning her attention back to who she was addressing, she cleared her throat and stepped closer. "*What are your names and ranks?*" This was something that needed to be done. They needed to see her as she was, by her merit, not her mark.

"Preston Connors, Lieutenant of Kunmei and the Neutral Territories, ma'am," Preston answered in common as he gave her another neat bow before offering her a smile. Preston was tall and lanky with dirty blond hair that was pulled back away from his face. On the collar of his uniform was a bronze star and on his chest was a pair of wings with the number four settled in between them. Morrigan didn't know much about ranking officers of the guard, but she assumed that the other male was his superior based on the color of his star.

"*Atyon Highwater, Lieutenant Commander. Ma'am.*" His ma'am sounded forced even in Rekru'e, and he frowned as he bowed to her as well. He looked older, the dark hair on his head having receded in some spots. He appeared several years older than Hawke and, for a moment, Morrigan felt bad. He had to have been in his rank for a while. His previous words and behavior made it more clear why Aquila had been trying to get rid of him as well.

Clearing her throat again, Morrigan turned her attention back to Preston. "How would you like a promotion?" she asked in common. Though her words were unsteady, Morrigan looked back at Aquila again, earning her a nod. Good. She had understood the ranking system.

"Ma'am?" Preston's eyebrows raised as he looked at those around him for some type of guidance.

"Morrigan?" Hawke stepped forward, but Morrigan gestured towards Atyon.

"*This thaber is dismissing Mr. Highwater for...*" Morrigan frowned for a moment, trying to find the word, but Aquila chimed in with "*Insubordination.*"

"She can't do that!" Atyon protested loudly.

"She can, and she did. You wear her mantle, Highwater." Santi's words were slow and vicious. Morrigan knew that referring to herself as thaber like Atyon had would be the only explanation the others needed.

When Morrigan glanced away to look at Hawke and Aquila, the shuffling of fabric drew her attention back to where Atyon pulled his mantle off over his head. As he dropped it to the floor with a vicious swear, he lunged at her.

Morrigan stepped back and turned, trying to protect Bec, but when no blow came, she looked up to see that Preston had stepped in front of her. Shoving Atyon back, Preston swung at him, punching him squarely in the face.

Atyon fell to the floor, swearing as he clutched his face over his nose and mouth. "I told you to watch your tongue. You did this to yourself, Ty." Preston murmured, shaking out his hand as he looked over his shoulder at Morrigan.

"I've got you, my lady."

Morrigan tried to shake off the vicious glee that came from seeing the man bleeding at her feet by focusing on the gratefulness she felt to see that everyone else seemed to be on her side. Hawke took her carefully by the elbow to turn her to him, his eyes flickering over her and Bec quickly. "Are you alright?"

"I'm fine." She was shaking on the inside and wanted to sit down, but she still felt like she owed the others an explanation.

"Aquila and I heard him speaking while we were in the hallway. He doesn't believe I should be in power because of my brand." She caught Nikaius' eye as she spoke. "It seems like Bastian has gotten into the ear of some of our guards. If any of your men believe their duty is to those with power and not with this house and the neutral territories, please advise they leave now." Nikaius gave her a brief nod. She wasn't sure if it was in understanding or agreement or both, but she continued anyways. They needed to know that their plans and people would be safe. "If they get found out later, I cannot promise a dignified departure. We have more important things to do than worry about infighting and sabotage.

Hawke, can you please escort Mr. Highwater to the infirmary to have his face tended to?"

Turning to Preston, she gave him a gentle smile. "Thank you for stepping up like that. It can't be easy to defend against a friend. I hope you'll agree to be the new Lieutenant Commander."

"Of course, my lady." Preston gave her another bow and a smile before returning to his position by the door, flexing the hand he had hit Atyon with.

"You can have your hand tended to."

"I'd like to stay and hear your ideas, my lady. Atyon was speaking nonsense about the lack of appropriate space and other things, and I would like to be able to advise towards these things if needed."

"I appreciate that. Please, everyone, be seated so we can start. I would like to get things done as quickly as possible." As she moved to sit in the chair that Aquila pulled out for her, Bec began to fuss again.

"I think it's his lunch time. I'll take him." Waric offered, making grabby hands for Bec as he approached.

"You're sure?" Carefully navigating Bec from the sling, she gave him a little snuggle and giggled as he tried to suckle her cheek.

"I can't make decisions, remember?" Waric whispered, pressing a kiss to her cheek before taking Bec and pulling a bottle from the ether as he stepped away.

"Right." Her heart gave a happy little flutter that pulled a smile to her face as she sat, looking at those gathered. She didn't know everyone's names, but she would learn them as she laid out her ideas, and they made plans for them.

Aquila and Silas would take men to the Western Keep to see what could be done about accessing it while Santi went back to The Pridelands to see if anything had been heard regarding Bastian's threats about calling the council.

Chapter Twenty-Four

Morrigan

Starsard

Morrigan, Aslin, and Waric were in the middle of lunch when Silas returned. It hadn't taken them nearly as long as Morrigan had thought, but when she saw him, she knew something was wrong. Silas was typically the more energetic of the De'Lyon triplets while Soren was more stoic and Santi a mix of the two. To see him without a grin was a bit jarring and sent warning bells of concern through Morrigan.

"My lady, my lord." His voice was soft as he dipped into a quick bow. "We've gained access to the land as close as we can, but there's no way to get into the Keep."

"What do you mean, 'no way'?" Morrigan patted Bec gently as she stood. She was mostly finished with her lunch and was eager to see another part of the world that was under her domain. As exciting as it was to have her world opening up more so she was able to go to more places, she knew that the trip wasn't for leisure, and she would need to keep the task at hand in the forefront of her mind. That excitement did, however, bleed over into the fact that there might be a new place for the people of Barnam to stay.

The blond male looked around for a moment before leaning down, dropping his voice even more. "The entire area is surrounded by ice."

"It's winter," Morrigan laughed. "Of course there would be ice."

"No, ma'am, ice that we can't melt." That was...weird. Was it like the ice golems they had faced a few weeks ago?

As Morrigan opened her mouth to ask what he meant, Waric stood as well. Clearing his throat, he cut in quietly, "This conversation would be better suited for other places," Catching Morrigan's elbow, he raised his eyebrows at her before gesturing with his head to the others in the room. Could he read her thoughts like she had picked up on his emotions the night before? Her eyes searched his for a moment before he gave a nod, turning his attention back to Silas. "Let's retire to the council chambers for these reports. Eat and rest first, we will reconvene in an hour." Morrigan frowned at him, but Nikaius appeared, plopping himself onto the bench beside where Waric stood with a soft groan.

Concern rippled through her. Had the events of last night been too much for him? Was he really up for travel? He had previously stated that he had to fight to get Santi bring him home. They hadn't figured out who would be staying behind to protect those who were currently residing in Starsgard. Perhaps if she brought her concerns up to him and Santi, they would agree. Nikaius would be the best choice to keep everyone safe.

As Nikaius reached for her, all signs of his distress had disappeared. He grinned playfully up at her, eyes dancing midnight and ice as he grasped behind her knee and tugged until it dropped to the bench beside him. She had to catch herself on his shoulders to stay upright.

She huffed, moving to pull away, but Nikaius grinned and grasped the back of her neck, bending her to him.

"Be patient. I know we're all eager to know what they know, but they've been working for hours to get back to us. The details won't change between now and then, and if you want to come with us, you'll eat something instead of just picking at your food."

With a fake angry pout, Morrigan let out a frustrated sigh and plopped down on the bench next to Nikaius, cradling Bec's head in an attempt to not jar him too much. Shifting to rest her cheek against Nikaius' shoulder, she nodded. "Fine. Whatever you want so that I can go too. I need to be sure it's safe for them." Looking around the dining hall, she thought about the number of people that had been displaced, the number of people that had nowhere to go.

"Good girl," Nikaius teased, catching her mouth in a kiss that reminded her of the night before. Fates, he could kiss. Being so easily lost to the world by a simple kiss was new, but it didn't last long enough. A throat clearing nearby sent Nikaius ripping away from her, snarling at whoever had interrupted them.

"Easy." Santi laughed. "I would let you finish your lunch, but this is pressing and cannot wait any longer. We've received word that the council will meet within the week, and our attendance has been requested." His eyes flicked to Morrigan. "All of us. Your parents wish for an audience as well."

"Go ahead and send them our acceptance. We can do dinner with them before the council event. Knock it all out in one go." Nikaius mused, glancing at Waric who nodded his approval.

It was weird to Morrigan that Santi would be the one to play messenger with Nikaius and his parents, but from what she had been told, the relationship between Nikaius and Nikola was one that was quite strained. Their issues mostly lay in the fact that he did not approve of Waric, nor Nikaius' methods of running Kunmei. How would he feel if he knew that Morrigan was now running the head of the Neutral Territories?

With the company she currently kept, it didn't really feel neutral to her, but she was still housing people from both Kunmei, Be'Sala, and The Pridelands under one roof, so that had to speak for something.

She had seen firsthand that people would reduce her to nothing more than her brand, and she would need to devise a plan to combat that.

Of all the things she had recently learned, the fact that sometimes magic had a mind of its own was the most baffling. She had never seen a house change its banners so easily as it had the day before when her people had declared her.

"I'll let them know." Santi gave them a smile, giving Morrigan's head an affectionate pat before he headed back the way he had come.

Finishing the rest of her sandwich, Morrigan caught Waric's eye and tilted her head, wondering if he could hear her.

I can. Waric's voice wasn't loud or as strong enough to give her flashes of events like the night before.

I don't think Nikaius should be traveling in his state. While she wasn't sure there was an explicit way to turn the thoughts off and on, she hoped that it wasn't needed in the long run.

I could argue that you don't need to be traveling either.

He just got back from being missing for several days because he was seriously injured. Mae and Santi are phenomenal healers, but they aren't gods. If my arm still aches, then his cannot feel good.

He's going to fight us on this.

If we get Aquila, Santi, and Hawke on our side, I don't think he'll have a choice.

"What are you two talking about?" Nikaius asked. Morrigan was shocked he somehow knew that she and Waric had been conversing, but before she could answer, he finished the last of his food and stood, offering his hand to her.

Unsure, Morrigan stared at his hand for a moment, wondering if he could somehow tell what she and Waric were talking about through their bond because he had heard it through the one he shared with Waric.

"Does sharing the bond between the two of us make you a sort of middle ground, Waric?" She knew the question was sudden, both Waric and Nikaius frowning down at her.

"I don't think so." Waric paused for a moment. "Nikaius, say something." Morrigan could instantly see what had prompted Nikaius to ask what they were talking about the moment before. Both Nikaius and Waric looked as if they were having a full conversation with just their facial expressions changing.

Did you catch any of that? Waric's voice flooded her mind for a moment. It was similar to when she touched people, but instead of going through her hands, it was like his magic was brushing against hers in her head.

I did not. Have you told him we think he should stay here?

I have not. I feel like that is a conversation that needs to happen in person.

Sighing gently, Morrigan knew Waric was right. Standing carefully, she offered her hand to Nikaius. "We have a bit of time before Silas comes back. Do you want to help me get Bec down again? I don't think I've quite mastered it yet." She knew using the baby as an excuse to get him alone was a poor one, but Waric was right, and addressing her concerns in private was the diplomatic thing to do.

"Mmm. I think I can do that." Nikaius' grin returned, and she accepted his hand hand, lacing their fingers together. The stars on his wrist matched up to hers, making it tingle. It was different from feeling his emotions because it was only skin deep and traveled quickly up her arm instead of making her feel like she was experiencing the emotions with him. It was weird that she could feel that way with him when all they shared at that moment was Waric's mark.

I'll go see if the others are ready and maybe catch Santi before he leaves.

Thank you. Morrigan accepted a gentle kiss from Waric before he nudged his nose against Bec's head and gave Nikaius a quick forehead bump.

Giving his hand a gentle squeeze, Morrigan led him out into the hall, and they headed towards the stairs. "Does it bother you?"

"What? That you marked him first?" Lifting their hands, he kissed Morrigan's knuckles gently. "I might be a bit jealous that you accepted his mark first, but in the long run, I don't think it matters too much. You're with all of us. As long as you don't start abandoning me for him, it won't bother me."

"I wouldn't dream of abandoning you." Morrigan smiled up at him as they climbed the stairs. She knew she needed to bite the bullet and just come out with her thoughts. Keeping them in wouldn't do anyone any favors. "I did want to talk to you about something though,"

"Oh yeah, what about?" He let her hand go to push open the door of their bedroom for her.

"It's about our marks."

"I have no idea what caused them. I'm also sorry I wasn't around when you got yours. I was so in my head, and Priamos was at the height of his nonsense. I was just not in a great place."

"Oh, no!" Morrigan stepped forward, taking his hand again. "No, I don't blame you for any of it. I got to experience Priamos in his true form for a bit, and I can see where he can be a handful when you're stuck with him all the time. I kind of get what it's like when you hit those dark patches. My demons sound like my mother and siblings. Sometimes it's hard to drown them out. But we're all working on it together." Holding Bec securely to her chest, she reached behind her to untie the wrap, letting it fall away from her shoulder. Bec blinked at her, and she smiled. "Hi baby," she whispered, pressing a kiss to his head as she worked the rest of the wrap off herself.

"That's very true." Nikaius agreed, carefully taking the wrap from her and folding it to set it on the table near the bed. "And now you have many different options of people who you can go to when you need them. You can't forget that you're building your own village as you go, Morrigan." He carefully took Bec from her, clicking his tongue as Bec stretched. The sound he gave made Morrigan giggle. It wasn't a whine but a gurgly coo that sounded quite happy.

"I'm glad he's getting settled, even though it's only been a day since we met." Morrigan pulled the things she needed to change Bec from one of the drawers as she spoke. Turning, she leaned against the dresser with a small smile. Seeing Nikaius with children did a funny thing to her heart. Any of them with Bec was endearing, both Waric and Hawke sharing the same amount of joy that Nikaius did whenever they held him. She was still unsure how their cautious peace would last, especially with everything else looming over them.

"It's really amazing how quickly the imprints work. I imagine Sable might have done it recently, but do you want to learn how to bathe him?" Nikaius seemed so serene swaying a bit as he cradled Bec in his arms, but Morrigan knew she couldn't delay much longer. The thought of ganging up on him made nerves twist in her stomach.

Turning back to gather the things she had set out, she blurted, "I don't think you should come to the Keep with us," into the quiet room. Preparing herself for backlash, she clutched Bec's things to her chest and cautiously turned to face Nikaius.

His eyebrows were pressed together as he looked down at Bec, tension bracketing his shoulders in a way that made him look more stiff than he had been moments before. "It's just..." She felt an overwhelming need to fill the silence and wanted to reach out to touch him, to know what he was feeling, but knew now would not be the time for that. "You just got back, and you're still injured. I can handle a stinging forearm, but your chest, Nikaius. That can't feel good."

"It only aches." Nikaius' voice was soft, as if he was talking to Bec instead of her. "But I understand where you're coming from."

"Someone needs to stay here to make sure Bastian doesn't come back, and who will stay with Bec? I know we won't be gone that long, but I couldn't, in good faith, just leave everyone here unprotected."

"So you think I'm well enough to defend a castle's worth of people but not well enough to travel?"

"Nikaius."

"You're being just as affected by this magic as I am, Morrigan. Are you going to stay back as well?"

"I..." She knew Aslin's belief on the matter would match what Nikaius thought, but she didn't know how to describe the burning desire she had to be there when they entered the Keep and to see it for the first time with the rest of them. "You've discovered so many new places, Nikaius. The entire world has been at your disposal since you were born. I can't explain it, but I just need to be there."

Whenever she thought about being there when they opened the doors to the Keep, she imagined it opening another door to herself.

"I don't know how to explain it, but I feel it in my entire being. This will change everything." She reached out to touch him then, to take his hand and press his palm over her heart.

The stoic look on his face dissolved. His hand curled into a fist, clutching her dress and giving it a gentle tug. Her hands flew to his chest as she stumbled towards him, bracing herself so Bec wouldn't get caught in between them. "I'm struggling with trusting you with your own mind, I must admit." His hand slid down, tracing over her chest for a moment before sliding across her waist to hold her to him as he adjusted his hold on Bec.

"I understand the draw to things. That's how we found you in the crowd during Selection Night. You were so tense and stressed. I worry about what will happen if I'm not there. I don't know what I would do if I lost any of you." His voice was soft as he rested his cheek on the top of her head, swaying them a bit. She understood the concern, could feel it when she slid her hand up his arm to stroke her fingers along the skin of Bec's cheek. Letting herself sink into his warmth, she gave a gentle sigh.

I think we're fine. Morrigan tossed into the ether, unsure if Waric would hear her but hoping she could reach him before he came in prepared for a fight.

Fine? Fine how?

He's worried about something happening to us without him nearby.

Of course he is. I think any of us would if we were put in his position. Waric's thoughts faded as footsteps in the bedroom alerted them to someone else's presence.

"You'll have to trust us to take care of her and each other." Waric spoke from the door. He smiled as he watched them.

"I do. This whole thing makes me nervous, though." Nikaius' words weren't a protest but more of an address of his concerns.

"Me too, but this might be what we're looking for. Once we've done a thorough sweep, we'll return, give a report of what we've found, and adjust our plan from there." Hawke stepped into the room, fluffing his wings as he entered. When they were in the privacy of their own room, he didn't wear them often, but with there being so many new people around, Morrigan wondered if he ever got tired of having his wings be on display.

"If something happens, you'll call me immediately? Bec can stay with Aslin or Sable for a while, he'll be fine. But I don't want to find out after the fact that something happened."

"You'll have constant access to me. I'll leave the bond open." Waric promised, reaching out to ruffle Nikaius' hair. The gesture made Nikaius turn and growl at him, which made Bec stir as well, giving his own squeal of approval.

"It's settled then?" Morrigan asked cautiously as she stepped away from the two tussling males. She wanted to reach for Bec, but he was staring at Nikaius and Waric with wide brown eyes as the two grumbled and growled at each other and at him.

"I'm not pleased about it, but I understand." Nikaius agreed with a nod.

The anxiety of there being a fight between them was eased by Nikaius' agreement, and Morrigan let out a slow, deep breath before giving her own nod. "Let's go ahead and settle Bec down for a nap and see what Silas has to say before figuring out what the next steps are." It was weird to be the one calling the shots, but she knew that if she misstepped, someone would be there to catch her.

Chapter Twenty-Five

Morrigan

The Western Keep

Her legs and hips ached. Everything ached.

Between the cold and sitting astride a horse for longer than she could remember ever being, Morrigan almost wished she had taken Aslin's suggestion to stay and wait. The unknown had driven her to insisting on joining the trip to the Keep. Every time she thought about it, the more convinced she was that this was the right move. This was needed to be done and something great would happen on the other side.

After spending more than an hour on the horse with Hawke, she understood why it had taken Silas so long to return to them despite there being a portal. Morrigan wasn't a good judge of distance, but Silas had said it was about a two-hour walk between the Keep and the closest accessible magic. For reasons they couldn't explain, no one was able to teleport into areas that were touched by the ice. It wasn't typical winter precipitation but something that felt *wrong*.

She couldn't explain how it was wrong, only that it made her feel restless and on edge, like an oily lotion on her skin.

Rolling her shoulders, she sighed, gently trying to find some semblance of comfort for the third time in as many minutes. "Just a bit longer, Morrigan." Hawke murmured into her hair as he pressed a kiss to the back of her head again.

He didn't know how far they had to go either.

Before she could let out an exasperated groan, they rounded a bend that opened into a wide-open clearing. She felt the tingle of magic that signified they were breaching some sort of ward, but Morrigan hoped that the area wasn't monitored by Bastian's people.

If it had been, they would have heard something about it before then, wouldn't they?

Roads spread out before them, their pavement cracked and worn. They weaved their horses cautiously between abandoned vessels, some overgrown with plants, small saplings twisting towards the sky on the side of the road. Others were turned over with nothing remaining but charred metal endoskeletons that had long since faded into rusted carcasses.

"What happened?" Though she whispered, her voice sounded out of place and louder than she intended.

"The continent used to flourish with an abundance of human, Fae, and Rekru'e. Things changed quickly when human scientists went too far." Hawke's response was distant, his arm banding a bit tighter around Morrigan's stomach as he held her closer.

"What do you mean, 'went too far'?" Morrigan tried to turn and look at Hawke, but he gripped her hip, spreading his fingers wide before curling them into the shirt at her side. Waric pinched the bridge of his nose as Hawke sighed heavily.

She hated how evident it was that they were only telling the story for her benefit. Everyone else in their party remained silent as their horses trotted through the slurry of mud and snow underfoot. She knew they didn't think less of her because of her lack of knowledge, but sometimes it did make her feel a little small. It was a reminder of the hit her education had taken when her role had changed within her family.

History, like religion, hadn't been something she learned. Especially things that didn't directly affect their family, including things that the Rekru'e went through.

"Medical advances at that time for us, well, Rekru'e in particular, had been great. About a century ago, changeling women were given suppressants that gave them the opportunity to go to school without being forced to miss time due to their heat. About two decades later, another suppressant hit the market, aimed at males so they could control their rut and no longer have to be segregated from others during volatile years."

Morrigan looked over her shoulder at Hawke. "No one ever mentioned—"

"This was over a hundred years ago, Morrigan. Things have changed."

Waric continued, and Hawke squeezed Morrigan gently around the waist. "After so long, the council, the mortal leader included, allowed genetic markups to be done on volunteers to suppress the Rekru'e gene altogether for those who had genetic histories that would make passing on the gene dangerous. Gnat's Syndrome was a thing they were trying to cure. It's a condition where once the beast presents, the person stays half beast their entire lives."

Morrigan gasped, "Like Gryffin?" She thought of the redheaded, cat-eared boy who had stepped up and offered his and his friends' assistance in the kitchens during the flood. He was kind and sweet.

"Mmm. Typically, Gnat's Syndrome leads to increased aggression and unstable personalities. Or it used to. In lieu of sterilization, the volunteers were allowed to procreate in captivity." Waric's face twisted, and he cleared his throat before looking at Hawke.

"What? Why that face?" She turned so quickly she almost fell off the horse, swaying with a yelp before Hawke hauled her back against his chest.

"Fucking Fates Morrigan, quit moving." Hawke's frustration bleed through into his tone, and they both froze, her breath hitching in her throat. She knew emotions were high and there was a lot going on, but Hawke had never raised his voice to her. The display of sudden aggression was startling, making tears well in her eyes. She gave a shaky little nod, tugging her cloak closer around her.

"Morrigan..." Hawke's voice softened, and his arms around her eased so he could take the reins from her. Gathering them into one hand, he maneuvered his glove off the other one and rested it, palm up on her thigh. "Sweetheart, you can get seriously hurt if you fall off the horse. You know this."

"I know," she whispered. Morrigan intimately knew the dangers of falling off a horse. It was how she and Mae had met Santi the year before. She would have died if they hadn't come across him when they did.

Giving another small nod, Morrigan tugged her own glove off and slid her hand into his, lacing their fingers together. His heat warmed her cold hand, and his worry seeped into her through the connection. Worry and affection.

"It didn't end well for the children who were born like that, Morrigan." Santi continued their story; his voice muffled a bit by the scarf covering half his face. He seemed even more bothered by the cold than the rest of them, but Morrigan couldn't blame him. Spending nearly all his life in the heated sands of The Pridelands would make the cold jarring and even more uncomfortable than it was to someone who grew up in the mountains. "The ones who had the genetic markers were killed, and the process started over. Basically, Changelings were being bred to have designer babies."

"They succeeded." Aquila responded from her right. "My grandmother spoke about it once. A healer by the name of Charles Alistar came out and told everyone the truth. The mortals weren't trying to purify Fae-blood. No, they were out to eradicate us for good. Full-blooded Fae and Changelings were having fully mortal babies. There were twelve being raised in captivity until the militia broke in and destroyed everything, including all the genetic material and the research that had been gathered over that century. Even the children were killed. Our kind called for the eradication of the mortals and when the time came, those who opposed were slaughtered. Anyone with Fae blood that could prove it were recruited under martial law to collect anyone that was found attempting to flee the continent."

"Our grandmother had a journal." Silas, who had been silent for most of the conversation, looked at Santi with a frown. "She had been eleven when it happened. Her best friend was playing with her one moment and then being stolen away the next. At one point, warfare began and the entire world just... stopped. Why do you think there is so much of the continent that is inhabitable?"

"I thought it had always been that way. I had never really thought about it, to be honest. My days were too full of other things that required my attention and no one to teach me." She sighed softly and shifting to settle her weight further back against Hawke as a chilled wind swept through the area. Even if it wasn't winter, she would still feel cold at hearing the story. "So, many people died?"

"Mmhm." Hawke leaned forward to rest his chin on her shoulder. He took a slow breath, and she mimicked him.

"They say the Fates themselves took matters into their own hands. The only recollections of any of this happening are in books and the memories of those who lived on the outskirts of the continent. The council is made up of the heads of each family..." Waric's voice died away as he looked back at them.

"There were twenty-four original families, I believe, but I think out of the twenty-four, only twelve speak for the continent now."

"Why only twelve?"

"Some of the families have died down or become encompassed by others, our mothers, for instance. They had no brothers, so the names died with our grandfathers. Many believe that was the consequence given by the Fates. In our parents' time, for every three females, there was one male. And then some of those males didn't want power. So, the names in power diminished to twelve, though heads for most of the twenty-four are still alive, it's just uncommon for a female to be given leadership of the family after her father's death but some—"

"—You" Waric laughed.

"Have achieved it." Hawke gave her another gentle squeeze.

"Hopefully it will be seen as an achievement once the council meets again." Morrigan sighed. She knew what she was doing was important and would affect many people, but she was still worried that the majority of the council would be like Atyon who only saw her mark, not her capabilities.

"We'll cross that bridge when we come to it. Right now, we need to focus on figuring out how to melt ice that cannot be melted." Silas, who Morrigan had met a few times when he came to her house with Santi, typically held the same playful, always grinning demeanor as Waric. But neither of them smiled now, their eyes alert as they kept their attention to their surroundings.

Though they had been debriefed about what they were about to encounter, neither Morrigan nor her pack knew what they would face when they entered the forest on the other side of the plain.

The freezing rain started as soon as they entered the tree line. It was similar to the winters she experienced as a child, the entire world encased in crystalline ice that shattered like glass when their horses brushed against the needles and twigs of the evergreens that surrounded them. There was evidence that something or someone had come through the area before them as not everything they touched broke, shedding ice, which led Morrigan to wonder if this was the same path Silas and Aquila had taken to get to the Keep or if they should expect visitors on the other side of the dense forest. The foliage was so thick that they could hear the ice hitting the leaves over their heads, and Morrigan watched as small fragments of ice tumbled to the ground, but she wasn't assaulted by the chill of tiny drops of ice.

Time felt like it dragged on with only the sound of ice and the hooves of their horses, and Morrigan wasn't sure how far they had come, or how much further they had to go because she couldn't see anything other than iced evergreens and foliage no matter which direction she looked.

After what felt like another hour, Morrigan noticed that the trees slowly became less dense and the temperature dropped quickly, making her tremble and shift back to seek out more of Hawke's warmth.

Where they exited the forest gave them a good vantage point for the entire area, and Morrigan gasped as she took in the view. Even covered in a thick sheet of ice, the land before her was beautiful. Though it was called the Western Keep, it reminded her more of what she pictured Starsgard to be on the outside.

Either no houses had been built between them and the steep descent from the hill or they had all been destroyed long ago, because the Keep stood isolated, nothing outside of its walls.

The first wall was encased in ice so thick it went up and over the wall, but she couldn't tell how far on the other side it went. A second wall sat between the first and the Keep, protecting it and the series of buildings set around it. The icicles that hung from every surface made it look like an angry maw of teeth snarling up at them.

As beautiful as it was encased in its dangerous ice, Morrigan wondered what it had looked like during the warmer months. It matched the thoughts that had drawn her to join them to begin with. There was a perfect amount of space to initiate as farmland, rows and rows of corn and beans could be grown on one side of the road, and root vegetables and other lower-lying crops on the other. There was plenty of space for farm animals as well.

A market like Kunmei's would take up one portion of the buildings inside the first wall, with residences on the other and everyone spreading out from there. The main building of the Keep was grand, several stories tall and with three areas each as wide as Starsgard. They could definitely work with it. Making sure it was habitable and getting others access to it would be the starting point, then they would need to figure out if there was a way to allow the people of Barnam to take it over.

"I don't think we can cross any further with the horses. The path is steep through here, and I'm worried there will be injuries we cannot fix if we try." Hawke looked around with a frown. Morrigan could see where he was coming from with his concern. The entire hillside shimmered in a thick sheet of slick ice, and she couldn't tell what the muddy dirt path hid.

There was no movement for a moment as everyone took in the scene below them. "I remember reading about this place when I was a child, during history lessons. This was where the research was being done." Silas murmured before being shushed by Santi. Morrigan was waiting for someone else to move first, to break the spell of curiosity and awe, to take the first steps into uncharted territories.

A gust of wind scattered snow around them, as if the world was angry at them for bringing up the atrocities that had happened.

"We'll make it right." Morrigan vowed. She meant it. She had plans to make the Keep habitable again, to give the people of Barnam some place to call their own once again. This place was part of her neutral territories, so they would be safe from any other lord trying to exert their rule over them. This would be a place of sanctuary for any who wished it.

As everyone dismounted, Waric waved to someone in the distance. "Soren and the others are waiting at the initial gate for us." He announced. Hawke held out his hands for Morrigan as she shifted so he could help her down.

"What do you think we'll find there?" she asked, tugging her hood over her head. Without Hawke's warmth bracketing her body, she was chilled. She knew she should have stayed home, but something important was about to happen, and she still couldn't figure out what insisted she *needed* to be here.

"I'm honestly not sure. It's been so long since anyone has been here." Silas turned to them, his eyes jumping from one person to another with an assessing gaze. Morrigan wondered what he was looking for, and what he saw that made him continue. "We have to be careful making our way down, there are some places where the ice is quite vicious. We've already had a few injuries."

"Stay close." Waric tucked Morrigan's hand into the crook of his elbow before Silas led them along the edge of the forest to where a set of stairs sat.

"At least there's a rail." Aquila gave a sarcastic laugh, reaching out to grab it as she made a tentative step down onto the first step.

Chapter Twenty-Six

Morrigan

The Western Keep

Climbing down the stairs was slow going, and Morrigan almost fell more than once. She was thankful that Hawke and Waric were both close when her footing became unsteady. "Finally!" she gasped when they found the end of the path and had met up with the rest of their party. "I'm so glad we're here."

"Stay safe, please. Your sister would have my head if you do otherwise." Santi gave her a pat on the head before turning to speak with those gathered.

Two of the people with them had drawn sigils into the ice and were working on connecting flames to them. Morrigan remembered that Silas had said that they hadn't been able to get through the ice by normal means, would fire work?

Their efforts blanketed their world with steam, making it hard to see around them, but she could still hear Santi discussing plans with others.

Come. Voices suddenly filled the air, coming from all directions, none of which she recognized.

This way. Morrigan's throat closed with the overwhelming sensation of fear that filled the air and coated her skin.

Over here. Whomever was calling her was afraid, so very afraid, and it terrified her. It was unusual to feel emotions throughout her entire body, but this fear was all-encompassing and blending with hers to make her whole body feel like ice. Like she was wearing nothing while standing in the icy rain. She looked around, hoping to see if someone else was having the same experience, but she couldn't see anything through the steam.

Come. This voice was different from the others, a deeper, more guttural sounding voice. Like someone who hadn't spoken for a long time. With it came an overwhelming surge of magic that froze her in place. She couldn't scream, couldn't move, and could barely breathe through the panic that welled through her.

This way. She felt completely paralyzed when dark figures materialized out of thin air.

Over here. Cold breaths on the back of her neck made her tremble and suddenly the magic scattered, causing her to jerk forward and stumble, slipping to fall on the ice she had forgotten was under her feet. Catching herself on her hands and knees was akin to Selection Night, but no one was around to torment or save her there. Not that she could determine anyways. When she tried to climb to her feet, she fell again, and it took several tries for her to be able to regain her footing. Once she was upright again, she found nothing was near her. The world was hazy and white, but not really a world at all. It almost felt like she had somehow stepped into another realm.

"Hawke?" He had been right beside her a few moments before. The steam was still so heavy around her, but the world had gone silent. It felt like someone stepped up next to her, but when she swung out with a hand, nothing was there. Everything tingled, and she felt like she wasn't quite attached to her body anymore, her heart fluttering a thousand miles a minute as she tried to scan the area again. She knew it was futile, but she couldn't help hoping that someone who could help her out of whatever was happening would appear.

You missed, try again, little girl. This voice sounded a lot like Elijah, the taunting jeer one he had used towards her when she was a child. There was no way he was the cause of this though, was there?

Was she finally losing her mind?

A spectral figure appeared, backed by ghostly others at his side and Morrigan let out another scream before turning and running. She attempted to return to her group, but the steam surrounding her was so disorienting that she wasn't sure where they were, and her feet felt like they couldn't make any traction on the ice even though she had only touched Waric a few moments ago.

Wrong way. Keep going.

Tears welled in her eyes as Morrigan ran, ghostly fingers pulling at her until her clothes were tattered, and her skin was shredded and bleeding, but she couldn't stop. She couldn't stop moving, couldn't stop running, no longer moving just out of fear, but compulsion as well.

Come.

Something swung into her chest out of nowhere, freezing her breath in her throat and knocking her back roughly, throwing her off her feet. The soggy ground she had just run over fell away from under her, falling into freezing water. She flailed as she tried to figure out which way was up, tried to figure out how to make her arms and legs work as they prickled with near numbness. She needed to get herself free from the water, her fear turning to pure terror as she accidentally inhaled a mouth full of water before finding her way to the surface. "Help!" Her voice was a desperate plea that escaped before she found herself underwater again.

She had never learned how to swim and there was nothing beneath her feet. Panic seared through her.

WARIC?! She tried to scream through the bond, hoping he would be able to find her through their connection. She couldn't hear him but could still feel a brief tingle of magic that seemed distant and far away.

As she flailed her hands, desperate to find anything to help her, she made contact with the edge of something rough and uncomfortable to hold on to. She tried to pull herself up, coughing and gagging around mouthfuls of water that she had swallowed in her panic. With some relief, she hauled herself up onto the outcropping of rock that seemed to lead further into a cave.

Her throat was raw, her skin and hair clung to her, and blood welled in the cuts that she had acquired by whatever had ripped at her skin as she cried out between heaves.

Come.

The cave that she was in was so cold that her skin stuck to the floor and made it instantly numb. She knew she would lose skin as she stood, but she didn't feel as if she had a choice but to stand and try to escape. The pain of removing herself from the ice was only brief, the world too cold and quickly numbing her again as she stood and stepped forward. The sounds of voices in her head, the feeling of chilled hands on her body, pressed her forward as water dripped from her shredded clothes and hair.

Looking behind her, all she saw was mostly darkness, the barest amount of light from the chasm overhead reflecting off the water she had just pulled herself out of, giving her a bit of illumination to see by. The only direction she could go was deeper into the cave, and part of her worried that leaving would make it harder for people to find her. A sudden gale of icy wind whipping through the cavern made her stumble back, her shoulders making contact with ice before she jerked away and turned. Morrigan lost her footing again, stumbling forward and catching herself against ice she hadn't noticed before. It was blocking the entrance to the rest of the cave.

She would be surprised if she had any skin left on her body if this ordeal ever ended as she pulled her palm away. The ache of her palm mimicked the one in her knees and feet, but the odd wall caught her attention again. Instead of cloudy, however, the ice was crystalline and clear, like the panes of a window or the glass of a mirror. She stared into the clear pane for a moment, only to see her own reflection before it morphed.

A figure, tall and fair with dark brown hair and a crown of thorns and roses, stood before her on the other side of the ice, replacing Morrigan's reflection. Jerking away, she turned to look behind her, anticipating him to be standing right there, however, here was nothing but the dim cave and the water. Turning, she faced him once again.

She surmised she was hallucinating at this point. It was far too cold for her to retain her sanity for longer than twenty minutes while her body temperature slowly decreased. The way her reflection had shifted was surely evidence of that. She felt too hot inside even though she was freezing on the outside, her entire body trembling with how she shivered. The only thing not making her dizzy was focusing on the form in front of her, even though she was sure it was a hallucination.

His outfit was made of foliage, and his feet were bare as well, but he seemed to feel nothing of the cold as his blood-red lips parted in a brilliant smile. "You have found me at last, little one." His silvery voice echoed around the cavern as he reached out his hand through the ice to offer it to Morrigan. "Don't worry, angel, I'll keep you safe."

"I'll keep you safe." When he repeated the phrase, his face changed, a dark, devious grin spreading across it.

Something within her screamed to not trust him, and she stumbled back, trying to get away. Her cold skin sliced against the stone of the wall of the cave as she slipped again, trying to keep herself upright, before landing on her back, her head smacking hard onto the floor. She saw stars for a moment and the world went black. When vision came back to her, the figure had become corporeal, leaning over her with that same dark grin. She threw up her hand, blood from her palm dripping down her arm as she tried to block him from view, to defend herself from him, or block him from her view. She needed to focus on something else. When he grasped her hand, they both screamed as electricity sparked across their skin, a keraunographic mark tracing searing patterns of thorns and vines up their arms and across their chests.

Morrigan screamed as he shoved her away, her head hitting the floor again. She wasn't sure how much longer she could deal with the sudden influx of pain she was beginning to feel. Starbursts clouded Morrigan's vision again as she watched the figure try to scrub the mark from his arm. "Who are you?" she asked.

A dark smile spread across the man's face once more as the voices in her head returned slowly, growing louder, from a soft moan to a full roar, louder and louder until Morrigan had to cover her ears. The pressure built until it hurt every fiber of Morrigan's being, and all she could do was hold her hands over her ears and scream.

The silence was so sudden, and the pressure disappeared so quickly, it made her dizziness worse. Bile and water and other unknown things spilled from her stomach. A word, a name flashed across her consciousness, and she scrambled to her feet. Kumnei.

Terror flooded through her again, making her bones ache as she turned and tried to run. She needed to get out of there. Now.

Looking around, she wasn't sure which way was out, but as she pressed her palm to the iced wall to stabilize herself, it vanished, leaving only smooth, dark stone underneath her hands and feet.

Somehow, the ice had receded, and she found herself in a large, wide room. The only furniture was scattered broken beds and chairs, a table on its side against a wall. Morrigan wondered what the room had once been. Other, more inconclusive piles of wood and fabric sat in the corners of the room, as if someone had simply pushed all the debris aside, and Morrigan imagined that was where the scent of rot was coming from.

"Morrigan?!" voices called for her and one of the doors to her left crashed open. Nikaius stood there staring at her for a moment before stepping forward.

Letting out a loud sob, she threw herself at him, clinging to him as he kissed every inch of her face he could find. "What happened? How did you get in here?"

"Kumnei. It was Kumnei. He's here. I felt him. I saw him! He's here."

His skin was so warm compared to hers that she snuggled as close as she could. "What did you do? Where did you go? You've been gone for hours." Though the timeframe felt ridiculous, it had to have held some truth, right? They had left Starsgard and Bec in Nikaius' care. For him to be there meant something had happened, and Waric had alerted Nikaius.

She shook her head frantically. "It felt like it was only a few minutes." She could hear her clothes dripping onto the floor, and her skin ached from where it had touched the ice. Twisting pain still lingered up her arm and through her shoulder, but she knew if she mentioned it, her men would be alarmed, and she would probably be sent home. She didn't even want to look to see if it was still there, afraid of whatever the truth held.

"Another temporal shift?" Nikaius questioned as he looked over his shoulder when the door slammed open again. His arms tightened around her, and a snarl ripped through his throat as he turned Morrigan away from the sudden entrance. Swords drawn, Waric and Hawke barreled in, looking around for any threats. Spotting Nikaius, Waric was the first to lower his weapons, but Hawke remained alert, his wings flared, and his eyes never resting on one thing for more than a moment.

"Are you alright?" Waric asked, taking off his cloak and wrapping it tight around Morrigan. His hand brushed against where the lightning marks had been seared into her flesh and it stung, making her jump a bit, but neither of her men said anything. Had they not seen it? Was it even still there?

Nothing about what had happened made sense, but it all did at the same time. "I think Kumnei has a part in this. I saw him." Nikaius frowned at her as others entered the room. She could tell from the way he looked at her that he didn't believe her. Neither Hawke nor Waric said anything even as she turned to look for them to see how they felt.

"Let's get this place cleared so we can find somewhere to rest and regroup so we can figure out where to go from here." Hawke announced before heading towards the door across the room.

"Aye. I agree." Santi nodded, gesturing for Silas and a few of his men to head to check the other doors off the room Morrigan had found herself in. "How are you doing?" he asked. She knew that he wouldn't be able to heal physical injuries without salve, and she was still unsure whether she wanted to know if the mark on her arm still existed.

"I've got a few cuts, but nothing that the healing salve can't fix."

"Once we get everything cleared, we can head home and tend to them. Right now, I don't think we have access to the ether. Do you have anything pressing that needs to be looked at?" Waric asked, reaching out to stroke his thumb along a spot on her cheek that stung.

"No. I think it's mostly just scrapes and scratches, nothing that seriously hurts." She wasn't lying. Of all the things she felt, pain wasn't one that came to the forefront of her mind. As she snuggled into Nikaius' embrace, all she felt was warmth where their skin touched. She couldn't pick up any emotions from him in the state she was in, but his expression didn't give her any reason to believe he thought she was lying.

As the others headed off to investigate more areas of the Keep, Nikaius kept Morrigan against his chest until her shivering subsided. "We'll get you some dry clothes once we're sure that there will be no more surprises," he promised.

"This portion of the Keep is clear." Silas stepped in through another door and smiled, wiping his hands on his pants. "Nothing seems to be in too poor a state. We're going to try to set up some portals in the galley to get supplies."

"This door leads out to a walkway that joins this side to the other, overarching the entrance. We're on the third story." Waric brushed snow off his pants as he entered from where he had come from. Morrigan wasn't sure if he was explaining it for everyone's benefit, or just hers, but Nikaius gave a nod as he rubbed his hand carefully up and down Morrigan's back.

"Are you going to send me back?" Morrigan asked softly, resting her cheek against Nikaius' chest. She wouldn't fault him if he did, but she didn't want to go just because of some mishap involving a rogue god.

Had it really been him?

"No darling," Nikaius leaned back to look at her, stroking her wet hair from her face. "There's no sense in sending you back. We don't really have an easy way to go back just yet."

"How did you get here?"

"The same way you did. It took us hours to find you." Right, she had forgotten that part. It had felt like only a few moments had passed when she encountered Kumnei. "Let's just get you settled and warmed up while Waric and the others gather supplies."

One of Santi's troops, the female who controlled fire, stoked an ember to life in the nearest fireplace. "Has anyone seen if we have access to the ether again?"

There were murmured answers, all to the negative. Turing to Nikaius again, she frowned at him. "Since the ice is gone maybe you can try again?"

Nikaius nodded and closed his eyes. Morrigan watched him concentrate for a moment before he reached out and snagged one of the blankets from their bed from the ether.

"Looks like the wards are down." Bundling Morrigan up in the blanket on top of Waric's cloak, he sat her down in front of the fire with a kiss to the top of her head. "Don't move. We'll take it from here and then we can explore later." Morrigan sighed gently but obeyed.

"I feel like I'm just in the way," she mused aloud, and Aquila hummed from behind her.

"You are." Before Morrigan could be offended, Aquila offered her a clean set of clothes and turned away with crossed arms, flaring her wings out, so Morrigan was mostly blocked from view as she continued speaking. "But that doesn't mean that you're not needed. Being trained to fight first and think second doesn't really leave room for much else when you're in a new place. Do I wish you could have waited until we had gotten the Keep cleared before coming? Yeah." As Aquila spoke, Morrigan began to change, letting her wet clothes plop to the ground in a damp puddle at her feet. It gave her time to look at the marks on her arm. If she didn't know it was there, Morrigan could almost think it was just scrapes along her skin. The mark was mostly hidden by Waric's along her wrist and forearm but spread up her biceps and across her shoulder. It was pale red but still burned to the touch.

"The fact of the matter is that if someone were to come here, they would need some evidence that Nikaius and Santi weren't just here to cause trouble." Aquila's words brought Morrigan from her thoughts, and she continued dressing.

"The same could be said about Starsgard, and I hope nothing happens while we're away. Aslin can only do so much." Morrigan agreed. To have Aquila's approval meant more to Morrigan than she realized. Every time she and Aquila or Aslin spent time alone, Morrigan remembered just how jilted she had been by the women she should have been closest to. As she changed, Morrigan thought about how far her relationships with others had come.

Aquila continued, her words mirroring Morrigan's thoughts in an interesting way. "Males are raised and trained to have a one-track mind, and that was to protect and conquer. We're socialized to be more caring and compassionate and though sometimes it does us a disservice, I don't think it's a flaw or should be overlooked just because it's your method of leading." When Morrigan had finished dressing, she stepped around Aquila's wings to give her friend a smile. "Watching you grow and learn yourself and what you want has been an honor. I hope you know that." Letting her wings fall, Aquila offered her hand to Morrigan. "I know we've been a bit absent, but I hope you know that Aslin and I both care for you very much and are proud of the growth you've made."

Unable to control the well of adoration and affection that flared through her, Morrigan let out a small, sobbed laugh and threw her arms around Aquila's waist to hug her. Having someone openly announce they were proud of her made Aquila's acceptance of how Morrigan wanted to lead even more potent. Amara and Delaney had always been the type to lead with force or backstabbing and belittling. Any way to gain control was acceptable in their eyes.

To have Aquila acknowledge that she agreed with how Morrigan was trying to do things made a world of difference to her. It made her feel seen and heard in a way that was different from how Nikaius, Waric, and Hawke made her feel. While they made her feel valued and understood to an extent, the support from Aquila was different and almost meant more in the grand scheme of things. This was another woman on her side. Someone who wouldn't tell her she needed to sit down and be quiet because Aquila had thrown the mantle of that expectation out the window when she had become the commander of Nikaius' guard.

Being prim and proper was not Aquila's style and to know that Aquila respected Morrigan as she was meant more to her than she could express in words. As Morrigan hugged herself close to Aquila, the other woman shared in the laugh, pressing her hand through Morrigan's hair.

"It's alright. I've got you. We all have you." Aquila hugged Morrigan back, and they stood like that for a few moments.

Chapter Twenty-Seven

Morrigan

The Western Keep

When Santi returned after several minutes, he offered her a container of salve. "This one is a bit more potent than what we usually provide, but it doesn't heal whatever magic created Nikaius' mark." Morrigan accepted it with a smile.

"I'm sure it will do fine." As he left again, Morrigan turned away to face the fire again. Aquila returned to her spot to hide her from view with her wings once again. Carefully, Morrigan opened the container and applied it to what scrapes she could find, smoothing it over both of her palms and her arms before sitting so she could apply it to the burning places on the bottom of her feet and her shins where she had knelt on the icy cave floor.

It only took a few moments, but after the cuts on her arms and legs had healed, she had put the smallest amount of the salve on the handprint on her arm and the mark she had gotten from Kumnei. Neither of them healed like the cuts on her hands had. Securing the lid of the jar, she adjusted her clothes and stood. She needed socks and shoes if she was going to continue through the keep with the others. Clutching the salve in one hand, she held out the other, closing her eyes and thinking about a pair of tights she had seen in her drawer earlier in the day. Still unsure about how exactly one pulled things from the ether, she wiggled her fingers and imagined picking them up from the drawer. When that didn't work, she imagined just pulling them out of thin air like she had seen others do, but that didn't work either. Letting out a heavy disappointed sigh, she turned to Aquila.

"You can tuck this away for now. We'll give it back to Santi." As she offered out the salve, she gave a surprised laugh. In her hand, under the salve, was the set of tights she had imagined grabbing. "Tights!"

Turning, Aquila looked at her with concern before she gave her own laugh, accepting the salve. "Did you get those on your own?"

"I got them on my own!" the flood of joy that spread through Morrigan was overwhelming, and she couldn't help the excited squeal she squeaked as she clutched the garment to her chest and bounced on her toes.

"Everything alright in here?" Hawke dusted snow from his hair as he approached the door, looking between Morrigan and Aquila.

"I pulled something by myself!" Morrigan announced, offering them out like an award she had won.

"That's amazing!" The same joy that Morrigan felt spread across Hawke's face as he stepped into the room and scooped Morrigan into a hug. "I think your magic is getting stronger."

"Me too." Stepping back away from him, she looked at her hands and then around the room. "I need shoes." Closing her eyes, she tried to remember what she had done to get the tights, but she didn't know when they had appeared or how, so she went through the same motions again. Opening her eyes, she instantly noticed that neither had worked.

"It takes time to do it on purpose every time." Aquila reassured her. "It's still a really new skill, like teleporting, so it's not going to work every single time for a while. Do you want me to get them for you?"

Morrigan knew she shouldn't feel disappointed, but her glee dampened a bit. "Please. That way, we can complete our evaluation and go home."

When Morrigan had her tights and boots on, they met the others in the room they had started in. It didn't take much time for them to go through the wing they were in and the main building, but when they reached the end of the eastern wing, Silas waited for them at the door that would allow them access to what had once been the chapel. "You'll want to move quick through this chamber, it's not a pretty sight." Silas whispered as he adjusted the cloak on his shoulders as if it made him uncomfortable.

Entering the chamber, Morrigan stared in horror at the scene in front of her. It appeared as if something had blown the entire roof off, something that they hadn't seen in their perusal of it from high up on the hill. Large columns were knocked over, shattered into a million places in some areas. What Morrigan imagined were regal stone statues were half dissolved and intersecting with large puddles of dark liquid. The entire room smelled like something had rotted, but also like hot, fresh blood.

It was silent except for the drips of water from the ceiling and the breathing of her party. She imagined it had been some type of art gallery. Though they were smeared with darkness, Morrigan imagined the images on the walls had once been beautiful as well. Winged women forever encompassed in eternal slumber.

As she approached the one closest to them, Morrigan reached out to touch it but gasped and jerked her hand away.

The woman she had touched was not a painting! Were any of them? Inspecting the one in front of her closer, Morrigan realized that these beings had been pinned to the walls by their wings. This one still breathed but didn't seem to be conscious. Morrigan couldn't imagine the pain that they would feel if they were awake. The sound of dripping she thought was water was actually blood dripping into the puddle at Morrigan's feet. The wounds on the people who hung from the walls were new, they had all been caused recently. Someone had come through and done this shortly before they had arrived. Were they trying to make it look like Morrigan, Santi, and Nikaius were leaving a path of destruction in their wake instead of trying to prevent it?

She wouldn't stand for that. "We can't leave them like this." Her voice was hoarse as she made her declaration. It sounded more like a plea than what she had meant but dropping her cloak to the ground, she looked back at the others. These were sentient beings that had their own thoughts and feelings, maybe even families that missed them, and she couldn't just walk past without trying to do something.

"Morrigan," Hawke caught Morrigan's elbow, and she turned to him with a frown. She wasn't sure if he was going to tell her no, or if he was going to help her, but she wasn't going to give him the choice. Not this time.

"No." Voice breaking, Morrigan's shook her head, wrenching her arm from Hawke's grasp. "This is my territory. It doesn't matter if we did this or not. If we leave them and someone like Bastian shows up, people are going to think that we did this. You cannot ask me to leave living creatures pinned to a wall even if I was in the heart of Be'Sala. These beings need saving." As she turned, she caught the look Aquila gave Hawke but didn't comment. Clenching her fists to her sides, she shook her head. "Even if all they do is succumb to their wounds, I would rather it be with dignity than to be strung up like an animal on display." Her entire body trembled as she stepped over the corpse of a stone wyvern, stomach turning as she slipped in the slick black blood that pooled next to it.

The impact of the stone ground hurt, sending a flair of pain through her hands and knees. The blood was still warm and had partly congealed, leaving a sticky, goopy surface underneath her hands. Someone reached for her, trying to offer their hand, but she refused it, swatting them away before standing again. The lives of others were not something she allowed to be taken lightly.

Her compassion did not end with the people of Barnam. It would encompass the entirety of Cav'Sara if she had her way. Letting out a trembling breath, she gagged quietly as she wiped her hands on the fresh clothes she had just changed into. The smell of hot blood and death was even stronger now that she was covered in it.

They would pay for this.

"Morrigan." She didn't look over her shoulder as Santi called after her. She squeezed her eyes tight and took a deep breath before wiping her hands on her pants again, trying to make them stop trembling.

Carefully, she hauled herself up onto one of the fallen pillars. The stone fixture had fallen between where two of the Valkyrie were pinned, but remained mostly intact, giving her a platform to attempt to help from. Grateful that her balance wasn't too uneven, she managed to make her way carefully to the wall.

That was where her plan faltered. Reaching as far as she could, even on her toes, she couldn't quite reach the bolt that was lodged into one wing. There had to be another way, but she didn't know of any weapon that could help her. She couldn't pull things from the ether, and she didn't want to ask Hawke for help. He didn't seem to agree with her decision to help, even though she was sure he understood her motivations.

This portion of the Keep was the last place that needed to be secure as they believed it to be closest to the encampment that Nikaius and Waric were making plans to raid. Though they had an idea of where the encampment was, no one seemed to be able to see it and, in their desperation, to get to it before anyone else did so there was little surprise in Morrigan's mind that they hadn't even stopped to evaluate the room she stood in.

Hot tears scalded her cheeks as she pressed her forehead to the wall, taking a heaving breath through her nose. Maybe she should have stayed at Starsgard. Maybe everyone was right, and she was more of a liability than an asset at times like this. No one had said it directly to her face, but she knew it had been mentioned.

But would they be where they were without her? She was pretty sure she was the reason the ice had disappeared. Whatever had happened between her and Kumnei seemed to have been the catalyst to that, as the ice was gone when she came back from wherever he had taken her. The people of Barnam would have a safe place to reside, and these beings would be saved by her. Though she had saved the people of Barnam with help it was her decisions that had led them down those paths, and she refused to accept that there would be any other outcome than them no longer being strung up on the walls on display.

She would accept the risk that they may die, but with it came an even higher chance that she could save them.

A hand at the back of her knee drew her attention away from where her thoughts were going, and she looked down to find Hawke standing on the floor next to where she was balanced on the pillar. His shoulders where he stood reached her shins. She braced for another reprimand, another explanation of why they couldn't, shouldn't, save the others, but none came. Instead, Hawke stepped closer, wrapping his arm carefully around Morrigan's ankles.

"If you stand on my shoulders, you can reach better. If we do it right, I might be able to keep them from falling too hard too." Gratitude flooded through Morrigan so quickly, she let out another soft sob before nodding quickly. It was still weird to not be forced into submission by those stronger than her.

"We don't have time for this," one of the De'Lyon's rangers grumbled, but Morrigan didn't look back to argue. This was something she could do. If he didn't like it, he could carry on without them. Two people did not make an army.

Carefully, she stepped onto Hawke's shoulders and steadied herself against the wall. With Hawke's added height, Morrigan was able to reach the bolt and relief curled through her. Wiping her hands around the wood, she tried to pull, to break it, but it was a thicker bolt, and it would take more force than she was capable of.

"I need something to break this with... I can't... I'm not strong enough to break through it, and I don't want to risk splintering it."

"Here..." Morrigan hadn't heard anyone approach but when she looked down, she found Silas standing next to Hawke holding up a pair of branch cutters.

"How do you have these?" Morrigan asked, giving a little laugh as Hawke accepted them and handed them up to her.

"I make arrows, and you never know when you're going to need to clip thick branches to make more, so I always have a set accessible, just in case."

It hurt the wrist she had fallen on, but she pushed through, managing to cut through the bolt with a loud snap. "I'm not going to pull the wing free until we do the other one, that way her weight doesn't damage them more. Can we move so I can see if I can wake her?"

"Yeah. Brace yourself." Once Morrigan's hands were braced against the wall, Hawke side stepped. Touching the face of the dark-skinned woman, Morrigan frowned.

"Hey." As Morrigan brushed hair away, golden eyes opened, and a pained gasp escaped. Pain and terror flooded through the connection

Morrigan shared through her touch. Sucking in a startled gasp, Morrigan dropped her hand away from the Valkyrie's face to her clothed shoulder. "Hey, hi. I'm here to help."

"My wings." Morrigan had expected a cry of pain or a wail, but all that escaped was a pitiful sob. As the woman tried to move, her body did nothing. It was as if she was completely cemented to the wall. Would she even be able to move her wings when they broke the other bolt?

"I've clipped one of the bolts. Look at me." Morrigan dipped her head down a bit to catch the other woman's gaze. "I'm here to help. I've clipped the bolt away from one of your wings, and I'm going to do the other. I'm here to free you, but I need you to pull your wings away from the wall when I tell you if you can."

The woman stared wide eyed at Morrigan for a moment. "Are you Eda?" she asked, her voice a broken whisper as she turned her gaze to her wings, looking at one and the other before giving a nod. "Surely I am dead, and you are her?" Morrigan wasn't sure what the woman was talking about, but she locked eyes with her again.

"I'm here to help. You have to do as I say, okay?" The woman blinked as if she was in a daze before her gaze cleared, and she nodded. "I'll finish clipping them, and when I get down, Hawke will help brace you, so you don't fall." Hawke side stepped again, and Morrigan clipped the second bolt. Hawke brought her back to the pillar, giving Morrigan a small smile and a reassuring nod before returning to the Valkyrie.

"I've got you," Hawke told her, his hands braced around her waist. "You can pull away." The sound of an agonized sob ripped through the pinned woman's chest; her hands braced against the wall so she could press away from it. Tears welled in Morrigan's eyes as Hawke settled them against the wall, both panting softly for a second. Morrigan's heart broke as she watched the woman try to flex her wings, but all they did was flutter uselessly at her side.

"It hurts," she hissed, letting her head fall back against the wall

"I know," Morrigan whispered, "I don't know what happened, but I wouldn't wish it upon my worst enemy." Kneeling next to Hawke, Morrigan reached out to gently touch one of the pale blue wings. Morrigan had always been told that the Valkyrie were larger-than-life women, with wings that were pure white. To see them in different colors was intriguing. "I'm Morrigan. What shall we call you?"

"Alydia."

"Alydia? That's a lovely name. Can you heal?"

"Not quickly. The only one who can instantaneously heal is our healer."

"Can you be healed by Fae healing? We have salve that might be able to help." Another cry echoed through the chamber, and Morrigan climbed to her feet, looking around in surprise. On the other side of the fallen pillar now sat another Valkyrie, Santi and Aquila speaking softly to her. "We found their healer!" Aquila announced.

"Rest for now. We'll see what your healer can advise us to do," Hawke told Alydia before he and Morrigan made their way to where Santi now sat with the Valkyrie healer.

"How long have you been here like this?" Morrigan asked, licking her slowly chapping lips. The temperature was starting to drop with the setting sun.

"I don't actually know. Whatever they put in the bolts rendered me unconscious in seconds. We were ambushed and Aeron disappeared." The response made Morrigan look at Hawke for clarification. She had heard the name Aeron before, but she couldn't place where.

"Aeron has been the most vocal supporter of Bastian's regarding court unity." Santi sighed as he shared a look with Hawke that Morrigan ignored in favor of speaking to the healer again.

"What is your name?"

"Skadi." Skadi rolled her neck and adjusted her posture as she tried to flex her wings again.

"That's a lovely name. Are your people able to be healed by Fae magic? Santi is the best healer on the continent when it comes to salves and things. The one we currently have might be of help."

"They can be. My healing is typically quicker, but I don't know how long it will take me. Whatever was in those bolts has left me feeling like I don't have a good connection to my magic. Usually, I can heal almost instantly from most wounds." She looked at her wings, which had slowly started to heal.

"That explains why we thought you were a lost cause when we came through before." Waric's voice was apologetic, and Morrigan looked back to see him standing in front of a glimmering portal. They had figured out how to get access to the grid.

"How?" Morrigan asked. She still couldn't believe that no one else had even stopped to check on them.

"With wounds that severe, not everyone would be suffering in silence. Someone would have been awake screaming in agony, but if you look around, these two," Hawke gestured towards Alydia and then back to Skadi, "are the only ones conscious. Which means the ones on the wall aren't suffering."

"At least Aeron gave them that." Santi sighed. Anger flared through Morrigan, and she crossed her arms over her chest. They may be more desensitized to acts of war than Morrigan was, but she felt that it was disgusting they didn't seem to have more anger about the entire situation. "I cannot believe Aeron did this to his own people. I refuse to let them die here, but I won't let him walk away from this unscathed. He attacked his own people." Morrigan turned to Waric, hoping he would feel the same as she already had heard Hawke and Santi's thoughts on the matter.

"He's not here to call for your retribution, Morrigan. There has to be more to this, and we can't just cry treason to anyone who will listen." Waric reached for her, gathering her close so he could wrap her in his new cloak, unbothered by the mess her clothes were. "We must play our cards right, especially considering people are probably already talking about you taking over the neutral territories. Once we get everyone settled, we're supposed to meet Nikaius' family for dinner and then we can voice our concerns, in private, to the council when that meeting happens."

While Morrigan hated the diplomacy in Waric's thoughts, she did agree with him. Doing things hurriedly left more room for mistakes, and if she went in with only revenge on her mind, she would get nowhere.

"Will they be there?" Morrigan asked. Letting her shoulders relax, she began to try to figure out what they could do and what would need to wait. She didn't have a definitive timeline for when the Solstice gathering would be yet, so she had time to formulate the best course of action. First, she would need to make sure the Valkyrie were taken care of.

"Bastian and Aeron? Bastian will be since he is the head of a court, but Aeron isn't the head of anything. Aeshira is the leader of the Valkyrie." Morrigan frowned at Waric's comment, turning to see if she could find the woman Waric spoke of.

"Aeshira's not here." Skadi's voice drew Morrigan's attention back to her. "We walked into a trap that was set up by Aeron. We're the primary infantry for the Valkyrie tribes, so we go where he tells us, especially when there were distress calls being sent from the neutral territories." Skadi shifted to stand. Her wings had healed, and she stretched them before turning to look over her people.

"Distress calls?" Santi sounded concerned as he stood with her. "The only distress calls we received were from the low-lying towns in Be'Sala."

"I don't know all the details, only that Aeron was enraged when we received the letter. Apparently, someone who claims to be a god is causing havoc."

"Kumnei?" All heads turned to Morrigan as she stepped away from Waric to look around the chamber again, her eyes focusing on where Hawke and Aquila were working on getting another Valkyrie down from the wall close by. "I saw him when I made the ice disappear."

The Valkyrie shook her head. "This man claims to be Balor."

Before Morrigan could ask which god Balor was, Santi cut the thought off with a scoff. "I find it hard to believe that the gods have descended upon us. It was probably just some ploy to hide whatever activities they have going on here." Santi's skepticism at the thought made Morrigan realize that perhaps she really was the only one who believed Ben and Ela. Even though they were the ones who had pointed Morrigan and her men in the direction of the Western Keep and had declared it being near the encampment they were looking for, no one else believed what they did about Ben possibly being a god.

Perhaps the Valkyrie could confirm that. Hadn't Hawke said that they would be the ones who might be able to confirm that Ben was writing the language of the gods?

Though she wanted to assuage her own curiosity, Morrigan knew there were more pressing things to do than to try to argue when no one else seemed to believe her. She let it go in favor of checking on the rest of the group. Doing a quick head count, she noticed that most of the guards that had stayed to help were her men. It appeared Santi's had continued on when Morrigan had decided she wanted to save the Valkyrie.

"Let's get the rest of them down now that we know they're still alive," she announced before giving Skadi a smile. "We'll take care of the rest if you want to start healing Alydia?" Skadi nodded, and they separated.

Morrigan, Waric, and Santi heading to help more Valkyrie as Skadi began her healing efforts.

Morrigan wasn't sure how much time passed but when they finished, her whole body ached and twenty-five Valkyrie sat along the walls, some looking worse than others but all alive and alert.

Morrigan turned to Skadi, reaching out to touch her arm gently. "Stay here and heal your people. When you're able, you're welcome to join us in Starsgard. I would like to continue our conversation about gods and how you ended up here. But we need everyone to be healthy and whole before that conversation can happen."

Skadi smiled, gripping her arm in a way that Morrigan had seen Hawke do to others previously, anchoring her hand to Morrigan's elbow. Morrigan returned the grasp and smiled up at Skadi.

"We owe you our lives. If you need us, you merely need to call, and we'll come." Skadi's palm warmed over Morrigan's hand, and she felt her own palm tingle.

"Thank you." Morrigan's hand still felt warm even after they disengaged and when she turned it over, she noticed that it glittered gold for a moment before the color disappeared. On her forearm was a pale blue feather. It was barely noticeable, and Morrigan only knew it was there because of its warmth unless she turned her arm just right to catch the sunlight.

"Is there more we need to see?" Morrigan asked Waric. She felt that they were no longer needed in the chamber, and she wanted to give the Valkyrie time to regroup and figure out what they were going to do without being watched.

"That was the last part of the building. The rest are just the courtyards and outlying structures. We haven't really come across anything promising though." Morrigan knew Waric meant the encampment.

The hope that it was nearby was what had led the men into coming out in the first place. Morrigan knew that her desire to help those in their care wasn't as predominant to them, but to her, both were of equal importance.

Clearing the Western Keep meant that the people in Starsgard would have a place to stay that hadn't been used in decades and finding the encampment meant possibly freeing people from some form of slavery if what Nikaius, Waric, and Hawke believed to be true.

When they exited the chamber, they were greeted with the cool winter evening. The sun was setting over the mountains, and Morrigan took a slow, deep breath of air. Even though they hadn't been in the room long, the air had been so stale that the fresh air outside stung as it went down. Coughing gently, Morrigan tried to clear the tightness in her chest before turning to survey the rest of the land. Thankfully, it seemed that the snow and rain had stopped.

If she hadn't been aware that there was magic in the air, she would have missed the glimmer that happened when she turned. None of the others seemed to have noticed, but as she stepped over to the edge of the bridge, the glimmer happened again. It was almost as if she was looking at the reflection of light off a mirror and when she turned a certain way, it changed minutely.

Of all the different magic Morrigan had experienced in her time with Nikaius, Waric, Hawke, and her new family, this seemed most similar to the magic she had felt in the bathroom. It caused the mark on her arm to burn in the same way it had when she had received it. Was that the entrance to what they were looking for?

Freeing her hold from Waric, Morrigan darted past Hawke, hope welling in her chest. If that glimmer of magic was where the encampment was hiding, then she could access it like she had when she got rid of the ice. She tripped as she made her way down the stairs but was able to keep herself upright and burst through the door out into the courtyard.

The way the light refracted off the magic changed, and it was almost as if Morrigan was back in the cave, staring at a fractured image of herself. It was a weird silvery crystalline kaleidoscope of images that blurred into one when she reached out to touch it.

Arms caught her around the waist, and Morrigan screamed as she toppled them to the ground. "What the hell are you doing?" Hawke' voice was worried as he righted them, taking her face in his hands to look her over. His hands were cold, but all she felt from him was affection and worry.

"There's magic. I can see magic." She was giddy with excitement. Was she the first one to see it? Was she the only one? Waving her hand towards it, she grinned at him. "That could be where they're hiding them, Hawke!" Morrigan wiggled free from him and moved to stand, but his hand caught her wrist.

"You can't just go running into magic you know nothing about, Morrigan. You need to communicate, and we need to form a plan about how to proceed." His frustration bled into his tone, but she didn't understand why he was focusing on her and not on the magic. Wasn't it what he and Nikaius and Waric had been looking for?

"Plan on how to proceed? There's no need for a plan when we can save people. Do you see the magic? I can." She gestured towards it again, anxious for him to see it. "We need to go towards it. We need to see if I'm right!"

Hawke let out a slow breath before moving to stand and pulling Morrigan to her feet. "It doesn't matter."

"It does matter. This is important, Hawke. These are people's lives we can save." She didn't understand the hot and cold she was getting from him. One moment he was a grumpy, broody guard and the next, he was helping her get Valkyrie down off the walls.

"Morrigan." He sighed softly as he tugged her to him. "That's not what I meant. Just because you can see and sense it doesn't mean that you should go running into it. We don't know what kind of magic it is. We just got you back from whatever magic had taken you earlier today." The sigh he gave was heavy as he pressed his forehead to hers. Worry and fear were at the forefront of his feelings, not anger, and it made Morrigan colder at the thought that she was the cause. "I promised you wouldn't get hurt under my watch and it still keeps happening." She had made the joke that it was a hard promise for him to keep.

Did he see her recklessness as a jab towards his skills at keeping her safe? Did he think she was doing it on purpose? Morrigan's chest felt tight, but before she could say anything, he continued, "I think you're more than capable of handling yourself. But we don't know what kind of magic is at play, like whatever marked you." His thumb brushed where the dark handprint was covered, and she gave a soft sigh. Of course he was right, he always was when it came to her safety. It was a frustrating fact that Morrigan didn't want to admit aloud, but she knew her other two men would back him up in this case.

Letting out a hard breath through her nose, she crossed her arms over her chest and nodded. "Don't expect me to leave. I want to be here. If this is what we think it is, and we can get people out of the encampment, they're going to need some guidance once they come through."

"I don't think any of us would ask you to not care about other people. I just hate that you keep doing it at your own expense." He nudged his nose against hers before pressing a kiss to her forehead. "We just want you safe. Just like we don't know what kind of magic is being used, we also don't know what state these people are in. If they're who we're thinking, many of them will be larger changelings and that poses a significant risk to you." Leaning forward, Hawke pressed a kiss to Morrigan's ear. "Plus, none of us would be able to focus with you near."

"Are you saying I'm a distraction?" Morrigan pulled away a bit, but the grin Hawke gave her soothed her.

"Absolutely." Waric laughed as he descended the stairs. "Your magic keeps changing by the day." Waric tucked her hand in the crook of his elbow and tugged her away from the others as Hawke and Nikaius turned to address the gathered troops. "Are you sure you're warm enough?" Waric asked once they reached the bridge overlooking the area again. It felt like he was trying to comfort her any way he could, and she hugged him to show her appreciation.

"I am. I wish there was some way I could help. I'm supposed to be the head of the territory, in charge of these people, but I won't be down there to greet them."

Wrapping her in his arms from behind, Waric leaned his chin down on her shoulder and nodded. "I understand where you're coming from. I feel that way whenever someone has to make a decision regarding how they rule without me being able to truly help. Everything I say and do is merely a suggestion. But just remember that you are a lot safer up here than you are down there. You've been exposed to a lot of unknown magic lately, and we don' know how that's going to affect you."

She wrapped her arms around his; sliding her fingers through his. The warmth the changelings gave off was something Morrigan didn't think she would ever get over. They stood like that for several minutes just watching as Nikaius, Hawke, and Santi formed a plan. They were far enough away that she could still see the magic and could watch Hawke and Nikaius examine it, but she wasn't quite privy to the conversation they were having.

Could Waric hear what they were talking about from where they stood? "Don't you need to be down there with them? You're going with them, aren't you?"

"Nikaius can relay everything to me while it's happening if he opens his mind to me." Morrigan had only just learned that her bond with Waric had opened their minds to each other.

Which is why she was surprised when Waric pulled away when she murmured, "I feel like I'm just an inconvenience." She hadn't meant to say it out loud and bit her lip as she kept her eyes trained on those gathered below.

"Life is complicated, but you're not an inconvenience, Morrigan. You're kind and compassionate and smart. Life has just dealt you a really shitty hand that we're trying to compensate for. A lot of this is just as new for us as it is for you. I can tell you right now that I never expected to find the Valkyrie here. I had started to believe that the encampment wasn't real, and I sure as hell didn't see that magic until you pointed it out, and I walked past it at least five times."

"You really didn't?" Hawke's reaction made a little more sense now. If they hadn't seen it, her running away probably would have looked bad. Letting out another sigh, Morrigan scanned the area. Aside from the faint glimmer of magic, everything looked normal. The courtyard was behind them, and they faced the setting sun. Morrigan knew that the temperatures were going to drop overnight, so she hoped they could get in and out of whatever the magic was hiding before the snow and rain picked up again.

"Are you staying here to make sure I stay put, or were you going to go with them?" she asked as she watched the group separate into smaller groups, and Hawke carefully raise his hand to touch whatever magic was there.

Waric seemed to hesitate, looking between Morrigan in his arms, and the men and women prepared to go towards the magic. "Promise me you'll stay?" he asked, and Morrigan knew he wanted to go, knew he would be of better use down there, protecting Nikaius, Hawke, and the others.

"I promise I won't move from this spot unless it is absolutely a life-or-death situation, or if I get too cold. Aquila and I will keep each other company." As if Aquila had heard her words, the dark-haired Avian approached with a smile on her face. They both waved to Waric as he descended the stairs to join the others.

"All the Valkyrie are awake," Aquila's voice was soft as she stepped up to the edge of the bridge and leaned on its wall. "Most of them have healed. I think Skadi is planning to return to Aeshira tonight, but it sounds like the rest of the Valkyrie plan to stay here. They're under the belief that if Aeron is trying something, their presence elsewhere might tip him off that someone is here and helping them."

"That makes sense." Morrigan nodded, but her attention remained focused primarily on where Hawke pressed his hand on the magic, even as she fought off a chill that was climbing up her spine. Of course she was cold, there was ice outside, they were in snow. The cold was a little distracting, especially when she breathed in and it stung her throat. She choked on a cough as she tried to clear it, which made Aquila frown, but she couldn't return to the warmth of the Keep just yet. She needed to focus on Hawke, Waric, and Nikaius. She needed to make sure they were safe, and that everyone came out alive.

When Hawke touched it, she held her breath, waiting for something to happen, but the magic only rippled. As Hawke stepped through completely, the tightening in her chest made it hard to breathe. She was terrified for them and the way her stomach dropped, and her breath caught in her chest made her cough again. She worried about what they might find on the other side of the wall. Would they be attacked? Would everyone in the encampment be dead?

Her head swam as she thought about those things, ignoring the concerned look Aquila gave her when she braced herself on the wall overlooking the area. Morrigan had to remind herself that she promised she would only move if it was life or death, but the urge to get closer was almost unbearable.

She needed them to be okay. If she knew that, maybe the world would stop spinning.

A moment later, Hawke stepped out of the barrier and spoke with the others. Her relief was profound, and her throat hurt at the harsh way her breath escaped her. Her shoulders loosened away from the tension she had been holding.

The three of them, Hawke, Nikaius, and Waric turned to wave at her, Hawke giving a thumbs up before the three of them disappeared.

Morrigan hoped they stayed safe and returned quickly.

Stay Tuned

What is behind the mysterious wall? Though Hawke, Nikaius, and Waric seem confident about what they will find, Morrigan is only worried about their safe return. Is Kumnei real or is there something more at play? Where did Bastian, Amara, and Elijah disappear to and will they return?
Stay tuned!

***

If you have some time, I'd love if you left a rating or a review! As an indie author, every review helps to get my books in front of the readers who love them, and I appreciate you taking the time to give me feedback!

Follow Me on Amazon to keep up to date on new releases!
Amazon Page

***

Want to hang out? Join the FB group for sneak peeks, arc signups, future projects, and more!
Facebook Group

***

If you would like physical copies of The Hidden Fates series I have signed copies available!
Signed Copies

***

About The Author

Siri has been writing short stories since she was 10 years old. At 13 she started publishing fanfiction on various sites and recently decided to make a huge leap of faith into self-publishing in 2022. When she's not writing the sugar to her author friends' spice, she's upholding her title of her work's Emotional Support Goblin, causing chaos with her bestie, and terrorizing her 14-year-oldson and their home office supervisor: an absolute unit of a black and white tuxedo cat named Figaro.

Acknowledgements

Oh Bestie, My bestie! Thank you for giving me sanity through work and the chaos that was writing this book. I can't wait to have a bajillion more adventures and at least 8 more books for you to read!

To Alicia: Thank you for whipping this into shape and for talking me down off the ledge when I decided to push back my release AND cut this draft in half! I had bare bones when you got this draft and look where we are now! Finally published! Wooo!

And finally to my amazing writers discord! KD and N.Slater have been so so so patient with me when I scream about everything going on in my head, even though this is the second time I've done this now. I hope you will be with me through my writing journey, always. Even when I feel like the most annoying person in the room.

Clan Names/Vocab

"Primal"(animal) changelings:
Rekru'e (Reh-crew-ay): Mammalian changelings (wolves, bears, lions, etc.) it is also the primary changeling.

<u>Clan/Pack/Family Names:</u>
Ayrden: Panther Shifters
De'Lyon: Lion shifters (both Large Cat and Mountain Lion)
Corinth: Nearly extinct Wolf shifters
Caan: Nearly extinct Bear tribe
Kitzira (Kit-zee-ra): An extinct tribe of Fox shifters

Kyilzar (Keel-zar): Avian changelings (Crows, Ravens, Owls, Eagles, etc.)

<u>Flock Names:</u>
Corviana

Velamo (Vel-uh-mo): Reptilian/Amphibian/Aquatic shifters (Dragons, Vipers, Mermaids, Sirens, etc.)

<u>Nest Names:</u>
Gorlassar

Rekru'evocab:
Atce'(At-see): Alpha/superior
Logar (low-gar): Water
Ie (EE): I

Ae (ay)-- you

Ie amar ae (EE ah-mar ay): Term of affection that loosely translates to "I adore you" but can have other meanings.

Aeonie (Ay-own-ee): Literally "You and I". Typically used for some kind of union/relationship (Can be used to describe marriage or sex)

Koen/Koea (K-oh-en) (K-oh-ah): Savior

Kumnei (Koom-N-eye) God of Mischief

www.ingramcontent.com/pod-product-compliance
Ingram Content Group UK Ltd.
Pitfield, Milton Keynes, MK11 3LW, UK
UKHW022237230426
12048UKWH00018BA/1302